Kiki Skagen Munshi

Whisper in Bucharest

Kiki Skagen Munshi is a fourth generation Californian and was raised in Southern California and in Tokyo, Japan. She attended Swarthmore College in Pennsylvania where she graduated *cum laude* with a BA in Political Science, History, and Economics. After a year on a Fulbright Fellowship in India she attended the University of California, Berkeley on an NDFL Fellowship for an MA in Asian Studies — Indian History and Politics. Ms. Munshi finished her education with a Doctorate in History from the University of Bucharest in Romanian History in 2006. She held various positions in California and India including five years working with print materials for television-based courses at the University of California San Diego until 1980, when she joined the US Foreign Service. Working with the United States Information Service and Department of State, Ms. Kiki Munshi served in Embassies in Nigeria, Romania, Greece, Sierra Leone, Tanzania and India. She was the Director of the American Library in Bucharest from 1983-1987 and the Counselor for Public Affairs there 2000-2002. She retired from the US Foreign Service at the end of 2002 but returned in 2006-2007 to head a Provincial Reconstruction Team in Iraq. She now lives in the mountains of San Diego County, California, where she writes and rides her Romanian horses. She visits Romania and India regularly. She has also written and edited a number of non-fiction books as well as a children's novel about India.

Kiki SkagenMunshi

Whisper in Bucharest

document.ro

compania

Layout: Compania
Cover Photo: Vlad Arghir (Bucharest, 1984)
Editor : Adina Keneres
DTP : Bogdan Constantinescu
        Vlad Predescu

Descrierea CIP a Bibliotecii Nationale a României
MUNSHI, KIKI SKAGEN
Whisper in Bucharest / Kiki Skagen Munshi. –
Bucuresti : Compania, 2014
344 p. ; 20 cm - (document.ro)
ISBN 10: 1530040019
ISBN 13: 978-1530040018
Second Edition 2016

821.214-31=111

Str. Tuberozelor Nr. 9, Sector 1, 011411 Bucuresti,
România
Tel. : 021 223 23 28 Fax : 021 223 23 25
Distribution Tel. : 021 223 23 37 Fax : 021 223 23 24
email: editura.compania@gmail.com,
compania@rdslink.ro
www.compania.ro

Acknowledgements

Authors of fiction are thieves, stealing bits and pieces of other people's lives and weaving them into the stories they create. This book is not about any actual individual, living or dead, but it contains snatches of many conversations and memories generously shared by Romanian friends and acquaintances.

The setting for the novel springs from the life of George Muntean, who was born in Bilca and for whom the loss of northern Bukovina was an unhealed wound. George's wife, Adela Popescu, gave generously of her time and knowledge as did others in Radauti and Bilca. It was my great fortune that Adela introduced me to Marian Olaru, the Director of the Liceul Hurmuzachi who also nurtured a passion for its history. Domitian Baltei, Vera Popescu, and Alexandru Brailean all shared their personal memories of World War II in Bukovina. Ion Talpes told me — not a great deal but I hope enough — of the workings of the Securitate; Larry Watts helped in this area and Mihnea Gheorghiu provided other details of Ceausescu's policies. Radu Toma shared coming of age stories and Antoaneta Ralian helped professionally but also personally through accounts of her own life. Mircea Raceanu provided corrections on the structure of the MEA and Andrei Filotti, Caius Dragomir and others shared their experiences of working in institutions overseen by the communist party. Matei Vintila told me of his pride in attending a *liceu* and Sodolescu Valerian recounted the story of the wolf and the sheep. Aura Munteanu, Sanda Brediceanu, Nae and Paula Constantinescu and Florin Codre all contributed in unique and valuable ways. Roda Tinis, Georgiana Punea and Ernest Latham provided useful commentary on early drafts; Roda and Vasile Avram recounted details of village life 'way back when'. Mike Macfarlane of Querencia in Murphys, California, made this second addition happen.

My colleagues in the American Embassy and the Biblioteca Americana during the 1980s are all behind the scenes but very much present because we lived together through those difficult years; similarly my friend and trainer Enache Boiangiu and others at the Olimpia Riding Club enriched the lives of many in the American Embassy during that time. For all of this assistance, however, the events and substantive characters in the books are fictional and they are not intended to represent any real person, living or dead. The horses, however, are an exception. They are real and it is to them I dedicate this book:

Haiduc, Hidalgo, Ropot, Igor, Bufon, So Brave, Blaze and all the other mounts who have put up with me over the many years I have been annoying them.

Contents

Historical Map of Romania

The map below illustrates changes to Romania's borders noted on page 353 and indicates where major locales in the story are found. Boundaries and locations are indicative rather than exact.

PART I

Cocktails at seven

Fane leaned against the bookcase, Scotch in hand, watching the cocktail party swirl and eddy around him. The gracious rooms buzzed comfortably as he lifted the tumbler to his lips, raised his chin and savored the whisky rolling across his taste buds. Someone was at his side. Turning, Fane found himself looking into the mild eyes of his American host.

"Stefan! I'm so glad you could come. Chay my fatchits?*"* *Peter Mellon, tall, angular, the perfect diplomat, eminently forgettable except for his atrocious Romanian pronunciation, addressed Fane with diplomatic enthusiasm.*

"Very well, thank you. And I'm honored to be invited to your lovely home again," Fane answered heartily with a genial smile that showed his gold tooth. He was careful to enunciate clearly so the American could understand. "I was admiring your wonderful taste in paintings."

Mellon was flailing to stay afloat in the sea of words but grasped the feeling of a compliment. "Thank you very much," he answered. "I like naïve art very much. I am pleased that you also like it." Fane waited through the man's struggling communication, looking interested in the childish sentences and almost feeling sorry because it was clear Mellon wasn't stupid. There were times when he wished he spoke better English but, as now, he usually enjoyed having the linguistic upper hand with the succession of American diplomats that was his job.

After a few more awkward pleasantries Mellon moved on and Fane returned his attention to the Scotch. He needed to be careful, there was important business to do tonight, but just a bit more wouldn't hurt. Finishing the glass he moved purposefully to the

10

bar, savoring the prospect of a second drink, some good food, and the easy warmth of the house.

The sturdy child balanced himself on the little ridge of dry earth, and carefully put one foot ahead of the other. 'If I don't fall off before the prune orchard,' he told himself, 'we'll have chicken for dinner tonight.' The well-traveled lane stretched ahead, a long way by a little boy's reckoning, past Fane's home before it turned towards other farmsteads. Late autumn sun warmed the earth with winter hiding close behind the light. The thought of chicken or maybe *sarmale*, plump pillows of rice and meat wrapped in soured cabbage leaves, made Fane's mouth water.

"Fane," his father's voice called, "hurry up. There are chores." Off-balance, the boy slipped and the chances of having a special dinner were lost.

"Someday I'll eat all the *sarmale* I want, and chicken every day," he promised himself, then added "and cake, too" as he ran toward his father across the family's cabbage field, catching his toe on the rows of dirt and righting himself again and again.

"Here, you drive." Fane scrambled up the step by the wagon wheel, bellied onto the footboards, and climbed on to the seat before his father could cuff him. Petru Vulcean handed him the reins. "To work." Fane chirruped and the horse moved forward slowly while the child dreamed of chicken soup. Haiduc's shiny brown hindquarters shifted down the long row to the regular thuds of cabbages landing in the wagon bed behind, his black tail swishing in rhythm. Autumn light slanted across the wide plain over the imagined shadow of the Carpathians in the West, infusing its beauty into a basically oblivious boy.

The sun was low and a chill had crept up Fane's arms to his small shoulders before Petru said, "Enough," taking the reins from the boy as he seated himself beside the child on the wooden board. Fane leaned against his father, enjoying the warmth and reflexively scratching his little blond head. Once home, Haiduc obediently backed the wagon into the shed opposite the house then stood quietly while Petru took off his harness. Fane stood in front of the horse, long reins in hand. Petru glanced at him with pride and didn't say anything — Haiduc would have stood alone but Fane liked to help. As for the boy, he looked at Haiduc's lowered nose and smelled the sweet spot between his nostrils, grateful for the warm breath on his cold hands. "Haiducule," he whispered, "we'll be warriors like Stefan the Old and Mircea the Great, or Stefan the Great or whatever, and I will carry a silver sword with a gold hilt and you will fight the enemies with your hooves. We'll gallop all the way to the mountains..." Haiduc snuffed in agreement, almost knocking Stefan over as he rubbed his itchy, sweaty head on the child.

Both men, large and small, washed before entering the warm kitchen to sit at the scrubbed table. Tonight's supper was *mamaliga*, cornmeal mush, sprinkled with cheese and with an egg for Father. Tomorrow it would probably be potatoes and peas. It was a good year with enough to fill everyone's stomach. Mother ruffled Fane's hair and talked of the day, the neighbors, the crops. Granny also talked, she talked incessantly, "God willing, we won't be hungry this winter," but no one paid attention. Mioara, Stefan's older sister, sat quietly, lost in dreams of young men and nice clothes. Petru and Fane ate, Fane savoring the grains of the hot *mamaliga* and the fleeting, sharp bite of homemade cheese.

"The Mayor's wife said today that the war would be here before the New Year," Mother ventured.

This caught Petru's attention. "I don't think so. At least it won't if Romania sides with the Germans. There's no choice, anyway, with Germany on one side and Russia on the other. But whatever happens, we'll suffer." He shoveled more food in his mouth and thought of the winter ahead. "Peasants always suffer."

It was the one point of constant agreement between Granny and her son. Granny eased herself up and put another stick in the great tile stove. "You're right. If only the Austrians would come back, things would be better." Petru had been a child during the First World War and didn't remember much about Austrian rule before Bukovina and their village had been transferred to Romania, but he did remember the hardship, the terrifying hunger and cold, and people dying. As did Granny, who recalled them at length and often. Turning back toward the table, Granny continued, "But this one is going to be worse. Wait and see." She moved slowly and painfully back to her seat. "I feel it in my bones."

"I heard that they will requisition horses and call up men soon," Mother continued.

"What does 'requisition' mean?" asked Fane curiously.

"That's where they come and take whatever they want for the Government," interrupted Petru. "And that's enough talk." He shoved back his chair and started to put on his coat. "I'm going to check on the animals."

"But they couldn't take our Haiduc," said Fane, "he's mine! He is mine!"

"They'll take anything..." began Granny. "Hush," said Mother, "Fane, would you like a pickle? I think they are ready." The specter of losing Haiduc was hidden by the great pickle jar as Mother began her usual questions about school.

After the dinner dishes were in their place, Mioara sat on the bench under the window, sewing her trousseau, face and light hair framed against the brightly flowered wool carpet on the wall. Grandmother helped, umpiring every stitch. The background murmurs hardly scratched Fane's consciousness as he lay curled into his little sleeping space high between the warm tile soba and the wall. Fane was looking at the little plate that hung between his space and the door. It was cream colored with a green and yellow sort of deer and flowers and Fane liked to dream of the world the deer lived in because it took his mind off other things.

Fane's problem wasn't a fiancée or Granny or war, it was Carol, big, lumpish, mean Carol, stupid son of the smart mayor. Carol who couldn't read. Carol who shared a bench with Fane at school even if he was supposed to be in the Second Class and Fane was in his first year. Today had been typical.

"How old is your sister?" Carol poked Fane in the ribs with his pencil, hard.

"What's that to you?" Fane replied, moving toward the edge of the hard seat away from the bigger boy.

"Answer me, how old is she?" Fane almost yelped as the end of the pencil bit him again.

"I don't know. Big, not as big as Mother and Father."

"Stupid. She's going to get married soon. And you know what they'll do then..." Fane's repulsion from the dirty voice under the meaningless words was broken by the teacher.

"Carol, be quiet." Carol knew he could get away with a lot but not a bad report from the teacher and turned his attention to the confusing marks in his book. Fane, for his part, peered over into the more interesting reader Carol was holding. The black letters promised new worlds until the teacher called his name and Fane obediently stood up to recite sums.

"The gypsies are in town," Carol whispered after Fane sat down. "Maybe they'll steal you and take you with them." Fane looked up sharply, not because he was afraid of that old wives' tale but the gypsies were a colorful break in the village routine. Rousing himself from his warm cocoon with this memory, Fane peered down from his nest and said, "Carol said the gypsies have come to town." It was more of an announcement to the family than a simple statement.

"What?" said Mother, "Gypsies," said Mioara. "Trouble," said Grandmother. "They'll be stealing for certain sure. But probably the child is wrong."

"He's not, they're here," interrupted Petru, unwinding his coat as he came through the door after a last check on the animals. "One of them is coming to shoe Haiduc tomorrow. Watch them," addressing his wife, "be careful while he's around, and don't let any of those children in the courtyard. You, Fane, come straight home from school and help with your horse. And now go to sleep."

Carol forgotten, Fane curled up again and thought of bay Haiduc with his black tipped ears and white star, the two of them flying through the sky to a place that was always warm and full of food.

Even Fane could see that the farrier wasn't very good. He had no patience with the horse and Haiduc, usually quiet, acted as if something were really wrong. Fane wished his father hadn't gone off to get the gypsy children out of the field even if they were probably stealing the crop.

"Hold that horse better," said the man. He wasn't really a man, not much older than Mioara, but he tapped the nails into Haiduc's reluctant hoof with authority. "He's not very well-behaved."

"He's fine," replied Fane heatedly. "But something's hurting him."

"Nonsense. There," the youth stood up. "We're finished." Fane looked down at the bright, cleated shoes on Haiduc's round feet and breathed a sigh of relief, sounding as grown-up as he could.

"That's fine. Father will pay you."

"He'd better." The gypsy was gathering up his few tools and rolled them in his leather apron before walking off to find his money. Fane walked a still unhappy Haiduc into his barn, patting him and assuring him that everything would be fine.

It wasn't. As the fall of 1939 moved day by day toward the winter of 1940 Haiduc wasn't his usual self. He didn't want to work, but the crops were in and there wasn't much he had to do. Perhaps that was why it was several weeks before Petru realized the horse was badly lame, not just a bit sore. "Looks like it's in his shoulder," Petru judged. "He'll just have to rest as much as possible." Petru turned to Fane. "You look after him. We'll want him to pull the sleigh when it snows."

"Will it snow soon?" Fane asked hopefully, remembering Christmas and tramping through snow to the neighbors' houses to sing, "*Morcova, Sorcova...*" and lots of people in masks, and being given sweets and cake to eat all jumbled together with laughter and feeling good inside and going to church.

"Dunno," answered Petru, his head now against the cow's flank, hands busy pulling milk from her udder. "Damn cow is going to go dry soon," he said more to himself than to Fane, trying not to think of frozen feet and ice to be broken on troughs and well day after day.

In spite of talk about the war the weeks moved by in the steady rhythm of years past. Just before Christmas all the families in Bilca who had pigs killed one or two, savoring the thought of fresh meat for the holidays followed by various kinds of bacon and cured meat through the winter. Mother made the bacon and small, thin sausages to hang from the ceiling and preserved more meat in great barrels, layering it with fat. Cabbages filled massive bins, apples lay fragrant in the cellar stored alongside dried peas from the field and potent tzuica made from prunes. Grandmother sighed, half content and half disappointed; there would be enough food, God willing, to last the family through the winter and early spring but next year would probably be worse. It was harder to get to school for Fane, slogging down the muddy lane or tromping through snow with feet fiery from cold, but Mother insisted. Mioara had stopped school before Fane could remember and Mother and Father still argued about it but Father said she was luckier than most, knowing how to read and write. Now she was needed in the house. Finish.

Fane was needed on the farm, too, but he was the family's fortune and future security. The teacher at school said, he was bright though peasant kids didn't usually go past grade school, but maybe, who knew. At seven, Fane carried the weight of his family's hopes lightly most of the time.

It was harder to deal lightly with Carol. Sometimes Fane thought his ribs must be black and blue from pencil jabs. Recently, Carol had been making fun of Fane's friendship with Mendl.

"He's a Jew and he's dirty," said Carol.

"He is not dirty, he's cleaner than you," replied Fane, thinking of Mendl's white hands and looking at the ground-in grime along the sides of his fingers.

"Don't say that," another pencil jab, "no Jew is clean. The Germans will get rid of the Jews. Or if not the Germans, the Russians and then your friend will be gone. Besides, all the Jews dress funny, like they're from town instead of villages. Why can't they be like us if they want to live here?"

"If they go, who will run the village store? And the mill? " asked Fane.

"I don't know," admitted Carol in a rare moment of candor. "And my Pa says that we need the Jews to give farmers money for seed in the spring."

"If Jews are bad, why do they give farmers money for seed anyway? Does your father think the Germans are coming?" asked Fane.

"No..." said Carol slowly, ignoring the first question on a topic neither child understood. "He said it'd be the Russians. But someone will come and take away everything that we have. That's what he said last night. Including your dirty Jew friend."

"Hush back there or someone will get beaten," said the teacher and both boys pretended to resume reading. Covertly Fane looked at his hands, the dirt ground in to the sides of his fingers and around his nails. Mother was always saying to wash, but on a farm hands got dirty and washing didn't seem to help. He glanced at Carol's hands which were the same. Carol's father may be the mayor, he thought, but Carol has to do chores just like me even if they have more land.

Mendl was smart. He and Fane were the best in the class. Why was being a Jew something special? Perhaps, Fane thought, it was a little like different kinds of horses, the horses he saw once pulling someone's fancy carriage and Haiduc, except Haiduc was as beautiful as those horses. Anyway, Fane thought, it didn't matter, Carol was lying. Father wouldn't let anything bad happen to Fane, and Mendl's father was rich and would protect Mendl. Fane turned his attention back to his reader, which he had already finished twice when the teacher wasn't paying attention.

In February the soldiers came for the villagers' horses, just as the peasants were beginning to plan their first spring plowing. "Use your oxen," they advised, "we need the horses for the cavalry. See, we'll pay for them" only they didn't pay enough or sometimes even anything. Mostly the peasants were asked to sign a paper with a sum on it that was about half the amount given them.

Fane heard about it first during arithmetic class in school. One of the older boys burst in the classroom door.

"They're taking our horses," he cried, "the soldiers have come." The class was in an uproar, boys getting up and looking around, wondering what to do, the girls sitting with bewildered looks. Fane's heart froze in his chest.

"Order, order," shouted the teacher, and the class calmed but no one could pay attention to studies. Finally another teacher came with the news that school was dismissed for the day.

Fane ran until his side hurt, panting as he slogged through the muddy track to the house, slowing to a walk, breaking into a trot every few steps and slowing again as he breathed too hard, the cold air hurting his lungs way down. He turned into the open gate of the farmyard to see three mounted soldiers talking with his father. Haiduc was standing by Petru, keeping his weight off his bad foot as usual but looking interested in the other horses.

"How long has he been lame?" one soldier asked.

"About three, no, maybe four months now," Petru replied.

"What's the problem?"

"I don't know. I think it's his right shoulder."

"Make him walk."

Petru led the bay horse around the farmyard. He was clearly limping.

"Better look at him, sir," the soldier said to one of his companions. "Our vet," he explained proudly, looking down at Petru.

The man swung off his horse and, looking around, handed the reins to a panting Fane. "Can you hold him?" he asked kindly.

"I kiss your hand. Yes, sir," answered Fane politely as he had been taught and grasped the leather reins tightly. The vet patted Haiduc's neck, ran his hand over the shoulder and down the leg to, finally, pick up his foot.

"Phew, this is full of filth. Don't you ever clean your horse's feet?" he asked Petru. "Get me something to clean it out with." Petru looked confused and the hand grabbed Fane's heart again.

The soldier-vet cleaned muck and mud from Haiduc's foot, then had one of his men pull off the shoe.

"Shit. Who shod this horse? When?"

"The gypsy farrier, as usual. About four months ago, it was."

"You ought to have the shoes redone more often, but that's not the big problem. That idiot didn't take all the nails from the old shoe out and now they've abscessed. He is probably lame—I'd guess in the shoulder—from the shoeing and now he's lame in the foot as well." He gently put Haiduc's foot on the ground and patted him. "Good boy, you're a lucky horse today. Let me switch horses with you," he said turning to a wide-eyed Fane.

"I knew he was hurting Haiduc," Fane blurted, "I was holding him and I knew Haiduc was being bad because he was hurt."

"You did?" the vet ruffled Fane's hair. "I have a son at home your age. I tell him to study hard and become a vet. Maybe you could, too." Suddenly he drew his hand back. "The Devil," he muttered under his breath, "the kid's got scabies." Fane's self-image moved from proud to dirty and poor, unconsciously, without quite knowing what was happening. The officer turned back to Petru. "Put seven parts water, three parts vinegar and one part lye in a bucket and dip the horse's foot in it twice a day. Don't let it touch his skin or your skin, and be careful when you put the vinegar and lye in the water. We'll come back next month. Remember, seven parts water, three parts vinegar, and one part lye."

"Yes, sir, I kiss you hand," answered Petru obsequiously, eyelids narrowed to hide his anger.

"Remember, seven parts water, three parts vinegar and one part lye. It will cure the abcess and may help if he has thrush, which he probably does under that muck given the smell. And keep the horse's feet clean." The vet swung up on his horse, the three men turned and rode up the lane toward Tante Elise's house.

"We got out of that one, at least for a while," Petru crowed to Fane. "Here, put the horse away and come to dinner."

"What about the medicine?" Fane asked.

"God damn it, you little bastard, always imitating your betters." Petru swung his hand, clipping Fane on the side of the head. Fane stumbled under the blow, scrabbling to find his feet and, failing, fell against Haiduc's leg. A wave of hate eclipsed his pain as it always did when Petru beat him. He'd show Father. Someday. Slowly, Fane got up, looking at his father's retreating back, then he turned toward Haiduc. "I'll make you well," he promised. "And we'll get even with Father."

It wasn't until the next day that Fane could ask Mother for lye and vinegar without Petru's presence. Petru had sat silent and late at the table the night before, drinking *tzuica* and staring at the wall.

"Why do you want them?" she asked curiously.

"The man who came, they called him a 'vet', what is a vet?"

"A doctor for animals. Did he say something?"

"Oh. Yes. He did. He said that Haiduc's foot had a sore and we should put water and lye and vinegar together and put Haiduc's foot in it. He said the foot was dirty. He said we should keep it clean. He said," Fane scratched his head reflexively, "I think he said we were dirty, too, but I'm not sure."

"Oh," said Mother with a glance toward the bed where Petru was sleeping off his binge. "I see. Did the officer tell you how much lye and vinegar to use?"

The lye made the cider and water foam and bubble and Haiduc snorted at the smell, but stood patiently as Fane lugged the wooden bucket in the stall and put it down. The child looked up at the enormous horse and down at the bucket. He moved close to the great feathery leg and pulled at the fetlock as he had seen the vet and Father do. Haiduc obediently raised his leg, all the while turning his head to look enquiringly at Fane. Fane looked at the bucket, out of reach, and let go of Haiduc's leg. He moved the bucket closer and lifted Haiduc's hoof off the dirty straw again. Taking the leg in his right hand, he reached for the bucket with his left. He couldn't quite make it. Again he moved the bucket closer, picked up Haiduc's leg and started to reach for the bucket.

Haiduc put his foot down. Firmly.

Fane swatted the horse's leg in exasperation and pulled at the fetlock hair again. Haiduc turned his head and shoved the boy amicably with his nose. Fane fell back, sitting on one of the places the horse usually peed and bumping the back of his head against the wooden wall. He sat for a second, drowning in the ammonia smell of urine. Then he heard a familiar voice.

"What are you doing?" In the doorway Carol stood looking down at him. Fane, warm with anger, shame and the smell of urine fought back tears, then he heard Carol swallow and gulp the same as he, Fane, was doing. What was wrong with big bully Carol? "What are you doing here?" Fane managed to ask back.

"They took our horses," Carol said, tears in his eight year old voice. "They took Tzigan and Tziganca. They...they hit Father." The world turned upside down. "I heard they hadn't taken Haiduc so I came to see." He looked at Fane sitting in the straw, the wooden bucket and the by-now dozing horse.

"What are you doing?" asked Carol again, as an afterthought.

"The vet, the doctor for animals, said Haiduc's foot had an...an...a sore and maybe was sick, too. I'm trying to soak it in the medicine but he isn't helping."

"Why isn't your father doing it?" asked Carol. Another wave of anger and shame silenced Fane and he looked down at the dirty straw under his legs. "Never mind," Carol continued in a rare moment of insight. "Let me help."

With one boy to hold the bucket and the other the horse's hoof, a routine was established. Night and morning Carol came. As time passed Fane began to admire Carol's way with the horse. "You're good with horses," he blurted out on the fourth day, half jealous.

"It's about the only thing I can do. Father beats me all the time because I can't read." Carol turned away, patting the big bay on his shoulder. "I like horses better than I like people."

"You can read," said Fane. "I bet you can. I'll help."

"Oh, you can't help, I'm just stupid." Fane was astounded at this admission. Carol was self-important and a bully.

And he wasn't stupid, except for reading.

They started that afternoon, the one-eyed leading the blind. They did lessons together, Fane delighting in being able to read Carol's lesson book, Carol beginning to see how the marks made letters and how they fit together. When the course of medicine had finished, the boys came to Fane's house after school to clean Haiduc's feet and brush his long, muddy winter coat with bundles of straw. "The vet said his feet and stall should be kept clean," Fane had said, and Carol took it to heart. The boys spent hours in the barn with Haiduc and the cows then went into the house to do their lessons.

"Hey," said Carol one day.

"Hay is for horses," interrupted Fane. The two were sitting in the stack of straw they had brought in to dry out from the winter snow. "Shut up," replied Carol amiably. "I bet we could get on Haiduc."

"What?"

"Get on Haiduc. Come on." Carol jumped up and climbed the side of the horse's now semi-clean enclosure. Clambering over the top board, he slithered up onto the bay's broad back. Haiduc looked back at him, mildly curious, and went back to his afternoon snooze.

"See," said Carol. "Come on!"

"I don't know," Fane said hesitantly. "Father..." but his voice trailed off and he followed Carol. Fane had driven Haiduc often when his father was alongside but he had never seen the horse ridden. Haiduc's back was broad and wintercoat furry warm. Carol lay back, then sat up, swung his legs over the horse's rump and, facing backwards, lay down again on his tummy, arms crossed under his chin. Fane sat ahead, facing forward, picking at a splinter he had gotten in his palm when he climbed the boards in the stall wall, beginning to feel comfortable on the horse's back. The boys talked about everything and nothing.

"This reading stuff is easy," Carol bragged one day. "I just didn't understand before. But I could've anyway even without your help." Fane didn't say anything. Both of them knew.

The friendship even survived the addition of Mendl.

Late one night about three weeks after the village horses had been taken there were slow footsteps in the courtyard, then a knock. With a worried mutter, Petru swung open the wooden door to find Mendl's father standing in the intersection of house warmth and freezing night, long coat blotting out the moonlight.

"Come in, come in," said Petru heartily but Fane, lying in his cozy bed by the tile stove, felt the note of caution in his father's welcome. "Come in. Sit down. A *tzuica*?"

"Yes, I'll drink a *tzuica*, thank you," answered Mendl's father, a hard edge cutting through his normally soft voice as he took off his brimmed hat.

"Here, Anna, bring something to eat. We have a guest."

"Please," said their guest, "I can't eat. I just need to talk to you."

"Just a little bite," said Mother politely.

"No, food is dust," was the strange answer.

Petru shifted uneasily in his seat, wondering if his guest had come to collect money. Surely the only shopkeeper of the village knew peasants couldn't pay until crops began to come in. Petru began to warm with anger as both men sat silent, the debt shimmering incarnate between them.

"I have a favor to ask, a great favor," Mendl's father said after a few more empty exchanges of polite words. "A great favor."

Stunned by the reversal of their usual roles, Petru merely said, "Yes, sir? Tell me."

"I want you to take Mendl to live with you and learn how to be a Romanian peasant. Teach him how to not be a Jew. I don't want him to be a Christian, you understand, but he needs to know how...how to appear to be one."

"What are you asking? Why? Why are you asking me?"

The shopkeeper shifted again, then settled himself. "You know," he began picking nervously at his cuticles, "about the war." Petru dipped his chin. "You know," he continued, "that I have relatives in Bukovina and through the north." Petru dipped his chin again though he didn't know, had only heard rumors.

Then Josef began to talk. He started with the German invasion of Poland, the refugees that had flooded Radauti on the way south, which Petru and Mother and even Fane knew about. He talked about the German bombing of Jewish villages in Poland, the rumors of things beginning to happen to Jews in Germany. He talked about his position in Bilca, how much he loved the village and how good he felt with the peasants. Here Petru felt he should speak. "You've always been good to us," he said, "and you are one of us." Warm feelings rose suddenly. "And," Petru added, "I know that my son Fane and your son Mendl are friends. I am pleased with that."

Josef relaxed a bit, his weight moving from his tight shoulders down into his hips, settling him onto the stool as if he belonged there.

"That's why I've come," he said. "Things are going to be bad for all of us, but they will be the worst for the Jews." Both men silently reaffirmed this. "After my wife died when Mendl was born the boy, he became my life. I want him to live, to have a good life."

"But what about you?" Petru asked, puzzled.

"I don't matter but, look," he said, drawing an imaginary map on the table. "Here is Romania. Here is Germany. Here is Russia. Germany and Russia are allies now but both want Romania's oil and Russia wants Bessarabia back. I have also heard," he hesitated, "that Russian troops are moving to the border of Bukovina..."

About this point, Fane's eyes were closing by themselves and he drifted off into an uncomfortable land of unwanted dreams.

The next morning, Mother said, "Fane, Mendl is going to come and live with us. Don't talk about it with anyone in the village except to say that his father had to go help some sick relatives. If anyone from outside the village comes, Mendl is your cousin."

"Mendl, my cousin? Mendl coming to live with us? How can Mendl be my cousin if he's Jewish?" Fane asked, feeling his voice rise with anxiety and anger.

"He won't be Jewish. And, uh, we won't call him Mendl any more. His name is Mihai. Like the King." Fane nodded.

"So Mendl..." "Mihai," his mother corrected. "Say it, Mihai."

"Mihai." Fane repeated. "Mihai is my cousin and will live with us. Where is his father going?"

"Away." Mother answered. "Your father may know where. I don't."

"Won't Mendl, no Mihai, won't Mihai be lonely without his father?"

"Poor little thing," said Mother softly, "I think he will. But he'll have us. We're his family now. And his father said an uncle would come to visit from Radauti." "Radauti," said

Fane reflectively. Radauti was where the high school was. It was a long way away. "But, Mommy, what's going to happen? It's bad, isn't it?"

"We don't know what will happen. God will decide that and God will take care of us." The conversation was ended.

Fane thought Mendl/Mihai, would come that day, but he didn't. In school, it was difficult not to say anything to Carol and even harder not to talk to Mendl, no Mihai. The two boys avoided each other, the shared secret creating a barrier, but the next they found themselves together during lunch break, walking together by the small river which flowed through the village.

"You're coming to live with us," stated Fane.

"Yes," replied Mendl, with a stony face. "And I will be Mihai. I won't be...I won't be Mendl anymore."

"What's going on with you?" asked Fane.

"I don't know, except Father said I can't stay with him because he is going to leave."

"Oh, okay," said Fane. "You can help with Haiduc, then, along with me and Carol," he added generously.

Mendl looked nervous but the school bell in the distance cut them short and they ran back to class.

The next day, at the time people were inside eating dinner, Petru hitched Haiduc to the sleigh and set off into the village through a winkling snowy night. Later he returned with such a load that there was hardly room for Mendl/Mihai beside him. He and Mother unloaded bags and bundles, helped by Mendl/Mihai, Fane and Mioara while Granny muttered "Jesus, martyr, killers" in the background. Mendl was crying silently, tears rolling down his thin cheeks.

Finally, Mother folded him in her arms. "Don't worry," she said. "Everything will be all right. You lost your mother and I lost a son, so now we have each other." Fane looked at her with surprise and a pang of jealousy.

"And from now on," Mother continued, "you are my nephew, Mihai, a part of our family. Your mother, my sister, died and you have come to live with us. That is how it will be to the rest of the world and that is how it will be in this house." She looked firmly at Grandmother who shifted and said, "Death and destruction will rain down on the family because of this."

Fane slowly neared the bar, greeting this person and that in the course of his journey. Out of the corner of his eye he glimpsed Greta, the German professor, slipping three cigarettes into her purse before she raised a fourth to her lips. "Could you give me a light?" she asked, turning to her husband. Fane mentally shrugged; the Americans had so much and real cigarettes were hard to come by these days. Good he didn't have that addiction. In another direction Mircea, clearly in his cups, was speaking rapidly to one of the diplomats, waving his hands. Jazz drifted over the group from the direction of the piano.

Fane reached the bar, a table covered with white linen and an impressive array of bottles. "Scotch, please, double" he said, extending his glass.

Victor, the host's chauffeur doing double duty as bartender, raised an eyebrow slightly, but poured a generous slug. Fane ignored the fleeting expression on the familiar fine-boned face. He could handle things. He turned back into the crowd, looking for Ellen Pelletier, the new Director of the American Library, Pam's successor.

"Where will Mendl sleep?" was Fane's first question.

"Mihai," Mother corrected him, "Mihai will sleep with you."

So now Fane shared his high space between the warm tile *soba* and the wall with his new cousin. This he thought, turning over restlessly, was the hardest part of having a "cousin" live with them. The space wasn't that big, really, and he hated having someone's breath on his face. He complained to Mother but she cut him short so that he was left alone with his resentment.

At school there was a flurry of interest the first day they arrived together but the new order relaxed into accepted fact before the week was over. Things were beginning to happen in the village, young men leaving for the army, other people visiting or passing by, and an implicit understanding that change was imminent had the curious effect of deadening interest in those things that had already been altered.

And there was enough food — something Granny had raised in the long course of her initial complaints. Somehow there was more food and better than Fane remembered from the hungry months of late winters before but that, too, soon went unnoticed.

It took longer for Carol to accept Mihai. The boys worked together to keep Haiduc and his stall clean because Carol had heard that good horses were brushed regularly.

"What nonsense," said Petru but he showed them how to twist straw to be used as a brush. It didn't work very well but they used it.

"I bet you," said Carol one afternoon, interrupting Fane and Mihai, "I bet I can stand up on Haiduc's back!" Almost before he finished, he was scrambling up the boards separating Haiduc from the cow. Quickly he slid onto the broad, brown back, drew up his knees, stood on them, and put a foot under him. Fane gasped as Carol, a little unsteadily, eased himself up and stood tall. Haiduc shifted in surprise and Carol slid down into a normal position.

"Wow," said Mihai. "I wish I could do that." Fane started with his second surprise of the afternoon. Mihai was scared of Haiduc. Or at least he had been scared though, come to think of it, that was last week.

As days passed the patient horse became accustomed to being stood on, slid from and generally used as an extension of the boys' play about the circus, battles against evil, and an imaginary airplane. Mihai, slight of build, and muscular but limber, and Carol were better than Fane but no one forgot that Haiduc belonged to Fane's father so everyone was even, Fane thought resentfully. And Mihai got them a real brush.

Each Sunday, after church, Mihai's uncle, Uncle Vanya, appeared to have lunch with the family. In the snow and rain when roads were muddy he rode a bony horse. As the roads began to dry out, he came in a little trap, pulled by the same animal.

"Why does Mihai have an uncle with a Russian name?" Petru once wondered to his wife, but this wasn't ever mentioned to Vanya himself and no one else could answer, including Mihai. "Is he your mother's brother or your father's brother?" asked Mother but Mihai didn't know. Uncle Vanya was just there, part of Mendl's landscape. And now he was here, in Mihai's new home, bringing news for the adults, sweets for the boys, and a small present for Granny or a thimble for Mioara. It didn't take long for Granny to sing his praises and, since he always had a special sausage or some sugar or some other delicacy for the house, he was a welcome guest at Sunday lunch.

The third week he came, he turned to Mihai as they were leaving and quietly asked him something Fane couldn't understand. Mihai looked surprised for a moment, then answered. A short exchange followed with Mihai obviously asking something back and Uncle Vanya nodding.

Later Fane asked, "What did Uncle Vanya say to you? I couldn't understand it. What was he saying?"

Mihai was surprised again. "Didn't you understand? He asked if I was happy."

"Are you?" Fane tried to ignore the fact that Mihai knew something Fane didn't.

Mihai shifted and looked away. "It's nice here," he said. "Let's go see what's for dinner."

"But why couldn't I understand what you were saying?" Fane persisted. "It sounded real strange."

"It's not strange." Mihai was vehement and uncomfortable. "It's how Daddy and I talk at home. I know it's different. Daddy said I shouldn't talk about it, but it's called German."

"German?" asked Fane, still confused.

"That's the kind of language it is. They used to speak it here more, when Bukovina belonged to Austria. Daddy said," Mihai went on hesitantly, confiding at last, "that's where our family came from and Daddy says everyone spoke German there and that I should know how to do it too."

"But aren't you from here, like us?" asked Fane. You've always been here. But..." he added, "you are different from me."

"I don't know," answered the child, "I used to be but now I'm not different," Mihai looked down at the clothes that Fane's mother had made for him, "I'm Mihai and I belong here now."

The soldiers never came back for Haiduc or the other few horses left in the village. Instead, more young men left, including Radu-who-makes-Mioara's-eyes-light-up, conscripted like the others into the army, leaving middle-aged to old men and the women to farm.

Haiduc and two mares who had been heavily pregnant became very popular. The first family friend who appeared to borrow the horse "just for a day or two to plough, you know we can't do it without an animal because my wife is ill," was soon followed by others. Petru lent Haiduc judiciously, wanting to help, not wanting to overwork the horse so he couldn't be used at home, appreciating the fodder and gifts people brought in return, afraid of the enemies he made because one horse can't plough fields for a whole village.

In spite of all Haiduc's efforts, those of the other horses, the few bullocks and cows who could plough, and the husbands and wives who dragged a plow through fields without an animal, not all of the land could be planted. It was going to be a bad year.

Most of this went over the boys' heads. Uncle Vanya returned with a brush the week after Fane learned there were more things he didn't know than he had dreamed, so Haiduc began to gleam as he shed his winter coat.

And things settled into a more normal routine. Mihai asked Granny to teach him Christian prayers and her grumbling turned to other targets. Carol and Fane told Mihai he really could fight after he'd been cornered by another boy and beaten up at school.

"What happened?" Fane had asked when Mihai appeared with a bloody nose and black eye. Mihai had just turned away without saying anything but eventually it came out.

"Why didn't you hit him back?" asked Fane, remembering vaguely that Mihai usually ran away from a fight.

Obviously that hadn't worked this time.

"I dunno," mumbled Mihai, trying to get away.

"Oh, no, don't leave," said Carol. "Tell us why you didn't hit him back." Fane recalled when he had come home crying after being hit the first time. "If you don't know how to defend yourself, stay home with Mother," Petru had said unsympathetically.

"We don't fight," Mihai was still mumbling. "We don't fight."

"Who we?"

"Us. We're different."

"You mean, you Jews?" Mihai-becoming-Mendl nodded.

"Oh, no, you aren't," answered Carol. "You're not different. Look at you." Mendl looked down at his clothes and up at Carol and Fane, dressed the same, all with dirt ground in along the sides of their fingers and felt like Mihai once again. At that point Carol stepped forward and shoved him on the shoulder. Mihai shoved back then leapt on Carol, tickling him mercilessly as they fell sideways. Fane watched the two boys scrapping and laughing on the ground feeling like an outsider for a moment, then jumped on the pile, playful puppies rolling in the dirt.

At that point Mihai stopped being different. He always remained slight but soon had developed a wiriness and tough agility that surprised everyone. Together, the three made a powerful team and they triumphantly ruled their small world.

Signs of spring appeared, pussywillows on the banks of the stream and nettle-soup, the first fresh green food of the year. Fane savored it, feeling the thick liquid's slight sharp thistle bite whispering along the side of his tongue. Mihai had never had it before and didn't like it much but ate anyway because it was food. Uncle Vanya continued to come and became a family fixture. He and Petru talked after lunch, walking out to the barn, watching the boys play or Mioara spin.

The weeks rolled past Easter and on to the end of the school year, tree branches swelled and burst into bud, bloom and leaf. Layers of clothing came off and the mud began to crumble into dust. The winds of war barely touched the children until Uncle Vanya appeared unexpectedly on a warm June afternoon, riding his now slightly fatter horse.

"Hola, what's up?" called Petru from the barn. Vanya swung down and led the horse to the fence, his face impenetrable. Fane and Mihai were weeding the vegetable garden behind the house and quietly drifted over to listen from shadow of the solid fence.

"Not much," Vanya answered. "How are you?" Formalities were duly administered. Eventually Petru asked, "Is it time?"

"My brother," answered Uncle Vanya, "it is. You should leave tomorrow morning, no later. And when you get to Brodina, go south, don't take the road to the north."

"But I don't know if we can take the wagon beyond Brodina de Jos. The road's bad. If there is a road."

"Please, it's important. Leave the wagon if you must and go by foot. I'm not sure exactly what will happen, but you must go south from Brodina to Brodina de Jos and from there to Carlibaba. Also, it will be better to be away from main roads. You can get to Brodina by tomorrow night, then early the next morning go south"

"It's about thirty kilometers from here to Brodina," said Petru, thinking of a heavily loaded wagon and one horse. "It will be possible if the roads are good."

"The roads should be good. It hasn't rained. Once you leave Brodina you can take it easy."

"What will you do?" asked Petru suddenly.

"I'll manage," replied Vanya who looked beyond Petru's shoulder and spied the boys. "Mihai, Fane, come here!" He put an arm around each of them. "Children, we are all going to have to leave on a long journey and I won't see you again for a while. Can you help your family and be brave?"

"Are you going with us?" asked Mihai. Fane remained silent and frozen with a pain in his chest moving toward his stomach, thinking suddenly of Haiduc and his stall and the house and his life.

"No, I'm not. I wish I could but I have to go another direction. But we'll be together again."

"What about my father?" Mendl/Mihai asked for the first time since he had come, beginning to cry. "Where is he?

When will I see him? How will he find me if I'm not here?"

"He is all right and sends his love to you," answered Uncle Vanya, drawing Mihai close to his reassuring bulk. "He knows where you are going, it's part of his plan to keep you and everyone here safe." Fane stepped back, feeling an overwhelming sorrow seeping into his soul. He began to cry as well.

"Here, here," said Uncle Vanya. "Go in the house and bring water for our guest," said Petru.

Vanya left quickly, but not before slipping Petru a small bag and a folded piece of paper. "In case of emergency," he said, "and an identity card for Mihai Sirbu."

Petru watched the big man ride out the gate and down the road, then turned to the boys. "Go tell Mother we're leaving tomorrow morning. We're going to visit cousins." "Cousins?" asked Fane.

"Yes," replied Petru. "Your cousins in Poiana Cozonac, in Transylvania. I haven't seen my family there in a long time. My aunt is sick and I want to see her once more in this life." What had seemed a disaster could be an adventure! The boys ran off, whooping and shouting toward the house while Petru watched. Then Petru looked around at his house, his barn, his land and sighed. He would be leaving part of his heart in its soil. Then he shrugged. The land would be here even if nothing else survived.

Granny was also pleased at the prospect of a journey. "I may die on the way," she announced, "but I will see my mountains again. And if I don't die on the road, in misery, as is likely, I will see my family." Fane looked at her in surprise.

"Yes, little chicken, my family." The old woman pulled him close to her side. "I was married here in Bilca but I was raised high in the mountains." She sighed, softly, uncharacteristically. "Once mountains are in your soul they never leave."

There were so many things Fane didn't know, even about his own family.

Mioara wasn't as happy. "But Radu is coming home on leave, his mother told me," she exclaimed. "I can't go." "You have to," said Mother, "You will," said Petru.

"No, I don't have to." Fane's mouth dropped at Mioara's defiance. Her pretty face flushed, Mioara declared, "I'll stay with Radu's family until you come back. We're engaged after all!" Other mouths dropped in a flurry of surprise, awe, excitement and despair. "Engaged!" "How could you be without the church and us giving consent?" "What?" "Shut your mouth!" This from her angry father. "You're going with us. You can't be engaged unless I say you can. No, shut up and get ready."

"No. I'm staying." Said Mioara, defiant. Petru slapped her, sending her reeling while Mother stepped back and cried out. The boys began to cry again and Grandmother muttered. Turning on his heel, Petru stalked out, leaving the family in tatters.

It was late before they had done as much as they could that night, loading food, seeds, tools, the plough ("Won't it be too heavy?" asked Mother. "We'll sell it or throw it off if we have to, but I want it if we can manage," replied her husband grimly.) preparing to pack clothes and bedding in the house. It didn't seem like a good start to a fun journey, thought Fane, but he and Mihai ran for this and that as bidden. On one of the trips into the house Fane looked up at the little cream colored plate with the green and yellow sort of deer and, on an impulse, grabbed it and stuffed it into his clothes. Mioara also worked, face set and shoulders tense, putting her spinning wheel in at the very last and tying it to the tailboard. Finally, after a supper of cold potatoes and cheese, the family went to bed.

Morning came with an explosion.

"Mioara's gone!" cried Mother.

"Damn chit," answered her husband.

"I'm going to get her." Mother put on her apron and started out the door. "She must be at Radu's parents' house."

"We don't have time. Besides, she's probably hiding until we go. We're going to have to leave her," announced Petru.

Fane watched his mother's face crumple into tears. "No," she cried. "I can't leave my child."

"If you don't," spat Petru at her, helpless anger suffusing his face, "if you don't you'll have to leave your other child. Take your pick. We're going." He threw the chicken coop on top of the loaded wagon, tied the two small pigs inside the cart, and told the boys, "Get in." Mihai obeyed. Fane looked from one parent to the other. "Get in, I said." Petru raised his hand and Fane scrambled up the step and into the back of the wagon, sitting beside Mihai and Grandmother on the quilts. Mother looked at them and looked down the road to the village. Slowly, tears streaming down her face, she climbed onto the seat beside her husband. Petru sat beside her and raised the reins.

"The cow! We can't leave the cow," howled Grandmother. No one replied as they set off in shambles.

Second Scotch in hand, Fane turned back to the party and spied Ellen, recognizing her from the receiving line earlier in the evening. He set off toward her, jovially greeting one person and another along the way. Suddenly his progress came to a halt, his arm caught by Dinu, the film director.

"Fane, how are you? I'm working on a film," Dinu began, "which is set in your period, one of your periods, that is, 19th century Romania, late 19th century Romania, that is, in Bucharest, of course, and I wanted..." Fane smiled genially over his annoyance. "God, how we Romanians love to talk," he thought. "What is he thinking about, setting a film in a period dominated by a royal family no one is allowed to mention." Fane settled into an interested pose, brightened his eyes, raised the Scotch to his lips and let his mind wander.

"I'm not sure about the hero, I've been thinking of Carol...you know him?" Fane's attention ratcheted up a notch.

The road skirted the main part of the village and by the time people began to come out of their houses, Haiduc was trotting smartly past the last buildings. Petru raised a jovial hand — "Going to visit the relatives," he announced and waved. Friends waved back and they were on the open road.

"I couldn't say good-bye to Carol!" exclaimed Fane. "No matter, you'll see him soon," his Father answered. Fane wondered about that a moment, but grownups knew what was going on.

Shortly the jagged layers of the Carpathians were clearly visible on the horizon and hills began to run alongside the road while the stream to their left ran more quickly. Haiduc leaned into the harness as the road rose. "Are we going there, over there?" asked Mihai pointing southwest.

"Not quite," answered Petru, once again the knowledgeable head of the family. "Those are the hills behind Putna, the Monastery of Stefan cel Mare, Stephen the Great, who Fane was named after. We're going there" — he pointed straight ahead — "just a little to the north, toward Brodina. We'll spend the night at Brodina," he expanded on the theme, "because Stefan from Bilca, another Fane," this in an aside to Fane his son, "works there at the stud farm. He's a cousin, I think." "Of course," interrupted Granny, "he's my father's uncle's..." Petru resumed, ignoring the details of relationship, "Then we'll go south, behind those mountains. It's a long road and hard, but we'll do it." The boys sat, taking in the enormous distance and great challenge. Haiduc clopped along, blissfully ignorant of the road ahead. Granny continued to talk about everything and nothing, Mother shrank silently into her seat.

By evening a very tired horse and five weary travelers saw the buildings of the Brodina stud farm lining the road behind a row of poplars. Petru swung the wagon into a great courtyard, filled mostly with hay and mud, and called, "Eh, Stefan! Stefan! Where are you?"

Fane started to say "Right here," but realized in time that it was the other Stefan who was being called. A short man in dirty clothes came out of the barn.

"Well, Petru. I'll be damned. What brings you here? And the family! By God, your horse looks tired, let's give him some water. Come in, come in, the wife will be glad to see you. Where are you going?" The other Stefan, Fane thought, must be a relative because he was just like Grandmother, busy and talking.

The men unhitched and watered Haiduc, then turned him into a pasture with some younger horses. "He'll be fine with the yearlings, won't you my good boy. He looks like he has a bit of Gidran in him somewhere, so perhaps they're related, too. But he isn't the right color." Stefan gave the boys and Petru a tour of the farm while the women went in to greet his wife. The great barns and pastures were full of red horses, beautiful ones, thought Fane, but not, he hastened to say to himself and the gods that be, nearly as beautiful as Haiduc. There were huge rooms in the stable, lined with wood to above Fane's head and whitewashed to the ceiling, some full of young horses or mothers and babies, others with two-year-olds, and some small rooms with beautiful stallions. Everything was neat and there was fresh straw in all the stalls. Fane nudged Mihai and said, "I bet Carol would like to see this! We've never been in a place like this before."

"But we've never seen much of anything at all, besides Bilca," Mihai reminded him.

After dinner the boys were put to bed in the wagon while the adults stayed at the table and talked. As they left the house, Fane sleepily heard Petru telling Stefan quietly something about war and Stefan saying, "Yes, okay, but you have to be careful about wolves..." Not much else happened in the two seconds it took him to go to sleep.

The next four days were effort beyond comprehension and overwhelming exhaustion. The road south from Brodina went through Brodina de Jos, then up, and down a bit, and up again and down yet again and up further. Great trees surrounded them, blocked their way, rivers almost swallowed them and the road disappeared. Petru kept saying, "Keep going," or "The forester said to...", but neither Fane or Mihai remembered anyone in particular, only a blur of lonely huts with strange people in them, feet that hurt first with blisters, then became numb, and always the exhaustion. The family walked to lighten the load, even grandmother, as Haiduc strained into the harness with the adults pushing the wagon at some points. Once, the wagon was stuck and Petru made them take everything out so they could lift it over a log after Haiduc had been unhitched and made to jump the barrier. Then everything, chickens and piglets included, went back in. At night they huddled against one or another lonely hut and once against some rocks with wolves howling in the background and a small fire in front of them, the boys too tired to think about being eaten. The load lightened a bit as Haiduc and the family ate their rations but by the time this made any difference they were going downhill more than up, Haiduc braking the wagon with his weight and the help of an iron rod against the wheel, boys walking again, everyone tired to the point of deadened senses and lack of thought. Finally they came to a bank that overlooked a real road lined with trees, an empty field on the other side.

"The Carlibaba Road!" exclaimed Petru. "We did get off the track. It should have taken us straight to Carlibaba."

"Now he admits it," said Mother, "but which way is Carlibaba? Left or right?"

"It should be to the right," said Petru confidently.

"No, to the left," contradicted Granny.

"It can't be. We have come out to the east of Carlibaba."

"No, we haven't," insisted Granny. "Look, there is Omului," she said pointing at a high peak, "and if we were east of Carlibaba it would be over there. Besides," she added, "I know that little grove of trees well, the one kind of hidden below the road."

"How do you remember that?" asked Fane in wonderment.

"Never you mind, little poky nose. I was young once," Granny snorted with laughter. "Go on," to Petru, "turn right on the road. We'll find our track south in a few minutes." Petru guided Haiduc down the bank, the wagon gave a last thump and settled its wheels gratefully on the real road.

They came to their turn in half an hour without seeing a soul. "Strange," repeated Grandmother over and over, "there should be travelers." As soon as they left the road they were in the forest once again but here there was a clear track, not good but traveled enough to be followed easily. It led down a narrow valley, the hills on either side stitching them and a small, fast flowing river together with multiple crosses and turns. Finally, just after they had gone through a small village where one or two people looked at them curiously while Granny grinned and waved at faces she hoped were familiar, they turned off the track at Granny's direction and Petru's assent. From the track it had looked like there was an unbroken wall of forest but inside the first line of trees it was possible to see a way through, large enough for the wagon, up along a narrow valley, the mountains so high on either side that the sun hardly touched the forest's top. "Are you sure this is the way?" asked Mother. "Absolutely," said Petru. "It's home!" said Grandmother, "God be praised."

Soon the valley widened into a meadow and the road was easier to follow though it was still climbing. Then into another small forested valley, almost hidden by surrounding hills. Haiduc and the wagon topped a small rise, descended through great dark firs and made one last turn. Here the family stopped of one accord, gazing over a high meadow, rimmed with trees and closely guarded by more forest-clad mountains. On the far side, up against a dark green backdrop of giant trees, was a village, surprisingly large for its isolation. "Poiana Cozonac!" announced Fane. "Poiana Cozonac," screeched Granny. "I guess we're here," said Mother softly.

"*Cozonac*?" asked Fane. "Do they have lots of that sweet bread, *cozonac*? I like it."

"It was better in old days," said Granny reflexively, Petru laughed aloud, and Mother said, "I'll make you *cozonac*, my son." Mihai sat silent as Haiduc eased the wagon over old ruts into the meadow, snatching bites of grass as he walked. Ahead there was a straggle and a flurry in the village, then a figure emerged, walking across the valley toward them. When the man was close enough to be seen, Petru shouted in glee, jumping down from the wagon to run toward him. "Grigore! Grigore!" "By my God, it's Petru. Petrica! Welcome, welcome! It's been years but you haven't changed! And the family! You've all come! You must have heard the news! Welcome!"

"News? What news?" asked Petru.

"You really haven't heard? Yesterday..." answered Grigore, taking his hat off as he neared the wagon and saw Granny. "Welcome, Missus," to mother and to Granny, "Auntie Varvara!" "Grigore!" screeched Granny, "Look at you! You've gotten old!" Grigore scratched his head in amusement.

"What do you think? It's been...how many years?"

"Let's see..." Grandmother began to calculate on her fingers.

"What news?" asked Mother softly. Grigore turned toward her. "You really haven't heard?" he asked.

"No," said Petru.

"It's the Russians," Grigore said. "Yesterday they took away not only Bessarabia but most of Bukovina as well. They've taken it away from Romania."

Fane and his family froze in place. Petru was the first to recover. "So it happened," he said, looking ten years older.

"Mioara!" cried Mother, tears running down her face again.

"My cow!" sobbed Granny, "those dirty Russians will take my cow!"

The men talked, wondering which side of the border Bilca might be on, wondering what Romania would do. The others simply listened in suspended, frozen silence as the small group traversed the quiet meadow, spring buttercups and lupine catching the last of the afternoon sun. Fane and Mihai held hands for comfort. Grigore said, "Yes, now that we have a radio we get all the news. No one knew...that is, we had heard Russia wanted Bessarabia, that's nothing new, but Bukovina..."

Fane nudged Mihai. "Uncle Vanya," he said. Mihai nodded and answered, "Yes, it must have been."

"But how did you know it was going to happen?" Grigore was asking Petru.

"I didn't. Just that it seemed that, one way or another, Bukovina was going to be invaded and that the family would be better off here. The army already came to take the horses, only Haiduc was lame at the time, God bless that rotten Gypsy farrier, and the younger men have been conscripted." "They've done that here, too," Grigore interrupted, "and soon it would be our..." Petru's voice faded as the men pulled ahead of the dragging horse and tired family. 'Grandmother is happy she's coming "home" but it isn't home to me', Fane thought, 'or to Mommy or Mihai and we don't have Mioara or even our cow...', a tear escaped and made a streak down his dirty face.

"Don't cry," said Mihai. "Wipe your cheek so no one knows."

"Why?" asked Fane.

"That's what my father always told me. Never let anyone know what you are feeling or thinking. It's safer."

Fane looked at Mihai a moment thinking that he did cry, Mihai did too cry, but then Petru shouted. They had come to the outskirts of the village and he was standing by a small, old house.

"Look, Ma," he said to Grandmother. "Your family house is still here and empty. It's ours. We have a place to stay." "Do you mean to say you brought us all this way without knowing there would be someplace to stay?" asked Mother all her anger erupting, bursting from every inch of her body. "All this way?"

"Of course not," said Petru, still pleased. "I knew we'd find someplace to stay — we're related to half the village and they'd help us no matter what — but the old house..." his voice trailed off as Grigore returned with his wife.

"Carol Cojocariu...the actor?" Fane prompted.

"Yes, that's him. Good actor. Good face. Very popular. And he can ride a horse, did you know that, and look good, which is important, you have no idea what we have to put up with..."

"I thought Carol was, um, not very popular these days," Fane interrupted one of Dinu's famous extended sentences. The joke around town was that bookies took bets on how many words he could string together without verbal punctuation.

"Well, that's true but it's been a couple of years since that unfortunate incident and about time that people forget the past and look into the future because after all..."

Fane remembered the 'unfortunate incident' well. Carol had vaulted off his horse during a visit of the Leader and his family to the Buftea film studio. He'd landed immediately in front of the daughter and looked meltingly into her eyes before turning to the country's leader. Horses and women, Carol's weaknesses, only he was picky about the quality of his horses.

44

"Maybe that's true," Fane said. "He's a good actor, as you said. Let me know what happens – you're a brave man." Fane smiled with a subtle hint of admiration, squeezed Dinu's elbow and moved on. Ellen had drifted into a quiet space by the bookcase and was looking around. Perfect.

Of the six years the family lived in Poiana Cozonac there were three things, Fane thought as they packed the old wagon, he would particularly remember. Besides the landscape, of course. He turned for a minute to survey the little house, the sloping meadow and the outline of Cucureasa looming above them. 'Maybe I have become a mountain person,' he thought along a diversionary line. 'Maybe there is a difference between people raised in the mountains rather than on the plains. But I was so young when we left Bilca – only seven. That was 1940 and now it's 1946 and the war is over but the Russians have run out the Germans and given us, Transylvania, back to Romania but they've still taken part of Bukovina even if our house is okay, like Tante Elise said when she told that traveler who told...but maybe we should stay here but', he turned back to the wagon, 'we'd have to go to school down in the Ilvei valley so we wouldn't be here anyway...' He turned his thoughts back to the last six years.

It was Mihai who had started them on this subject, mushing on about what they would remember. They were ready for sleep, comfortable in the hayloft over the barn now that it was spring. They had just learned from Petru that he planned to take the family home to Bilca.

"Home," said Mihai. "Where is home anyway, now? Maybe I'll find Father – perhaps he's come back, maybe Uncle Vanya will know where he is – but will we ever live in our house again?" In six years Mihai had received two letters from Uncle Vanya, both warm and reassuring but without details.

"I feel funny about going to Bilca," Fane confessed. "I hardly remember anything about it now, except maybe we can find Mioara. Mother doesn't say anything, but I know she's hoping."

"Remember..." mused Mihai. "I remember my Father and his store and working there. And I remember Carol and the time you and Carol told me I could fight back."

"Really?" asked Fane. "We had to tell you that?" Fane thought of the scraps he and Mihai had been in together in Poiana Cozonac. They had had to fight their way into acceptance by the boys who were already there, but it didn't take long. Fane grinned to himself. Of course, there weren't very many, either. It was a small village. But that one, when was it...

"Yes, you did," Mihai's voice interrupted Fane's memory of a particularly good fight and brought him back to the hayloft. "But now, what will we remember in six years or ten or twenty years about Poiana Cozonac? Besides our friends, of course." Both boys lay still for a moment thinking of the other kids in the village, who'd shared the schoolroom with them, who'd played with them, who'd fought with them through the years.

"That we didn't get *cozonac* all the time," joked Fane, breaking the silence, "only at Easter and Christmas, the same as in Bilca."

"And that the houses were made of wood, not white plaster," said Mihai, "and that there are wolves here." "And that time when the wolf jumped on the sheep and made it walk into the woods," interrupted Fane. "I still don't believe it," interrupted Mihai in turn, "or wouldn't believe it except we both saw it, the way the wolf was guiding the sheep by its neck, walking along on its hind legs, and making it go into the forest..."

"And we weren't brave enough to go out and rescue the ewe."

"But, seriously, what happened here that was really important?" asked Mihai again.

"Well," pondered Fane, "when Transylvania was given to the Hungarians and we had to learn Hungarian in school. And then when Romania got us back and the war ended."

"No, I don't mean for history. I mean for us. Like the time that..." The boys talked back and forth a bit more before falling into dreams of roads and forests and the open plain.

Fane shook his head and turned back to the house, ready to carry out the next load but Mother met him halfway. "We're done," she said. "Go get Haiduc. The boy, still slightly awkward in his long adolescent bones, turned back to the barn and walked toward the horse. Haiduc looked at him, hoping as always for food.

"We're going home, Old Boy," Fane said softly into the pointed black-tipped ear, blowing on the hairs lining its interior and running his thumb along the soft edge. "We're going home and, lucky for you, we're going by a real road this time." He remembered how astounded everyone had been when they heard the family came through Brodina de Jos and up the mountains.

"Impossible," Grigore had said. "There's no road there anymore. You can barely get through on foot." Grandmother and Mother had looked at each other, prudently keeping their mouths shut. Grigore's wife and the group of neighbors had all nodded.

"Well, we did, and here we are," was all Petru would say.

Fane put the collar over Haiduc's head, threw the harness across his back and began drawing rough straps through iron rings, "I wonder where Carol is," he thought. "Or...IF he still is..." Fane stopped thinking abruptly, shying away from the unknown. The news that out of Moldova hadn't been that good.

"Not that it was easy here," Fane told Haiduc. "And I certainly know one of the three things Mihai will always remember."

It was, let me see, thought Fane, two years ago when we were eleven...

Poiana Cozonac was so isolated that few cared to make the effort to visit it except the postman and tax collector. The village men who had been left by the various armies — mainly because they disappeared into the mountains with the sheep whenever there was a rumor of more conscriptions — occasionally went to town to sell wool and cheese from their sheep and to buy necessary supplies, but women and children rarely left the village and didn't see many strangers. So any visitors were an event — usually unpleasant — and the ones who came that day aroused both interest and fear. They had arrived on horseback, two men in foreign uniforms, riding into the village and asking to see the mayor. Grigore limped forward, a slight limp that became worse whenever strangers or officials appeared.

"We're making a census and want to know how many people live in the village," one announced, speaking Hungarian badly and with an accent. Fane and Mihai nudged one another; their Hungarian language studies actually were useful. The rider looked around, mentally counting the houses.

"Should I count the men who have been conscripted?" asked Grigore.

"Which army?" asked the officer.

"The Romanian Army in the spring of 1940. None has come back. Then two more by the Hungarian Army," Grigore shifted his weight, emphasizing his bad leg. "They haven't come back either."

"Just tell me how many families."

"We are twenty-three families and two widows."

"You say that the younger men were conscripted," the officer said. "What about you and the others of your age?"

"They didn't want me or the priest." The riders considered this, looking at Grigore and then through the women and children. Fane started to look for Father but stopped himself, realizing that the only grown men present were Grigore and the priest.

"What nationalities are the families here?" Fane and Mihai knew that this didn't mean citizenship, but ethnic origin.

"This is a pure Romanian village," said Grigore.

The second man, by now obviously the senior officer, said something to the other in a language Fane didn't understand but that seemed a little like something he had heard before. Suddenly Mihai's hand gripped his arm so hard that Fane started. Then he held absolutely still, hardly breathing, sharing the tight pain of Mihai's tension. The two riders conversed a short while then turned back to the villagers. "All right," said the first officer abruptly in Hungarian. "That's all."

"But won't you come and sit down, let us offer you something to eat," protested Grigore politely.

"Thank you," said the older man, obviously an officer, in Romanian, also obviously making an effort to be cordial, "but," he continued in Hungarian, "we have a long way to go this afternoon and we can't stay." They turned their horses, conversing in what Fane now knew must be German, as they left the village.

The inhabitants of Poiana Cozonac stood silently to watch the men leave, worried by the visit, examining it in the light of stories that had been brought in by the school examiner or the tax collectors or villagers returning from the market. Fane and Mihai had a difficult time getting through the small crowd without making a fuss. When they were out of everyone's hearing, Fane said, "Was that German?"

Mihai was shaking. "Let me sit down, no, I want to walk." Fane looked at him, puzzled.

"What's wrong?"

"They were searching for Jews," Mihai said. "They wanted to know if there were any Jews in the village."

"But we don't...oh..." Fane caught himself. Even in Poiana Cozonac stories about what was happening to Jews in Romania and Germany and other places were common, though no one paid much attention and, anyway, they were Jews after all. Except probably, Fane thought for the first time, Mihai probably did pay attention. He squeezed Mihai's hand.

"But they are also after men and horses," Mihai continued. "They said they'd come back and get them. Did you notice how they kept sort of, sort of like counting people?"

Fane had noticed the way they looked around. "But there aren't that many here," he protested.

"I don't know," answered Mihai, "but that's what they said. They said that they knew there were some men and they must be hiding."

"Then we've got to tell everyone," Fane exclaimed.

"But...", started Mihai. "But...then people will want to know how we know."

"Oh," answered Fane. "But," he continued with a new thought, "we can tell Father."

"Yes, but then he'll have to tell people."

"We have to warn them. They might also take Haiduc." Both boys thought of Haiduc, the only horse in the village.

"I guess so," said Mihai slowly.

In the corner of the shed, mending harness when they found him, Petru wasn't surprised by the news but he was disturbed. He looked at Mihai all the time the boys told him about the officers' German conversation, glancing only occasionally in Fane's direction.

"I'll talk with Grigore — he can keep a secret — and we'll figure out something," he said finally. He reached over and cuffed Mihai on the shoulder. "I knew taking you would bring us luck," he added. "You've probably saved my life."

The next day five men—the only males who weren't very old or very young except for the priest—left with the village sheep for pastures on the Romanian side of the border. Petru vaulted on to Haiduc's back and bunched the long reins together, much to Fane and Mihai's surprise. "I didn't think anyone except us..." Fane started to say then fell silent.

Three days later another detachment of riders came across the meadow from the southwest. This time they were Hungarians.

"Where is the mayor?" they asked.

"He left with the sheep for summer pastures over there, across the border," said Father Ion, now the spokesman for the village, gazing serenely toward the strangers.

"What in shit do you mean by that?" swore the leader.

"Only, good sir, that we always take the sheep in May to summer pastures, to save the grass near the village and that is where our summer pastures have always been. He is being helped by two boys, both thirteen."

"We'll take you then," one of the others said, "we have a quota of laborers to fill."

"But, esteemed sir," the priest responded, "I am useless. Don't you see that I am blind?"

In a rage the leader rode his horse into the priest and began beating him with his whip. Fane and Mihai didn't see much more because Grandmother shoved them and told them to run for the woods, but Fane heard a crack of bone and a muffled cry of pain as he turned.

No one followed the fleeing women and children but later they found Father Ion lying on the ground unconscious and the houses ransacked. Not that the riders could carry that much and the women had hidden most of their food in the forest as soon as the men had left with the sheep but Father Ion...he was badly hurt. Fane shivered as he remembered trying to help by holding their teacher as Granny and another woman pulled to set his broken leg. It sort of...popped and Father Ion cried out briefly, then lay very still, hardly breathing. Just like those Hungarians, he thought to himself, to beat a priest, a blind man. But everyone said the Germans were worse, that if the Germans had been there they would have killed everyone in the village. A blind man, though, beating a blind man, a priest. Fane snapped the last strap against its buckle, patted Haiduc and walked back to the tiny house.

"It's going to be hard, leaving," Mihai interrupted his thoughts. Fane turned to see the other boy at his shoulder. "I've been saying good-bye," he explained.

"I guess I should have gone around with you," said Fane.

"Don't worry," answered Mihai, "everyone will be here in a minute." Fane looked up the road to the rest of the village and saw Mihai was right. Led by the priest with a cross, a procession was coming down the lane and each person was carrying something. A loaf of bread, a piece of bacon, everyone brought something for the road, scratched out of nearly empty larders, "They really care," he thought and a tear came unbidden to his eye. No one ate well these days and to give away food...

"We've come to bless your journey and wish you a safe return to visit us again," said the priest. Fane gazed at this man who was teacher and priest and would be his example of a good man for the rest of his life and responsible for the second thing he would never forget.

It was the second winter they had been in the village that the priest had come through the snow to their house. Fane and Mihai often wondered how he managed to make his way, with only a cane but he walked so surely that you wouldn't know he was blind if no one told you. His eyes were clear and always appeared to look at your face and through it into your soul.

52

Mother and Father invited him in as he stomped the snow off his boots, and asked about his health before anyone approached the business at hand. That business, it seemed, was Fane and Mihai.

"They're behaving themselves in school, isn't he?" asked Father. "Tell me they aren't and I'll beat them for you."

"No need of that," said Father Ion, looking at Fane with approval. "He and Mihai are the best students I have."

"We are beholden to you for teaching them," murmured Mother. Priests weren't usually schoolteachers, but it was a small village and these weren't normal times. And Father Ion seemed to like his job and do it well.

"That's why I've come," continued the priest. "I wanted to be sure you understood."

"Understood what?" asked Petru.

"That both these boys are very intelligent and will go far. You need to encourage them, to make sure they have time to study. I know how difficult it is when you need an extra pair of hands in the fields or the courtyard, but this you must do. You must promise me, before God, that both these boys will be given time to do their schoolwork, that they will continue to the *liceu* and, after that, to the University if it's possible, and that you will not, you will NOT stop them." Father Ion's face, usually calm, was flushed with the intensity of his emotion. Petru sat open-mouthed and Mother shifted on her stool.

"I promise you before God, that we will do this," she said firmly. And so does Petru. Don't you Petru." "Yes, yes, I do", Petru finally managed to say.

"You promise before God," insisted Mother.

"Yes," Petru repeated as if in a daze, not quite understanding. "I promise before God."

After that, Fane thought as the loaded wagon rattled across the meadow with Poiana Cozonac behind them, Father Ion was even more demanding about schoolwork.

"But," he thought to himself, "I learned a lot, especially about history, but the best part of what I learned is that I don't have to grow up and be a drunken peasant like Father." Fane pushed the last words away and looked ahead at the track down through the woods toward the rest of the world and Bukovina.

"And the third thing...I know what it is but I don't want to think about it right now."

"Buna seara, *Ellen," Fane said from behind the petite blond. "I am Stefan Vulcean from the Institute of History – we met earlier this evening. What are you thinking about, so serious?" Fane had heard she spoke passable Romanian, almost good in fact, but this was the acid test.*

"Oh," *startled, Ellen turned toward the large man. "Stefan Vulcean, the Institute of History...how nice to meet you...again. I... don't know exactly what I was thinking about."*

"Come, come, now. Surely diplomats don't allow their thoughts to roam," *he joked.*

"Well," *Ellen withdrew slightly, then opened up. "My father...he's sick and I was wondering if I should go be with him. I've just arrived here, but..."*

"Is your Mother there?" *asked Fane, thinking that perhaps these Americans were human after all.*

"I'm afraid she...she passed away last year. "I'm so very sorry. It's difficult to lose a parent. You must be very worried about your father." Fane naturally fell into a rhythm of short, easier sentences with people who mattered...and whom he could teach.*

"Thank you," *she said simply. "Have you lost a parent?"*

"Have I lost a parent?" *Fane thought ferociously. "Hell yes, at the gates of hell, yes." Aloud he said, "I lost my mother when I was fourteen, shortly after the war." The two fell silent, separate and together.*

The road to Bilca was long and after they had come to Carlibaba (and passed the forest they came out of but didn't have to go back into, Fane thought, and thank goodness for that) it was well-traveled. There weren't many horses other than those ridden by Russian soldiers, but no one tried to take Haiduc.

"That's because he's old and tired," said Petru. Fane looked down from the wagon seat and saw his beloved friend through others' eyes. It was true Haiduc was tired and now, six years after he had hauled them up the Carpathians, he did look old, his back sagging into sharp hipbones, his neck thin and a bit sunken in front of too-prominent withers. Poor Haiduc. Fane jumped off the wagon and began to walk alongside. Petru looked down at him and snickered.

"Thank you, old boy, for getting old," Fane whispered into Haiduc's black tipped ear when they stopped to rest at noon. "That was smart of you because if you were young the Russians would take you from us." Haiduc seemed to nod in agreement, or perhaps it was weariness.

And one by one, all the family except Granny tacitly began to walk rather than ride in order to lessen Haiduc's burden. It was a long road and hard though, the boys agreed, more interesting than the way through the forest. They passed through towns larger than either had ever seen, with two-story buildings, one night they bathed in a hot spring and they went over great gorges on long bridges.

Near the end of the journey they stayed across a rutted dirt road from the great stone walls of the Sucevita Monastery. Fane and Mihai broke away from evening chores as soon as they could to visit the massive fortress. Cautiously they walked through the grey gates and stopped, astounded at the riot of color splashed across the outer wall of the church before them. Blues and reds and the ladder from heaven stretching down caught and held them still.

Fane felt a tap on his shoulder and turned to see a young monk, slight like Mihai but fair and with light brown hair like Fane. He felt a stab of fear — maybe peasants like them weren't allowed inside the walls — but on hearing their story the young monk took them in to the church and explained the meaning of the paintings. Here at the right of the church door was a river of fire with all the sinners being tormented by demons. To the left was heaven and those waiting to enter. At the top, God who sat in judgment.

"Wow," said Mihai, nudging Fane as they followed the monk into the church. "It almost looks like hell is more interesting than heaven." Fane stepped back in shock, awed, embarrassed and a bit scared, hoping the monk hadn't overheard.

"That was what I thought the first time I saw it," the monk turned back, laughing. "Then I thought about it a bit longer." The boys could see that he wasn't very many years older than they were and asked his name.

"I am Brother Augustin," he said. "I had another name before I came here, but that isn't important now."

"Why?" asked the ever curious and much bolder Mihai. "Why did you become a monk?"

"Let me show you the church first, then we can find a place to sit down in the last bit of sun and talk," Brother Augustin replied. When he mentioned sun, Mihai and Fane looked at each other, realizing how cold it was in the church but, even so, they were in no hurry to leave.

They had been in churches often before, of course. There was the dark wooden church in Poiana Cozonac that they knew so well because they helped Father Ion with the service, and the little church in Bilca, barely remembered, but neither was anything like this. The great iconostasis separating the people from the priest was an ornamented work of what seemed like pure gold, the eyes on the icons looked straight through you, and Christ gazed down from the great dome with awe-inspiring strength. Fane felt as if the world around him, every object in it, glowed with the glory of God. Each detail was clear, almost etched on his eye, and immense joy together with a great love for God's creation surged through him. Could this be God speaking to him?

The feeling lasted through the conversation with Brother Augustin and lingered into the night. When they left the church, the three climbed the great surrounding wall and sat on the parapet while the young monk told them a little about the war in his village, his vision one lonely night, his trip to the Monastery, his difficulty convincing the guard at the gate to let him in. "I think God was in me," he said candidly, "for when I walked through the Gate I saw the Bishop and went straight to him. I knelt and told him of my dreams and my desire to be with God. He was visiting from Putna...just by chance and he...he said I could return with him. Then, after a year, he said I could study to be a regular monk, rather than one of the brothers who serve though I still have much to learn and still must serve."

"So you don't live here, in this monastery?" asked Fane.

"No, we are just visiting. We'll return to Putna tomorrow." At that Fane truly felt that God must have some plan for him, to have given him this meeting.

"But what about your parents?" asked Mihai, less interested in God than in the person he was talking to.

"My family was gone. My father was killed in the war and Mother died, spitting blood, soon after...and I was the only son since all the other children had died while they were babies." Fane thought a moment of Mioara with a pang, then of the mysterious brother, whom Mihai had replaced; Mihai thought of his father and wondered. Both boys shifted positions on the hard stone wall. The long day's sun hung above the mountains in the west and lit the slopes of the hills to the east with flat rays.

"When did this happen?" persisted Mihai, ever curious about the lives of other people.

"Four years ago, I have been here four years now. I received the vision the night of the day my mother was buried." All three fell silent.

By the time they returned to camp, Fane was sure he wanted to be a monk but there wasn't much time to think about it. "Hey, boys," said Petru, "get us some firewood from that grove or it's all over with you." He took a swig from his jug as the boys hurried toward the trees.

Two days on they trundled in to Bilca late in the afternoon. It was June but there were no crops to be seen, no moving carpet of young barley, no baby cabbage, no animals on the road, no people. "Really does look like there hasn't been enough rain," remarked Petru. Mother agreed quietly but Granny told Petru several times that everyone they had met on the road had said there was a drought and they shouldn't have returned, as if Petru and the whole family hadn't been there and heard them, too. Fane and Mihai didn't know enough to do anything but listen.

The lane toward their house looked the same and different. Trees had been chopped down, once neat courtyards were in shambles and everything looked really small. Finally they turned in their own gate which hung open rather than being firmly closed as it should be. The scene in their courtyard was heartbreaking. The house was half-destroyed, window and door frames ripped away. Half the barn roof hung over empty, open space, the courtyard itself and the long wagon shed were bare. It would have been dirty if there had been anything left but it was picked clean.

"God save us," murmured Mother. "I told you they'd take my cow," screeched Granny.

"Shit," said Petru.

"Eh, Petru, Petrica!" A voice came from the gate, their neighbor Ion, Tante Elise's husband. "Eh, welcome, welcome."

"Good that we've met thee!" chorused the family in reply, relieved that this desert of their past wasn't completely empty.

"By God, you've come back to misery," Ion said, "but it's good to see you. Good to have you here in spite of everything."

"What's happened?" asked Petru. "What's happened?" screeched Granny." "Tell us, tell us, who is here?" said Mother, her voice caught by her swollen throat.

"Get down, get down, let's put the horse away, I'll tell you, let me tell the wife you're here, she'll have some dinner for you, it's been a long time..."

While the boys unhitched Haiduc and led him into his old stall, trying to clean out burnt rafters and the ashes as they went, Petru and Ion cleared debris from a room in the house then Mother swept it clean. "Did you hear," Ion related, "the family down the way, Tante Viorica and her husband, came back after they were gone two years and found their dog, skin and bones, waiting for them...after all those years," the family nodded with polite amazement.

"How was it with the Russians?" Petru asked when this tale was done.

"What do you mean, the Russians? We had everyone through here. We fled to the forest when the Russians came the first time, just after you left, then our side went through, not much better, and then the Russians came again and that was, let's see, the summer of '44. But we weren't here then, it's what we've heard because that first autumn, we couldn't stay out in the woods any longer and the Russians took us and sent us to Botosani to work the land. We were there two years — we've only been back a few months ourselves."

"Are the Russians why there aren't any crops?" asked Fane.

"I'd blame the Russians and maybe it's their fault, but it's God's will and worse. We haven't had any rain since

March." Fear was in his voice and the others caught it. No one said anything for a moment, then Mother spoke.

"Do you know anything about Mioara?" she asked, her throat swollen and words misshapen.

"Mother of a daughter," Ion turned to her in sorrow. "Mioara was taken by a Russian officer in '44. He liked her, a beautiful, lovely maid. I haven't heard anything about her since."

Fane watched his mother, the strength of the family, cry out and fall to the floor. The world he tried so carefully to hold together broke into pieces. Everyone rushed in and helped Mother to lie down on blankets and said useless, soothing things to her while Granny put wet cloths on her forehead. Unable to leave the subject of change the men began talking again, Fane and Mihai listening.

"At least we found the village on the Romanian side of the line," remarked Petru.

"Part of the village, you mean, may they be cursed to Hell and back again," swore Ion. "The frontier is up the lane, not half a kilometer from your house."

"But that's the common grazing ground, there are families there," protested Petru.

"There may be grazing, there may have been families, but we aren't supposed to take sheep there and the Russkies have arrested several shepherds. They took the families who lived there, some say to Siberia but they always say Siberia when they take people away in Russia these days. I don't know, but that's the line and better not cross it!"

"How will we know where it is?" asked Mihai from the background.

"You'll know. Just don't go there," answered Ion.

That answer stayed in Fane's head for the rest of his life, drawing a line where none should be, cutting part of his life away along with his lost sister and leaving a dull, burning anger. But the Russian army helped drive out the Germans

60

who would have taken Mihai and who let the Hungarians do such awful things. It was confusing.

"Maybe she'll come back to visit," he tried to comfort Mother later that night. Mother simply turned away in silence. Fane watched her for a minute, then went out and came back in with the little cream colored plate with the green and yellow deer. The nail where it had hung was still in the wall. Fane put it up — he didn't have to reach above him, he had grown so much — and stepped back into Mother's arms. She was looking at the plate, then she held Fane against her and wept. Fane patted her shoulder awkwardly. "No," said Mother. "No. It's all right. It's just I'm so glad to be home. Thank you."

The next day more people came by and more news poured in. "Did you hear about the Mayor?" asked the first visitor.

"Carol's father?" chorused Mihai and Fane together, all ears.

"No, he's probably with his family in the West, somewhere, if he survived the war, that is. They were evacuated there, to Timisoara. No, the *primar* who we chose when we returned. When the Russians came back, they wanted to move the line they had made earlier further south, to the Suceava River, so that all of Bilca would be Russian. Our mayor was brave — he protested and, in the end, somehow, he succeeded in keeping the line just there," the man gestured up the lane toward the Known Unknown, "but the Russians got him in the end. He's gone, maybe in Siberia. Poor man. Just goes to show — 'He who puts his head above the others gets it cut off.'" All nodded solemnly. Fane thought about that saying later that night in the hayloft — he and Mihai were too big for the old space by the *soba* now — and wondered whether he would dare to put his head above the crowd. But he didn't think of it again as the next days were a blur of work, ploughing with Haiduc straining to pull the plow through dry hard ground that hadn't been tilled for years, planting a garden in the hope that it wasn't too late and watering it by hand from a well that, thank God, still had water in it, rebuilding, reordering, cleaning. Bit by bit their old lives began to come together except for the lack of rain which hung over all of them like an angry sun.

When they had been back a week, Uncle Vanya arrived on his same old horse. The animal was ancient, skin and bones, but managed to pick up his head and snort at Haiduc. "There, there, old boy," said Uncle Vanya as he swung off Rocinante's back. "You'll get a rest now. Welcome home," he said, turning to the family and holding out his arms to Mihai. Mihai hung back a second then threw himself against Uncle Vanya's chest, trying to hold back tears.

"Your father is well," said Uncle Vanya. "Don't worry." At this good news the whole family wept, the strain of homecoming finally rolling away down their cheeks in the faint hope of a return to normalcy.

"Where is he, when can I seem him?" cried Mihai. Fane looked at Mihai and thought, "Will he go back and be Mendl again?" and, in passing, "I'd be the best student then and wouldn't have to have him around all the time" but shied away from those confused feelings.

"He's in Romania and he'll come to visit," said Uncle Vanya. "Not quite yet, but he'll be glad to hear you have grown so well." The older man held Mihai at arm's length and looked at him, still slight but nearly as tall as a grown man, wiry and strong. "You look as if the war hasn't treated you too badly, as if there has been enough to eat." Uncle Vanya turned to Fane's parents. "I thank you for this great favor," he said.

"Oh, no," answered Petru. "It is you who have helped us. Without you we would have...we wouldn't have..."

"Never mind," Uncle Vanya clapped Petru on the back and turned to Granny. "Missus, I'm glad to see you back and looking so young. Did Mihai behave himself?"

"He's a rascal like any boy," cackled Grandmother, taking a loving swipe at Mihai, "and he's good at his school work but a little lazy in the fields." The family laughed, knowing that Mihai was grandmother's favorite. Fane, still a little jealous, laughed with the others.

"Come inside," said Petru. "It's a mess," Mother demurred. "I wonder if he brought anything to eat," Granny said to Fane in an aside. They finally decided to stay outside on the porch, women sitting on the long bench while men and boys leaned against the wall or rested comfortably on their heels.

"Do you still have Mihai's papers?" asked Uncle Vanya after a certain amount of news had been exchanged.

"But of course," Petru said in surprise. "They're with Fane's and the family's."

"I, well, 'we' because I discussed this with Mihai's father," started Uncle Vanya a bit hesitantly, "we think that, that is if you wouldn't mind, it would probably be best if he continued to be Mihai. Bilca was lucky, not like Radauti. Most of the Jews from Bilca survived — not that there were that many." Petru nodded. He had already heard. "But Mihai's father can't return right now and it might be safer..." Vanya's voice trailed off for a moment as the family murmured in unison and understanding. "No one will wonder about Mendl, since so many people disappeared, and if there are any who remember when he joined your family after all these years and all this suffering," Uncle Vanya waved his hand toward the north and then all around, "they'll probably forget quickly. Especially since the boys will be leaving for school in Radauti before long."

Fane and Mihai both gasped and started to talk, but Mother hushed them. "Listen," she said. Uncle Vanya smiled and continued. "Yes, to school, to the Liceul

Hurmuzachi, the best secondary school in Bukovina now that we have been split in two, good preparation for the University."

"High school! University!" exclaimed Petru. "Maybe Mihai, he's a...a...but Fane, Fane is a peasant. He's a peasant like me, like us, he..."

"You promised the priest," interrupted Mother. Uncle Vanya looked at her questioningly. Mother smoothed her apron over her long skirt and looked up at him, her eyes gleaming. "The priest in Poaina Cozonac was also the schoolteacher. Father Ion. Father Ion came and told us both the boys were intelligent and could go far and we shouldn't stop them. We both promised in the name of God we would help."

"But we don't have any money for Fane, woman!" said Petru angrily, "and we won't take charity!" He looked at Vanya almost, Fane thought, almost like he was an enemy.

"Don't worry, Petrica," Vanya said, using the diminutive to sooth things over. "We'll manage the liceu — you kept Mihai safe and strong all these years and a little help for Fane isn't charity, my God! After all you've done! And there are changes coming. Changes that will mean students go to the University on merit rather than because their parents are rich. By the time the boys are ready, the changes will be here and they'll have a good chance if," he looked at Fane and Mihai meaningfully, "if they study hard and do well."

"Changes?" asked Mother. "Changes bring trouble," said Granny. "But..." interrupted Petru, "what are you talking about? Are you...is this...the Russians..."

"Of course," said Uncle Vanya spreading his hands deprecatingly, "no one can predict the future, least of all me."

"You did pretty well in the past," cackled Granny, "so we'd probably better listen to you now." The family laughed a little too loudly and went on to discuss the drought.

Before he left, Uncle Vanya turned to Mother. "The exams are next week," he told her. "I'll pick up the boys on Monday morning, an hour after daybreak. Petru should have Haiduc hitched to the wagon."

"But what will they wear?" Mother asked.

"Their Sunday clothes. The boys from the country wear national dress to the school."

"But they don't have time to study. What should they study?" worried Mother. Petru stood to one side and listened to this conversation with a grim face.

"Don't worry, they'll be fine," Uncle Vanya reassured her. After he left, Petru burst out angrily.

"What is this idiocy? Peasants don't go to the University. Besides, I need Fane to help me on the farm." Mother, who usually agreed with her husband, put her hands on her hips and said, "You swore before God. They are going." The boys saw Petru raise his hand and, unconsciously, the two teenagers stepped forward as one. The older man looked at them, moved back, turned on his heel, and went out of the courtyard.

"He's gone to the village pub," Fane whispered to Mihai as Mother wiped her eyes with the back of her hand and turned to wash the dishes.

"Yeah, I guess so," was all Mihai said.

"Go, start studying," Mother said over her shoulder in a muffled voice. The boys looked at one another and walked toward the barn.

"What does Uncle Vanya do?" asked Fane.

"Do? What...I...I don't know. I never thought about it." Mihai looked down and scuffed his feet on the ground. "I never thought about it."

"Neither did I," said Fane.

The following week was consumed in study in spite of Uncle Vanya's reassurances. Petru, somewhat the worse for wear the day after the family fight, sullenly worked the fields while the boys worked inside. No one in the family spoke much except Granny, who talked incessantly as she went over Fane and Mihai's Sunday clothes, letting them out here and mending a bit there.

Uncle Vanya picked them up on schedule. They had hitched Haiduc up to the wagon while Petru watched. Petru stood to one side as the boys climbed into the wagon but as the horse negotiated the turn onto the lane in front of the courtyard he strode over and scrambled on to the seat beside Fane. "Better go along to see that you behave. Move over," he said gruffly, giving Fane a shove with his shoulder and taking the reins from his hands. Fane looked at him and noticed that Petru, too, had put on good clothes this morning. All three, Petru, Fane and Mihai, had white baggy pants tied from the knee down with the leather laces from their shoes, the pants in turn covered to the hips by billowy sleeved homespun shirts, cinched in place by a wide leather belt. In June there was no need for a vest or coat but all three had caps on their head to complete the outfit. 'We look pretty good,' thought Fane as Petru turned Haiduc toward Radauti, Uncle Vanya riding ahead in his city clothes, 'like a parade.'

It was a long journey all the way to Radauti and their road took them through most of the spread out 'town' of Bilca, houses set along the road with fields stretched behind. Neighbors waved and called to them. "Going to take exams for the *liceu*!" Petru replied proudly. "They'll probably fail!" "*Noroc*, good luck!" was the reply with an occasional "God Bless".

Neither Fane nor Mihai had been to Radauti before and Uncle Vanya pointed out various landmarks as they passed: the great Orthodox Church, the Synagogue, the market. But when the party arrived at the corner with the school Uncle Vanya stopped and turned to the three in the wagon. "You don't need me with you but," he said addressing Petru, "when you're done come by my house for a drink. It's on the block behind the Synagogue, cross the street behind it and I have the third house on the left." Petru touched his hand to his hat in assent and turned back to the Eudoxiu Hurmuzachi High School, an imposing building with the weight of history behind it.

They had arrived along with other boys who would take the entrance exam, a mix of country and city, some trying to bolster their courage by swaggering around, some standing quietly. All of them were accompanied by family members. 'I'm feeling out of place here,' thought Fane to himself, 'but Father is more nervous than I.' He squared his shoulders, put his courage in order and walked towards the school with Mihai, Petru behind, down the neat front walk between well kept little hedges separating it from an equally well kept lawn. 'After all,' thought Fane looking around at the other small family groups going in the front door, 'there aren't very many if you don't count parents. Maybe we will pass and...' He couldn't think further — there was too much to see.

Neither Fane nor Mihai had ever been in a building like this. It was so big, two stories high. The entrance hall opened through glass-paned doors — glass! And so much of it! — into a great round space with a vast stairway before them. On either side were long halls lined with doors. It was built of fine stuff, fine stuff indeed, Petru muttered. Most of all it had a smell, a special smell. A school smell? Books? It smelled of study and hope. The students and parents climbed the stairway and were seated in a hall on the second floor.

One by one the applicants were called into a room with a panel of examiners. One by one they came out looking pleased. Mihai, who went in before Fane, emerged with a radiant face just as Fane heard his name, 'Stefan Vulcean'. For a moment it felt as if Haiduc were galloping around in his chest, trying to get out and when he went through the door, Fane could hardly see anything for the pounding. Gradually the air cleared and he saw three serious men dressed in suits. He'd never been this close to such people before and he automatically dropped his eyes and, returning their greeting, mumbled, "I kiss your hands."

"Don't be nervous," said the man on the right, "and look at us." Fane raised his eyes to meet the gaze of a youngish man who smiled at him and introduced himself and the others. The names went in one ear and out the other for Fane but he remembered the middle man was the Principal and the younger man taught history. "Now I would like you to..." The questions, on Romanian history and language and geography were surprisingly easy and Fane found himself answering automatically, as he would have answered Father Ion in Poiana Cozonac. As more questions came and were answered everyone relaxed. Fane could tell from their bodies, as he could tell from the bodies of animals, that the professors were pleased. Finally the Principal asked, "Did you study any foreign languages in your school?"

"Yes, sir," answered Fane. "We were in Transylvania and had to learn Hungarian. And Church Slavonic."

"Slavonic? That's interesting," said the young professor. "Were you in a monastery?"

"No, sir, we were in a very small village and the teacher, he was also the village priest. We, my cousin Mihai and I, helped him in the church and he said we should learn everything we could, so he taught us."

The man in the middle turned to the young Professor. "Mihai, we just saw him, a very bright boy but he didn't tell us about the languages."

"We didn't ask," the younger man replied. "Remember—we started talking with him about Romanian literature and time ran out. You," he turned back to Fane, "you two boys had a remarkable education in your small Transylvanian village." "I'm sure," added the older man in the middle, cutting in and asserting his leadership, "you will do very well here at the Liceul Eudoxiu Hurmuzachi. Welcome." They stood up and Fane did so as well, mumbling his appreciation before he fled from the room half floating, half afraid he'd stumble and fall.

He didn't need to say anything as Petru and Mihai embraced him. On the way out they all looked back and forth at the other students who, in turn, looked at them, everyone pleased and curious and all knowing they would be classmates. Fane wanted to talk to them but couldn't quite find the right words and before he knew it they were untying Haiduc and getting into the wagon. Some of the families were leaving in carriages, some on foot, one in an automobile and several in wagons like theirs. "Think of it," Mihai nudged Fane, "all of us, all these rich city boys and all of us from the country, we'll all be together. What did they ask you in there?"

Uncle Vanya's house was like the others on his street, set in a modest courtyard with an enclosed porch and glass in the front windows which had lace curtains behind the panes. "I've seen more glass today than I think I ever saw in one place in my life," Mihai muttered to Fane as they went toward the front door. Fane agreed, thinking of the village where glass was such a luxury. It seemed everyone in the city was rich.

They entered to find a comfortable room with stuffed chairs. There were pictures on the walls and a table laid with food and drink. "I thought we'd celebrate," said Uncle Vanya as Petru looked at it. "It isn't every day boys are admitted to the *liceu*."

"How did you know?" muttered Petru. "How did you know they would be admitted?" he asked more loudly, suspiciously.

"I didn't have anything to do with it," said Uncle Vanya as he motioned the boys toward the food. "I've talked with the two of them and could tell they had a very sound —

maybe an outstanding — education in that village, what was it, Poiana Cozonac? You were truly fortunate to have the teacher/priest because they aren't simply well-prepared, they've probably studied much further than most of the other students. And this," he turned smiling toward a small, plump woman coming in to the room with a tray and more food, "this is my wife, Anna. Anna, Petru Vulcean, Fane and Mihai." Anna turned and smiled at Petru and held out her hand. Petru grabbed and kissed it awkwardly, mumbling, "I kiss your hand, missus," then stepped back, face suffused with red. Fane hadn't felt out of place until that moment when the difference in their social stations hit him. Uncle Vanya was educated, he was rich, the man who sat so comfortably in their kitchen so many times lived like, like... he was jolted out of his thoughts by a motherly kiss on the cheek. "I'm so proud of both of you!" Anna said. "And so pleased to meet you — Vanya has told me all about you and I've wanted to see you for such a long time!" She put her hands on her hips and looked from Mihai to Fane and back again, smiling. "Come and have something to eat — boys are always hungry."

"We don't have children," Fane heard Uncle Vanya explaining to Petru as they moved toward the table, "and Anna has been waiting for the boys to come so she could mother them." Fane and Mihai caught one another's eye before they were pushed gently into taking plates and forks and food. It was, Fane thought, some of the best food he had ever had though Mother's salami, he mentally added, was every bit as good as this. When they turned into the courtyard at home, harness creaking as the traces tightened on the right and loosened on the left, Mother and Grandmother hurried out of the house to ask what had happened. Petru swung his legs over the side of the wagon and said, "Stupid boys...they are admitted. Now we'll have to provide fees by giving the school food supplies." He could barely conceal his pride under the grumble.

Grandmother cackled happily and Mother added her soft voice of congratulations with a glowing, happy face but Fane thought something was wrong. He looked at her closely and it was like seeing Haiduc on the Carlibaba road—she was thin and much, much older. What had happened to her this year? And she didn't look well.

"Oh, nothing," she said when he asked, waving a dish towel at him. "I've just got a bad headache." She turned aside and coughed then went briskly back to cooking.

That night, after a special dinner, Mother lay down early. When Fane was ready for bed he walked over to her bed and kissed her forehead. "You're the best mother in the world," he whispered into her ear, feeling her hair tickle his cheek and the heat rising from her face. "Go on with you," Mother answered softly. "But...you are the most wonderful son in the whole world. I am so proud of you, my Fanica." "I love you," said Fane very softly and went off. It was the first time in his life he had said those words, he thought later, except of course to Haiduc. "I hope Mother is all right," he said to Mihai before turning over and falling asleep to dream of long halls and the smell of knowledge.

In the morning, Mother was worse, burning with fever and aching all over. Petru went for the doctor and came back alone. "He said he's busy, that we should take her to a building where they've decided to put the typhus patients, he can see her there."

"Typhus!" screeched Granny, "Typhus!"

"I'd heard it was in town," replied her son, "but I didn't think..."

"Just like in the last war," said Granny shrilly, "war and famine and typhus come together. I thought we might escape the plague because of the lumber."

"What does lumber have to do with it?" asked Mihai. Fane could see he was badly frightened and trying to hide it. So could Granny and she reached up to pinch her adopted grandchild's cheek as hard as she could. "Ow," said Mihai. "Don't question your elders," Granny screeched then lowered her voice to explain. "It's because the men in this village earn money with wood from the forests so we have some food. Not enough, of course, but it keeps us going. Typhus is worse when people are thin and weak." The boys looked at each other, thinking of the talk of famine they had heard but they hadn't paid much attention. They were used to never having enough food and the hunger hadn't been worse than usual in spite of the dry fields and bad crops. But thought Fane, Mother always seemed to eat less than they did and she...he shook his head to clear it.

Petru went out for medicine but there wasn't any. There wasn't any question of taking Mother to be with other typhus patients. "That charnel house would surely kill her," snorted Granny. "Besides, it might not be typhus at all since that stupid doctor didn't even come to see her." They all took turns sitting by Mother and putting cold cloths on her forehead, trying to get her to eat something. Granny took over the cooking. The boys went through their chores in a haze of misery and worry, not quite feeling, not quite knowing what to feel, simply numb when they weren't frighened. It seemed as if the end of the world had come. Mother lost consciousness at some point. A day later she died. The family stood, stunned, going to look at her body then walking away, nowhere, confused and helpless until Tante Elise arrived from next door and took over, calling the priest and giving orders.

Arrangements for the funeral were simple, "But," said Petru, "it's still going to cost money we don't have. We need a coffin, we need..." He stomped off angrily, telling the boys to go hoe the barley field.

When they returned, Haiduc was gone. "Petru took him to be sold," said Granny brusquely, turning away. "That's why the wagon is still here."

"Sold?" asked Fane incredulously. "Haiduc? Sell Haiduc?" Fane thought of the lovely black-rimmed ear, the kind eye, the sweet spot on his nose. "Why would Father sell Haiduc?"

"He needs a younger horse," said Grandmother, "and, besides, we need money right now for your Mother's funeral."

"But where would he sell Haiduc?" Fane felt his heart rise to bursting with fear, all the fear he had kept away while Mother was ill bunched up and seemed about to erupt from his throat. He could hear himself shouting, "Where?" But he knew the answer.

"To the horse dealers from Sibiu," answered Granny. "You know that. Now go away and do some work." Fane turned and left.

Sibiu. Famous for its salami. Even if horses didn't actually go to Sibiu to be slaughtered it meant the same thing. He thought again of Haiduc, of the hours they had been together, playing, working, of the heroic effort to get them to Poiana Cozonac. How could Father do this? But he knew the answer. Oh, Haiduc, scared and bewildered and finally being hurt and...Fane shoved the thought out of his mind. "Never again," he said to himself. "I won't love any horse again! I won't love anybody again! I don't ever want to feel like this again!"

"My mother died of typhus, the summer I was fourteen," he found himself telling Ellen.

"I'm so sorry," she replied sympathetically. "It must have been terribly hard for you." Fane murmured something about Ellen's own situation and asked where in the United States her home was. "Oh, it's in the middle of the country, Iowa," she replied and her face softened with the memory while she pushed blond hair away from her green eyes. "It's rolling farm country, like a lot of Romania. I grew up feeding chickens and riding horses... though," she added, "people here find that hard to believe."

73

"Not at all," said Fane although he was surprised that a capitalist diplomat could have such a background. "Tell me about it, but why don't I bring you a drink?"

It was a bad summer and the boys were glad to leave it behind. Without Haiduc farm work was more difficult but without rain there wasn't much of a crop anyway, only constant worry. Petru, as far as they could tell, spent some of the money from Haiduc on the funeral and the rest on alcohol because he was either drunk or hung over most of the time. Granny did her best in the house but it gradually became disorderly and dirty and her cooking wasn't like Mother's. Some days she didn't feel well enough to cook at all so the men ate whatever they could find which usually wasn't very much.

The one shared diversion was provided by a collision. Late one afternoon Fane and Mihai were racing down the lane toward their house. They flew around the corner by Tante Elise's and Mihai collided with a uniform. Stunned, the boy and the uniform stepped back and the two looked at one another. The uniform saw a small and wiry but goodlooking teenager with dark hair. Mihai saw a tall, blond man in Russian dress.

Fane saw disaster. He looked at Mihai and the two Russian army officers but Mihai and the Russian continued to look at each other leaving Fane and the second Russian bonded in discomfort. Simultaneously, Mihai and the blond began to laugh so heartily the sound dragged all four into shared mirth.

When the moment passed they fell silent and looked at each other again, a little embarrassed. The blond officer — a 2nd lieutenant and young, Fane noted — broke the silence. "You were really running pretty hard," he said inconsequentially in accented but understandable Romanian. All of them relaxed. "We are looking for Mihai Sirbu. Can you tell us where he lives?" Fane froze, wondering what could be wrong but Mihai didn't seem worried, just a bit surprised.

"I'm Mihai Sirbu," he said.

"Great!" exclaimed the Lieutenant. "I was asked by my Colonel to give you this." He drew a letter out of his breast pocket. "We were traveling to Chernovitsky and he said it wouldn't be far off our road." He held out the letter and Mihai took it without looking at it. "Thank you," he said. Fane wondered how he could be so calm, the letter must be from Mihai's father or could it be Uncle Vanya? But who knew Russians well enough...

"...in and have a drink," Mihai was asking politely. Fane tried to keep the surprise, then the dismay out of his face as the two accepted.

The four walked through the little gate at the side of the large wagon entrance and into the courtyard. "Oh-ho, Granny," called Mihai, "we have visitors."

"Visitors?" Granny screeched, wiping her hands on her apron as she came on to the porch. "Why..." She fell silent when she saw the Russian uniforms. "Good evening, Missus," said the blond officer politely. "We should introduce ourselves, I am Pyotr Ilyanov and this is my friend, Vladimir. We were delivering a letter to your grandson," he nodded toward Mihai. "We were on our way to Chernovitsky and," he repeated, "my Colonel said your village was on the way."

"Welcome and thank you for saving us from the Germans. But it's late," said Grandmother. "You can't travel in the dark." Fane looked up and saw that the sun had, indeed, sunk behind the trees by the empty stable. In the east the long light of evening was fading quickly into blueblack with a few stars beginning to twinkle their way into night.

"...we'll manage to find someplace to sleep," he caught the other officer, was it Vladimir, saying.

"Well, come in, come in, don't just stand there, child," said Granny regaining her usual screech and perching on her great age to give her courage. "We don't have much but you're welcome to share it and there is the haymow where the boys sleep. You are probably used to better, but that's what there is. I'm an old woman, but..." the screech continued as she turned and went in the house. Vladimir and Pyotr caught each other's eye and smiled.

"Sir, I'm afraid this isn't what you usually have," said Fane with some embarrassment, stepping forward as the man of the house. Where was Father? Probably in the village tavern he guessed, "but you are welcome..."

"Don't worry," said Vladimir. He was blond too but shorter than Pyotr, about Fane's height. "We both come from good peasant backgrounds and we both grew up sleeping in haymows in summer."

"Besides," added Pyotr, "we've been sleeping whenever and wherever we could for the last six months."

"Six months?" asked Mihai, thinking that the war was over a year ago.

"That's when we were commissioned and sent here. We missed most of the fighting," Pyotr said regretfully, "even though they hurried the officers' course."

"They were running short of patriots because, uh, you know..." Vladimir started to say then stopped.

"We heard that a lot of Romanians died at the Front and I guess that they killed their share of Russians...and, er, I mean..." said Mihai, treading into swampy ground himself.

"Soldiers fight wherever they are told to fight in a war but that's over now," said Fane diplomatically, "and we thank you for saving us from the Germans. We were in Transylvania during the war and..." Mihai was amazed at this unknown side of Fane—so was Fane, truth be told. He led the conversation to Transylvania and the villages where Pyotr and Vladimir had grown up and Bilca, all participants including Granny skirting areas of difficulty.

'It wasn't bad at all,' thought Fane later before falling asleep. Granny had somehow managed to pick up the house and you couldn't see the dirt in the night and also somehow she had produced a good, simple meal. Vlad and Pyotr ate as if they hadn't had food in days while the family held back to be sure there was enough for the guests. Father hadn't come home by the time they went to bed, probably asleep under some tree on the road dead drunk.

In the morning the Russians bid goodby and left early after addresses were exchanged along with mutual assurances about writing and improving postal systems. "We'll find some transport going north and catch a ride," Pyotr said cheerfully. "Write us when you get to school," he added. Maybe we'll come back this way. Or you come visit our families! You'd like my village." It was like saying good-bye to Romanian friends Mihai remarked later.

"Yeah, they were really nice," replied Fane. "Even if they were Russians and took half of Bilca and...but, you know, it is true they helped us, too. It was going to be the Germans or the Russians, and the Germans..."

"You don't have to tell me!" Mihai exclaimed. "And I wonder...do you remember what they said about it being GOOD to be a peasant?'

"Maybe in Russia," said Fane shortly. "Not in Romania." He turned as the courtyard gate opened to see a blearyeyed Petru coming in. "Uh-oh, watch it. He looks like he's in a bad mood." Both boys greeted Petru quickly and left for the fields.

As they walked away, Mihai told him what was in the letter. "It's from Father," he crowed. "He's in Bucharest, he has a good job and has already paid the school fees for us!" Fane grabbed Mihai's shoulders with both hands at this news and the two hopped in a circle dance.

"Will you go to visit him?" asked Fane when they were walking normally again.

"He said it isn't time yet but maybe we'd meet during the year!" The rest of the day went by on a summer breeze and even Petru was cheery when he heard the news about the school fees. Granny cackled as she served them a vegetable stew over mamaliga and things seemed almost normal for the entire evening.

The other event of Fane's summer began with a dream. In it they were back in Poiana Cozonac and the boys were peering through the slats of the bathhouse at a naked Petru. "Look at the size of that rod," hissed Mihai. Fane nodded, hearing Haiduc below and the cow moving and Mother singing in the distance all mixed up. Mihai reached over to him and said something about the afternoon, then touched him under his clothes. In the dream Fane didn't pull away in horror as he had years before, but let the excitement build until exquisite feeling pulsed through his body.

He woke suddenly to find his own hand under his pants, both hand and pants wet and a bit sticky. Fane looked over to Mihai, moving only his eyes. It looked like Mihai was sound asleep. Fane then wiped his hand on the hay slowly and quietly, tried to get pieces of hay off it, and wondered what had happened and if he could do it again.

In the morning, his clothes were stiff and he felt unclean. It reminded him that Granny didn't do the washing very often and...maybe he should help her. Granny cackled in delight at the obviously strange idea but gave him instructions punctuated with "Who would have thought a boy..." Step by step, Fane learned the mechanics of washing clothes.

"It's hard work," he said to Granny in surprise, "really hard."

"You men!" Granny crowed, "You don't know half of what women do! You'd die of the effort if you tried!" Fane didn't quite agree but he was gaining new respect for Mother and her work and, to his surprise, he began to like the process of washing and ironing. He could see the results and he controlled what happened, not like trying to grow crops in the drought stricken fields under Petru's increasingly unclear direction.

After that he was careful to move off his sheet and over the hay at night. Every night that he managed to stay awake until Mihai had gone to sleep he brought secret pleasure into the hard round of survival.

As the days shortened towards autumn the bad summer continued to get worse. Typhus had spread through the village and there were deaths every day — soon there weren't any coffins left and people were buried without them. In their lane Mother was the only one who died, but other nearby houses lost young and old and sometimes those in between. And under unremitting sun, the prospect of winter hunger began to affect everyone, even the boys.

But they were going to the *liceu!* All they had to do to lift their spirits was look at each other, then one would mouth the word and they'd both smile. It never failed to produce a shiver of excitement and anticipation as the hot dreary hours dragged on.

The Day finally came. Petru had to hire a horse and cart to take them to Radauti with their sheets, blankets and small bundles of clothes. They kissed Granny good-bye and she cried proudly at their departure. Fane was the last out of the house and as he passed the little cream colored plate he looked at it for a minute, noted the green and yellow spotted deer, then took it down and hid it in his black and white wool shoulder bag, carefully tucked inside his clothes.

At first school was a high tension blur of new faces and events but in time the days and weeks at the Liceul Hurmuzachi quickly settled into a routine that became familiar and comfortable. Knowing adolescent boys, the authorities kept them fully scheduled with classes, sports and study. To their surprise, Mihai and Fane had no difficulty finding their places in a social hierarchy profoundly unsettled by war, displacement, and rumors of changes to come. Both were outstanding students. The classes and studies were difficult enough to keep their attention but Father Ion had stretched them much further in the little Transylvanian school though neither quite realized this. They only knew that their studies weren't nearly as hard as they had feared.

And Fane found he loved the school. He loved the wide corridors, the classrooms, being somebody—a student! People looked at students with respect and he, Fane, was one of them. Fane especially loved the smell and feel of books, loved sitting inside on a rainy autumn day reading by electric light, loved burying himself in the worlds of other times and places. He could bury his hunger, bury his hatred of Petru, bury Mother by plunging into the past.

Hunger was always present through the autumn and into the spring of that first year and later they joked that Carol kept them alive through the winter. This was an exaggeration but in that terrible year of famine it wasn't far off the mark. The school food was poor and scant—a cup of tea with a slab of mamaliga fried in rancid oil for breakfast, sprouting potatoes and not many of them for lunch, some sort of gruel for dinner. Once there was powdered milk—the word was that it was sent by Americans but that word was street gossip. Whoever sent it, the milk was welcome.

Each of the boys received occasional packages of food from home though, in Fane and Mihai's case, it was from Uncle Vanya since Petru and Grandmother were themselves hungry to the point of death, grubbing roots and trying to eat leaves and, again, subsisting only with Uncle Vanya's help as the boys learned later. Liviu, the son of a priest in a village to the south, received *coliva*—the remains of food for wakes—and shared it, Eusabiu was sent cakes of grain and honey. Whenever someone in their dormitory room received a packet they would lock the doors against uninvited guests from the other dorms, sit on their beds and share the spoils.

But Carol, coming from a wealthier family, had an ironbound chest which always seemed to hold something, perhaps a bit of cheese, perhaps some bread. He shared it judiciously and generously, giving a bit more to the boys who had less from their families, ensuring that everyone had something. He enjoyed the power, thought Fane, but you had to admit that he was really good about it.

Carol had come in the second week of school, arriving along with a windstorm, blown in by the breeze. An older boy brought him to their dormitory to occupy the last empty bed. Carol was larger, still blond, handsome and easily recognizable. Fane was the first to speak, moving forward from the knot of boys gathered to watch the newcomer.

"Carol?" he asked, though he didn't need to. Carol looked into his face and broke into a grin. "Fane! Fane! I'd heard you were here. Also," he looked around.

"Mihai's here, too," Fane said quickly. A flash of asking and understanding flickered in Carol's eyes, then they were neutral. "Mihai!" he said, turning and looking as Mihai, hands in his belt, moved forward with a wary smile. "Mihai!" Carol repeated and the two embraced. "You rascal, are you still climbing over horses? I am!"

"No time," said Mihai, "Were you? Where were you?" "How did you come here?" asked Fane at the same time. They turned and introduced Carol to the rest of the dorm's inhabitants and helped him unpack, talking all the while.

"We were evacuated in 1944, just before the Russians came," Carol related to a circle of curious faces. "Father had been conscripted and was at the Front so Mother, my younger sister and I loaded the wagon — all the horses had been taken, of course, but we still had a bullock for plowing — and went south to Focsani. It was a long wagon train and the road was lined with furniture and things people had tried to take but the animals couldn't pull." The boys nodded, they'd heard this before. "At night we'd stop in villages — it was before the famine and people had food so they usually gave us food to eat and somewhere to sleep. Finally we were at the Focsani railhead and loaded on trains and...guess what!...we went all the way to Timisoara and we were quartered with a family in Pastureni, where the famous stud farm is, and..." Carol went on to talk about the horses and his adventures with them until he sensed waning interest in his audience. Toward the end of the War, his father had been able to join them before they returned and arranged entrance to the *liceu*. They had just come back.

"I'd heard about the famine," Carol said, "but we didn't really know how bad it was up here in the North until we got here. It's terrible! But what happened to you, where were you? We heard you went to Transylvania to visit relatives, but you must have known something because the Russians came just after you left!"

One by one the other boys went back to their studies as Fane and Mihai told of the trip to Transylvania, the years there, Mother's death and the hardships when they returned while Carol talked enthusiastically about what he had learned on the stud farm.

"How is Haiduc?" he asked suddenly. "Did you bring him back with you?" Mihai looked sympathetically at Fane as Fane turned away, a tear in his eye. "Haiduc was sold," said Mihai, gesturing with his head toward Fane's back.

"Oh," was all that Carol said. "And how are studies here?" Carol never again mentioned Haiduc to Fane; later Mihai told him privately what had happened. He didn't need to explain Fane's pain because Carol shared it. Horses, Mihai thought, were as important to Carol as people. Maybe more important.

It wasn't until the next day that the three were isolated enough for Carol to ask, "What, um, about Mendl?" "He's gone," replied Mihai, looking steadily at Carol.

"Disappeared in the war, I think." Carol looked at Fane and Mihai, neither of whom said anything further.

"I see. Probably best, all things considered."

Carol sometimes went with them to Uncle Vanya's after church on Sunday but usually he had to stay and study if his father hadn't come into town. Outstanding at sports, certainly smart, popular yes, but he hadn't had Father Ion, Fane and Mihai agreed when they talked about Carol's dismal marks. They both helped Carol but the big blond got through school more on the strength of his personality and general intelligence than devotion to classwork.

Sunday afternoons at Uncle Vanya's became a tradition. Uncle Vanya helped Petru write a note giving permission for the boys to visit and they always found the small house was warm and welcoming even if, at times, the always delicious food Mrs. Anna served was carefully arranged to hide scarcity. It didn't take long for them to discover that Uncle Vanya was a doctor, respected and sought by the rich but also one who treated the poor. These days the poor, more plentiful than ever, paid as much as they could in food but even that didn't come regularly.

"It's funny we never thought about what Uncle Vanya did," said Fane one day. "Too young, I suppose," replied Mihai and the matter disappeared into the well of childhood.

The conversation, on the other hand, was always rich and plentiful. Friends dropped by to discuss current events, politics and the future. At first the boys could only listen — no one they knew had ever talked as these people talked. Yes, they knew when King Carol had abdicated to be replaced by King Mihai and that King Mihai had arrested Marshal Ion Antonescu, but details, gossip, speculation, and ideas about reform, growth, social justice now swirled about them in a soup of letters and countries and half-started sentences during long intense sessions of pure thought. The content of the discussion changed according to the visitors—now art, then the latest about the town library and again politics. Gradually both the boys not only increased their understanding but noticed that some things were only discussed among a certain group.

"People have different interests," Uncle Vanya explained when Mihai asked him one unusually quiet afternoon. "I find that I learn more when we discuss the things that others are passionate about."

"Oh." It seemed a sensible explanation. "I think it's a little like reading a book," Fane said when they were back in the dorm. "You go with what the author's interest is."

"No," said Mihai. "I think it's more than that. Some things can be said to some people but not to others...sort of like what you would tell me but you wouldn't tell, um, Liviu or Eusebiu or other students." After this Fane watched and listened with more attention and both boys began to absorb the important lesson of being careful about what they said to whom and under what circumstances.

It was during these afternoons that Fane began to develop not only his love of food and conversation but an interest in music. Mrs. Anna loved it, classical music, light music, almost any music. There was a phonograph and a few treasured records but also a radio. Fane was quick to pick up tunes and often went away humming from the songs he heard sung by Jean Moscopol or Titi Botez or another popular singer. He especially loved the older songs of a lighthearted Bucharest, "Let's meet Saturday night" or "I'm Crazy about You". They were so different from the songs Grandmother taught them or that they had learned in Poiana Cozonac. That music, accompanied by Pan pipes or only the sound of wind in the fir trees always seemed sort of...dark, maybe, with sadness underneath, no matter how fast and happy the melodies might be. That was the music, Fane thought, that fit times when he remembered

Mother or felt sad but most of the time it was, well, just nicer to be lighthearted. If there was a choice, that is.

One spring afternoon as they were on the long walk back to school a thought occurred to Fane. "Is Uncle Vanya Jewish?" he asked Mihai. "I mean, I've always thought he was because your, uh...but there is an icon in the living room and, uh...I..."

Mihai punched him in the arm. "You're embarrassed!"

"Well, I mean, the Jews were driven out of Radauti, but Uncle Vanya wasn't, but he has a Jewish last name..."

"How do you know that?" asked Mihai, genuinely curious.

"Because there's that man who came once who was the head of the Jewish something society who had the same last name."

"Uh...I guess you're right. I'm not sure, but I think Uncle Vanya is Jewish and Mrs. Anna is Christian. It, it...it doesn't seem very important, maybe."

"I guess not," answered Fane. "I was just curious." But privately he continued to wonder about it, being not only a visitor but almost a family member in a Jewish family and, then, why didn't they do any, well, have any Jewish rites or whatever they did. Eventually, Fane simply pushed the whole matter out of his mind since Uncle Vanya was the kind of person he wanted to be when he grew up anyway.

Even if he was Jewish.

Spring moved into summer and a break in their lives. Mihai stayed with Uncle Vanya to study German and English while Fane went back to the farm to help Petru and Granny. It was a smaller farm, since Petru had sold a piece of land. "With just two people we don't need all we had before," he explained to an astounded Fane. It was also evident that without a horse, since Haiduc had never been replaced, it simply wasn't possible to grow as much. Still, Fane burned with the loss of the field he had known so well and resented the fact that another man walked on it and thought it was his.

It was another bad summer. The rains were better than the year before but Fane was lonely without Mihai, bereft without his books, and though he loved his village and home he kept looking around and wondering how he had lived this life so happily. Carol wasn't there very much either as he was being tutored in Radauti and spending his free time at the racetrack. The best thing about the whole vacation, Fane thought, was going back to school and finally getting his hands clean again. And Granny's beloved screeching — not quite as strong and loud as before but still pithy and unique. Fane helped her as much as he could, mostly with the wash but also with preparing some of the food for dinner which was, more often than not, only for the two of them. During these times, Granny rambled on about events in the past, mixed in with tales of magic and witchcraft, pithy sayings and an occasional raspy song. Fane listened patiently, rejecting most of what she said as he knew it wasn't true but absorbing the lore of his heritage without knowing it.

The second fall Mihai's father came.

The boys had arrived at Uncle Vanya's and Mrs. Ana's house after church as usual one bright autumn noon. They knocked, wondering who would be there that day. "Welcome, welcome, come in," said Uncle Vanya happily when he opened the door with a wide smile. "I have a surprise for you." They walked into the entrance hall and turned into the parlor when a man was silhouetted against the lace curtained window. Turning, Fane saw a familiar figure and face he just couldn't quite place. Was it the writer who had...or maybe...

"Father, Father?" Mihai said from Fane's side. Fane felt him stiffen and tremble slightly. "Father?"

"My son!" Iacob Eichmann stroke forward, his arms opened wide. "My son! My beloved son! I've been half dead all these years without you! My son!" Fane turned away, his eyes stinging a bit, as he automatically followed Uncle Vanya into the kitchen with Mrs. Ana.

It was only a few moments before Mihai or was it Mendl now? and his father crowded into the cozy room and sat at the wood table with Uncle Vanya and Fane. There, while Mrs. Anna finished cooking a festive meal the years began to be knit together. Under skillful questioning the boys tumbled into their past, telling Mihai's father about the trip to Transylvania through the woods, about Poiana Cozonac and Father Ion, their return, school and on. "He's amazing," thought Fane to himself. "He knows exactly how it feels to be a teenager, and he really wants to know about us!"

"But Father," Mihai finally said, "We've told you all about us, what about you? Are you in Bucharest? What are you doing there? Will you stay here? Will we, I...we...uh...go to Bucharest?"

"You certainly will come to Bucharest but perhaps not right away, my boy. I'm working there, trying to do something useful for once in my life, maybe to build something enduring but it's not at a point where I can see the outcome clearly yet. And," Iacob shifted uncomfortably, silent for a second and suddenly stiff as he had been that long ago night he came to ask Fane's family if they would take Mihai, "it isn't a life for a son to come to. Not yet."

"Am I still your son?" asked Mihai with a bitter turn to his voice, hands clenched into fists under the table. "Who am I?"

"You are my son before anything else, my most-loved son, but you always have to be many people at the same time, it's the way life is." Iacob Eichmann leaned forward, intense and taut. "You are my Mendle, the child of my beloved wife, your mother, the light of my life. That is to me and always will be. You are Mihai, Fane's cousin, to your school and your public life." He shifted to one side. "Here in this house I am your father. For the rest of the world, for the time being, I am Vanya's friend from Bucharest who will come to visit occasionally." With this he rose from his chair and walked around to stand behind Mendl/Mihai, placing his hands on the boy's shoulders and leaned down to hold his cheek against Mihai's dark hair. "The world is a difficult place. You know that already. I have done the best I could to keep you safe and for the moment, this is how it must be." There was a long minute of charged silence, no one looking at anyone else, until Mrs. Anna said, "Come, let's eat."

Was food, Fane wondered, an answer to every awkward moment?

As usual Mihai and Fane talked about the afternoon as they walked back to school. "I feel funny about my father," said Mihai. "I don't know what's going on, but it makes me worry."

Fane scuffed fallen leaves in an arc, first from one foot then the other, watching them intently as he replied slowly, "I see what you mean, but he said it was for you."

"If it was really for me wouldn't he..." Mihai didn't finish the sentence. He didn't need to. Both boys had seen too much to think life was that easy. "I just hope he's not doing something dangerous for him or, or...against the law or something."

"I think whatever your father is doing must be all right. Maybe it's something political." Both boys fell silent, thinking of the swirls of conversation in and out of the school about the Russians and what they were doing, about the Romanian government. It hadn't been terribly important to them compared to who would be chosen for the soccer team or who got the best marks or, for Fane, the latest book he had discovered in the rich depths of the school library but now the currents of politics and domination and resistance seemed much closer.

And much more important. As the weeks and months of their second year in the *liceu* passed, both Fane and Mihai began to pay more attention to the discussions at Uncle Vanya's. They absorbed the pros and cons of alliance with Russian, the anger about the reparations Russia was extracting to "pay" for their soldiers on Romanian soil and gradually realized that Romania would be influenced by the Great Bear to the north no matter what the Romanians said, wanted, or did. Almost unconsciously they learned the names of the players in Bucharest and even in Radauti as they listened to discussions or arguments about tactics, motives and outcomes. They were enraged by stories of what was happening in northern Bukovina, the lost land, the deported villagers gone, it was rumored, to Siberia, the overtures at friendship to Southern Bukovina, still in Romania, from the Russian occupiers to the north, and they absorbed the suspicions about a possible Russian move further into their own country. They heard of the Austrian rule years ago and its benefits and failures, of the Romanian rule and its benefits and failures, of the glories of their homeland, this lovely Bukovina, their corner of the earth, and the longing to unite it again.

Above all, they learned to keep their mouths shut until they knew how the land lay in any group.

The first time they heard a discussion about collectivization they were astounded. "But they can't take our land!" said Fane later.

"It sounds as if you might not have much choice," replied Mihai. "And they already took land from war criminals and the really rich."

"But that was different."

"How?"

"Well, they can't. I'd...I'd...I'd kill them. I'd join the Resistance. I..."

"But you hate farming, you said so yourself!" Mihai pointed out.

"That's different, that's...it's...it's our LAND. I hated it when Father sold that field. I don't want to plow it, but I don't want anyone else..." Fane stopped, confused.

"I understand," said Mihai consolingly. "I understand, I think, but you know we can't, well, we'll just have to wait and see what happens." Just today it sounded like it's going to be something bad.

"Going to happen? Has already happened. Lots of it," Fane said bitterly. "And just thinking about it makes me want to, to..." He turned away. "I think I'll go do my history lessons." Mihai looked sympathetically at Fane's retreating back, noting the stiff shoulders, and envied his ability to lose himself in his beloved books.

"Thank you," Ellen said as she took the glass of wine from Stefan. "It was kind of you to get it for me."

Fane smiled and brushed the words aside. "You were telling me about your childhood in, what was the place?" He settled himself in to listen, interested as always in other worlds and hoping to find that chink, the one place in the armor of diplomacy that could draw her out into his plans.

Over the summer of 1948 theory and speculation turned into reality and hit the *liceu* like a blow to the side of the head. Change was coming to Bilca as well. Fane was working in the family's courtyard, weeding the area right by the house that had their small orchard and vegetable garden, when he saw Carol's father coming up the lane.

"Good morning, sir," Fane said respectfully, wondering why their former Mayor was visiting this part of the village. He also wondered, as he looked at the tall, well-built visitor, why he hadn't resumed his duties as Mayor.

"Good morning, Fanica," Ion Cojocariu replied. He still had the bearing of an important man and moved easily as he leaned over the wooden fence and surveyed Fane's work. "How are you doing?" They exchanged pleasantries for a few minutes, Fane explaining that Mihai was spending the summer studying in Radauti again, then Ion Cojocariu said, "Fane, Carol tells me about you and how you are close friends, just as our families have been close for many years."

"Yes, sir," said Fane, wondering what was going on.

"I have something to ask of you," Carol's father continued.

"What could that be, sir?" A stab of fear darted around Fane's stomach. What could be wrong?

"Carol says that you write very well. That is, that your handwriting is the envy of all the other students and that you can imitate old style penmanship." Fane stepped back in surprise. It was true he was proud of his handwriting and of his ability to imitate the flourishes of the last century, but what could it have to do with Carol's father? "There is some work I need done," the former Mayor continued, "work that requires your skills and absolute discretion and I could use your help."

"Of course, sir, I would be glad to do anything for you." Fane replied. He was curious. Besides, there was no way he could refuse.

That was how he found himself in a quiet room, warm with summer dust and the hum of a lazy fly, copying old ledgers of land records and...changing them. Land that had belonged to Carol's family was recorded as sold in bits and pieces through the years to other people, names Fane didn't recognize but seemed vaguely familiar. It was careful, tedious work on old ledger pages that looked the same age as the originals. Fane found the old records fascinating, some with mistakes, some involving families he knew and lost himself in the task the way he lost himself in history. This was history! He worked on odd afternoons when he told Father and Granny he was going to see friends and it lightened the long, dull months of summer farming. Carol's father was often with him, ready to talk about any of the families in the ledger except the ones who had "purchased" his land, and was nothing but praise for Fane's work. At home praise was an unknown word — it was hard enough to keep Father from trying to hit him — and through the weeks that they met, Fane developed a feeling of deep affection for the older man. "What," he sometimes wondered, "what would it be like to have him as a father..." but he pushed that thought away. He never saw Carol's mother but he didn't think much about that either.

Two weeks before school the last page was done. "What are you going to do with them?" Fane asked as Carol's father looked over his shoulder at the pile of ledgers. Fane felt he was treading on forbidden ground but his curiosity drove him.

"They'll be rebound and taken back to the records office," Ion Cojocariu replied, his hand on the boy's shoulder. "You know a lot about our family now and I would appreciate it if you don't mention this to anyone. I will, of course, continue to keep an eye on your Father and Grandmother. Here is a bit of something to help out at home." Money had never been mentioned nor, in fact, had Fane even wondered if he was going to be paid. He opened the hand the former Mayor had taken and saw enough there to buy...a lot!

"I can't...you shouldn't...Sir, this has..."

"Don't say a word," the older man interrupted. "You will learn eventually how you have helped Carol and his family. We'll repay you. It's always good to be in your position — having people owe you favors helps you in life." Ion Cojocariu clapped Fane on the shoulder and added, "Go home, don't show your Father any of this but get some of the supplies he needs." He then embraced the boy, waited while Fane put his writing implements away for the last time, and walked with him to the gate.

When students returned to the *liceu* in the fall, they found that the Government of Romania — that is, the Russians, the whispers said — had changed the school curriculum. Decadent foreign languages were now to be replaced by Russian and, to Fane's unconcealed outrage, Romanian and world history were pushed to the background by History of the USSR and History of the Communist Party. It was bad enough, all the boys agreed, that the name of the Liceul Hurmuzachi had been changed to an undistinguished "Boys High School" but making them study Russian History...Fane was so angry he forgot to hide his teenage contempt for the stupid idiots who had done this.

"Hey," said Mihai after one particularly virulent outburst. "You need to take it easy." Mihai pulled on the illfitting pants of his new, Soviet-inspired uniform. All the boys had them and no one knew whether to be pleased, angry or ashamed but at least, Fane and Mihai had agreed, there weren't any obvious differences any more between the town boys and those from the country. "You could get in trouble," Mihai continued as he buttoned his coat.

"I don't care," replied Fane shortly shrugging his own shoulders into his new jacket. "They shouldn't have..." He turned away angrily and stomped off, resolved to uphold his principles, but when Professor Brebean asked him gravely to meet him in a quiet corner he anxiety hit his stomach. 'That stomach,' he thought in passing, 'seems to be my weak point.' The anxiety was immediately replaced by another burst of righteous anger and he bristled as he approached his favorite professor.

"Fane," began the Professor. "It is all over the *liceu* that you object to the changes in the history curriculum, and..."

"Of course I do," Fane interrupted. "Don't you?" almost accusingly. "What horrible nonsense this all is..."

"Shut your mouth and don't talk to me or anyone else that way!" Professor Brebean grasped Fane's arm, hard, then let go. "We need to talk," he continued quietly, "There are a lot of issues here. Listen to me." Fane nodded, jolted by his Professor's anger.

"Look," Brebean said. "I understand how you feel. I feel the same way and I don't like having to teach the 'History of the Communist Party'...but I have a wife and two children to support, to live for. You could be severely punished for opposing these changes—and it's not just you."

"But Mihai has nothing to do with what I'm saying, he even told me to be quiet," Fane said quickly.

"Not Mihai, you little fool. Me, my family," said his Professor angrily. "I could be punished because I'm your teacher. What you do reflects on me. I..." Professor Brebean hesitated and Fane saw his face had flushed and there were, could it be? tears in his eyes. "I am ashamed that I have to talk to you like this, that I'm being a coward, but it's not just me it's my family as well. Already...you perhaps have noticed that Liviu didn't come back to school this fall. And that some professors are gone."

"Yes, but...I didn't...is it that bad?" whispered Fane, thinking of Uncle Vanya and how people seemed to be ever more careful about when and to whom they could talk even in the small house that always seemed so safe. He thought of the change in Sundays, now that they no longer had to go to church, weren't even supposed to go to church, and though many of the boys continued, it was sort of...not talked about. Had the world changed so much without him noticing it?

"I think it is, and if it isn't that bad now it will be soon. It's...it's going to be a bad time Stefan."

"But what will I do?" Both knew Fane was referring to his love of recent Romanian history and how he had been looking forward to the rest of the year.

"You will study the subjects that are required. And I will tell you about books that you will enjoy reading. You

94

will continue to get the best education possible in history and...you'll learn how to hide it. And you will also go to the meetings of the young communists and say the right things."

Over the course of that year and the next, Fane learned not just to talk but to think on two levels. He continued his exploration into the past that he loved, but not in the classroom. In the classroom he learned what to say whether or not he thought it right. That part was public; what he really thought could only be discussed with Brebean and that didn't happen often and when it did Fane didn't need to be told again that it was strictly between the two of them.

Brebean had gotten permission for Fane to take books off campus with him; he kept them at Uncle Vanya's but he noticed that there wasn't any record of this in the logbook and he knew, without asking, that he needn't bring them back. Other books, Fane noticed, seemed also to be out of the Library but the librarian simply kept his passive face on display and said nothing. No one else was interested in these titles and as cards disappeared and records changed no one else at school seemed to notice. There were, of course, Uncle Vanya and Mrs. Anna and Mihai and they didn't bring up the subject until Fane did.

That is, he didn't quite bring it up. One quiet Sunday afternoon when snow had kept all guests except the boys away Uncle Vanya was talking to them about the need to help the ordinary people of Romania and they were discussing the corruption of public officials under former governments and how to stop it.

"Shouldn't they all just be arrested?" Mihai asked.

"It's a bit more complicated than that," replied Uncle Vanya. "They were paid very small salaries so they had to make money in other ways. The Government knew it and simply turned a blind eye to under the table payments."

"Then they need to be paid better," interjected Fane. "That only makes sense."

"True, but in order to have the money to pay them better, the Government needs more money. And though the typical way for a Government to raise money is to increase taxes, the best way really is to increase the wealth of everybody because, as you know, most of our people don't have any money for extra taxes." The boys, thinking of Bilca and its peasants, nodded. Then Fane spoke, "That's what they say will happen, but what does history have to do with increasing production? And all the other things we are hearing about?" Fane could hear himself voicing the subject that had gnawed at him for months. "Why does...the school..." fearing even here to name Professor Brebean, "not want me to bring books back? What's happening?"

Uncle Vanya looked at his hands. Fane did as well, then looked at his own, noting with pleasure they were also clean like Uncle Vanya's, but didn't have blue veins on the back. Fane's hands were strong and still calloused, not really a scholar's hands. Yet, he thought. Not yet. He shifted imperceptibly in his chair.

"Sometimes," Uncle Vanya began, then paused. "Sometimes there are disagreements about the best way to do things." The boys nodded. This wasn't exactly a new idea.

"We in Romania have to admire the Soviet Union for its many accomplishments but we don't have to like all its methods, especially regarding Romania. History seems to be the first casualty of Russian occupation — no, the second. The first is a country's wealth which is hauled away," Uncle Vanya said with a quick flash of bitterness, then he regained his usual equanimity. "And we have many things for which to be grateful, especially those people who suffered under the, ah, previous regimes. But...but." He stopped again to search for the right words. "There are problems and will be greater problems in this fight to transform Romania so that there is no more inequality, no more injustice, no more poverty. And we can only hope that some of them, like the perversion of history, are temporary and will disappear as things get better." The boys nodded thoughtfully.

"But there are difficulties and problems will get worse," Uncle Vanya added. "And it will be necessary to be very, very quiet about them if you want to survive." He looked at the boys, noting how they were trying to appear calm and worldly while under the surface there was a desire to rush in with questions. It was time to change to subject.

Tramping through ankle-deep snow and skittering across icy roads to the *liceu*, flakes swirling around their heads and blurring vision, Fane said in a muffled voice, "Mihai. Uncle Vanya said exactly the same thing that Professor Brebean told me. The problems will get worse."

"Yeah. I think they're right," was Mihai's rejoinder.

"What will this mean for us?"

"We already know we've lost some of our professors while others have come to teach...Russian and stuff." Fane nodded in unseen agreement. "And like I told you, I heard that some of the boys from rich families might..." Mihai paused, not wanting or needing to go on. After a few steps Fane said, "I wonder if Carol..."

"I...I think Carol will be all right. His father...he's pretty smart."

"Well, at least we don't have to worry."

"Because we have a poor family?"

"Yeah. We're peasants, remember?"

"Don't be so sure. We're all right as long as we keep our mouths shut. Remember what Uncle Petru always says, If you don't stick your head up, it won't be cut off." The boys tramped on through the thickening snow in silence, returning to a haven that somehow didn't seem as safe as it used to until Mihai broke the tension by scooping up a handful of snow and tossing it into Fane's face. Fane returned the favor and they were in a regular great snowball fight until Mihai, usually accurate, missed Fane only to hear the missile thunk against another target. Fane turned around and saw a Russian uniform brushing the snow off its face. "Oh, no..." he began to think when Mihai went running past. "Pyotr? Pyotr!" "Why...it's you, my young friends from...what name...the village like mine!" The two hugged, Fane followed, Pyotr turned to his companion, "I was going to...when..."

"What are you doing in Radauti?" "What brings you here?" all three asked at once.

"Do you have time for a coffee?" Pyotr asked. Mihai and Fane looked at each other, wondering about the time, wondering if they wanted to be seen with a Russian officer. "Yes," said Mihai. "Unfortunately..." began Fane. "Come," said Pyotr, "let's walk...you must be at school. Do you have to get back? We're here on some business and we were looking around the town, perhaps..." They walked together toward the school, the boys pointing out sights, Pyotr talking about Bucharest where he was stationed. They talked about the *Liceul* Hurmuzachi and the boys' studies. They didn't talk about what Pyotr did, or politics, or the Russian occupation. They all knew where to stop. Once again they exchanged addresses on parting. "This time," Fane thought, "we probably really will meet again," though he wasn't sure why.

"And what do you want to do while you're here in Romania," Fane asked Ellen. "Not in your work, but for your own pleasure."

"Oh," she replied eagerly, "I want to travel and see the country and get to know the people. You know, my Romanian teacher had me read a lot, Caragiale, the Miorita, Luceafarul, *and he talked a lot about how beautiful this country is, so I want to see as much as I can."*

"He certainly prepared you well. And who was your teacher?" asked Fane.

"Oh," Ellen withdrew her warmth, "someone settled in the US." Fane mentally kicked himself for reaching too far, too soon,

and noted that Ellen had already learned, somehow, an important lesson. 'I wonder,' he thought, 'who that teacher was.'

In spite of the currents of history that swirled in and out of their lives most things stayed the same. Fane and Mihai studied, exercised on the sports field and helped Carol. "I just don't know what's wrong with Carol," Mihai told Fane at one point. "He's plenty smart and he spends time with his books, but he never seems to learn anything!" "He's thinking about horses," said Fane.

"More likely about girls," corrected Mihai.

They were both right. Everyone 'knew' about 'women' and one of the older boys bragged so continuously about his 'conquests' — limited, everyone was aware, to the two prostitutes near the marketplace — that he became a laughingstock when he said one of the women was paying him for his 'services.' Carol, on the other hand, didn't talk until one day he took Fane by the shoulder.

"Hey," he said.

"Hay is for horses," Fane replied automatically.

"No, listen. Why don't you come with me Sunday afternoon."

"I have to go to Uncle Vanya's," Fane said sullenly and turned away, hiding the surge of interest in his groin. He knew very well what Carol meant and he also knew that it cost money.

"Look," said Carol forcefully. He grabbed Fane's shoulder and turned him back. "You and Mihai have been helping me out a lot. I could do it by myself, of course, but...anyway..." his voice trailed off. Fane waited uncomfortably, wondering what to say. "I..." he started when Carol interrupted again. "Look," he repeated, "It's my treat. I want to do it for you and Mihai."

"Have you asked Mihai?"

"Not yet. I thought it just might be easier for both of us to talk to him." Carol fell silent for a moment while Fane nodded in agreement. Mihai never seemed to talk about girls in the same way the other boys did. He was interested in them, of course — who wasn't? — but much more quiet. 'I wonder,' Fane thought to himself, 'if being Jewish has something to do...' He stopped the thought and said, "Come on, let's go!" Carol grinned and they set off to find Mihai.

Two weeks later Fane walked with Carol through the Radauti marketplace. They were supposedly visiting Carol's father and Fane realized with a start that Carol probably knew a lot more about Radauti than he or Mihai had dreamed of, that he had a lot more freedom than anyone thought possible. 'And why,' he thought to himself, 'does his father...' but the thought wasn't completed.

"Here we are," said Carol, stopping before a plain doorway, set into a solid row of buildings lining the side street. "Up two floors, you'll see a man on the landing. That's her father. Thumbs up, pay and go in. Thumbs down, she's busy so come wait with me. I'll be in that coffee shop." He pointed to a small place back toward the market. "Have fun!" Fane looked at his friend and the door, then turned and entered.

The stairs were narrow, dark, and very steep so Fane blamed his pounding heart on the series of upward steps. He wondered what he should say but as he was composing something in his head he reached the second landing. A nondescript older man looked at him without interest but, Fane saw almost with alarm, he had his thumb up. He used the thumb to gesture at the door so Fane fumbled forward, somehow got the money into the man's hand and opened the door.

Inside was a bare room, a bed, a chair, a stool and a woman in a robe on the stool who smiled at him. Fane hardly noticed anything about her as he wondered where to look. "Come in and make yourself comfortable," she said. Fane looked around again and again wondered what to do but he obediently sat on the chair, hands on his knees and looked at the woman. He saw little beyond a female form through his excitement and pounding heart.

"Not that, sweetheart. Take your clothes off. I'm Rosa." Rosa stood up and began undoing her robe so Fane, in a panic, dropped his pants and started unbuttoning his shirt when she came over to him. She had nothing on and Fane's body responded beyond his ability to think or direct. A step, a tumble on to the bed, he entered a special place that burst into waves of pleasure.

Then it was over. 'Is that all...' was a fleeting thought but he found the woman stroking his face. "Your first time?" she asked.

"Uh, yes..." Fane turned his cheek feeling the coarse bed sheet under his face.

"Raise yourself on your elbows, hon, you're a big young man and you're smashing me." Fane put his elbows on the bed to support his upper body and looked down at Rosa, still between her legs but not really in her any more. It made him feel halfway between a reprimanded child and a powerful man; he unconsciously centered on the latter.

"You did well, but you'll be even better next time. You're a fine young man. Come back soon," Rosa said. Fane looked at her face, realizing she was older than he, almost as old as...he stopped before he completed the thought. Still, it had been just fine and he had done it! Rosa moved under him and Fane found himself swinging off the bed and standing. "Now put on your clothes, hon. I'd love to spend more time with you but I'm a working girl." Before he quite knew how he had been helped to wash with the jug and basin, dry, dress, and suddenly he was running down the stairs into daylight and a normal but changed world.

'Do I look different? I've done it,' he wanted to ask Carol, but all he could do was grin. "Hey," Carol said, "have some coffee. How was it?" "Pretty good," Fane said as he sat and took his place in the adult world.

When they finally got back to school, he wondered if the other boys would notice that he had...changed. Surely people must see it...but no one said anything and the usual routine took over. The next Sunday was Mihai's turn while Fane went alone to Uncle Vanya's. "I hope that cold you boys passed to each other wasn't too bad," said Mrs. Anna. "I'll send back some good cough syrup with you," then the conversation turned to an upcoming exhibit by an artist from Suceava and meandered on.

The last autumn of their high school years slid into winter as more rumors of land reform, changes in Bucharest, and growing unease alternated with intense study. Most of the boys hoped to continue to University but they knew that there weren't very many places. Uncle Vanya and Mrs. Anna now turned conversations on to subjects that might be useful to Mihai and Fane and at school Professor Brebean quietly began tutoring a few boys outside of class as did many of the professors, each working with the best boys in his area of expertise. Even Carol started to take studies seriously. By the time the Christmas break came it was a relief.

"Except it isn't a Christmas break any more," noted Fane. Mihai nodded as they climbed into Ion Cojocariu's wagon. Carol's father had come to pick up the three boys for what might be the last Christmas at home for a long time since they'd be at the University...of course, Fane thought, if they didn't get into the University...he stopped the thought. "I kiss your hand," he said politely to Carol's father. "How are things in Bilca?"

"They are...progressing. They're taking land from the mid-level peasants and turning it into a collective farm," Cojocariu answered. "They're taking some of the mid-level peasants, too, since they're resisting and we all know they're class enemies." His face was grim, then he changed the subject and smiled, "But we still have a pig to kill for the winter. I hope," he nodded toward Fane and Mihai, "you'll bring my friend Petru and your granny to join us for the festivities." The boys, knowing that Petru probably didn't have a pig this year, nodded gratefully. And now Fane understood why he had spent so many hours in Carol's father's house redoing old records — and why Carol treated him to occasional visits to Rosa.

The rest of the year raced by. Exams came and went and even before the results were out a group of hopeful graduates prepared to go to Bucharest. Just before they left, Fane and Mihai visited home where Granny pulled their ears, screeched happily about her grandchildren the high school graduates, and cooked special meals meant to increase their brain power. Petru was silent most of the time but proud. The house and courtyard seemed particularly shabby but all this was soon lost in the rhythm of the train, headed South toward the capital. Carol, Mihai and Fane traveled together along with several other boys from the *liceu* who were also going to take the University entrance exams and the hours went by quickly as they moved out of their own rolling hills into the great Danube plain. The weather was warm and they kept the window open in spite of the soot blowing in, creeping into their clothes and hair. By late afternoon they arrived.

The Gara du Nord was immense and dark, crowded and noisy. The three stood a moment on the platform beside the train, looking around and wondering what would be next as their classmates were met and dispersed. "Uncle Vanya gave me the address of where we're staying," said Mihai uncertainly.

"Come on," said Carol, "let's go out," and he led the way as if he knew what he was doing. Fane and Mihai began to follow when they heard their names. "Fane, Mihai...and you must be Carol...I'm over here."

"Mr. Eichmann! We thought you'd be here!" Fane exclaimed. Carol looked a bit puzzled for a second, glancing first at Mr. Eichmann, then at Mihai before composing his face into a bland mask. Mihai, hung back, not quite sure how to handle this public meeting.

"Vanya told me you'd be coming on this train and asked me to meet you," said Mihai/Mendl's father. "Good evening," he turned to Carol. I am a friend of Dr. Vanya and I've known you since you were a little boy." Carol looked straight at him and said, "I remember you. I was so sorry to hear about Mendl's death. It must have been a great loss." Fane was shocked but Mihai's father registered a barely visible admiring flicker before he answered sadly and smoothly, "Yes, it was a great sorrow. Everything about the war was a great sorrow but I'm glad you three are here now. Let's go find your rooms and then have dinner."

Before they knew it the older man had hailed a carriage, or perhaps it was waiting for him? and climbed in after them. Go to Strada Ostasilor, it's near Cismigiu. Do you know it?" "Yes, sir," the bearded coachman, "yes, sir, I know the street," and cracked his whip.

The roads were paved with cobblestones and full of people, carriages and automobiles. "I've never seen so many cars," Fane thought, "nor so many big buildings. Suddenly Radauti seemed small in memory and very provincial.

"...I think they'll do..." Mihai's father was saying. Fane realized he must have been talking about the rooms. "The three of you get on and sharing a room won't be too bad. Ordinarily you should be in a dormitory, but you can't get one until...unless, of course...you pass the exams. Mrs. Radu is a clean woman, honest, not a very good cook but there's the canteen when..." Fane's attention wandered back to the surrounding scene noticing particularly the well-dressed, beautiful women on the streets and hearing strains of music from an occasional open door. He even recognized some of the songs!

The "rooms" turned out to be a small attic with two windows, three beds and two desks. There was a washstand. "The toilet is downstairs," the small, round woman who had met them and introduced herself as their landlady, "and to bathe, the public baths aren't far on a Saturday night." It was all very strange and yet somehow familiar, as if it had happened before.

"But...but..." said Mihai as they left the building to walk to a small nearby restaurant, "...we haven't even sat for the University exams yet...but she acted as if we are going to be there a long time..." The three entered the restaurant and were shown to a table where Mihai's father asked for a bottle of wine and, naming the cook, asked what had been prepared this evening. Then he turned his attention to the boys again.

"You are going to have to wait for the results of the exams and that will take some time," he said, lighting a cigarette, "and, in any case, I am hopeful you'll be accepted." Fane looked at the long menu and his own glass of wine— "In celebration," Iacob Eichmann had said—and wondered what he should order. The prices seemed so high.

"But even if we pass the exams," Fane burst out awkwardly, surprised at himself and unable to help it, "how will we pay for the University, to stay...I mean, I've heard there were scholarships, but..."

"You're all well-prepared and from an excellent *liceu* and, at the same time, have good backgrounds, which is important these days. The Government gives scholarships to poor students who qualify and I'm fairly confident you'll qualify—both on scholarship and income." Mihai and Fane glanced simultaneously at Carol, who always seemed to have money. "I have corresponded with Carol's father," Mr. Eichmann seemed to read their minds! "...and with Vanya and have the necessary paperwork for all of you. The scholarships," Mr. Eichman raised his glass, took a sip of the wine, and put it down again, "include food and a place to stay. And this summer..." he added, "this summer it may be better to remain in the city." The boys nodded without really comprehending. "Now," Mihai's father continued, "don't pay attention to the menu. They usually don't have much of it on hand but I'm known here and we'll eat well." Fane and Mihai had never eaten in a restaurant before — who knew about Carol? — so perhaps, Fane thought, this was normal. There was so much to think about. He watched Mr. Eichmann carefully, noting which utensils were used for what and was thankful for Aunt Anna's gentle unobtrusive instruction in table manners.

Over the next week what they thought about was the exams they were taking. Both Mihai and Fane took time to tutor Carol and they discussed their choices of Faculties. Fane's was clear — his love was History, "In spite of everything," he said and the three needed no more explanation. Mihai wanted Law but Carol wasn't sure. "What I really want," he said, "is to study horses."

"Go on," said Mihai, "don't be silly."

"No, I mean it. Breeding is a science. Training is a science."

"Well, get over it. What have you put down?"

"Oh, I couldn't think of anything so I put history, so Fane could, um, you know..."

"Keep you in!" said Mihai. "History!" said Fane. They should have known but somehow this hadn't come out before. "History!" repeated Fane. "You don't care at all about history!"

"History of war," muttered Carol, "that's what interests me. Why, then horses were..." the discussion went on until they all turned over and fell asleep to dream of exam rooms without pens or paper or having enough time to finish or realizing they had come without any clothes, all the sleeping and waking nightmares students have about exams.

The exams themselves were grueling, days in summerhot rooms without enough time for eating or even thinking. There was a water jug in the middle of the room for all the exam-takers and occasionally someone would go up and drink but mostly rows of hopeful students wrote and wrote and wrote. Then came the nerve wracking days of waiting for results until one evening they were walking through Cismigiu Gardens in the long twilight, idly looking at the lake and talking about the swans' long necks. Down the path ahead of them they saw another hopeful student, known from long hours of writing and awkward discussions during breaks, coming towards them at a trot. "They've posted the results," he said as he passed.

"Let's go," said Carol, turning first and leading them down to the Boulevard, up the long blocks, past the Military House, on to the great buildings by University Square all three half walking, half running sometimes Mihai behind Carol, sometimes Fane, Carol always in the lead. There was a large crowd of hopeful students shoving to get onto the downstairs hall and crowding among the pillars of the great hall to see the lists. The three couldn't begin to get close in spite of their anxiety until Carol turned to Mihai. "You look for all of us. You can see really well." Fane stepped forward to help lift their slim friend onto Carol's shoulders while the big blond told Mihai, "You direct me." "Straight ahead, to the left a bit, it's by last name. Fane! You're there!" Fane's heart leaped! He was a University student! "Now to the left...yes...I see... There I am! And...more to the left...let me see, at the top of this column... Carol!!! You, too!" They went through the crowd toward the exit with faces that told everyone the results. Other students pushed forward to see if their own names were on the list. Some stayed and searched and searched, hoping that perhaps the list was out of order...others whooped and clapped one another on the back. Somehow the three managed to exit the hall and stumble down the University steps where they embraced each other and their future.

The rest of the summer disappeared and classes began. Fane found that as much as he had loved the halls and library of the Liceul Hurmuzachi with a deep, abiding affection, he loved the University even more. He loved reading in their common garret where they had remained, he wasn't sure how or why, the rain against their windows. He loved the walk to the Faculty of History through a bit of the Park and down the great Boulevard. He loved weaving together pieces of the past into a seamless whole. He loved the city of Bucharest, and explored first the nearby streets, then further on in each direction, as he thought about assignments. Following the increasingly strict party line was a bother but Fane found he could provide professors with what they needed to hear and continue to search for what he came to think of as the "real" past on his own. It was the same game he had played in Radauti, a solitary pursuit, but gradually he realized that there were professors and students who did the same thing. They didn't really talk about it, but here and there the odd remark made it clear.

And he made friends. There were a few boys from Bukovina and with them there was always the bond of a shared homeland but Fane found it was easy to talk to other students as well, draw them out, amuse them. He had a good eye for faces and remembered the details of people's lives, so he could always ask them how a sick mother was doing or if the results of the last whatever were good. Every once in a while he said to himself, "I'm getting to be good at this...but it comes naturally to Carol," but even this thought was eventually lost as building relationships became part of his being.

News from home was mixed. Father wrote sporadically and with great difficulty; Granny dictated letters to Tante Elise down the lane. She explained in her first letter that Bucharest was so far away the boys needed her advice. Fane wondered why Bucharest was "different" in this than

Radauti but enjoyed Granny's colorful missives; he and Mihai took turns writing back. Collectivization was a topic much on Granny's mind and she didn't like the idea at all.

"Naturally," said Mihai, "she's set in her old ways."

"But peasants will never give up their land peacefully," retorted Fane. "I know. I wouldn't."

"You're here in Bucharest, you're not going to be a peasant, so the question is academic. Besides, production has to be increased for people to live better."

"But..." started Fane, ready to contradict Mihai, when Carol intervened. "Romanian peasants will always manage, you know that, and life could hardly be worse for most of them than it has been the past few years. Could you lend me your notes from the last lecture?" Mihai spent most of his time studying that year, Carol spent a lot of time elsewhere, and Fane soon found his own pursuits on his long walks, mostly linked to his studies, as he missed the exercise of the playing fields at the *liceu*. His sport now, he thought once as he hurried through the Lipscani, was hunting books at the *anticariats*, the used book stores, of Bucharest. Fane had almost no spending money but still managed to pick up a few volumes when the proprietors would hold them for him. Mostly he sold one of the two daily meals he had on his food card, filching extra bread against the lean evening ahead but occasionally he went to the Bank of Carol. Always generous, Carol tried to refuse repayment the first time he did this.

"But..." Fane protested. "You have to take the money."

"Come on, you're always tutoring me. Go ahead, take it."

"I can't," Fane protested in frustration.

"Why not?" Carol turned to his friend. Both were in their garret and Fane sat, outlined against the window with the blue and white of a spring sky behind him, a spray of cherry blossoms cutting through one corner. Carol automatically held up his hands to frame a picture. Cinematography was his current love.

"Well," Fane searched for words. "If I take the money from you, I can't ask you again and then I'd never be able to get any books."

"Look," said Carol, "you spend...how many hours a week...taking notes in lectures which I use, not to mention tutoring me. I'd have to pay anyone else for it."

"But you're my friend," Fane cut in.

"I know," Carol replied patiently, "but I'd have to pay someone else. So let's not talk about it any more. Now," the big blond came over and put his hands on Fane's shoulders, pulling him up, "let's go have a coffee and you can explain..." Fane occasionally wondered that the attacks on 'rich peasants' and even 'middle peasants' never seemed to affect either Carol's status as coming from a 'poor peasant' family or his finances, but then he remembered the summer spent copying old land records and shrugged his shoulders. It wasn't his place to complain.

The arrangement lasted and Fane became a familiar figure in the bookstores though both Mihai and Carol protested from time to time that Fane's books were crowding them out of the room.

For Fane, the great trophies were those few "suspect" books that had somehow been overlooked by the authorities — books mentioning the Royal Family, about Romania's historic bouts with Russia. Most, of course, had been taken out of stocks and the rare items that had slipped through the system were trophies, hunted with passion and found with carefully hidden triumph. The chase eventually led to the back room at the Curtea Veche Anticariat.

Fane usually entered the dark shop near the great Obor Market after looking carefully through the items in the windows to see if there was anything new or exciting, heart quickening in anticipation of the possible unknown. Then he went through the door, turning to the shelves at the back left for history before going on to look at old postcards and peruse other subjects. In the course of his routine he had struck up a casual acquaintance with the young assistant who was about his age. They occasionally chatted about books, cautiously at first, more openly as they recognized a mutual passion. One cold, gray February day only the two of them were in the shop, talking about the number of encyclopedias there were about Romania, arguing heatedly about what could be considered an 'encyclopedia' whatever might have been put in the title, when they hit a silent spot.

"Look," said the assistant, "what's your name? I'm Andrei. Andrei Roveanu. I feel as if I know you but we've never introduced ourselves." Fane started at this, half suspicious but with the same thought.

"I guess you're right—it's a wonder we've talked so much about books and never introduced ourselves. I'm Fane, Fane Vulcean."

"No one's here, let's go have a cup of tea."

"Can you leave the shop?"

"No, but there's a hot plate in the back room. The bell on the front door will tell me if anyone enters and not many people come at this time of day." As Andrei led him to the back of the shop and through a door, Fane wondered why he'd never really thought about what might be behind the wall. Probably because he was always stopped by the history books and...his thoughts stumbled as he looked around the little room, one of two. It was full of books! He looked at the books. Rare books, books that were...

"Yes," said Andrei interrupting his thoughts. "These are the books that aren't for sale because..." He didn't need to go further. He also didn't need to tell Fane the risk he was taking in introducing a relative stranger to this space. Fane's thoughts flickered back to the previous week when Mihai had told him and Carol about one of his classmates. "Velu's been arrested!" "What?" "Velu who?" "Velu who's in the Faculty with me. He used to go to the French Library to study. Yesterday, when he came out, two security

111

officers were waiting for him at the door, they took him by his elbows and put him in a van. Liviu saw it, no one knows where he is..."

"The books, of course," continued Andrei as Fane returned to the present, still shaken at the thought of one of their colleagues being taken to...probably the DanubeBlack Sea Canal because there were rumors..."the books will be, um, turned over to the State because they are incorrect in their historical approach." The two young men looked at each other and from all that wasn't said began a friendship that would endure for years.

In the summer they all went home for the long vacation. Iacob Eichmann brought them train tickets and a small knot of people waited for them in Radauti, a welcoming committee. Feeling like heroes, the boys jumped down from the train to embrace Uncle Vanya, Aunt Anna and Carol's father. "Welcome." "You'll come home with us to wash before going to Bilca." "It's so good to see you." Fane felt tears come to his eyes, realized he hadn't actually missed anyone before this, and wondered why. He looked around as they went down familiar streets and thought, 'Radauti...it looks shabby and small...' but it was home.

In the wagon on the road to Bilca they asked for news of the village and what changes had happened. "We're managing," said Carol's father. Fane noticed that his hair was thinner at the temples and greying a bit. "They haven't completely collectivized us yet but it will happen." He turned to the boys and grinned. "We'll manage," he repeated, "rather than be managed. That's how we do it in Bukovina."

"How do you get ready for something like collectivization?" asked Mihai, "Who's in charge?" asked Fane. "How are the other horses?" asked Carol, looking at the matched grays who were pulling the wagon. Ion Cojocariu flipped the reins against the horses' rumps and laughed. Fane didn't think the laugh was very happy but

Cojocariu simply said, "You boys, full of questions. Carol —
I've arranged for you to spend some time in the stud farm
at Brodina. If you are serious about horses, you need to
learn from professionals." Carol whooped and the subject
of collectivization was lost in other news.

Granny and Petru came down the lane to meet the
wagon in a flurry of exclamations and hugs. Granny had
prepared the boys' favorite foods and the bare little house
was clean but to Fane's eyes, smaller and very poor. Both
Granny and Petru were visibly older and Fane himself felt
old and worldly and...apart.

For Mihai and Fane arrival and departure were the two
best days of summer. They worked hard in the fields,
visited Radauti and Uncle Vanya's little house when they
could, met some classmates from the *liceu* but not many.

Toward the end of the vacation, Mihai remarked to
Fane that there were two things he had forgotten about
living in the country. "What?" asked Fane.

"The first was how good the food is even though it's
plain and there isn't much — well, any these days — meat.
The student canteen really is terrible, there's never a lot of
choice, and even in restaurants the ingredients in Bucharest
aren't that fresh."

"Agreed. The second?"

"How poor everyone is. Look around you! Look at
Tanti Elise's clothes. Look at how thin people are. Look at
how Granny can't see but can't afford to get glasses. Look
at your father's hands, almost crippled with arthritis and
hard work and he can't afford to go to the doctor." Fane felt
a pang of guilt and thought of life in Bucharest, not easy by
any means but not... "And," continued Mihai heatedly, "it
almost makes me wonder if some sort of collectivization,
not the way they're doing it now, but something...
something has to be done. Because we've been poor here
ever since I can remember. Only we didn't know it. We
were kids. We just didn't know...but the adults knew. They

knew how close we all were to disaster every year...like the Famine...how close to illness and death. If she'd had proper food, Mother..." Mihai's voice trailed off and he turned away.

That night as they dropped into sleep Fane's thoughts returned to that conversation, logic and the new realization that the life he'd always taken for granted was really...terribly...hard, all this at war with his fierce love for the fields he worked, for the little house and its courtyard, for the kitchen garden and animals. And over all this love was the hard fact that he didn't want to stay in those fields and be a farmer, not at all, no way.

"I don't know," was all he could finally say to himself, so he turned over and closed his eyes.

"What I'd really like," said Ellen a bit hesitantly, "this is just personal, is to..." She searched for the words in Romanian, "do riding with horses."

"Ride horseback," Fane corrected with his genial smile. "Your Romanian is so good...I hope you don't mind if I help occasionally..." "Of course not," Ellen rushed to say.

"So you like to go horseback riding?"

"Oh, yes! I grew up with horses. For some years after University I didn't ride but I started – you might laugh – I started to ride again in Nigeria, of all places, at the Polo Club there. It wasn't a very good horse, the one I was riding, but I enjoyed it and would like to continue."

"Did I hear the word horse?" said Dinu the film director joining them. "Hello," he said turning to Ellen, "you must be the new Director of the American Library. Welcome. Welcome to Bucharest. Fane here should introduce you to his friend, Carol, if you like horses. And I, I..." Fane thought, not for the first time, that Dinu had a big mouth then let his mind drift to the nearly empty glass of Scotch in his hand as Dinu's endless torrent of words rushed on and eddied around Ellen's head into the rest of the party.

114

That summer set the pattern for the next two years, a striking contrast to being at the University. "I wonder if they" 'they' being the adults in their lives "have any idea of the total divide between city life and country life," said Mihai later. "Father did say something about establishing our poor peasant credentials and has made a few remarks, but he's been away a long, long time."

"I don't know," replied Fane. "Certainly Granny and Dad have no idea what Bucharest is like and, did you notice? After the first two days neither treats us any differently than they did when we were kids. But it's good to remember the real world." "What is the real world?" Mihai asked rhetorically. The two fell silent, thinking of the changes that were taking place in the countryside and in their lives, their long discussions about the unequal relationship with Russia, the need for economic development, the excesses of the Government driving change and the endless arguments they had on the subject before the conversation turned back to classes, friends and women.

In the spring of their Junior year Fane was reading in their garret when his two roommates tried to get through the door together, both panting from the flights of stairs. The two were talking at once. "Stalin's dead!" shouted Mihai. "I just heard it on the street." "I've been kicked out of the University," announced Carol. "How do you know Stalin's dead?" asked Fane. "It's a rumor but...it's true, I know it." "Hey, I'm leaving the University!" repeated Carol. The three, now all in the small room, looked at one another.

"Oh, shit." "We need to talk." "What?" In the moment of silence that followed there were several firm raps on the door.

"Good God, what now?" said Mihai turning to open it. On the outside was a grizzled, gray man with a familiar face. Fane stared. Mihai spoke slowly, "Grigore? Grigore?"

The man nodded. "Grigore from Poiana Cozonac?" The man nodded, smiled, enveloped him in a great hug and said simply, "My, you've grown."

When the flurry of greetings subsided, Grigore was seated in one of the three chairs with a glass of *tzuica* from the bottle Carol always seemed to have tucked somewhere while Fane perched on his bed. At that point they began to fill in the blanks.

"We're fine. Just fine," Grigore said of the Transylvanian village. "Most of your classmates are grown and gone. Vasile and Bebe went to the University in Cluj, Little Ion joined..." the list went on through living and dead. Finally, in response to the unspoken question, Grigore offered, "I've come to Bucharest on some business and Petru wrote that you were here and...I thought I'd like to see how you were doing."

"You haven't mentioned Father Ion. How is he?" Mihai asked eagerly.

"Well," Grigore hesitated, the chair creaking under him as he shifted his weight. "I, um. Well, that's why I've come to Bucharest. Father Ion...Father Ion's been arrested." "What?" "How?" "Not Father Ion!"

"For a long time," Grigore continued, "no one bothered about us or him or Poiana Cozonac...you know how it is up there and we still don't have a decent road into the village or any electricity...but the school authorities finally reported who was teaching and...and they came and arrested him and took him away. They sent some sort of school teacher but she hates it there. And hates us."

"What are you going to do?"

"Well...I...I wrote Petru...Petru said you might know someone...He didn't say anything else, but...we've tried with people we know in Lunca Ilvei but they are too...small..." Grigore's words trailed off lamely into a pit of hopelessness as he looked at the three confused young men.

Finally, Mihai spoke. "Grigore, I don't know what we could possibly do, but we'll do something, whatever we can. Please give me as many details as possible. And then I must go as I have a class."

After Grigore had answered Mihai's precise and probing questions, 'He already sounds like a lawyer!' Fane thought to himself, Mihai stood up and left. Grigore stayed for a bit longer as they talked over old times but no one had much heart to reminisce, the specter of Father Ion in a bare cell, perhaps ill or injured, perhaps even being tortured, filling their minds, all the whispered tales of prisons suddenly made real. Finally they agreed to meet the next day and Grigore excused himself, leaving Fane and Carol alone.

"Mihai doesn't have a class," Carol said after Grigore's footsteps faded down the stairs, "not at this time." "I know," answered Fane. "He's gone to his father." Carol nodded. "What happened to you?" Fane asked.

"Oh, that. Well, I got in a fight. A fist fight. About horses — the policy of killing horses for mechanization. It was in a class...they haven't expelled me yet, but I know they will." Fane himself had felt sick when they heard that the Government was going through the countryside, killing horses so the peasants would have to use tractors, and he knew Carol's fury, but still...

"Shit! You might be arrested! What will your father say? What will you do?"

"I'm not worried about being arrested, not much. What will my father say..." Carol looked worried in spite of his words, an unusual expression for him. "I suppose that will depend on what I do and..." his handsome face was more cheerful, "and I already have a job as a stunt man for the movies. They really need me, so I don't think I'll be arrested."

"What? What's a stunt man? And being 'needed' isn't much of a reason not to get arrested!"

"The thing is, they don't want to mess up the hero's face if there's a fall or something, and most of the heroes can't ride horses and occasionally the 'hero' has to 'fall off' his horse, or fight from horseback, so I'll do the riding, in the distance of course, whenever the hero has to do something like that."

"Oh," said Fane dubiously. He paced their room, three paces, avoid the chair, two more paces, turn back and take two steps before the chair... It was a small room, he thought, for worrying.

"And, in the movies," Carol continued, "well, there are people with connections..." Fane wondered what that meant but Carol's next remark, about Father Ion, deflected his train of thought.

Mihai returned well after dark. He came in the door, looking tired but satisfied. "How...?" "What..." "Sit down," he replied. "I'll tell you. I went and telephoned Father and asked him to meet me. I said I had a problem at school I needed to discuss immediately so we met in the Garden" — he didn't need to say Cismigiu — "by the lake and walked. I told him about Father Ion and everything he had done for us and the other kids in the village, about the time when he got beaten up during the war. Father," Fane realized this was the first time they had talked openly in front of Carol of Mr. Eichmann being Mihai's father, "Father said he would do what he could. That being beaten up by the Germans during the war might help."

"But he was beaten up by Hungarians," said Fane.

"That's true, but it sounds better if it's Germans."

"When...?"

"He told me to meet him tomorrow morning. In fact, he said he'd like to see all of us, that it's been a long time since he's gotten a progress report."

"Oh," said Fane. "Um..." said Carol...and Carol's story was related to Mihai.

"But, coming back to Father Ion," said Fane finally. "I know that religion is supposedly used to divert the people's attention from social problems, but there's a lot of good in it, too." The discussion continued, ending as usual in more questions than answers.

The next morning was warm so Mr. Eichmann bought everyone pretzels in the Park and they strolled to some nearby benches. "This isn't exactly fancy," said Mr. Eichmann, "but it's so beautiful out it seemed a shame to sit in a restaurant though it would have been nice to celebrate somehow."

Celebrate! The boys looked at one another. "Then..." Mihai started.

"Yes, your Father Ion was unfortunately detained as the result of some false information and the Government released him about," Mihai's father looked at his watch, "an hour ago. He's all right and apparently a very good man, even a good communist although he's not, of course, a Party member,"

Mihai's father said smoothly. "I think the matter is closed and probably shouldn't be discussed any further. But there's one thing..." The older man hesitated.

"What?"

"You didn't tell me Father Ion was blind."

Mihai and Fane looked at one another. "We, we didn't think of it," Mihai finally said.

"But how did he teach you if he couldn't read? Couldn't illustrate letters easily?"

"Sir," said Fane, "he had us help. The older students wrote for him and helped the younger ones."

"We all read to him as well," added Mihai. "There were a lot of books he wanted to read, so we took turns reading. Fane and I...I guess we read the most because we liked it so much."

"If we didn't understand a word, or something that was in the book," said Fane, "Father Ion would explain it to us,

119

or ask questions until we did understand. It was," he paused, "looking back, I see it must have been an unusual education, but one that was..." his voice trailed off.

There was a moment of silence before Mihai changed the subject, "Why are there so many arrests?" His father sighed and was silent.

"I suppose," he finally said, "that when a Government is trying to do something as radical and far-reaching as change the very nature of a country, to bring about new kinds of relationships among people so that you no longer have wealth concentrated in the hands of a few, but distributed fairly and, more than that, so you are increasing production and, therefore, increasing the wealth for everybody, that there inevitably are people who are in opposition. Normally, I suppose the best way would be to convince them by demonstrating the worth of the new system, but they are powerful enough to stop the new order and we can't take the chance that they'll derail everything and take us back to where we were. Unfortunately, in people's haste to do good things some become, shall we say, overly zealous. Or they act on the basis of false or incomplete information as in this case."

Fane absently threw some crumbs to the pigeons on the pavement in front of their benches. The answer sounded reasonable, but too...smooth? He also thought he heard some things that weren't said...how could that be? "But what about history?" he asked, putting his other thoughts aside and thinking as he so often did of the disconnect between what was taught and what he read in the older books.

"History, Fane...I know this bothers you a lot, Mihai and I have talked about it." Fane looked at Mihai, startled to think that he had been the subject of their conversation. Fane also realized that Mihai apparently had spent more time with his father than Fane had known. "History is part of a people's self-image. If the self-image is unhealthy then the people won't be able to progress and grow in good ways but will return to the old ways. So we have to help in every domain possible."

"But what about the, uh, the role of the Russians?" Carol asked. Fane was a bit surprised — Carol usually stayed away from political discussions. "They took our land, they have taken our wealth, they are forcing change in the countryside, they..." his voice trailed off.

"Here, too, some have been overzealous and...badly behaved...but we're coming into a better balance, I think. The Russians have led the way in Socialism but sometimes they don't realize that each country is different. And they don't discipline all their troops very well," he added under his breath.

"Stalin," interrupted Mihai, "I just heard that Stalin is dead. Is that true?" The conversation took a turn into international politics and prospects. Later, back home, Fane and Mihai talked again. "Well," said Fane in conclusion as he often did, "I have to come back to the fact that if it weren't for Socialism, I would still be a peasant on the farm, and that things are getting better." "And we don't have time to let Capitalism come to this country and run its course, as it will in the West, it's too slow for what we need to do — and we need to help our people," Mihai added. "At least, that's what they say." By this time they were lying in their beds, with Carol snoring lightly in the corner. Fane turned sleepily and drifted away.

"And," Mihai continued sleepily, "I would be in the village, like Father was. I wonder how..." Mihai, too, drifted into night.

The spring moved toward summer with Carol traveling and away much of the time. It wasn't long before he was in charge of all the movie horses and, Fane thought later, with his good looks and physique it should have been no surprise that somehow Carol soon became an actor rather than a stand in. And as for Father Ion...Grigore had been grateful and wisely asked no questions though Fane thought he looked at Mihai with a sort of funny look. Grigore later wrote a long, newsy letter which mentioned that Father Ion was teaching school again, frail but in reasonably good health after being 'ill'.

As the last year of University was drawing to a close and spring was finally pushing a particularly hard winter aside, Fane realized he had fallen in love. It took him a while to come to this conclusion, the feeling was so...unexpected. So... something else. And unwanted. At least, Fane didn't think he wanted it.

Fane had met Leri about six weeks earlier as she was hurrying to get through a blizzard to a class. In fact, her head down to protect her face she had run smack into him and with the force of the wind behind her Fane was knocked backwards into a snow bank, the girl on top of him. Fane automatically put his arms around her, rolled both of them over, and stood while pulling her up as well.

"Oh, I'm so sorry," the girl said, brushing snow off her head and pulling her hood back up. "I'm so sorry," she repeated. "Let me get the snow off you." She started to run her gloved hands over his shoulders but the snow was falling so fast it came back immediately. The girl looked at her hands and at Fane helplessly, then they both broke into laughter.

"That's all right." Fane looked down at her, not very far down as he realized she was tall for a woman, on to fair skin with tendrils of dark hair escaping the hood of her heavy coat. "Where were you going?" The snow swirled around them and he cleared a few flakes off her eyebrow with his thumb, feeling its softness under his touch. She didn't object.

"To my class," she said.

"They cancelled classes today because of the blizzard. I've just come from the Faculty of History. Hey," Fane smiled, "let's go have a, um, a cup of tea and get warm.

There's a little place just here." She nodded and smiled, flakes of snow again on her lovely, dark eyebrows.

They hurried down the stairs into a small coffee house students frequented, looking around at the almost empty room. The waiter approached them, towel in hand. After they'd sat down, Fane introduced himself.

"My name is Stefan, Stefan Vulcean. I'm in History." He looked at her, seeing dark brown hair, hazel eyes, that flawless skin and features that were individually pleasant but somehow, all put together, were completely beautiful. Why? Maybe her smile and sparkling eyes? Fane didn't care.

"Hello again, Stefan, I'm glad to meet you. I'm Valeria Matei. In Philology." Silence took hold for an eternity, perhaps ten seconds. At once both of them spoke, "Where are you from?" "Isn't it bad weather?" and burst into giggles. The waiter, polishing glasses behind the bar, smiled and poured something into two small glasses. "Look," he said as he came to their table with a tray, "I don't know if you young people drink but this weather calls for something more warming than tea. Here's a *tzuica*, a hot *tzuica* with a bit of pepper in it to warm you up." Fane smiled and thanked him. Valeria hesitated.

"I, I...don't usually drink," she said.

"And that's good, but you really do need something warming now," the older man said kindly. "A little sip won't hurt you." He put the glasses down and left. Fane raised his little glass in a toast. "Here's to green eyes," he said.

"And here's to brown," Valeria said in exchange. They both sipped and smiled at one another, then Valeria coughed.

"Wow! It's strong!" The ice was broken.

"You haven't told me your name," said Fane.

"Oh, but I did. I'm Valeria. Valeria Matei.

"Valeria, Valeria, Leri...you are Leri..." Fane said losing himself in her green eyes.

"Leri?" she laughed. "If you want." They then began to exchange bits of information about themselves. Fane mentioned winter in Bilca. Valeria had grown up in the foothills of the southern Carpathians, and knew snow very well. "Did you come to Bucharest for University, then?" asked Fane. "No, my parents, my father was transferred after the war to a village that didn't have a secondary school. They sent me here to live with my aunt so I could go to the *liceu* and when I was admitted to the University, I just stayed," she answered. "Father is a veterinarian and he tried to get another post, a transfer but...it wasn't, it's never been, uh, quite the right time..." her voice trailed off. "And you said you were in the Faculty of History," Leri continued and the conversation turned to school and courses and teachers and a search for common friends.

Time passed unnoticed until the waiter stood by them, towel over his arm, smiling down. "Look, children," he said, "it's getting late and I want to close. Fane glanced up, startled to realize it was dark outside. "Let me walk you home," he said to Leri.

Leri's aunt lived near the new Opera House, not as close to the University as Fane but not too far. Fane didn't go upstairs with her but they shook hands at the door. "Can we meet again?" he asked, wondering if she would want to, wondering if he wanted to risk... He thought he saw Leri blush but it was too dark to be sure. He sang softly, "Let's meet on Saturday evening..." "...and walk on the Avenue..?" Leri hummed back. Fane was lost in spite of himself. So they did meet again. And again. They walked on the Avenue talking about music, they sat over endless cups of tea talking about nothing. It seemed that they ran into each other all the time...perhaps because Fane went to some lengths to find out her class schedule and just happened to be in the area when she came out on the street.

124

He was antsy and couldn't eat and there were butterflies in his stomach when he was waiting to see her, then a burst of happiness when she appeared drove all other feeling away. Fane continued to study, of course — final exams were coming — but for once history seemed less important than what might happen today.

"What's up with you?" asked Carol one soft warm May day as Fane gazed out the window, unusually idle. "Are you in love?"

"In love? That's the first thing that always occurs to you!" It was true that Carol seemed to have an endless parade of girlfriends, passionate about one today, passionate about another the next but not exactly forgetting the first...or second...or twenty-fifth. Of course Fane had gotten to know girls, too, but that was different. No one, except maybe a couple of the girls, had ever thought it was serious.

"Well, why else are you mooning around, in a hurry to get out some times, being useless at others. Who is she?"

"Who is she?" Fane repeated stupidly, then shook his head to clear it. "Maybe I am in love, so what?"

"Hey, it's great, love is wonderful...I wish it would happen to me." Fane looked at Carol in surprise. "But you're always 'in love'!" he said.

"I love...I love women, they are wonderful, all of them, fillies and mares, all kinds and colors and shapes..."

"Are we talking about women or horses?"

"Both, probably," Fane had never seen Carol so serious. "I love both in general, almost all of those wonderful creatures, but not one...not one enough to stay only with her. I've wondered..." his voice trailed off. He took the thread again after a pause. "...what it would be like to love one so much there were no others."

"I guess...I don't know...but Leri is different than the other girls I've met. She's...she's just Leri. But I don't want to be in love! I don't want to love anyone."

"Why not?"

"If you really care about somebody or something you get hurt. It's better not to care."

"But what about Mihai? About me?" Fane didn't respond to this question and Carol, knowing he had him, changed the subject. "Tell me something. You've talked about your mother quite a lot over the years, and about her death, but you've never mentioned Haiduc once. I know the horse meant a lot to you but your mother..." Carol halted, uncharacteristically at a loss for words.

"I guess," Fane said slowly, "that Haiduc's death hit me so hard because it wasn't necessary. It was a betrayal, of him, of me. Father sold him to be killed after he had worked for us, after he had practically saved our lives on that trip to Poiana Cozonac, after he'd been part of our family. He didn't have to die," Fane's voice rose, "and he was sold for..." Fane didn't complete the sentence. "But, speaking of my mother and these things, why do you never talk about your mother? She's still alive, you see her. You talk about your father but you never mention anything about your mother."

"I'll tell you about my Mother. She's a drunk. A disgrace. We hide it as well as we can but if you still lived in Bilca you'd know by now. And she..." Carol turned away slightly, "...she never wanted a child, she didn't want me, never cared for me. Maybe that's why I don't fall in love but you...don't miss this." Both young men were silent, slightly embarrassed and wondering what to say next when they heard Mihai's footsteps coming up the last flight of stairs.

"Hey, here's our nonexistent roommate!" Carol said, "You must be in love, too, since you're around even less than I am." Mihai flushed and said, "No, just studying, something you wouldn't know about."

"Then why are you red?"

"Because those stairs get longer every day. Especially when I'm hurrying to tell you my news."

126

News! Fane almost forgot his mental note that Mihai really had been gone a lot recently.

"What?" "Huh?" "Tell us."

"Let me put these books down." Mihai swung his bag of books onto a desk and leaned against it. "I have found out what I'm going to do." He didn't need to say 'after we graduate' — it had been on everyone's mind as they and classmates wondered about jobs and assignments.

"I'm going to Moscow to study diplomacy."

It was clear that Dinu was talking too fast for Ellen to understand much but Fane saw that she was nodding politely and looking interested and that Dinu — the self-absorbed twit — didn't even notice. Horses...culture...perhaps here was a chink in the diplomatic armor. He excused himself unnoticeably and drifted toward the bar.

Finals were almost on top of them before Fane found his future profession. Carol, of course, was well-placed in the movies and would continue to do what he was already doing, at least for the moment. Mihai was preoccupied with the thought of Moscow and the preparations for advanced study in the Russian capital, with all its opportunities and pitfalls. Mihai was also studying Russian on the side not having paid more attention to the mandatory language, like all of them, than absolutely necessary to pass exams. Fane had thought he might teach or do research and had asked around a bit, knowing that in the end he would be sent somewhere by the Government if he wasn't able to work the system somehow, but nothing quite seemed to happen until Professor Rapeanu stopped him in the hall. A bit surprised, Fane smiled warmly and said, "Yes, sir?" in response to his greeting. Rapeanu, sardonic and possessing a razor sharp mind together with a wicked sense of humor always seemed to be several steps ahead of the class, which Fane admired and thought wistfully of emulating someday.

"Stefan...do you know what you will do when the University year ends?"

"Not yet, sir."

"Tomorrow go to the Institute of History and ask for the Director. Tell him I sent you."

"The Institute of History?" Fane repeated. Of course, he knew about it—this was the research Institute for History belonging to the Romanian Academy, but he had never been there and...

"Yes. Near the Piata Victoriei, not on Kiseleff, but on the street just to the east the one that leads to the statue of the aviators. Left side. It's the last building in the Park." This triggered a memory of a walk and someone saying...

"Yes, sir," Fane replied, now sure of where it was even if he didn't know what. "I know where it is. What time? And, what..." Fane's voice trailed off.

"Be there by eleven in the morning. You'll see," was the reply, and while it wasn't exactly warm, it was, Fane thought, friendly. Maybe even satisfied?

It was a long walk up Calea Victoriei from their digs but Fane thought it would be good to calm his nerves before the interview because, although Professor Rapeanu hadn't been very specific, he knew that this visit was probably about a possible position there. A position at the Institute of History! But wasn't it supposed to come through the Ministry? On the other hand...But the whole thing was almost unbelievable. Maybe it wasn't for that but something else...

Fane was also walking because he didn't have money for tram fare. Unfortunately, it was a warm day and he arrived at the Institute sweaty and hot and feeling very awkward. His self-confidence wasn't helped by the disdainful look he was given by the badly dressed older woman who opened the door.

"The Director?" she asked with what Fane thought was an air of total disbelief.

"Yes," he replied. "Professor Rapeanu sent me." "Oh," she said and invisibly shrugged her thin shoulders. "Come in." Her manner wasn't exactly warm but it maybe had thawed just a bit. Fane followed her into the dark, cool hall and found himself in a spacious room with a large window, a larger desk, and a still larger man behind it. The man, older, not very old but very heavy, rose with some difficulty, motioned toward a chair, and sank gratefully back into his own seat.

"Stefan Vulcean?"

"Yes, sir,"

"From Bukovina, I hear."

"Yes, sir, from Bilca."

"Were you there on June 6, 1940?"

"No, sir. My family had left to visit relatives in Transylvania."

"Hmmm. Interesting. Lucky." Fane's hands were sweaty. "Now let's talk a minute about your studies..."

The interview went well, Fane thought as he left the Institute and...he looked back at the boxy stucco building...maybe...the Director had said he was well-prepared... there was paperwork and official permission and, of course, exam results...who knew, perhaps...

'Perhaps' took a week to become real. The three went out to celebrate. Mihai was leaving for Moscow in a few days and busy packing and putting various permissions and papers together. Carol was getting ready to move to a room near the film studio. Fane was exulting in his good fortune.

Finally Mihai shut him up. "You idiot, of course they want you. You're good, you're one of the top students in your class. But you're also a great addition to their quota of employees with good backgrounds."

"Huh? Good backgrounds?"

"Exactly. All of us have that advantage. Look around you. We're all from healthy origins, poor peasants though,"

Mihai grinned at Carol, "how you manage to be in that category..." Carol grinned back and Mihai left the subject. "Seriously, look at the backgrounds of the others who are really good in class. All of them have bad social origins. Intellectuals, bourgeois..."

"I hadn't thought of it," Fane realized this was true. He knew practically everyone quite well but until now...but Carmen's father was an engineer, and Antoaneta's in Roman a former banker, and Dinu's a...He sat speechless as he realized that they, many of his friends, in fact most of the people he really enjoyed talking to, were from the former middle and even upper classes. Light dawned and with it horror and self-doubt.

"Do you think I'm good enough...am I only there..." Was all he could say.

"Don't be an ass," said Mihai. "Of course—you really are good, look at your marks. It's just that almost no one else from our 'good' background was well-prepared for University, as we were, almost no one else had the kind of education we got, first from Father Ion and then from the *liceu*. So it stands to reason..." his voice trailed off, something that rarely happened with the self-possessed, always smooth Mihai. Carol broke the moment's awkward silence.

"Where are you going to stay when we all leave?" he asked Fane. Fane looked at him in distress. Stay?

"I hadn't even thought of it," he said but he realized that he would have to find someplace to live after the end of the school year. Which was soon. "I mean, I knew, but I didn't really..."

"Are you and Leri going to get married?" Carol went on. "That would make a difference. You can stay with me until you do," he added generously. "What is Leri going to do? Maybe she can get a place to live for you," he added.

"Married?" Somehow Fane, for all his thoughts of the future, had unthinkingly assumed that things would stay

130

the same, that life wouldn't change even if the place where he went every day moved from the University to someplace else, now the Institute. Even his dreams and the almost constant ache in his loins would stay the same, titillated by holding Leri close in dark corners but foiled as much by that absolute lack of any place to be...really private...as by morality. "Leri's going to teach in the girls' *liceu*, the one by Gradina Icoanei. I guess she's going to stay on with her aunt. They share a room..."

"You idiot," Carol added. "You never think of practical things."

"Who was the one who thought before he got into a fight and was kicked out of University?" Fane said hotly.

"But look where I am now," Carol retorted. "I have a job and someplace to live and you..."

"I have a job, too, and..." Fane's voice trailed off.

"Come on. Or, rather, go ask Leri to marry you and then find a place to live. In the meantime you can stay with me as I said."

So Fane found himself walking aimlessly, wondering where Leri was since classes were over and everyone was studying for exams, except for idiots like him, what she might do if he asked...said...did she love...? His footsteps led, still aimlessly, to Leri's house where he rang the bell. A strange woman answered.

"Is, uh, is Valeria Matei in? I, uh..." "Upstairs, the room to the right," the woman answered. Fane thought she wasn't exactly unfriendly but... "Thank you," he said, feeling even more awkward, and brushed her as he went past. "Uh, excuse me..." Color mounted to his face and he rushed up the stairs, not seeing the woman's indulgent smile behind him. Fane knocked on the door to the right.

"Yes?" It wasn't Leri's voice, it must be her aunt. The door opened and he saw a middle-aged figure in dark clothes and, behind her, Leri!

"I'm, uh, I'm Stefan, uh, a classmate of Valeria's, and I..."

"Come in," said the woman, of course she was Leri's aunt, with a smile. "I'm sorry that we weren't expecting you, but Valeria has talked about you..." Fane walked in, feeling as if he were bumping into every piece of furniture in the crowded room, feeling as if he had come at a bad time, feeling like a big, awkward idiot with sweaty hands. "Sit down here," said Leri's aunt, "I'll go make a cup of tea." She smiled and Fane smiled back, feeling better. As the aunt exited, he turned to Leri.

"I'm sorry if I'm disturbing you," he said.

"Oh, it's all right, it's not a bother," Leri replied with a nervous smile.

"I, uh..." Fane, the young man with dozens of friends and the right word for each one, was tongue-tied. "I...would you marry me?" he said before he could think straight.

Leri blushed and tried to look as if she were in complete possession of herself. Then she burst into tears. Fane stepped forward and took her into his arms. "I'm sorry," he said, "I didn't mean to make you cry. Forget I said anything."

"I'm all right," Leri replied shakily, beginning to laugh through her tears. "I thought you'd never ask me. I thought you didn't...I don't know..." Fane drew her closer and laid his cheek against her dark hair. "You silly girly, I love you," he whispered. Neither of them noticed the door behind them open and close, very gently, very quietly.

Exams came and went and Fane hardly even noticed. That May and June, unusually fine weather, trembled with change. Fane, Leri, her aunt and Carol all looked for a place for the young couple to live. Fane thought about his new job which would, among other things, mean he would need to continue studying and eventually write a PhD dissertation. Fane and Leri talked about when and how and where to get married. Fane wondered what he would write about. Leri's parents came to Bucharest to meet Fane — a difficult time for him but it passed, like everything else, and Fane found he could actually talk to Leri's father about animals and farming and how the older man worked in his veterinary practice. Fane wrote Petru and Granny about his job and the wedding plans. A letter from Granny via Tante Ani appeared what seemed the day after.

"Granny says we need to have a religious wedding. We can't do that," Fane told Leri. "How can I tell her?" Leri looked at him strangely.

"I always thought we would be married by a priest," she replied.

"But Leri..."

"Don't you believe in God? You told me one time..." She looked at him again, at this point confused.

"Well, yes, but that's private, not something one...you know..." his voice trailed off. "You know..." Fane said again, "...I mean, you're a teacher and I have my job and if..." he started again. He didn't need to continue.

"Idiot," Leri said softly. "Everyone does it. Just not very publicly. Don't you know a priest...?"

"Not really. I mean, I go to church but just not very often and not always to the same one and, no, I don't. And I'd lose my job." Fane's thoughts turned to Father Ion. Suddenly he wished he could talk to him, tell Father Ion his problems and ask his advice. It was always so good. If only...why not? "Wait! I have an idea! Would you mind terribly much if we had a private religious wedding? I mean, not everyone coming? Would your parents mind?"

"I don't think so, as long as they could be here for the Registry marriage. And as long as we DID have a wedding that would be recognized in the eyes of God." Leri's eyes shone, maybe with tears. Fane took her hand tenderly. He hadn't known she felt like this and he realized he loved her the more for it. It seemed to be so right. "I know that some people wait a couple of years before they have a religious wedding," Leri continued, "and we could, but I wouldn't feel...I just don't want to. I want us to be really married, not just inscribed in some registry."

"Great! Wonderful!" Leri looked at Fane in amazement. "How about Transylvania for a honeymoon? We're going to do it!"

And so it was that in Bucharest Leri and Fane were married at the City Hall with Leri's aunt and parents, Mihai and Carol, a few other friends in attendance. Petru and Granny couldn't come and Fane, with a twinge of shame, was relieved. Mihai's father represented them as a 'family friend' from the same village and Fane barely noticed that the other guests were deferential to him but warmed as the older man drew them out. After the ceremony they went to the Carul cu Bere as guests of Leri's parents for a late lunch. It was the first time most of them had been in the famous restaurant. The food was good, the wine flowed freely, and neither Leri nor Fane could eat. Finally Leri's mother spoke to her quietly. Leri nodded and her mother tapped her wineglass for attention. "The young couple are going to excuse themselves and leave us now," she announced. Everyone clapped, Fane pushed back his chair, stood, and thanked the group. He looked at them and thought he knew exactly what they were thinking and blushed. Leri was also blushing. In some confusion the couple gathered their things and left for Leri's room as her aunt had arranged another place to stay for the night.

What followed was, Fane thought with satisfaction, as good as it got.

The next week they were on the train to Cluj and Bistrita, then Nasaud, where they found a ride to Shantz. It was a better road than the part from Shantz north to Carlibaba Fane thought, then he remembered that years had passed and maybe the road was improved. What about the road to Poiana Cozonac? What if Grigore hadn't gotten

134

the letter about their visit? He had mentioned honeymoon, he didn't want to make things obvious to the authorities. Would Father Ion marry them? They didn't dare bring a letter from a priest in Bucharest saying they were members of a church even if they could found a priest...but Father Ion knew that Fane, but what about Leri... What if...Fane fretted, the familiar knot in his stomach taking his attention away from the sparkling day and the conversation between Leri and the cart driver. "She really does know how to talk to peasants," Fane thought in passing, "guess growing up with a vet for a father helped."

Toward late afternoon they finally reached Shantz where, to Fane's unspoken relief, Grigore and his old wagon were waiting for them. Grigore climbed down and embraced both of them, then held Leri at arm's length and looked at her with a smile. "You've done well, my boy! Welcome to Fane's home. He's very important to us, which you may not know." Leri smiled delightedly.

"If I didn't know, I'd guess! He's important to me as well." The three continued to talk as they climbed up into Grigore's wagon. Grigore slapped the horses' backs with the reins and they started off.

As the cart climbed higher into the mountains, Fane eagerly looked at the trees that closed them in, hoping to recognize something. Then he mentally kicked himself — he had only been over this road twice, once coming, once going. How had they managed so many years in isolation, without even leaving the village? He hadn't even thought of it then, the village and its valley and the mountains around were his whole world. Kids.

Finally, they came over the last of the hills and entered the remembered valley. The sinking sun caught the tops of the great fir trees and the mountain beyond. There at the far side, wagon tracks running to it through the meadow, was the small cluster of houses. Were these tears in his eyes...maybe from the chilly mountain air.

"It's beautiful!" whispered Leri. Grigore smiled at her from the other side of the wagon seat. "You can talk out loud here," he said. "It's safe." They all laughed in relief. "But there are no fruit trees, and I don't see any corn or wheat. What do you eat?" Leri continued. Fane looked at her in surprise, realizing that she was right.

"We're too high for most fruit trees," replied Grigore comfortably, "though we have a few prunes to make *tzuica* — up here we need a drop now and then in the winter! Mostly we have potatoes and meat and the vegetables we grow in the courtyards. And berries and mushrooms from the forest." Fane listened, remembering the days when someone got a deer or even a rabbit in a trap set along a hidden path through the trees.

"Do you, um, still, um, eat deer?" he asked, curious but hesitant to speak about something he knew must have been illegal even then.

"Not so much now as during the war...things are different. But not all that different. Hayup!" Grigore moved the horses into a faster trot across the valley to a waiting group of people. The entire village had come out to meet them it seemed, led by Father Ion. Fane got their suitcase down and asked where they would be staying. Grigore's grin belied his gray hair and weathered face. It was almost wicked.

"You, Fane, will stay with my family and your bride with your old neighbors."

"But...but...we're married!"

"Not here. Not till tomorrow." Everyone was laughing, expectant. "We're old-fashioned here," Grigore added. "You didn't tell us anything except that you were coming on a honeymoon but...we got some other news so we're ready." Fane wondered how this "news" came as first he then Leri climbed down from the wagon to a sea of embraces and good wishes but before he knew it Leri was gone with the women and Fane was seated with the men, a *plosca* of strong *palinca* passing from hand to hand, bad jokes and good wishes passing with it.

The next day both Fane and Leri were dressed by the villagers. Fane could hardly believe his eyes when a Transylvanian girl, beautiful in her traditional dress, was brought to the church but then he looked down at his own clothes. 'We should have brought something better,' he thought but then, 'no, it's perfect this way.'

And indeed it was. Father Ion presided, Grigore and his wife were the godparents, and all of Poiana Cozonac filled the tiny church, spilling out over the steps. As they exchanged crowns, Fane looked into Leri's eyes and felt they were exchanging pure joy.

They spent a week in Poiana Cozonac, staying in the same small house that had been Fane's home so long ago. Everywhere Fane turned he felt Mother's presence...and her love and happiness. He wanted to talk to Leri about it but couldn't find words.

Fane did talk with Grigore, Father Ion and the other men about politics and what was happening in the city, trying to explain things, perhaps to defend them, also realizing uncomfortably that he was now their means to solve problems, their Man in Bucharest, however unsuited. "We're too high in the mountains to be collectivized," Grigore explained, "and so far no one has really noticed us, except for..." He didn't go on and started in another direction. "But we know that change will come and...in one way we need it. We don't have a doctor, Father Ion could use some help in the school..." This was, Fane realized, a kind way of saying, "Father Ion is getting old". The beloved priest walked with a cane now and was obviously in pain when he moved. "I wish I could do something for him..." Fane thought. "He did so much..." We can manage without electricity," Grigore continued, "but these days people want a bit of...comfort...I don't know...we've heard..." It was clear that the desire to continue their traditional lives and for stability was at war with a very real need for change. "The young people want another life..." As Grigore's voice trailed off Fane looked around and realized that the familiar faces were, with a few exceptions, quite old. Most of the kids he'd been at school with weren't there, gone first either to the *liceu* in Lunca Ilvei or to the army and then...Fane thought of the life that had been lived in this village for centuries and wondered how long it would last. He wondered if Father Ion would be blind if he'd had good medical attention. He looked at the hands of the older men and wondered how much they ached at night, like Petru's, gnarled and hardened by unremitting work. Fane loved the life in the country but he couldn't pretend it was ideal or easy or always rewarding. At the same time there had been so much destruction because of the desire to change things quickly. 'I'll do better for them,' he thought then kicked himself mentally. 'You can't do anything. You're just a historian, lost in the past. But still...'

"Well," he began awkwardly, "I think that the best of the people in charge are really trying to do good things. The problem is that many others, those who in the past...and those who want to profit only for themselves..." He found himself repeating Iosif Eichmann's arguments but...they made sense. Sort of.

And Fane worked with the men since there was too much work simply to watch others try to get it done. He found he fell into the rhythm of farm life in Transylvania as he had during the summers in Bilca and when he realized this might be the last time he worked on the land his heart lurched in loss. 'It's good to work like this...except,' he thought one evening he and Leri were sitting by the front door in the long twilight, 'for getting dirt ground into my hands again.'

"What are you doing? Why are you looking at your hands like that?" Leri asked from his side.

Fane put his hands down, curling his fingers so she couldn't see the dirt under the nails. Leri reached out and grabbed the hand nearest her and lifted it from Fane's leg to examine it. Fane pulled it away. "Don't."

"Don't? Don't be silly. Are you hurt?" She captured the hand as she spoke and started to examine it, holding it firmly. "Don't...my hands are so dirty from the farm work."

"But that's natural," Leri said. "You should be proud." She turned his palm away from her and ran her own forefinger over the side of his where each crack and whorl was dark even though he had washed when he came in.

"I can't get it all off, but it will be clean after a few days in Bucharest," Fane said with embarrassment.

"You are always so fastidious about your hands and nails. I had wondered." Leri leaned down and kissed his fingers. "I'm proud that you can work and get dirty, It's a...manly thing to do." Fane felt himself warm with embarrassment and pleasure and love and grabbed for her in response. "No, don't," Leri protested, "not where people can see." "So come inside." Night crept over the valley.

From Poiana Cozonac they traveled—catch as catch can—to Bilca. Fane told Leri about their wartime journey as they went. He also told Leri about arriving in Moldova during the famine.

"I remember the famine," she said. "I was young then, but we heard about the terrible problems in Moldova and food was short even in Horezu. We had powdered milk from the US...they didn't tell us at school that's where it was from but somehow everyone knew."

Fane looked at her and smiled. "We had powdered milk, too, exactly the same..." It was another shared bond tying them together.

They stayed in Radauti, at Uncle Vanya's, for a perfect evening. Books, art, music and ideas flowed across the dinner table. Leri sparkled. Uncle Vanya and Auntie Anna were charmed. Fane looked proudly from one to the other, enjoying the exchange, enjoying the way things should be.

Bilca was different. Carol's father came to pick them up and that was fine though he looked much older than Fane had remembered. Uncle Vanya was older, too, Fane thought, but in a different way...maybe peasants aged faster because of their hard life. But Mr. Cojocariu wasn't exactly a peasant, not like Father.

"We've heard news of you from your grandmother and father," the older man was saying, "and it seems you are doing very well. Unlike that ne'er do well scamp of a son of mine."

"Carol?" Leri replied in astonishment. "But Carol is a movie star!"

"I know he's in the movies, if not exactly a star yet," Cojocariu smiled, "but it doesn't seem like real work, does it?"

"They pay real money," Fane said.

"True, and it's also true that everyone has heard of him but I'm not sure it's a fit profession..." Cojocariu's smile belied his words.

Fane looked around eagerly as they came up the little lane to his house. The fields looked untended and some of the boundary markers were gone. The orchard was half gone, too! Granny hadn't written anything about that. The gate had a broken bar and the courtyard was dirty but Granny's smile erased everything as she hobbled out to greet them.

Erased everything for a few moments, Fane later thought. Granny was obviously ill, Petru wasn't drunk, not exactly, but his whole body smelled of alcohol. Granny had fixed a good meal and their welcome was warm but it was hard to feel proud of the family. Still, Granny and Leri had hit it off. "Come here, child," Granny had said and reached up to touch Leri's cheek with her hand. The hand shook a bit, Fane noted, and was ropy with veins but tender.

140

"You're Granny!" Leri exclaimed. "Fane has talked about you so much!" The young woman took Granny's hand in both of her, then embraced her warmly while Granny grinned with pleasure. "Welcome, welcome," she repeated in a happy screech, bringing back the old Granny to the world. Fane smiled to himself, realizing how important these two different women were to his life. If only Mother...another thought to push out of his mind.

On the way back to Radauti, Carol's father ("You shouldn't go to so much trouble," Leri protested. "Our families are very close," Cojocariu answered with a smile and a squeeze to Fane's shoulder) talked of the different collectivization campaigns and what they had meant to the village. "We've done okay, especially compared to some of the other villages," he said, "but the young people are leaving for the city since they have the opportunity and they don't have their own land. The Government wants more of them to stay here but one way or another, they manage, especially the hard working youngsters who have gotten an education. Those of us who remain do what we can but it isn't easy."

"What does 'okay' mean, that we've done 'okay' here in Bilca?" asked Fane. The wagon bounced across a wooden bridge and between deserted fields.

"Well, no one was killed or kept in prison..." Cojocariu started.

"That's ok? You're not serious!"

"No," he said grimly. "I'm serious." Fane suddenly felt isolated and out of it. "In some of the other vil...I mean communes...it was really bad. Bilca cooperated well, put a good amount of land in the collective even though we didn't have any really rich peasants or large landowners." Fane thought in passing about that quiet, dark room through the summer of copying records. "After the early days when a few of the middle peasants were arrested for resisting, the rest of the people came together and cooperated. Because of that we managed to keep plots for each family's use. Rather large plots, in fact. Measurements aren't terribly, uh, precise here in Bukovina, as you know. It's because of the Austrian background," he added whereupon both he and Fane burst into laughter while Leri looked puzzled. Cojocariu smiled at her. "Now tell me about you, Leri. You've been very quiet."

When they returned to Bucharest Fane and Leri found unexpected good fortune. Leri's aunt met them at her door with a happy smile. "Welcome, welcome, come in, I think I've found you a room!" Instead of resting, they cleaned up and went with her to see their possible home.

"It's in a little villa in an area behind Kiseleff," explained Aunt Sanda on the tram. "The people who live there, the Dumitrescus, are distantly related to..." Fane lost the connection in its ins and outs, "then the uncle died and now there is a vacant room. Someone will be put there if it isn't occupied and they'd rather have people they know who are decent and clean than just anyone off the street. So we're going to see them."

Ady Endre was a street of houses built before the war and its cobblestoned length stretched from the *Piata* Filantropia — now called *Piata* May 1 but everyone still used the old name of course — to the back of a large residence on Kiseleff. "That was Ana Pauker's house," Aunt Sanda whispered, gesturing down the street toward the high wall. Fane shivered mentally at the thought of the famous former Party member, now fallen from grace and, what? Working at some publishing house. She was lucky...

Number sixteen was half of a two-story villa, a small garden in front and another down the side where the door was. "A cousin lives downstairs, I think," Aunt Sanda said as they opened the door onto a little glassed in entry which led, through a second door, into a dark, crowded and not very clean hall sort of space. "We're here," she called up the stairs. "Come in, welcome, welcome," a voice came down

142

followed by footsteps belonging to a small, round woman of, Fane guessed, about sixty, maybe a bit more. "Come on up," she repeated, and led them up the curving, narrow staircase into a hall.

The house was two rooms, a bath, a kitchen and a storeroom. "We're fortunate," their hostess said, "to have this large hall at the top of the stairs which, as you see, holds two big cupboards. It's not counted a room but gives us some extra space. On the other hand..." Fane and Leri glanced at each other as they realized the rather dark room they were being offered was also the way to the kitchen. In the corner was the *soba*, a brown and, Leri whispered, rather ugly tile stove. The room had a bed, not very big but large enough perhaps, a table and chair, another cupboard. There would be, Fane looked around, some room to put bookcases. "...it's lovely," he heard Leri saying with a start. "Just what we would like, a quiet street and people like you to share the kitchen and bath. And so clean."

"I do like a clean house," he heard the lady say. "Unfortunately, Daniela, who lives downstairs..." her voice trailed off as Leri and Aunt Sanda made small noises of agreement and sympathy. The women had already developed their own solidarity. "Here in the storeroom," she continued walking through the miniscule kitchen featuring a wood stove, a sink and a small cupboard, "we have room to put the root vegetables in sand for the winter. I make *zakuska* and *muraturi*..." "Oh, I love to cook," said Leri. Solidarity notched up another layer.

"What do you think?" the woman's husband said. "Perhaps we should both have some time to decide," "No, no," said Leri and his wife together. "It's perfect," said Leri. "We couldn't ask for a better place and clearly we have the same...values." What she really meant, thought Fane as he looked approvingly at the books in the hall and mentioned a few titles he knew to the husband, then asked if he could build some bookshelves, was 'We're not workers or...

peasants...we're all intellectuals. But,' he wondered, 'what am I if not a peasant...' then he stopped his thoughts in discomfort and the offer of a cup of tea.

As they walked away from the house after shaking hands on the agreement, Leri bubbled. "Oh, I know it's a bit awkward with our room being on the way to the kitchen but think, it's a nice bathroom and we are only four people sharing both bath and kitchen. And the area is so pretty...did you notice the lilac they've planted in back?"

"I wonder about the cellar and the little storehouse building in back, by the lilac," mentioned Aunt Sanda. "We didn't talk about them..."

"How do you like it?" Leri turned to Fane as they approached the bus stop. ("Not very far at all," said Aunt Sanda approvingly, "very convenient...it will make up for being a ways out of town. And you're so close to Kiseleff to walk in the evenings...")

"I..." Fane began and he paused to turn to Leri. "I feel strange, as if I'm really an adult. And I love you." They looked at each other and the world receded.

It didn't take long to move into their new home. The room already had furniture which was fortunate. Leri came with her clothes and personal items, Fane with his and with books. When he took the little green and yellow plate out of his suitcase and put it on the wall, he felt that this might really turn into a home.

"That's beautiful," said Leri. "It's from Botosani, isn't it?"

"Botosani? I don't know..."

"I'm sure it is — that green and yellow on cream is typical of plates from that area. Does it have a history?"

"A history?" 'Yes,' Fane thought. 'I can tell Leri.' And he did.

Life began to assume a form that seemed at first to be a game of 'house' played by someone else but eventually became so familiar neither Leri nor Fane thought about it.

144

Fane walked to work while Leri took the bus to her school. Leri enjoyed cooking and Fane enjoyed eating. He also, to Leri's delight, knew enough about cooking to appreciate the little flourishes and experiments she liked to try. They got along well with the Dumitrescus who had no children and slowly began move into the young couple's world as if they were close in kinship as well as physical space, providing advice on some of the ins and outs of being adults and running a household. Leri and Fane disagreed, mildly, on politics with Leri thinking that the old ways were better than the current regime. Fane knew Leri wasn't alone in this and he had to admit that not everything was perfect—but Fane remembered only too clearly how hard life was for most people and kept trying to convince Leri that the changes were, overall, for the better. "You were in villages," he said, "You saw the children with lice and...scabies," Fane paused remembering a distant child and the vet who drew back in disgust. "They deserve a better future!" he would say. "But..." Leri would start and their private discussions went on. None of this, of course, was anything that could be raised with most other people but that was so much a part of life that neither thought about it.

Only one thing wasn't right, Fane thought one morning, finally facing the problem. Leri had begun turning over at night, putting her back to him, pleading fatigue, a headache. She was loving and close during the day but when it mattered she...withdrew.

This thought and unresolved longing were with him when he met Carol for their by-now weekly lunch in which they shared their lives and the latest news from Mihai in Moscow.

"He really hates it there, I think," said Carol, "though of course he doesn't say anything."

"Mmmm."

"Hey, Fane, what's up?" Carol looked at his friend, noting the slightly expanded waistline as well as the palpable gloom that had settled over him.

"Oh, nothing but, there is something...it's Leri." Fane muttered.

"Leri? I thought you two were as happy as can be."

"Oh, we are. No...well," Fane wanted to talk but couldn't bear to expose himself or Leri. "It's sex," he finally said in a low voice, looking steadily at the table. "She doesn't like it."

"Whoa. So...problems. But that's often pretty easily solved." Fane looked up sharply, met Carol's blue eyes, and looked away. "It's in your hands, boy, literally in your hands."

"Well, I know it's my responsibility, but she has to..."

"No, wait. Let me explain." Fane drew slightly away, not wanting to talk or hear this but Carol kept on. "Remember how Haiduc loved to have you rub that one spot on his back?

How he'd stretch his neck and lift his lip?"

"What does Haiduc have to do with Leri?"

"Because the principle's the same. Women, horses, God love them, they all need a bit of petting."

Fane stared at Carol, half angry. "I guess you should know," he muttered.

"I do," replied Carol matter-of-factly. "Look," he continued, "women aren't like men."

"Tell me something I don't know."

Carol ignored the remark. "They aren't like men and they are slower to want IT. So you have to help them. Touch a little here, nibble a little there, tell them pretty things they want to hear like how beautiful they are, how much you love them."

"Okay. Then?"

"Then, when they begin to feel...soft...ready for the bit as it were...you go for the magic spot. It's," Carol lowered

146

his voice further and became serious, "it's what they all want. Down there."

"You want me to touch her there?"

"Yes, but if you haven't done it before, go slowly so she doesn't shy and run off." Still with the horse metaphor, Fane thought. "Start a ways away and move closer," Carol continued. "Down there above her lovely sweet well touch lightly and you'll find a sort of button. Go gently with it, more on the side I find than the top, like behind a horse's ears...it's absolutely magic."

Fane's face was flaming but he couldn't stop asking questions. It's like research, he said to himself in passing, I need to know. Carol was patient and became even more explicit in his answers. Gradually Fane's embarrassment receded as he took on the task of learning, exciting in a way that even 19th century history wasn't...quite.

Fane was late getting back to the Institute but everyone was buried in various projects and only the porter at the door noticed and said nothing. "He's good at keeping his mouth shut," thought Fane as he smiled, exchanged a few words with him and offered the man a cigarette. They both came from the North, the porter from Falticeni, and found a shared kinship. Almost everyone, Fane found, had some point that made them seem related in one way or another.

The rest of the afternoon dragged.

That evening, after dinner and when the Dumitrescus had finished in the bathroom and gone to bed, Fane began to kiss Leri, nibbling on her ear and whispering outrageous compliments. She giggled but said, "It's so late..." Fane didn't stop until, almost with a sigh of defeat, Leri began to kiss him back. Fane slid his hand under her blouse and cupped her breast and moved his thumb over her nipple. He listened to her breathing, acutely aware of her body and remembering Carol's instructions. Leri began to relax, to move toward him, to seek his body. Holding his breath, Fane gradually moved his caresses down, undoing clothes and whispering distractive words in her ear. It was easy to find the spot— the minute his fingers encountered the hard little bump under slippery flesh Leri shivered and moaned. Just enough, not too much, they came together in a burst of flame, clinging to one another at the end of the world.

Afterwards Leri snuggled close for a minute, then pushed Fane away, turned over and began to cry."What's wrong? It was good this time for you, wasn't it?" Fane touched her shoulder but she pulled it away from his hand.

"Where did you learn to do that? Who have you been with?" she whispered angrily through her tears. "Do you think I wouldn't notice?"

"Leri, Leri," Fane put his cheek between her shoulder blades glad the bed was too small, shoved against the wall, for her to move further away. "I'll confess. Don't worry...I haven't been with anyone but promise you'll never tell?"

"Tell what?"

"Carol...he...Carol, um, told me..." suddenly Fane couldn't find any words but they were no longer necessary. Leri was shaking. Giggling. She turned over and buried her face in his chest. "Carol?" he heard her muffled voice. "Carol? He told you?"

"Well, yes." Defensively.

"We owe him. Let's...do it again."

I wonder how Ellen would be in bed, Fane thought in passing as he wove his way back through chatting groups of people. It was an idle thought – Leri was the only woman he really wanted – but still, an American would be interesting. Were they different in bed or were all women the same? He shrugged mentally; he'd never know. That was one of the things he had told his bosses he'd never do.

Maybe Carol? Would he take it on as an assignment?

Dinu was still talking a mile a minute. "May I interrupt?" Fane said politely. "I realized I know someone who is connected

*with a riding club. There might be a chance you could join." Ellen
turned toward him with a radiant face.*

*"My goodness, this is wonderful! Do you really think I might
be able to ride while I'm here? You think you can, how do you say
it in Romanian, manage it?" she asked with obvious pleasure.
Dinu's face showed the same question without quite as much
pleasure.*

Fane's first hurdle at the Institute was his dissertation.
He needed to find a topic that was interesting, not already
explored, and not likely to become tangled in the
complexities of the official view of history. It was proving
thorny enough that Fane was seriously thinking of
transferring his loyalty from the Nineteenth Century to
Medieval Romania, so much further in the past, so much
easier politically in the present. He was, after all, already
doing a bit of research for the Director of the Institute on
the great northern monasteries and their linkages with
Romanian rulers, but the 19th century...it was so close, so
real, so pertinent... Finally, as he told Carol, he found his
solution.

"It's brilliant, I'll look at how traveling artists saw
Romania in 19th century!" he exclaimed enthusiastically.

"Why is that brilliant?"

"Because, well," Fane wondered how to condense his
thoughts. "First, most of them drew peasants, in costumes
that looked like European peasant costumes."

"But the cut of the cloth was different," Carol
interrupted.

Fane looked at him in amazement. "How did you know
that?"

"Oh, some background for a movie or something I
think. What else about artists?"

"The thing is, I believe they saw Romania as a European
country, not 'oriental'. The authorities will like that. There
are a couple of tricky points, like Amedeo Preziosi the

149

Italian artist, no, not Italian, Maltese, but most people think he's Italian...he was hired to come here by King Carol I, but I think I can get around that. And a lot of them drew churches...but that's part of my thesis that Romania was seen as a European country, so perhaps it can be part of..." Fane continued enthusiastically until he saw Carol was struggling to stay awake and changed the subject.

"By the way, I have a letter from Mihai."

Carol's attention snapped into gear. "What does he have to say?"

"As usual, not much," they both knew Mihai was severely limited in what he could put on paper, "but he does mention a young woman. Her name is, let's see, Svetlana..."

"That's a bit odd. Or maybe not," remarked Carol.

"Why odd? It's about time for him to think of marrying."

"Because..." Carol paused for a second, cleared his throat and continued. "You know, the Russians try to catch people like Mihai by getting them married to Russians. I'd think he'd be too smart to fall for it."

"You're right, but maybe...who knows. Anyway, he mentions that his marks are good and the classes are as interesting as Professor Radu's at the Liceu!" They both laughed heartily, since all three had regularly fallen asleep as Radu droned on interminably about chemistry.

"Shouldn't he be coming home soon?" Carol asked. "It's been two years almost."

"He doesn't quite say, but I think he has to complete a couple of special assignments first. In any case, it's just as well he's out of the country now," remarked Fane worriedly. "Why?" asked Carol.

"Haven't you heard what's going on at the University, they're kicking people out right and left. It hasn't reached the Institute, yet, but who knows..."

"You mean that movement against 'intellectuals'? Led by Iliescu, isn't it? Do you know him?"

"Not really, I've met him once, I think, but yes, that's it." "You're not worried are you?"

"How can you not worry?" In fact, Fane had been preoccupied with the subject almost as much as he'd been preoccupied with his dissertation topic. Well, not quite as much to be honest. He didn't feel a stab of fear in his gut when he thought about the dissertation. Not like he did at the idea of being thrown out of the Institute, sent back to the farm...

"I'll admit it's pretty bad from what I've heard but remember..."

"Remember what?"

"We're not intellectuals. We're peasants. Don't forget. Growing up in Bilca has taken us a long way, we have a lot to be grateful for. And so does Mihai. I wonder if he'll come soon."

"I wonder," Fane looked down at his hands, smooth clean with well kept nails, the hard farm labor pushed to the back of his mind so far, so deep...but Carol was right. Maybe. A peasant?

It was over a year before Mihai returned and then he arrived with a metaphorical bang, the same day as Sputnik. The first news to arrive was of the space launch. Fane was in the Curtea Veche Anticariat hunting through the art history section when Andrei burst out of the back room. "We've done it!" he said. "We've put a rocket in space!"

"Huh? Who's 'we'?"

"We, the Eastern bloc. It was the Russians, but it's a great step!" Andrei slapped Fane on the back and they embraced, laughing. "We've shown the West, we can do it, too!" The two momentarily forgot their shared hatred of the USSR in a wave of pride. The feeling of accomplishment, of vindication, was still with Fane when he opened the gate into their little courtyard. It creaked, the usual signal to all inside that someone was entering, and as he swung the rusty latch loop over the iron fence post he heard Leri calling from the bathroom window. "Hurry," she said. "I have a surprise."

"You mean Sputnik? I've already heard! Isn't it great?" Fane called up as he walked to the door.

"No,"Leri leaned further out the window as he passed and spoke to his back. "Something more important!"

It was more important. Mihai, along with Carol. The two sat in Fane and Leri's two chairs, crowding their tiny room, while Fane and Leri sat on the bed. Mrs. Dumitrescu passed through to the kitchen apologetically but it didn't make a dent in the conversation. There were years to exchange. The four of them talked for an hour then Carol suggested they go out to get a glass of beer.

"Oh, no," said Leri. "I have a bottle of wine I've been saving. Let me open that."

"I really feel like beer," said Carol.

"Me, too. It's been a long time since I've had Romanian beer," added Mihai. Leri looked from one to the other in confusion. "Come on," said Fane, making it all into a joke as he often did. "These two are set in their ways so we'll set them down and set down beer and set up..." "That's enough 'setting'," laughed Mihai. Leri joined the laughter saying affectionately, "You guys are impossible. I know you want to spend some time together. Go out and have a drink, then come back for something to eat." Fane looked at her in wonder — he didn't think they had enough food in the house for four people, but Leri was amazing. He said it aloud, "You're amazing," and they all laughed again.

Instead of going to the bar by the market they walked toward Kiseleff and Herestrau Park. "I need to stretch my legs after all that traveling," Mihai said to no one in particular. When they reached the park they kept up their pace in case someone might be watching, but the conversation changed.

152

"So how was it really?" Fane asked.

"They're really good, the Russians, in some ways, but they fell down in a couple of places. The first, they just couldn't hide it though they'd like to, things in Moscow aren't that much better than in Bucharest."

"Did anyone expect them to be?"

"What about the music, the film?" asked Carol.

"Music is great, film so-so, not better than ours, but I'm talking about the way people live. You can tell from their shoes, just like here. Of course," he said remembering, "they do all have some sort of shoes, which is something. But you can see it on their faces, most people don't have good food, clothes, crowding is bad..."

"But they are still feeling the effects of war...even if they made up some of them from us and other countries. It sounds like Romania."

"That's true, but I expected more, especially after they had taken..." The three fell silent, remembering the trainloads of goods, food, raw materials heading always northeast. Mihai continued, "I think it's really better here. And I thought that they had 'real' communism...that things would be...more evolved, maybe." He stopped for a minute, then continued. "And then there were the camps...in Siberia and other places, just rumors but rumors like our DanubeBlack Sea Canal, but bigger. With more repression...some of the stories..." Mihai paused. "I think Siberia is where the people on the wrong side of the line in Bilca were sent."

"Sent to prison camps?" Carol asked.

"Some, maybe, but I heard that most were just dumped, dumped in the middle of nowhere and left to survive if they could. Like our Jews in Transnistria. I wonder..." He stopped talking again and the three remained silent.

"Who's this Svetlana person you mentioned?" Fane asked, changing the subject. Carol looked at him strangely.

Mihai shrugged. "A very nice young woman their 'boys' were trying to get me interested in. I wrote about her so they might think I was serious and leave me alone. It worked. We had a tearful farewell."

"What was wrong with her?"

"Nothing. She was lovely. But if I get married, I want to marry a person, not a government." They all laughed aloud, their laughter bouncing back from the crackling of the autumn leaves underfoot. At this point they came out of the park into an area of small houses, found an open bar and sat down for the much-discussed beer. "Leri will be disappointed if we don't drink it," joked Fane. The conversation turned to news of mutual friends. Not until they were walking back through the deserted park did Carol ask Mihai what he would be doing now.

"I'll be in the Ministry of External Affairs, of course," he answered. Carol gave him a friendly shove. Maybe not so friendly. "Come on. We've been together too long for you to treat me differently than the way you treat Fane." Mihai looked surprised then thought a minute.

"Look," he said, "I can't really talk, even here, and you really don't want to know. Let me just say that in the Services there are factions. One faction has its primary loyalty to Romania. That's me. The other to the wider, um, picture— to Them." He tilted his head northeast. I'm going to be a diplomat and I really will be in the MEA, but with an agenda. And that's as far as I can go."

They walked in silence for a while. Fane digested Mihai's statement which put into words something he had felt for a long time, both about Mihai and about politics. He also realized that Carol had asked to be a full member of the group while Fane had thought he always had been, especially since the incident with Father Ion. Funny how people could see things differently.

"What's happening here?" asked Mihai. "It looks like there is some improvement."

154

"Sometimes I think we're the only Stalinist country in the bloc," answered Carol, "but things are getting better, don't you think, Fane?"

"Yeah, I guess so. It's a bit easier to get stuff — Leri and I have been discussing getting a refrigerator and they're available. All you need is money. And space. We can't figure out where to put it. They abolished compulsory delivery of crops from the peasants at the beginning of the year." "I heard about that," interjected Mihai. "We're also," Fane continued, "getting out from under Russian influence and control more and more. You probably know that better than I, but I see it in the Institute and how we approach history. Some history." They walked on a moment in silence before Fane continued. "If you stay away from the politics at the top, you're okay and more is available all the time. Speaking of that, how's your father? We see him once every few months, here and there, but of course he doesn't talk about himself."

"He's fine," Mihai said, "working hard. He doesn't tell me too much but I've basically found out that he's really good at keeping his head down."

"He who raises his head gets it cut off," Carol quoted and they all laughed.

"Have you really found someplace for her to ride?" Dinu asked when Ellen was drawn away by a writer who wanted to know about publishing his books in the US. "I thought that kind of thing was off limits for foreign diplomats."

"I have an idea," Fane smiled. "Have you tried some of those breads they call 'pizza'? They're really good." His thoughts were at odds with his easy demeanor but he was fairly sure he could swing something with Carol's help and with the new dispensation. After all, Ceausescu himself had said that they should identify diplomats who could come to recognize Romania's worth as a culture as well as be political allies, then give them the opportunity to love the country. Not that I, Fane thought, sit in on those meetings. If I could be a fly on the wall...

155

Life continued to weave its patterns as the months and years passed blending one into the other with small markers that were later occasion for discussion about when, who, exactly, what had happened. Was it this year or that they had met so and so? Was it that month or this, no it must have been spring because there had been pussywillows... When did they discover the Turkish yoghurt shop, that one, the one near Calea Mosilor...oh, yes...is it still open? Remember, when so-and-so got a sack of American records and...Patterns were set and became part of the rhythm of daily existence. Leri visited her aunt regularly and Fane continued to haunt the *anticariats*. Both wove nets of acquaintances and connections, the kind that made life sometimes more pleasant, sometimes easier, as the circle of people who had this or that or could do that or this widened. Leri began to meet former students, ones who had studied in her class one year, two years...I can't believe how many years it's been. Fane found his friendly geniality worked as well with his colleagues in research as it had at the University. He was always ready to listen and respond with a joke or a neat turn of phrase, to be helpful wherever he could and to find that individual bond that made each person feel he and Fane had a special relationship. Few days went by without someone coming for this favor or that introduction and each act of...assistance...was eventually rewarded.

Politics were always present but Leri remained aloof and though Fane heard a lot, he managed to be so neutral that no one knew what he really thought. Often the center of attention, Fane honed the ability to draw back so no one thought he was putting himself too forward. His inward, private life grew steadily away from the public Fane everyone "knew" and the Fane everyone knew was already ready to use his growing connections to help. But, he sometimes thought, everyone lived like that, a world with concentric circles of trust and another set of circles of

156

influence, sometimes overlapping, sometimes completely separate, always changing and never really neat but always important to remember or, not really remember, have as a constant whisper at the back of your mind. Who do you trust? Who can do what? Who wants...

There were some markers that were so important they couldn't be misplaced in memory and became events or periods that defined everything else.

The first abortion was the hardest. "We just don't have room, money, we can't have a child," both Fane and Leri said to each other, over and over. It was all true because, Fane thought, they lived in the city. If it were the country it would be different. But here...he looked around their little room, not that it took much looking to see all of it.

Leri went off alone, with a friend she said. She didn't want Fane with her but when she returned in tears he held her tenderly. It was his child, too, he thought, his son, of course, it would have been a son, but it did no good to think like that, to think of a little Vulcean growing up, no good at all. Fane kissed Leri's hair as she tried to hide her sobbing so the Dumitrescus wouldn't hear.

That wasn't to say the second abortion was easy, or the third. "Damn us," Fane thought, "we could have had so many children if we were in the village." But there was no alternative and they were still young, really. And thank God they had found a good doctor, clean and discreet even if he was expensive. He was also a cousin of Aunt Sanda's late husband so it was doubly safe.

It was after the third abortion that they went to Sucevita. Leri's school was out for the summer and Fane was given the opportunity to do some original research there, another gift of Father Ion, he thought. It was a pity that Father Ion had passed away and he couldn't tell him about it. Funny also that he felt so sort of lost without Father Ion in Poiana Cozonac. It wasn't as if he had ever turned to him for advice or even heard from him except through occasional letters from Grigore who was also, Fane realized, getting on in years, but maybe because he always could have gone to Father Ion if he'd needed to. Or because he had 'gone' to talk with him in his head when he needed good advice and somehow the Father Ion in his head had always come through.

Fane had been at his desk at the Institute, happily reading about Michel Bouquet, studying the few pictures that were in the Institute Library and thinking he would need to go to the Cabinet de Stampe at the Academy then call again on the Goga family who had several prints when the Director's secretary tapped him on the shoulder. "Comrade Vulcean," she said. "The Director wants to see you. Now." Fane pushed back his chair in alarm at her tone and the not very usual request. He followed her through the hall to the Director's office where someone was sitting in a chair talking with the head of the Institute.

"Comrade Vulcean is here," she announced and left. The two men in the room turned toward him and Fane's heart leapt. It wasn't...it couldn't be...

"Fane, my boy," said Professort Brebean, "I would have recognized you any place!" He rose and they embraced warmly. "What a pleasure to see you," Fane said. "I didn't know you were acquainted with the Director. How are you? How is the *liceu*?" "Please sit and join us," said the Director. "Relu and I were in the faculty together and he was set for a brilliant career, but he couldn't stay away from Bukovina."

After Fane heard various pieces of news from Radauti and the *liceu* and had described, modestly, his research, Director Dragomir turned to him and said, "Relu tells me that you can read and understand Church Slavonic. You never said anything about it."

Fane looked down, wondering what to say. It was a difficult subject. If you could be sacked for being seen too often in church, what would it mean to know Church

Slavonic? "It never seemed very important," he started, searching for the right words and explanation. "When my family was in Transylvania during the war the village we lived in was so small that the priest was also the schoolmaster." "Rather unusual," noted the Director. Fane politely continued. "He taught us. At that time it wasn't..." he stopped as Professor Brebean stepped in.

"I found out about it when they, Fane and his cousin, came to Hurmuzachi. It was before the reforms so I arranged for them to have some tutoring so they wouldn't waste the early education. They were both bright boys and learning is always useful even if it wasn't on any formal record." The two men nodded in accord. Fane sat with his hands clenched under the table. "After 1948, of course, we stopped but the foundation is good." It was astonishing, Fane thought, how openly Brebean was speaking — the two men must be very good friends — but also now he realized consciously for the first time that the change in their studies wasn't, as had been said at the time, because they needed to begin working toward University entrance exams. Or, maybe, the thought flickered, it was that, too. Anyway...

"This is a great piece of luck for us," he heard Director Dragomir say. "As you know, my own field is Medieval Studies and I needed someone who can help me really get into the history of the monasteries in Moldova and Oltenia. You know how I've been interested in the similarities and differences between their development in the two Principalities. There is, of course, a lot of material in Romanian but some key documents...I can't leave here easily...and these days you simply can't find..." Fane kept one ear on the conversation while he looked at the face of his beloved Professor. Brebean had aged, but gracefully, the fine lines of his face simply etched more deeply. But...he hadn't aged that much. He couldn't be all that old, Fane thought, in fact, he's not all that much older than I, perhaps fifteen years or maybe twenty. It seemed such a great difference just ten, no twelve years, no could it be fourteen, fourteen years ago. How time passed.

"Come, let's go have something to eat," the Director was standing. Fane stood quickly and started to say good-bye. "No," said the Director. "You come with us — we need to talk some more. I need someone to look at documents in the Sucevita Monastery's Library."

"I know the monk in charge of the Library there," interjected Professor Brebean. "An interesting man with quite a story..."

This began Fane's second academic career, adding yet another layer between the public Stefan Vulcean and the private. More and more he worked in medieval studies, burying himself in ancient documents and half-remembered history. It needed to be modernized and updated to serve the Revolution, of course, but was far enough away that the truth usually didn't pose a threat. Except, Fane thought, perhaps to the Russians as it was clear that part of his job was to prove that Romania had a long, proud and Western history. And wasn't all that close to Russia.

On another level, he continued his work on the 19th century. Part of that was his dissertation, which everyone knew about but in any case was nearly finished. Completely hidden from all except Leri and Andrei at the Curtea Veche Anticariat was his interest in the 19th century history that had been erased by the communists. Even his book collection was layered. Fane had deliberately built his bookshelves deeper than the width of his books so that most of the collection was neatly arranged, spines of books to edge of shelf, while certain books were tucked behind them. Fane didn't really think about whether the necessity to keep things to himself was good or bad, it simply was. Like the concentric circles of friends he sometimes catalogued in his head — a very few like Mihai and Carol, others you could share some things with, and on until you reached those 'friends' with whom you were very affable and to whom you said absolutely nothing of importance while watching them carefully.

When he told Mihai and Carol he was going to Sucevita, Mihai immediately asked if he'd see the priest they had met as children. "Do you remember?" he said, "The one who had lost his family and became a monk?"

"Yes, and who took us around the Monastery. I was afraid that they wouldn't let peasants like us in." Fane smiled. "We've come a long way."

"Speaking of old times, do you remember the Russian officers we, I, ran into that summer in Bilca, the ones we met again in Radauti?"

"You mean the one you hit with the snowball and we thought we'd be shot?" Fane chuckled.

"Wow. You're lucky to be here," said Carol. "I hadn't heard about that. What happened?"

"We were walking back from Uncle Vanya's to school and having a snowball fight," explained Fane. "Mihai missed me and caught the Russian in the face." "And we had actually met them in Bilca when I had run into the same one, sort of in the same way!" added Mihai. "Why," Fane turned to Mihai, "are you remembering this now?"

"I'm not sure I mentioned to you that I ran into the same pair in Bucharest while we were at the University."

"No, you didn't." Fane wondered why Mihai hadn't said anything. He must have said it aloud because Mihai answered.

"Probably because we were all busy with exams at the time and it didn't seem important. Anyway, we occasionally had a cup of coffee together. Then I left for Moscow and we met again there. Vladimir was at their Headquarters and moving up into an impressive career while Pyotr was studying diplomacy on a short course so he could work in the Military sections of Russian embassies—most notably Romania. I didn't see much of him since we had different classes and it would have been...tricky. Anyway, he's back in Bucharest with the Russian Embassy and wants to meet all of us."

"Why?" asked Carol. "I'm not sure that's a great idea," said Fane. Neither wanted to get mixed up with a Russian diplomat or, more important, with the Romanian Security Police.

"Come on," said Mihai. "It's all right. In fact, it's a little official. I've," he glanced around to be sure no one could hear them, "I've been asked to cultivate him. It would be easier if we could all meet."

"If that's the case," said Fane reluctantly. "Let me know when."

"Yeah, okay, if you want," added Carol, not entirely graciously.

"Thanks," said Mihai. "Now Fane, your turn. Why did you bring up Sucevita?"

"Oh, nothing much," replied Fane feeling somehow deflated and a bit angry by Mihai's riff on the Russians, on his stealing the spotlight. Mihai was always two steps ahead, had always been...Fane stopped an ugly thought and went on, "I'm being sent on a research trip to the Monastery. Since Leri's on summer vacation, we're going together. I'll be able to take a couple of days and go to Bilca as well." There were cheers all around. They all went to Bukovina for holidays, not always and not always together as Fane and Leri also had to spend time with her family but Mihai's remark was true. "You made me realize that none of us has really visited any of the monasteries in Romania, seriously, I mean, not just passing them in an afternoon, or a lot of other important places."

"I have," said Carol. "We've done filming at Marasesti, that film on World War I we made last year, and..."

"Oh, you do all kinds of things," interjected Mihai. Which, Fane thought was true, just as it was true that he and Leri had spent vacations at the seaside when they

162

weren't with one family or another. It was time to learn more about the rest of Romania first hand and not just in books, time to make new resolutions, time to...probably time to go back to work. He pushed back his chair. "Sorry, but it's getting on..."

The not very clean rural bus rumbled along the bumpy road toward Sucevita and there was a flutter of excitement in Fane's chest. What a different arrival this would be from that in the wagon pulled by...Fane shoved the thought of Haiduc aside. Here he was, coming back as an official researcher, not a poor peasant kid. "I could get used to this really quickly," Fane had told Leri earlier that day.

They had stopped in Suceava to call on the Council of Culture where Fane found himself treated like someone important. Someone really important. He was from Bucharest, from a prestigious Institute, a politically sensitive institute. He won over the head of the Council by an adroit combination of subtle flattery and references to their common Bukovinean heritage then provided a measure of relief to the hospitable but hard-pressed bureaucrat by declining to use the Council's car.

"I want to go to Radauti to meet some people and, since it's much closer to Sucevita we can just go on from there." Fane had actually been given an allowance for gas that would have provided the same relief to the Director, but this was paying Leri's expenses. Besides, he really did want to go to Radauti and he had already made sure they could get to the Monastery by bus.

After calling on Professor Brebean at the *liceu,* closed for the summer, empty of students and with that special smell that schools have when they are unoccupied, they spent the night at Uncle Vanya's. Fane felt very much at home.

"I feel like a different person when I breathe this northern air," he told Leri. "There is something about your birthplace, your heritage..."

"You know," said Leri, "Romania isn't that enormous. And the whole country is your heritage." Fane couldn't find a proper argument, for once, but he knew she was wrong. Not Romania but Bukovina was his home. There was something in the light, the smell of the air...not, of course, that he wanted to live there now but...someday.

Professor Brebean had provided them with an additional letter of introduction to the Father in charge of the Monastery Library to add to their more official collection. "You'll like him, I think," Brebean said. "He's a remarkable man."

"I thought Sucevita was a convent," Fane said, half question half statement.

"It was, after about 1936 or 7 I think, but now that the religious bodies have been disbanded they wanted someone...responsible perhaps, at least someone who knew what he was doing, to be in charge of the treasures they have and felt a man, of course, could do the job better than a woman," he explained. "He's not alone, there are a couple of other monks, one of them a brother, I think, to help," Brebean added. "They're the ones in charge of the rooms for people like you."

People like Fane usually came by car and he wasn't surprised when no one met them. He helped Leri down the steps and the driver pulled their bags out, then the bus pulled away, no longer blocking their view. They had seen something of the Monastery through the dirty bus windows but now they beheld the great gray stone walls and buildings clearly and as a whole. Fane heard Leri draw in her breath. "It's beautiful," she said softly. "Is this what you remembered?"

Fane was suddenly thrown back into his history, the hungry, scared boy wondering what was ahead in a halfremembered Bilca, whether they could avoid Petru's drunken blows when they got back, whether they would even be allowed to enter the great gates. As in a dream he

164

saw a black robed figure approach them, familiar and not familiar. He moved forward, not quite knowing what he was doing. "Brother Augustin?" he asked, standing outside himself and watching without believing.

"Why yes," the monk answered. "I am Father Augustin. Have we met?"

Fane returned to his senses and the present. Smiling broadly he held out his hand. "Yes, just after the war, many years ago. You were kind to two peasant boys. You showed them the church and told them about the frescos. You probably don't remember but neither of us ever forgot you."

"God has his ways!" Father Augustin exclaimed in delight. "I do remember. I don't recall your names but your family camped here one night. You came at a critical time for me."

"How is that?" Fane asked. Leri remained silent at his side, almost invisible to the two men.

"I remember talking to you about my family," Augustin answered, "the family I lost in the war. That day I had had a crisis of faith, wondering how God could visit so much suffering on me but, somehow, being with the two of you and telling you how I was led to this monastery brought me back into my real beliefs. I saw great purity in your face, absolute faith as you wondered at the beauty of this place. It was important to me."

"And after talking to you I felt I wanted to become a priest, a brother like you," said Fane quietly. "I have taken a very different path in my life, but it is also a good one and perhaps not so far from yours in some ways."

"But I'm forgetting myself. I was expecting a visitor from the Institute of History in Bucharest."

"I am your visitor, Stefan Vulcean," said Fane. "May I introduce my wife, Valeria."

"God is great," said Father Augustin. He embraced Fane and smiled warmly at Leri. "I had come outside the

Monastery on a whim. He led me to you. Please come and I'll have you shown to your quarters."

Leri and Fane stayed at the Monastery for a week. Fane spent most days in the Library, poring over documents, talking with Father Augustin and taking copious notes. Leri went for walks, read and talked with the women from the peasant families in the area. Each evening they dined with Father Augustin and talked, sometimes about Fane's research, sometimes about God. "This was a special time for me," said Leri when they left. "I feel closer to God, closer to this country of ours, closer to you. The only trouble," she added, "was that I was cold most of the time there."

"It was cold," Fane agreed, not really comfortable talking about God outside the Monastery walls though he knew that even there it could be dangerous given the official position that religion was simply an opiate for the masses. Another of the unresolved tensions it was better not to think about. "Maybe it's so cold because of the mountains?" His speculations were lost in Marginea where they got off the bus. "Oh, look!" said Leri. "That man is selling the most beautiful black bowls. Let's get some!"

"We don't have room in our luggage," protested Fane as they approached the elderly man sitting in a small stall on the side of the road. "We don't have room in the house, for that matter."

"Just one," said Leri firmly. "Well, two. I want to take something to the Dumitrescus." She examined the various pieces, bargained half-heartedly with the man, then took her prizes.

"You should have gotten a better price," grumbled Fane.

"I know, I could have," she replied calmly. "He looked so poor."

"Hmmph. I do love you."

"Hush, here comes bus." They climbed on and asked the driver if he stopped at the road to Bilca. "Sure," he

166

replied, "I can stop there. Not really a town there, between Lower and Upper Vicovul, but it's a place where people occasionally get off. Why are you going to Bilca?" The bus was rumbling down the rutted road, both Leri and Fane hanging on. "I'm from there, Vulcean family, perhaps you heard the name..." Fane answered. "Of course," the busdriver replied. "I met your Father once at..." the conversation continued in a cloud of dust.

Finally the two got off the bus, waved to all the passengers who had now become acquaintances, and started to walk towards Bilca. It wasn't long before Fane hailed a man with a wagon who had come up behind them and another set of explanations began. Reaching home was, he thought, a relief as they turned wearily into the courtyard. Fane heard Granny's welcoming screech, weaker now but still penetrating, and braced himself to face Petru.

When they entered the house, Fane stopped in surprise. The stools at the table had been replaced by chairs. There was a new pot by the stove and, in a place of honor on the old dowry chest, covered by a piece of handworked lace, was a radio!

"Eh, you're seeing our radio!" squawked Granny happily. "Look, we can get two different stations on it. We can even," she lowered her voice although there wasn't another house within a quarter of a mile, "get Voice of America but," she hastened to add, "we don't listen to it. Except Petru once in a while. And the music programs. I like that man, Louis Conover..."

"Louis Conover, the jazz man? Petru? You? Jazz? Granny! And the radio! What happened?"

"If you came more often you'd know. Things have been getting better here. Not as good, of course, as when I was young and the Austrians were here, before the First World War, but much better than they used to be. If you came more often, you'd know," Granny repeated.

"I'm glad to see everything," Fane deflected the justified criticism. He felt guilty, of course, for not being in Bilca much more often but he was so busy and he did send money and...he mentally ran through his litany of excuses but they were for himself as Granny was off on another subject. Clearly, though, there had been real improvements in the countryside. Come to think of it, Father Augustin had said something similar.

"...of course," Granny was saying, "if your Father didn't spend all his money on alcohol, we'd be even better off. But I did get another cow...come see her...she's..." Fane and Leri obediently followed Granny as she hobbled excitedly out the door.

It was a pleasanter visit than he had thought it would be and it was of course good to be back in Bilca, and great to see Uncle Vanya and Aunt Anna in Radauti but opening the squeaky courtyard gate on Ady Endre in Bucharest was the real homecoming. Mr. Dumitrescu came down the stairs to help them carry the luggage up and Mrs. Dumitrescu stood in the hall to greet them. Leri embraced her warmly and gave her the black bowl as the older woman said, "Welcome, you must be tired. I have some *ciorba* I've made..." They were fortunate, Fane thought as he often did. It was hard to get along with other families in such close quarters, but they did really well. Perhaps if the Dumitrescus hadn't lost their son in the War it wouldn't be so easy...he turned to the older man and asked reflexively if everything was all right while they were away. Of course, was the easy reply.

When he returned to the Institute, greeting the doorman and slipping him a small bottle of *tzuica* 'from our Bukovina,' Fane completed his financial report and took it to the Chief Accountant before he turned to putting together his notes for the Director. At the Accountant's desk Fane doublechecked the report and receipts. "I want to be sure nothing is wrong, and I'd appreciate your advice since it's my first time," he told Popescu. The older, rather severe looking man wasn't someone that Fane had had many dealings with but, as with everyone, he had made sure their relations were pleasant.

This time Popescu glanced at the report then looked more penetratingly at Fane. "You're beginning to move up into a responsible position here, aren't you," he said.

Unsure of how to reply, Fane deflected the question with a deprecating remark. "No," said Popescu, "you are. I hadn't really noticed you — you haven't quite finished your Doctorate yet, have you, a little slow on that, perhaps? — but I've been asking around and gotten some good reports." Fane had no idea at that point why Popescu should be interested in him. It wasn't until he was called again to the Director's office that everything became clear. This time the third person in the office wasn't a visitor but Popescu.

'Come in, Fane, and close the door," said Director Dragomir. A bit surprised at this, Fane did as he was told and stood until he was invited to sit down. Mentally he went over a checklist of ways he could possibly have done something wrong in the accounting for his trip to Sucevita.

"There is something I'm afraid I've overlooked," said the Director.

"Yes?"

"You aren't a Party member." A light went off in Fane's brain. Of course. Popescu was the head of the Institute's Party cell.

"No, I'm not."

"Is that, ah, because of any ideological...no, let me put it differently. Is that by choice?"

Fane knew he needed to be careful though, in fact, he didn't particularly have ideological objections. After all, he had been a member of the UAER in high school, like everyone else. When the UAER was changed, merged rather, with the UTM, the Communist youth organization, as a "poor peasant", Fane was automatically enrolled even though some of his colleagues, like that priest's son, what was his name, who used to bring them *coliva*, had a hard time getting in. He went to the obligatory meetings and functions — everyone did, mixed up in the alphabet soup of organizations that were more important to those who didn't belong than to those who did.

And when he turned 28 and his membership in the youth organization lapsed, Fane hardly noticed since he'd sort of been 'lost' when he moved to the Institute and was happy not to have time taken from his research. And now... he simply didn't want to have to spend time going to meetings or, in fact, get mixed up in political activities at all but it didn't look as if there would be a choice. Not if the Director was involved. "No," he replied. "In fact, I have benefited personally very greatly from Party policies and their promotion of people like me who, as you know, come from poor families. Without the Party I probably," here he felt he was stretching the truth a bit, "would still be a peasant in Bukovina."

"Then, why not?"

"I was, of course, a member of the Communist Youth from the beginning but when I began work here, to be candid, I never really thought about it and the membership lapsed with, um, age. I am happy spending my time in research and writing and haven't paid much attention to politics."

Director Dragomir smiled. "I understand — you are truly a scholar. But this Institute is, ah, important politically and we need to be certain that our collective is comprised of, ah, persons who have understood, ah," Dragomir paused longer than normal at this point, "the importance of working together for the benefit of all."

"Are you," Fane asked, "advising me to join the Party?"

"I would not interfere in such a private matter. At the same time, if you want to advance within your profession,

170

perhaps even to remain in your profession, it might be advisable. I might add on a personal level that your work has been of considerable value to the Institute and to me, and that I hope you have a bright future with us." Dragomir concluded then remained silent, letting Fane consider his words.

The decision wasn't difficult. 'It's not as if I felt strongly one way or another,' thought Fane to himself. Aloud, he said after a suitable silence, "I would be honored to be accepted into the Party. I confess I should have applied much earlier, but it has been such a positive and continual presence in my life that taking the actual steps to join hasn't seemed so important to me. Comrade Popescu," he said, turning to the older man. "Would you please guide me in the application?"

"Of course," Popescu said. "Naturally, your background and work will have to be considered at a meeting, then it goes to the District Party committee for review but from the enquiries I've made about you, there should be no problem. The only question mark was why you hadn't been asked to apply earlier." Fane felt vaguely guilty about this although it was clearly their business, not his. Thinking of a proverb he had read in a book about Mexico, "Flies don't get in a closed mouth," he simply smiled and waited.

The Director broke the silence, saying solemnly as he folded his hands over his vast stomach, "You are making a wise decision, now let us hope you are accepted...I think you will be," but as he spoke Fane thought he saw a sardonic twinkle in his eye. Fane almost winked back.

And so it came to pass that Fane made an application, was interviewed in a meeting of his colleagues in the Institute, and faced public criticism. He came from the "right" background — impeccable, he said to himself with satisfaction — and had never done anything remotely political, which was the main criticism levied at him. The right words came easily since he had heard them on the radio most of his life and, besides, Carol had told him what to do. He said, "Tell them that it's your firm decision to be a full member of the Worker's Party of Romania (PMR) because you want to dedicate all your energies and future activities to the leading political force in the country." Popescu was leading the gathering and solemnly accepted Fane's statement. Fane's application was duly forwarded to the Bucharest *raion* committee of the PMR but everyone at the Institute correctly thought this was pro forma and indeed it was.

The only real hitch was Leri. "Aren't you a hypocrite for doing this?" she asked.

"Hypocrite? Why?"

"For pretending you believe in something like that?" Fane was taken aback at this. Surely Leri understood that some things were simply necessary, like attending an obligatory class at the University with a bad professor where you didn't learn anything. Maybe a waste of time but you had to do it. Besides, the Party WAS helping Romania progress—just think of Granny listening to jazz on the radio! Fane conveniently suppressed the accompanying thought that it DID have to be a bit of a secret, listening to that station and program, but... They segued into a familiar discussion that became an argument which was finally put aside when Fane, with his usual ploy, began kissing Leri and moving her toward the bed as his hands roamed her beloved body.

Except for obligatory meetings, in which he made friends, spread good cheer, and said nothing of importance, his Party membership remained simply another minor duty through the rest of the decade. And, he thought, it's not too bad, just once a month and sometimes the meetings were interesting, especially when there were odd topics, like the lecture on Mozambique when the Leader was visiting

172

there. And when they were boring it was a bit like church with Leri, a chance to think about other things.

It turned out that the journey to Sucevita was the first of many such trips, back to that Monastery then to other places where material lay in dusty archives and forgotten corners, some taken with Leri, those during the school year without her. Fane finished his dissertation the following year and received his Doctorate in History with Distinction. He was surprised at the number of people who showed up at his Defense in the Faculty of History and pleased that he was able to invite his Professors and other important people to the customary meal following it. He published a well-received article arguing that Western artists perceived Romania as a European country, backing up his point with illustrations. "Interestingly enough," he said to Mihai at one point, "no one raised the question of the portrayals of churches."

"Probably because it was important to your point about our European ties — churches, not mosques. But I note that you didn't say much about King Carol and Preziosi. Wasn't leaving Carol I out of this picture intellectually dishonest?"

"You've got to be joking..." Fane started, then he realized Mihai was, in fact, pulling his leg. "Damn you," he said reflexively.

"Oh, I'm quite damned," replied Mihai and they both laughed.

"How's your work coming?" asked Fane, knowing he wouldn't get much of an answer.

"It's fascinating, tense. The story with our friends," Mihai nodded very subtly to the north, "gets more complicated every day. But we're beginning to develop better trade with the West and ties with them and other...friendly countries. The problem, as always, is to profit economically and develop political allies but retain our ability to pursue socialism at home." Fane looked at Mihai wondering if he were joking or serious this time. He couldn't tell. Mihai and his father were both mysteries more often than not. A part of their work, he assumed.

But at the same time, he had to admit things were getting better, not only in Bilca but in Bucharest as well. More food in the markets and shops, better choice of clothes in the stores. The Government had started to build really nice apartment blocks along the major avenues so the housing shortage could ease.

"I think we could manage to get on the list for one of those apartments," he told Leri. "I have a friend who could help and it wouldn't cost too much."

"No thanks, I like it here," she replied.

"You what? I mean, I like it here, too, and we're lucky with the Dumitrescus, but wouldn't it be nice to have a place all to ourselves? Not to share a bath or a kitchen? Not to..." Leri knew he meant 'not to have to keep quiet all the time, even when we make love' because it had come up before. But she had a surprise.

"The Dumitrescus have talked to me about a possible change in their lives," she said.

"What?!"

"You know that Mrs. Dumitrescu has a sister who is much older and who lives in Craiova," Leri answered. It was hard to think of anyone being "much older" than Mrs. Dumitrescu. "Her husband died last month." "I didn't know," said Fane. "If you would take your nose out of a book and talk to people, you would." "I talk to people all the time." "Only 'important' ones." Fane was taken aback at this. Leri continued as if it hadn't been said. "It seems that she has a very good house in Craiova but she doesn't think she can live alone in it. The Dumitrescus are going to go stay with her for a month or two and see how they like it there. If they do, they want to try and work out an arrangement with us to sell us this flat."

Fane sat down heavily on the bed. "Wow." It was all he could say. "Wow." Leri looked at him expectantly. "Aren't

174

you happy?" she asked. Fane didn't tell her he had dreamed of a clean, new flat, laid out precisely, with square corners in rooms that didn't have the ground-in dirt of decades in every crack and crevice, maybe an elevator, certainly no mess in the entry like the one spilling out from the apartment of Daniela downstairs. Instead he smiled and said, "I'm just stunned. How long have you been talking about this with them?"

"Oh, a couple of months since they first brought up the subject."

"And you never said anything to me?"

"You...you've had your head going back and forth between the 19th century and medieval Romania like a ping pong ball, first on one side and fully there, then on the other and fully there but so fast I can't follow, and never here, in Bucharest, now."

"I'm sorry." Fane got up and put his arms around Leri. "You deserve better. I'm sorry. I love you and..." ...and as usual, they were interrupted, not this time by the Dumitrescus on the way to the kitchen but by Mihai bounding up the stairs. "Forgive me for not knocking," he said breathlessly, "but I heard Carol is in trouble and I'm meeting him to talk about it. Can you come?" Fane and Leri looked at one another. "Go," she said wordlessly and looked at him with such love that Fane knew it would be all right. He kissed her ear and murmured, "Thank you," then turned to Mihai. "Where are we meeting Carol?"

On the way to the workmen's bar they often visited Mihai filled Fane in. "It's over a horse, this time, not a woman."

"That's a change. Go on."

"The director of his latest film wanted to show horses going over a cliff during a running battle scene. They constructed a cliff that Carol thought was dangerous for the horses. Typically, he didn't say anything about the actors."

"So did he refuse to act?"

"Worse. He told the director exactly what he thought of him in," Mihai grinned, "words and phrases that would make every ear in the country burn if they could have heard them and that would have left even Petru openmouthed with wonder."

"Carol always was good at that." They burst through the door to find a relaxed Carol flirting with a waitress. "Hi. What's your hurry?" Carol asked, looking at his two friends quizzically. The waitress took one look at the three and decided she had duties elsewhere.

"I..." Mihai was at a loss for words for once.

"We heard you had problems," said Fane, "and asked Mihai to bring me and meet with you."

"I'm always glad to see you but I haven't talked to Mihai for a week unless," Carol reflected a moment, "unless I was really drunk and don't remember. Did I?" he turned to Mihai.

"Well, no, I just heard..."

"About the horses and the fake cliff? Quite a fight. Where is that pesky waitress when we want her? Excuse me? Can we order?"

Orders given, Fane asked for an explanation.

"I think the director will be given a documentary on dancing in Vaslui or something exciting like that to do next," Carol said with satisfaction. "Dina loves horses, too."

"Uh..." said Fane "...Dina who?" Mihai glanced at him warningly and signaled him to lower his voice. Fane sat back in astonishment. "Not THAT Dina? The one who..."

"Who taught our esteemed leader table manners? Taught him to wipe his mouth with a napkin and not to pick his nose in public? Exactly." said Carol. "It helps to have...friends... Come, let's have a beer and catch up and, Mihai, don't believe everything you hear."

Mihai, sweeping together his equanimity and becoming his usual in-control self, leaned back against the wall and changed the subject. "I saw Pyotr last week and

176

he'd like to visit a movie set. Not work, just an interest. Can you help him out?" Carol began talking about the possibility and Fane excused himself as soon as possible and returned to Leri. He couldn't say why he was uneasy about Carol's episode, perhaps the power Carol had, maybe being too close to the center of politics. He couldn't even tell Leri, not yet, and simply deflected her questions to the developments on the housing front. His dreams of a clean, new apartment were, he realized, dust in the face of Leri's enthusiasm for the old and familiar, the echoes of a past Romania that the two of them remembered differently. Or, more precisely, he thought, that their parents remembered differently. Leri loved their cobblestone street with the old villas and their quirky roofs. Fane's head may have been in the past but he wanted the comforts of the present when he emerged from books into his life. He shrugged mentally and resigned himself to Ady Endre. At least for the time being.

"But," he asked Leri later, "How can they manage?"

"Well, the apartment wasn't nationalized — we sort of knew that because we pay our rent to them," she replied, "and as for selling it, I mean, I'm not sure but the laws are changing and I don't know exactly, but they have a friend who helped them when the nationalizing was going on, he's in the Housing Authority..."

"...the one who helped us when we moved here?"

"I think so..."

"And now the same friend might help with further paperwork if they decide to sell it?"

"They haven't said anything specific, but I have the impression that it might be managed."

"Romania is a land where everything can be managed." Fane was half joking, half upset but if it made Leri happy, she was the one who did the most in the house. He hugged and congratulated her for putting this together. "It's splendid!" he said.

It was all right, Fane later thought. In fact, it was more than okay. The Dumitrescus found they enjoyed Craiova ("Much more than I had thought we would," Mrs. Dumitrescu confided to Leri, "though of course we missed you...") and though managing various transfers of residence permits and property was a lengthy and difficult — and expensive — process things eventually fell into place and the Vulceans found themselves the owners of a small, not very convenient apartment with an untidy entrance and a growing, lovely lilac tree outside their kitchen window. Leri was thrilled and insisted they celebrate when everything was finally concluded. Carol and Mihai were invited.

"I have a problem," said Mihai. "I'm not sure I can come that evening."

"Why not?"

"I'm supposed to have dinner with Pyotr. I need to see him but...could I bring him?...It might work well, since he would see firsthand some of the progress Romania is making."

"But," Fane felt a bit trapped. "We couldn't begin to give him the kind of meal that would be appropriate."

Mihai laughed. "You're forgetting that he slept in our hayloft! Don't worry — I'll bring some wine. And I know the kind of miracles Leri can work with food. And so much is available now."

Leri fretted for the rest of the week about the event but in the end produced a superb array of food set prettily on a tiny table in the front room that was formerly the Dumitrescus'. The evening light filtered through trees into the curtained, high windows on the street side of the house and the atmosphere (except for Daniela's mess in the entry, whispered Leri as the two stood by the front door) was magical. Since it was summer the market was full of fresh vegetables so summer squash and dill, eggplant salad, and a lovely platter of radishes, green onions, boiled eggs and cold cuts together with country cheese and fresh bread invited them all to eat well.

"We don't exactly know how we're going to arrange the house," Fane replied to Carol's question after they had talked of this and that and the old days just after the war. He took a swallow of the white wine that Mihai had brought, savoring its dry sweet scent of summer—he'd have to remember this brand, if he could ever find it again. "The arrangement is a bit awkward but some day we want to make a little dining room where the kitchen is now, then a kitchen where the storeroom is..."

"Might there be a need of, um, a second bedroom for a small addition to the family at some point?" Carol didn't usually beat around the bush. "You have the room now."

Leri blushed and said, "Maybe now..." Fane smiled with pleasure then deflected the question with another one. "But why aren't you getting married? You have plenty of women—surely one of then must be desperate enough to want you? You'd be a good father."

"I'm not sure of that but I am sure that I'm still the happy bee, buzzing from flower to flower."

"I envy you," Pyotr put in. By this time his Romanian, though accented, was flawless—one of the plus points for Soviet diplomatic training, noted Fane. "I'd love to get married but don't have things in place to do it yet." Mihai looked at him and looked away without changing the expression on his face.

"Why not?" asked Carol.

"It's a matter of my position here and...I don't have a girlfriend in Russia and girlfriends in Romania aren't..." Pyotr stopped and Fane, realizing what he was going to say but couldn't—that Pyotr couldn't risk getting involved with a Romanian woman and, in any case, it was probably forbidden, changed the subject again. But that night he and Leri decided that it was time to have children. Then they acted on the decision with enthusiasm.

Starting a family was easy to think about and certainly the way to do it was more than pleasant, Fane reflected some weeks and months later, but getting results...there simply weren't any results. Leri was as regular in her monthlies as always except when, before, she had been pregnant. Come to think of it, there hadn't been any accidents in the past couple of years...

"It was so easy when we didn't want to," she said. "I don't understand why it's so difficult now."

"Don't' worry, it'll happen," Fane comforted her.

"But when?"

Finally they decided Leri needed to see a doctor. She made an appointment with the gynecologist she had gone to for her abortions, but this appointment was during regular clinic hours and didn't have to be secret. After the examination, he sat and talked to her. "I can't find anything wrong. The next step should be to see if there is any problem with your husband but some men don't want to even think that they..."

"I'll talk to my husband," Leri interjected, understanding his meaning. "I have no idea..." But to her surprise, Fane agreed readily to be tested. The two of them met the doctor in his clinic, nervously waiting to hear the results.

"I'm happy to say that you, Mr. Vulcean, should have no trouble becoming a father."

"But then," asked Leri, "am I the problem?"

"My dear lady," the doctor replied, "not that I can see but sometimes certain...procedures...can be very hard on the body. You have seen me, how many times, four?"

"Five," said Leri, her face white. She held herself together until they reached home, then turned and sobbed. "Fane, I knew it. I knew it."

"What?" he asked.

"God is punishing me for killing my children. This is a punishment from God." Fane put his arms around her and they sat on the bed, still in its old place. "No, no, you'll be all right, we'll try some more, everything will be fine," was all he could say but they both knew that it wouldn't be all right, not about children. Some time later Leri asked, "Will you still love me if I can't have babies?" At this point Fane wept.

"You are my life," was all he could say and he kept repeating it, holding her, rocking the two of them back and forth in pain.

It's such good whisky, Fane thought, swirling the last bit of faintly colored water around melting ice cubes in the faceted crystal glass. And good, heavy crystal. We make crystal here, why isn't it as good? This glass makes the Scotch taste better, but that's nonsense. Fane swallowed the bit of liquid and wondered if he dared face Victor again for just one more drink. It was cold outside and...

"Hello, Fane, my dear!" Silvia, the journalist, kissed him warmly and Fane returned her embrace, mentally moving into a state of high alert. The woman was invariably trouble.

Silvia didn't beat around the bush. "I just heard a rumor that Mihai Sirbu is working for the Voice of America in the US! He was your friend, wasn't he?"

"Really!" Fane answered. "Mihai Sirbu! You do have a talent for finding interesting stories! How did he ever..."

"You hadn't heard?"

"Nothing. I don't think I've even heard Sirbu's name for years. Tell me all about it." Fane took her by the elbow and moved her toward the bar, leaning close to hear a confidence.

He should have seen the signs, Fane thought after the sorry business was finally behind them. But the whole thing was so unthinkable, who could have known? Probably Carol, who always had been so much more worldlywise and was certainly exposed to more through the world of film. I mean, he justified it to himself, I knew about, had heard of, but Mihai...

Fane and Carol learned, after Mihai had returned from Moscow, that he was to be in the First Directorate, dealing with the Soviet Union. "I wasn't part of the elite group," said Mihai once, sometime later and a bit bitter. "I missed out on that—those people were chosen right out of high school and then given a really first class education in diplomacy.

Our training was okay and, in any case, diplomacy wasn't..." "...the primary focus," Carol finished the sentence for him.

"You said it, not me," replied Mihai. "THOSE people didn't come back to Romania to work at menial job in the Ministry as I did..."

"Come on," interjected Carol, "you weren't exactly a janitor."

"You know what I mean," Mihai brushed the interruption aside, hardly noticed it, "but they got to intern in a Soviet Embassy in their country of specialization before getting plum assignments. I studied English—I'm good at languages—and hoped that this would at least get me Canada but it didn't. I'm here. But I've gained a lot being here that they haven't, I've learned, I've developed some allies, and there are other factors..." The other two knew he meant his real profession as well as the ongoing dogfight between the faction in the 'forces' that wanted 'closer ties' with the Soviet Union and those that were more nationalistic in orientation. "Anyway, I've done all right and I should be posted abroad, to a good Embassy, maybe US but more likely Moscow, in a couple of years."

"If it's the US, you'll have to invite us to come visit!" joked Carol.

"My splendid apartment next to the White House is at your disposition," retorted Mihai, bowing formally. "Come tomorrow!"

"I can't come tomorrow, unfortunately, as I have to make another date. Fane," Carol turned his body along with the conversation, "tomorrow is your anniversary, yours and Leri's, isn't it?"

"Yes, that's right."

"Would you do us the honor of joining us for dinner in Cismigiu? At the restaurant there? And you, as well, Mihai. I would like you to meet a friend of mine."

"A...female friend? Has the butterfly found his flower? I'm all ears," Fane's questions fell over each other. "Pyotr and I were meeting..." Mihai tentatively started.

"Bring Pyotr, and it's definitely a flower but whether the nectar will keep this butterfly remains to be seen. Still..."

They all met the following evening for a stroll through the Park before dinner. The weather was perfect. Trees and flowers were reflected in the still lakes, their images broken only by serenely floating swans. Carol's lady friend was beautiful and friendly, eager to make a good impression. "Come, Leri and Fane, let me take your anniversary picture!" Carol had bought a new camera and was eager to try it out. "You two look like movie stars tonight!" Carol's date nodded enthusiastically, Leri blushed and murmured a deflective word while Fane, looking at her, thought it was true, she was the loveliest woman he had ever seen. "Go stand on the bank, so I can get the swan behind you...Fane, kiss Leri...no, like you meant it...move just a bit to the right...more..." SPLASH "Oh, my God!" SPLASH SQUAWK Leri screamed, the girlfriend screamed, Fane swore, the swan screeched, "You've killed the swan!" "You'll drown!" "God damn it!"

"SQU-WAKKK!"

"What's going on here?" The policeman's voice cut through the laughter and screaming. Fane and Leri managed to stand up in the shallow lake. The swan they had fallen on, his dignity offended but otherwise in good if loud form, squawked once again and sailed off, outrage in every line.

"Come with me, I'm going to have to arrest you for trying to kill a swan."

In the ensuing babble of voices Pyotr's Russian accent, suddenly much more pronounced, cut through the noise.

"Officer, was there any harm done?"

"Who are you? Let me see your identity card."

"I'm with the Russian Embassy...here it is."

"Yes, sir." The policeman, not wanting to become involved with a foreign diplomat, mentally stepped back. At that point Carol moved in. "Thank you very much for understanding", he said, patting the policeman on the shoulder and expertly moving his hand down to slip a note into the officer's hand. "We do need to get our friends to where they can dry off, especially as it's their wedding anniversary."

"Well, I wouldn't want to dampen their spirits on this occasion." Everyone laughed at the policeman's humor and ignored his surreptitious pocketing of Carol's money. "Just don't do it again."

"We won't!" promised Leri. The group watched the policeman depart and dissolved into helpless laughter. "I can't believe..." "I'm such a mess..." "Pyotr, you saved the day..." "You looked so funny standing there!"

Carol's 'flower' was quite fetching and, Fane and Leri later agreed, all wrong for Carol. Apparently Carol thought the same as there was no further mention of her.

At another time Fane asked Mihai a question that had been nagging at his orderly mind. "If your specialization is Political...where does Pyotr fit in? He's in the Military. Or does Political include Military?" Mihai looked uncomfortable as Fane raised the subject.

"He doesn't fit into my work profile, in fact, not just because of the geography but because my specialty is political relations and treaties, not defense but...there is our history with him and Vladimir and it was an opening that 'they' wanted followed up on so the Ministry agreed..."

This was more than Mihai had openly admitted to either before, and the whole conversation was perhaps more than Fane wanted to know, so he changed the subject and stopped thinking about it.

Eventually Mihai was posted abroad. He had a short assignment in Lagos ("On the surface because I speak English and there was a vacancy, but it really was because X in the Personnel Section hated me but I fixed it...it just took a little time," he said after he returned) and some years later he was finally sent to Washington. In both Embassies he wrote Fane letters to be shared with Carol — letters which didn't really say much but which Fane kept in spite of Leri's grumbling about a lack of space.

None of this was in Fane's mind when he was unexpectedly called to meet Popescu. Over the years the Chief Accountant and Fane had become, if not close friends, colleagues with mutual understanding and warm respect for one another. It hadn't taken Fane long to realize that the Institute employees who were responsible for the mechanics of the place, from the doorman to the Chief Accountant, were desirable 'friends' and he genuinely liked Popescu. He was, therefore, a bit surprised by the tone of the summons as well as by the place. 'Protocol' was the term used for kind of the meetings held in the small room just to the left of the entrance hall of the Institute, but Fane and everyone else knew that it was for meetings with people who should be kept at a distance from the Institute's work and people. Everyone also believed, with some basis, Fane thought, that the room was wired for recording.

When Fane entered he saw Popescu, a mid-level researcher from the Institue who never seemed to get anything of importance completed and whose name Fane had somewhere in the back of his mind, Radu, yes it was Radu, Radu something...as well as another man, someone Fane had never seen before, seated at the long, green felt covered table that nearly filled the room. Some papers were on the table top, there was an old and dark oil painting on the wall and there were a few books to be used as gifts on a bookshelf behind them. Otherwise the small room was empty, devoid of life or activity and exuded the smell of a space seldom used. "Come in, Comrade Vulcean," said Popescu formally. "Take a seat. Comrades," turning to the other two men, "may I introduce Comrade Vulcean." He didn't introduce the other man. By this time Fane knew something was wrong but he kept his face, if not smiling, dialed to a pleasant setting. "And now," Popescu continued, "I will excuse myself." Avoiding Fane's gaze but otherwise with an impassive face, the older man rose and left the room. The other researcher glanced at Fane and looked down at the table.

"Comrade Vulcean," began the strange man, looking first at the papers spread in front of him, then glaring directly at Fane. "You ARE Comrade Stefan Vulcean."

At this point, Fane knew there was a problem. "Yes, Comrade, I am."

"I also believe you know Mihai Sirbu."

"Yes, Comrade. He is my cousin."

"You know him rather well, it seems."

"Yes, Comrade. His parents died and he came to live with my family when we were both...six or seven years old. We went to school together and roomed together at the University." Fane's palms started to sweat but he continued to hold his face in pleasant neutral.

"When did you last see him?"

"Before he left for Washington, in the United States."

"I know where Washington is, Comrade."

"Yes, Comrade."

"Where is Mihai Sirbu now?"

Fane was dismayed at the question but didn't show it.

"I...in Washington at our Embassy as far as I know."

"Have you received letters from him?"

"Yes, Comrade, I have."

186

"Do you have the letters?"

"I have them at home, Comrade."

"You knew, of course, that your cousin, Mihai Sirbu, is a homosexual?"

Fane suddenly felt sick. Unbidden, the thought of that long ago summer night Mihai had reached over and touched him came to mind and Fane wondered if he could keep from vomiting. He hardly heard the two men speaking through his shock until the stranger said, a bit more sympathetic, "It seems you didn't know."

"No, Comrade," Fane managed to say, "I didn't." Of course, he should have realized, he thought to himself. The talk about girlfriends but not a single one ever produced but, no, wait, don't think, pay attention.

"It seems he hid it well," the interrogator remarked. "And now you can think of signs that you didn't notice, is that so?"

"Perhaps I can, Comrade. But there was nothing I ever saw," he had to be careful, to protect Mihai if it was possible, "that positively indicated such a thing to me or others."

"Absolutely nothing?"

No one would know about the hayloft, ever..."No, only the fact that we never met any of the girls he was dating. None was serious enough, he once told us."

"That's because those 'girls' were men. Or a man. You know that homosexuality is not only a sin in the eyes of God, but a crime in the eyes of the State."

"Yes, Comrade," Fane answered though, his thoughts slipped away again, there certainly must be far worse crimes than what one did in private. The researcher — Fane now realized he was the Securitate agent for the Insitute and wondered, fleetingly, why they had chosen such a dud — shifted uncomfortably. His slight movement made Fane wonder something else.

The interrogation continued for nearly an hour, going over every aspect of Mihai's and Fane's life. Fane answered as openly and honestly as possible, concealing only those few things that really needed to be concealed. Strangely enough, neither Mr. Eichmann or Uncle Vanya was mentioned and Fane volunteered nothing. Finally the exhausting session was brought to an end.

"This is enough for today, Comrade. Please come tomorrow with the letters you have received from Mihai Sirbu." It's strange, Fane thought, that he keeps using his full name. "And don't speak of this to anyone, not even your wife. I would like to thank you for your full and continued cooperation." Fane murmured some appropriate response, pushed back his chair and edged out of the room. As he closed the door behind him, he heard the researcher's voice, "...that he's a decent man, good reputation, and didn't..." He hoped the man would help him, Hristu, that was his name, Radu Hristu. Would he? He'd always been friendly to him, he thought, just not close. Fane didn't want to go to prison, be taken away from the Institute, damn Mihai, what was happening to him, was he all right? Was he...

The Institute's closing time had come and gone so Fane gathered his things, passed through deserted rooms, left through the door saluting the doorman only by rote, and walked home in a fog. By the time he reached Ady Endre he could barely hold himself together. He had to talk this over with Leri...no, they had told him not to, but...the telephone he had managed to get last year with such difficulty and use of this and that contact, not to mention money...was it tapped? Leri said most phones were tapped but that was different than having a microphone in the house, but she said they had microphones...could they talk anywhere? Maybe he shouldn't talk...

Fane pushed through the gate barely noticing where he was and mechanically climbed the curving, dark stairway to his haven, his safe place. Leri wasn't home yet. It was, he remembered, the day she said she was going to visit Aunt Sanda, who hadn't been well recently and she wouldn't be here for another, he glanced at his watch, hour or so. WHAT did Mihai do? The telephone interrupted his thoughts. Fane didn't want to answer but it might be someone from the Party or the Prosecutor's Office since that man...he picked up the phone.

"Hey, Fane," Carol said, and the world jolted back into some normalcy. "I feel like talking. Meet me for a beer in half an hour?"

"I really don't want to go out right now," Fane answered. He simply didn't have enough energy to deal with Carol tonight.

"Look," he heard Carol saying, "I had something bad happen today...my favorite horse, Haiduc, the one you like so much, the bay with the white star, he broke his leg. I really need to get out." It was, Fane thought, total nonsense. Fane had never seen any of Carol's horses and the only reason Carol would talk about Haiduc was that he was sending some sort of message.

"All right. Where?"

The two met in a new bar and Carol talked about nothing in particular as they downed a quick beer. Then he stood up and said, "I'm so restless, I want to walk. Come with me," and they set off.

They walked briskly toward the park and when there was no one nearby, Carol said, "I've got some bad news."

"Mihai?"

"Oh, you know then."

"I spent the afternoon being interrogated."

"Wow. I suppose I'll be next."

"I never guessed, though I should have. I mean, I'm not exactly innocent, but still..."

"How could you possibly have known?" Carol said. "He never gave either of us the slightest hint he was going to do this."

"But the signs were there. I should have seen them..."

"What signs? Wait...are we talking about the same thing?"

"Mihai's homosexuality, isn't it?"

Carol slowed to a stop and turned to face Fane. "That's been around a long time. Mihai defected to the US yesterday."

"How do you know?" Fane's thoughts were racing back and forth across his mind till he thought his head would break. "They didn't say a thing about that to me."

"They're probably trying to find out if you knew about the defection."

Fane remembered a series of questions that were sort of...non sequiturs unless they were put into another context... "You're probably right, but why...?"

"Why not?"

"But what will happen to Mr. Eichmann...Mihai's father? They'll put him in prison, they'll..."

"That would have been a good reason except that he hung himself last night."

Fane sank onto a park bench, grateful it was there. He felt as if...as if the ground weren't under his feet any more. Mihai...his father...how could Mihai do this? How could he destroy so many lives to...to what? Have a free life in a rich country? That wasn't...

"How do you know?" was the only thing that came to him. How did Carol know all this?

"I have friends..." Carol answered vaguely and sat down beside Fane on the bench. "I don't know what's been going on, either," Carol continued, "but I suspect that Mihai has been planning it for some time, his father obviously knew something, and Pyotr was probably a key player in all this."

190

"Pyotr? They did ask me about him, quite a lot."

"Fane...did you really not know?"

"Know? About...Mihai...it was Pyotr. Of course." Fane didn't know how he had missed it and said so in despair. "I should have done something! I should have made him..."

"Do what?"

"Shit. I don't know. I just don't know."

"For once, neither do I."

Fane brought his letters to the Institute the next day and went over them with the nameless Comrade and over, again and again, his knowledge of Mihai, his whole life both that day and the part of the following day. It was both more difficult and easier to answer, now that he knew what was going on but apparently his answers were good enough to satisfy the authorities. At the end of the interrogation, he still didn't know the 'Comrade's' name and he was never officially told what it was all about.

He didn't ask, either.

The final piece of the puzzle fell into place when Carol found out that Pyotr abruptly returned to Moscow. There were no good-byes.

"So Pyotr was..."

"Either trapping Mihai on orders or he wasn't, and if he wasn't he's in deep shit."

"I don't know whether to feel sorry for him or not. He's always been good to us."

"Right. We'll probably never know."

"Poor Mihai—do you suppose he knows?"

"Why poor Mihai?" Carol asked, puzzled. "He's in the US where he can do whatever he likes."

"Because if he cared about Pyotr, and I think he did, he's either been betrayed or his friend is on his way to Siberia. And his father is dead."

"Yeah, I see what you mean. It's a putrid mess."

It was and maybe, Fane later thought, 'putrid mess' described the way the ground felt under his feet for the next days and weeks. As soon as he could, Fane traveled, this time without Leri, to see Uncle Vanya and Aunt Ana. He wanted their wisdom and comfort but he found them as shaken has he had been. Uncle Vanya, looking much older than he had on Fane's previous trip a few months before, tried to explain as they sat in the cozy, familiar sitting room. As he talked, Fane looked around, trying to concentrate but also thinking of all the conversations, heated and cerebral, eager and angry, that had taken place in this room. And now Uncle Vanya was telling him that so much was useless.

"I've come to believe," the older man said, "that the Party has too much power and isn't using it wisely." Aunt Anna nodded in agreement.

"Uh, why? It is because of this? Because things are really getting better, much better. And we've gained much more independence from the USSR." Fane thought back over the various steps first Gheorghiu-Dej and now Ceausescu had taken to lift Russian control from Romania — including restoring the founder, Nicolae Iorga's, name to his Institute. And rehabilitating not only historians but writers and artists. Not the Royal Famly, though...but there was more stuff in the shops and...

"I think this incident, the loss of my beloved friend Iacob, the loss — because he's lost to us forever as well — of Mihai, these things may have been the tipping point for Anna and me, but it started much earlier." Fane focused his attention on Uncle Vanya's words again.

"For me, it really started with the purge of intellectuals in 1956, where so many of our friends suffered for no good reason," said Aunt Anna quietly. Uncle Vanya nodded and proceeded to name several people, some of whom Fane knew, who had been dismissed from employment and given menial labor, thrown in prison, persecuted in various ways through the fifties.

With some surprise, Fane said, "I hadn't realized...I guess being in the Institute and buried in research...I heard stuff, of course, but tried to stay away from politics, even discussing it at that point, and didn't know how much was true and in any case, a lot of it seemed justified." As he talked, Fane found he sounded lamer and lamer even to himself. There was no real excuse. He had known. He just hadn't wanted to think about it.

"I don't think it was justified, Fane," replied Uncle Vanya interrupting Fane's thoughts. The older man stood up and walked around the small room, agitated. "I knew these people here in Radauti and Suceava—you did as well—and they were true patriots. Some of them might not have believed in the Movement, but they were honest, good people and I have to believe they weren't the only honest and good people who suffered. But that was just the start. We'd already had problems with collectivization up here and with the way it was administered, but it kept changing, and no one knew what was going to happen. Then Anna and I wanted to visit some friends in Austria."

"But it's almost impossible to get a visa to leave to the West!"

"That's it. That's exactly it. We couldn't go. Why? Why shouldn't we be allowed to travel if things here are so good? Why can't we see how other countries are doing things and bring back ideas? And why are you looking so astounded? Do you think I don't ponder things like this? Haven't you thought about them?"

Feeling like a chastised child, Fane squirmed in his chair. Of all the adults in his life, Uncle Vanya was one of the two or three most influential, one of the two, along with Professor Brebean, that he respected most. Why hadn't he thought of all this? What was wrong with him? "I don't know," he finally said. "I guess I've been so wrapped up in the details of living, buried in my research, and so pleased with what I saw around me, the new buildings, the better food..."

"You're right," said Uncle Vanya sitting down again and lowering his voice. "You're right and you're probably representative of a lot of people in the country, and that may be part of the problem or it may be why it's not going to be a problem at all...the way our Movement is going. You don't know what it was like Before...but I also have to remember that Before there was great hunger and poverty for many..."

"But you've always been..." Fane's voice faded away.

"...a passionately convinced communist?" Uncle Vanya finished the sentence for him. "I was, which makes all of this," he made an inclusive gesture at nothing in particular, "all of this that's happening, that Iacob gave his life, for...shit?" "Vanya," Aunt Anna protested softly.

"And Mr. Eichmann's death, Mihai's defection...what do they mean? I guess I know what it says about our country, but what do they mean for us? It's important, right?" "What do they mean?" echoed Uncle Vanya thoughtfully. "You don't know this either." It was more a statement than a question.

"Uh...I do." Fane had put this part together but hadn't made it real by saying it. "I know that Mr. Eichmann has been a sort of...protector...for us, Carol and Mihai and me. He paid the tuition at the *liceu*, helped us out with the University. I don't know whether he had something to do with my getting the job at the Institute but..."

"You did that on your own merit," said Uncle Vanya, realizing immediately Fane's self-doubt and moving to erase it. "But your merit might not have come to the attention of the Institute of History without Iacob's help. Or it might have been more difficult to...arrange things."

"And, of course, you helped us enormously as well, helping my family during the famine..." Fane rushed to say.

"I was glad to do what I could but that wasn't much with Iacob's extra..." The two men remained silent for a few seconds then Uncle Vanya sighed. "But it isn't all in the past

194

and that's the problem. Iacob is gone, my best friend, and with him the protection and assistance he gave all of us. And THAT is part of the problem with the system," he added savagely. Fane had never seen him so angry before. "Why do we have to have 'someone in Bucharest'? Why don't things work...normally? What is normal? Why don't things work without having to have connections, people, bribes..."

Fane was nonplussed, remembering without wanting to the stream...no, not stream, trickle, but still...the trickle of little requests that came to him from Poiana Cozonac and Bilca and occasionally from other places he visited and did research and made friends and connections. He'd not really thought about it, done it consciously, built his network, he had just...talked to one person or another on behalf of...for a position in the military...admission to a school in Bucharest...they weren't important or difficult things like Father Ion's arrest...but people needed his help to...get things done...that was just...how it was...

"And now, Mihai's defection..." Fane's stomach, as usual, knotted at the thought. Not just the loss of Mihai but the problems Mihai might cause him and everyone else, and he hated himself for putting that before Mihai's welfare or absence from his life.

"Fane, we'll get through this," Uncle Vanya put his arm around the younger man, reaching up slightly but seeming to Fane to be the taller and stronger of the two...for a fleeting moment. "We'll get through this," Uncle Vanya repeated, "even if it might be difficult. Don't worry."

The three continued talking for a long time, exploring not just the present but history and what life had meant to individuals living at different points in Romania's past, then returning to and debating the present with an honesty and openness Fane hadn't encountered before. Later he looked back at the conversation and realized two things. The first was that he rarely talked seriously about the present with anyone. Carol had no taste for such discussions, Leri's views were firm and different than his and, well, she was a woman...and there was no one else in Bucharest besides Mihai he trusted enough.

And Mihai used to be busy and evasive. Now he was just gone.

The second was that, for the first time in his life, he seriously disagreed with someone he loved and respected and admired. Uncle Vanya had a lot of right on his side but in the end, Fane thought, he was wrong. The advances were worth it, worth the sacrifices, people's lives were all right.

"It was lovely, as always, talking to you." Fane took Silvia's hand, leaned down and kissed it, lingering just enough to flatter her into thinking he found her attractive. He had managed to work the conversation around to where Silvia felt good about giving him news...not that there was much of it. Someone had heard Mihai talking on a Voice of America program about the US legal system and there were unflattering comparisons to the ways things worked in Eastern Europe. No surprise, that last, coming from VOA. But Mihai...

One thing, though, Fane realized. It had taken all his will power to focus attention on Silvia and avoid saying anything he shouldn't have. He gazed regretfully at the empty whisky glass and put it down on a nearby end table. The party was nearly over anyway.

It seemed as if both Fane and Carol had satisfied the authorities that they had nothing to do with Mihai's defection and knew nothing about it. As the days, weeks and months went by neither was contacted again. Life gradually settled into the rhythm it had had when Mihai was in Moscow or abroad except now there were no letters to share with Carol over their weekly meal. There never would be letters, any contact, it was like Mihai had died along with his father and with him part of Fane's life. Fane lived with a constant ache somewhere in his heart.

Mihai...not even a real relative, he thought angrily, but at the same time his brother in the truest sense of the word. Gone.

Fane threw himself into work and into redoing the storeroom at the back of the apartment, making it into a small kitchen where they were able to put the refrigerator, have modern cupboards and a gas stove.

"You can't imagine how convenient it is," said Leri. "What a wonderful kitchen and now we have a real dining room. Sort of." She looked around the small cheerful space that used to be the kitchen. It was tiny but there were two windows looking out on the courtyard and the lilac tree. Between the windows was, of course, a bookcase; on the wall opposite the stove was a sleek new matching breakfront for glasses and china and a host of other things. It was, in some ways, the pleasantest room in the apartment. Fane's little cream plate with the green and gold deer was moved to the wall above the table just below a painting.

"Then why," asked Fane from his seat by the table, "did you still keep the old wood stove in here? It takes up a lot of room."

"Because it provides warmth in winter and, besides, there are some things that just taste better if they are cooked over a real fire." Fane didn't point out that the modern stove had an open gas flame. Women were just stubborn about some things.

In time the tiny dining room turned into the "everything" room, where Leri sat at the small table and planned her lessons or where Fane wrote. They had kept their bedroom in the same room, the one that they had to walk through to get to the kitchen, and used the front room for reading, entertaining occasional guests, and watching television. Fane had, as Leri knew he would, filled it with more bookshelves. A few spaces were left open for some small paintings Leri had received from her family and one entire wall was devoted to Fane's print collection. It was, he often thought with satisfaction, quite good—he had managed to find prints by many of the artists in his dissertation, Raffet, Mayer, Bartlett, Bouquet...even one after Cherubino who had visited Romania in 1826 although the print was done later but... and the ongoing hunt for more was now as exciting as the hunt for books.

Leri used the odd unfilled or semi-empty bookshelf for momentos and knickknacks. The apartment had turned into a comfortable home where the only annoyance was Daniela downstairs. In an inherited arrangement, Fane and Leri had the side yard to use and Daniela the front. The front was overgrown. "Thank goodness there are so many bushes so people can't see what a mess it is," said Leri. The side yard was Fane's and in the narrow, tiny space he grew an assortment of flowers that passersby invariably complimented. 'The peasant part of me," Fane sometimes thought as he surveyed his handiwork.

Fane's professional life bloomed like his flower garden. The work he and Director Dragomir had done on medieval history had been well-received—very well-received as first Dragomir then Fane as well had put in flattering references to current leadership in the last few articles, comparing Ceausescu with Stefan the Great or Michael the Brave. As he did this, insertions after the meat of the work was already finished, Fane remembered the distant boy who talked to Haiduc of the deeds they would do and smiled at the dreams this history evoked even then. He was even able to remember Haiduc with only a fond pang, resolutely pushing away the anger and hatred for his father surrounding the horse's death.

Both men were in considerable demand as speakers and, as Fane privately admitted to himself and occasionally indicated to Leri, Fane was the more popular as he had a folksy, engaging way of presenting the same facts that were dry as dust in Dragomir's talks. Fane was careful not to be perceived in the Institute as the more sought-after of the two though he suspected Dragomir knew—and didn't care. The Director had continued to increase in bulk as well as in age and moving about was clearly laborious, even with the Institute car at his command.

Fane continued to travel, with and without Leri, to give lectures, to do research, on vacation. They both visited the Monastery at Sucevita at least once a year, spending time with Father Augustin. It was there that they met their neighbors in Bucharest.

Leri had gone into the forest to look for the wild strawberries of June. Dappled sunlight filtering through the trees made it hard to see and she had bent over to examine a profusion of plants at the edge of a small clearing when she heard another woman's voice, obviously educated, obviously not from the area.

"Good morning. Have you lost something?" Straightening up and shaking her head slightly to clear it, Leri saw a slim blond about her own age. "Oh...no," Leri replied. "I was looking for wild strawberries."

"Strawberries? Do they grow here?" Leri wondered how someone wouldn't know such an elementary piece of information but answered politely. "Yes, and it's just the season. Look!" She leaned down and picked one. "Silly me—I have been looking and looking and not seeing anything and here some are, right under my nose. Try it." She held out the tiny red object.

"It's so sweet! I never thought...let me help you."

As they picked and looked and ate and picked they exchanged bits and pieces of information. Rodica was staying in the village with her husband. They were on vacation. She worked in the Meridiane Publishing House and her husband was a hydrologist. No, they didn't have children...they had wanted to but... Leri changed the subject. "Where in Bucharest do you live?" she asked.

"On a small street behind the May 1 market. It's called Ady Endre."

Leri stood up and gasped in delight. "Don't tell me that. Ady Endre is our steet. We're at number 16!"

"The house with the lovely side garden and..." Rodica paused in consideration of her new friend.

"...and the overgrown front garden, you meant to say? Our downstairs neighbor..." No more explanation was needed on that topic as both laughed together.

Rodica and Leri wasted no time introducing their husbands and the friendship, begun in Bukovina, continued in Bucharest. Shortly after they had returned from Sucevita, Leri met Fane one afternoon with the news that Rodica and Emil had invited them to a concert.

"A concert? Where?"

"In their house. Not exactly a concert", she said, "but Emil and his father both play the violin and they meet with friends to read through various pieces. When I talked with Rodica about how much we enjoyed music, she invited me." "Talked with Rodica? When was this?"

"Just yesterday, we were both at the Piata at the same time. You know, I've seen her there before but..." Leri continued to talk and Fane continued to listen.

Sunday afternoon they walked through warm summer sunlight to the other end of the street. Rodica and Emil lived in a larger house, obviously it had been quite grand at one point, with Emil's parents. The families had the ground floor and at the back a room, more like a conservatory with its glass windows across the rear had been cleared for the players and a group of about six guests. A bed shoved against the wall showed that the room wasn't dedicated to music but any other activities became immaterial once the four musicians raised their bows and began to play. The sun caught a few motes of dust through the windows, the music wove itself around the audience, it was how things should be, Fane thought. After the music the musicians and 'audience' had tea and Fane was able express his pleasure at being able to see the interaction among the musicians, to really hear the music as it was meant to be played. Emil, who had played second violin, was visibly pleased.

Walking back to their apartment, Fane contemplated the day and his life, the Institute and his work, Leri, their little house with satisfaction. "It really doesn't get much better than this," he said to his wife.

"It was wonderful, wasn't it? I think," Leri said wistfully, "that this is what it must have been like Before."

"Before?"

"You know, before...the war, everything."

Fane's ebullience leaked out, deflating the day. "Oh," was all he could say but he thought to himself,

Before...before...I was a peasant kid with dirty hands and an empty stomach and a head that itched. Doesn't she undertand the real world?

In spite of the momentary unpleasantness a good memory of the afternoon lingered and it proved to be the first of many such afternoons and of other points of mutual bonding. All four enjoyed good food and light music as well as classical. They met almost weekly, Sunday evenings, sometimes after a musical soiree, sometimes not, eating at first one house then another, and Carol soon became a welcome part of the group.

The bonding was complete for the women when Leri learned that Rodica had wanted children but couldn't have any.

"I...I'm in the same position," said Leri. "When we didn't have the room to have children..." her voice trailed off and tears came into her eyes.

"Oh, my dear!" Rodica moved toward Leri and took her into her arms. "The same thing..." With that, the women were united and the men, almost in self-defense, began sharing their own experiences and opinions.

"You know," Fane told Leri after a particularly interesting discussion on Romania's international position one evening, "I think I can talk with Emil about almost anything." Except, he added privately to himself, "Mihai."

"I'm glad you have someone to be close to now that..." she paused. "I mean, you talk with Carol about a lot but he..."

"He doesn't like political subjects and, once in a while, it's good to explore ideas."

"But I'm worried about one thing," said Leri.

"What?" Fane's attention was caught. A problem?

"I'm not sure Rodica and Emil are getting along as well as they might," Leri said hesitantly. "She's said a couple of things...

Fane was relieved...Leri's worry wasn't about Emil or Rodica's betraying confidences. He didn't think...but still...Leri had a good instinct for such things. Then he kicked himself — he, Fane, should worry if his friends had problems.

But the discussions continued and there was a lot to talk about. Over the same years external events had come and gone without the opportunity to discuss them outside the family circle. Fane and Leri were both proud of Romania's support of Czechoslovakia in 1968. At the same time, the President's visit to China had introduced some elements into his talks that the chattering classes, to which Fane listened without putting forth more than genial good will, found potentially unpleasant. On the other hand, there were some openings to the West. The American Library was established, quietly and without fanfare but still, it was actually allowed to open and although Fane wasn't among those invited to any events there and although nothing was ever in the newspaper about its activities, gossip went around about movies, concerts, and talks. There was an individual in the Institute who would borrow books for others there and at the French and British Libraries. It was, in fact, Hristu who had been at the meeting about Mihai which Fane didn't want to remember...but Fane had little interest in their collections and didn't, in any case, read easily in either language.

"I do wish, though, that we could see the movies and I understand there is a jazz performance next week at the American Library," he told Leri.

"Could your person at the Institute borrow books for me? Novels?" Leri asked. She did read enough English, Fane thought, but the risk... Nothing ever came of it.

Two events jolted Fane out of an increasingly comfortable existence.

The first came about with the return of another friend, a specialist in American history who had gone to the United States on a Fulbright grant. He lived in one of the identical rows of apartment blocks lining May 1 Boulevard and Fane ran into him as they waited for milk in the *piata*. He'd just returned the day before and Fane was interested in how US universities were organized in comparison with Romanian, a safe topic in a crowd that cared little about it. After they had stood in line and finally received a liter of milk each, Fane asked as they walked away from the crowd, "Is something bothering you, Caius? You seem upset."

Caius looked around to see if anyone was listening. "I shouldn't say anything but...we got in last night and our son was hungry. He wanted some milk, so I started to go out to buy it."

"But you can't get milk at night, the shop isn't open," Fane said, puzzled.

"That's just it. 'There' you can buy milk—anything, coffee, meat, a refrigerator, a car—whenever you want. In the cities there are stores selling food and other small items that are open 24 hours a day."

"Oh, I see. But they're capitalists..."

"And with all the problems of capitalism. We're lucky to live here, where we don't have the bad influences that are ubiquitous there. I am particularly glad to have my son back here where he isn't subject to that degenerate stuff." Fane glanced back and saw two men standing suspiciously close.

"As I said," Fane replied smoothly, "things are going very well here in Romania—you'll find enormous improvements since you left last year." The two exchanged a few more sentences then bid each other farewell and went their different directions. Fane was relieved that neither of the men followed him or Caius. Probably they weren't anything special but you never knew...

But why should it be a problem? And why, if things were going so well in communist Romania, did milk have to be rationed? Why, in fact, was there less in the shops now, come to think of it, at least it seemed that way, than there used to be? Uncle Vanya's words, never far from the surface, rose again in his mind. "It's not working..."

The second event was a face to face encounter with the Securitate—with the same man, in fact, who had interrogated Fane about Mihai. This time he introduced himself. Fane had just come out of the Faculty of History where he had given a lecture when he felt, rather than saw, someone beside him.

"Excellent lecture," the man said. "You are a very good speaker." Fane's stomach clenched into a tight ball as he recognized the Comrade of, how many years was it now? "My name is Stefan—Fane, like yours—Fane Antonescu."

"It's a pleasure meeting you under different circumstances," said Fane smoothly. "I didn't realize you were interested in the history of Dragomirna."

"I find many aspects of Romanian history interesting, especially as my degree is in the subject," responded Antonescu politely, "but that's not why I'm here today. I wonder if you would mind stopping by my office for a few minutes to chat."

The knot in Fane's stomach got tighter. "Of course not," he replied, as easily as he could manage.

"It's not far," Antonescu said. Fane followed him toward the National Bank, then down a small alley and through a nondescript door. The narrow stairs to the floor above weren't very clean—cleanliness, Fane thought in passing, wasn't something you found in public places or government offices— but the small office he was ushered into was, on the contrary, well kept and neat.

"Please sit down," Antonescu said, gesturing toward a wooden chair in front of the desk. He, himself, walked behind the desk and sat in a leather chair, rather shabby but originally of good quality. Otherwise the office was quite empty except for a few papers on the desk. A window looked out onto a blank brick wall.

"Have you heard anything from your cousin? Mihai Sirbu?" Antonescu asked. Fane was afraid he might throw up but replied smoothly. "No, not a word since we last met."

"It was an unfortunate business, very unpleasant all around, but we..." there was a slight emphasis on the 'we', "...were impressed by you and how you handled yourself then and since then." Fane stayed quiet, wondering what was coming. Better let this man lead the conversation where he wanted it to go.

"Since then we've had occasion to hear about you, mostly about your professional success but also that you are a helpful person. Many persons in..." Antonescu consulted some papers in front of him, "uh, Poaina Cozonac and Bilca owe a great deal to you, then there was that request you had from Horezu that you dealt with very adroitly. Not, let me hasten to add, that there is anything at all wrong with this. You have, on the contrary, shown yourself to be a good communist, a good comrade, helping others when they don't understand the system. And you have gained an impressive array of contacts."

"Thank you," said Fane. He waited for Antonescu to continue.

"I see that you are regular in attendance at Party meetings, though not really active in them, and that you have written a great deal about history, history that supports the Movement and shows how Romania is on the path to true Socialism." "I try to do my best," said Fane noncommittally.

"That's why I wanted to talk to you today," Antonescu leaned back in his chair and gazed directly at Fane. "In spite of this business about your cousin, which seems to be the only black mark on your record," he paused to let the words with their thin icing of threat sink in, "you are a patriot and a committed Communist. Would you agree, Comrade?"

Fane nodded gravely. "It's an honor to me to hear you say this."

"Our country needs a bit more help from you. Are you ready?"

"How could I not be ready to help my country?"

"I'm glad you see things our way. Have you heard of the American Library?"

"The American Library?" Fane was astounded. "Behind the National Theater?" he said to gain a bit of thinking time. "Not much. I don't work in American History so there isn't much there that interests me."

"It might be useful if you were to attend the occasional film or concert, perhaps even a lecture."

"I'm not sure I understand," said Fane, by this time totally mystified as well as uncomfortable. "I don't speak English and though that wouldn't matter at concerts or films, I just don't...perhaps you could explain." Antonescu looked pleased and Fane, though he wasn't a fisherman, realized he was being played like a trout on the end of a line.

"It's quite simple. At times there are persons who...shall we say...who don't have the best interests of the nation at

206

heart and are using events at the Library as a way to, uh, develop contacts that...perhaps I shouldn't go further."

"Yes?" Fane resisted the natural temptation to ask what this had to do with him.

"What we need is simple. You go to an event, enjoy yourself, and note who else is in attendance. Nothing more." "Do I have a choice?" asked Fane in a rash lunge.

"Of course..." Antonescu let his voice trail off and the meaning was clear: Not really.

"I would be glad to do whatever is necessary for the greater good of our country," Fane said, almost by rote. "And, it's true," he added to lighten the conversation, "that my wife and I are both lovers of music."

"I regret that your wife won't be able to go with you."

"What?"

"As a teacher, she's in a sensitive position and she can't be seen at such a place."

All Fane's anxiety and anger at everything seized him on this point and his sense of caution was overwhelmed by the emotion. "It's no deal then," he said while he pushed his chair back and started to rise.

"Wait, wait...sit down...don't be angry." Antonescu saw his fish almost off the hook and about to escape. "Let me see if it might be possible...I can't guarantee anything but I'll ask."

"That's kind of you," it wasn't clear whether Fane was sincere or ironic but he then modulated his voice further. "I hope you understand. I am where and what I am as a result of the Party and its support and, in turn, I naturally want to do whatever I can to make a contribution in return, but my wife and I do almost everything together. If I were to go off without her there would be...explanations...perhaps bad feelings..."

"I do understand and, it's true, you have been quite... devoted," Antonescu really meant 'faithful' Fane realized and felt a stab of outrage at this, too, being a subject of their snooping, "to your marriage and suddenly beginning to change that pattern might...yes, that makes some sense. Changing patterns isn't a good thing." Antonescu leaned back and sat for a minute, face completely impassive except for a slight movement of his jaw. Considering something, Fane thought, and wondered what. Having clearly made some silent decision, his interlocutor began to speak again.

"Let me be honest with you. There seems to be some sort of plot, we don't know what. We aren't sure that it involves the Americans, although it might, but we are fairly sure that people are using the American Library and Embassy events as a meeting place. We need someone they don't know, someone who mixes well, who has no linkage with us, to be there, to listen. It's important to the country. I'm taking a chance with you, some of my superiors objected because of your cousin but," he paused, "I've watched you and come to believe that you really are committed to your country and its welfare. That's why you and I are sitting here today. Will you help?"

Fane felt a small stirring of pride. He could do something more important, perhaps, for his nation, for history even, than being a scholar. There was an equal stirring of doubt but it receded. "Yes, Comrade. I will do my best for you." Antonescu smiled and Fane was warmed by his charm, by the proffered friendship. They chatted a bit more, easily, and Fane began to feel almost as if he were making a new friend. Finally they rose and clasped hands.

"Thank you, Comrade," Antonescu said and smiled that warm smile again. "You are a good man." Fane left feeling good.

Until he began to think of telling Leri about the encounter. She wouldn't understand, she was so against everything to do with... Perhaps...should he not tell her? If he didn't it would probably be the first important thing they hadn't shared since their marriage but women, women didn't really need to know everything.

But Leri wasn't just a woman. She was Leri.

In the end Fane compromised, a bit uncomfortably, by telling Leri the Institute wanted a reliable person to attend events there and to know what resources there might be.

"But you aren't a specialist in the history of the United States, you don't speak English," Leri protested, "so why are they asking you and not someone else?" Leri put down a plate of stew beside the yellow *mamaliga* and went into the tiny kitchen for the bread.

"At the moment there isn't anyone else," Fane replied from his seat at their tiny dining table. The two rooms were so small and close they could converse from one to the other without raising a voice or even thinking the other wouldn't hear. His statement was, in fact, true as the only older specialist in the history of English speaking countries was indeed very old and the younger specialist was still without a doctorate and only beginning his career. Leri accepted the explanation and the following week an invitation to a concert arrived for Fane at the Institute. It was delivered by Hristu, the mid-level researcher who never did much of note.

"I gather you've been, uh, in conversation with someone," Hristu said with a bit of asperity.

"To my great surprise," Fane replied. "It wasn't anything I exactly looked for."

Hristu smiled, putting the uncomfortable moment behind them in an effort to mend fences. He was smart enough to know when to stay on good terms with people. "I suspected that you didn't know 'they' were talking about you." Fane realized that Hristu needed to be sure Fane hadn't gone behind his back to higher authority. He contined, "You'll forward your reports through me."

"Without any question, and I'll rely on your guidance."

"And it might be well if you let me know when you talk to our friend."

"Of course." Hristu was, Fane realized, worried about Fane's contact with Antonescu. 'I wonder what's going on,' Fane said to himself, and made a mental note to find out if he possibly could.

The following week Fane and Leri found themselves outside the iron fence of the American Library. It was an old building, well kept and freshly painted in contrast to the buildings around it, with a rose garden in the courtyard behind a wrought iron fence, a circular sort of drive between the garden and the three-sided buildings, and wide open gates where the two ends of the drive met the little street. "Look," said Leri, "it originally must have been two matched buildings facing one another and somehow they've been joined."

"Not quite matching," said Fane, indicating a few differences in the façades, "but close." Leri took his hand. "People are going in that middle door, shall we follow?" A mixture of power and nervousness pushing his feet forward through the open, unguarded gate, Fane led them into a small line. He tried to look around discreetly, to see if there was anyone they knew who might see them going in then mentally shrugged. He had permission. He gave their invitation to the person at the door, they found themselves handing their coats to an older woman in blue at the cloakroom, then they followed a cheerful crowd into a small auditorium with a red curtain pulled back to expose a grand piano on the stage.

"Everybody is talking so loud," whispered Leri. "Oh, look, there's Alexi." Leri waved and they both felt better. After the concert ("Very nice, I'm surprised the Americans have such good classical music," Leri whispered to Fane) they talked a bit to Alexi and overheard other friends greeting one another as they left. People seemed to be staying around but Fane felt it would be better to leave quickly.

"So that's the stronghold of the capitalists," Fane remarked once they were well away from the building and walking past the National Theater toward the bus stop. "I had expected something more...well, less ordinary I guess."

"So had I," said Leri. "It was really nice. I particularly enjoyed the Gershwin...but..." they stepped into the bus still talking and it was all very normal.

That, Fane realized, could be a problem. There was nothing, absolutely nothing out of the ordinary about the exchanges they had had and had overheard. 'Maybe next time,' he said to himself.

The 'next time' was an exhibit opening, photographs by an American photographer. The works were lovely and there were refreshments at the event. "Look," Leri said, "salami and ham and cheese...I wonder where they get them." "Look,"

said Fane, "they have Scotch whisky and gin..."

"...and juice...real juice, not flavored, colored sugar water!" added Leri. This time they saw a number of people they had seen at the concert. Alexi, who introduced them to some of the others, asked why they hadn't come to the reception after the concert. Leri and Fane looked at one another in confusion. "I hadn't..." "I didn't..." they started to say but Alexi simply laughed and said, "These Americans, they're rich. They always have receptions."

But, again, nothing out of the ordinary seemed to be happening.

"Don't worry about it," said Antonescu the next time they met. It was outside a pastry shop, seemingly by chance. The two men strolled down the street together, chatting easily. "I'll check in with you from time to time, and perhaps there won't be anything. That's all right. Do please let me know who was there and if any conversations you see seem unusually, shall we say, intense...you know, not appropriate to the relaxed setting."

"Sometimes people become very involved with ideas or points of view. At the photography exhibit, for instance, I saw Ion Miclea arguing with someone else...Radu Steflea, perhaps...but it was just about the quality of the work."

"I know about academics," Antonescu chuckled easily. "You know what I mean. Speaking of academics, have you heard..." The conversation, the first of many, continued on to general topics and Fane felt increasingly comfortable with Antonescu and their relationship. He dutifully chatted with Hristu after each meeting with Antonescu but it seemed as if Hristu wasn't quite as interested as before. Or something.

Eventually, attending events at the American Library became a normal part of life. And valued...especially for Leri. "Why do you like it so much?" Fane asked at one point. Leri looked at him in amazement.

"Don't you enjoy it?" she replied incredulously, putting her fork down on the table.

"These 'beaten beans' are wonderful, it reminds me of how Mother used to make them, lots of garlic," Fane said in passing, then returned to the subject. "Of course I enjoy a lot of the events but sometimes it's hard, going out again at night after a long day and I thought you might find it tiresome."

"Not at all! But now that you ask..." Leri reflected a moment and continued. "I think it's just pleasant—I mean, the events, the movies or exhibits, or even the talks though sometimes the translation isn't great, they're all interesting and then there are the receptions after most of them with generally mostly the same people...a lot of them we already know, some are new, there's always someone different but it's sort of...comfortable. By the way, have you heard that there will be a new Director for the Library this summer?"

"Yes. Apparently they always change after a two or three years."

"I wonder if things will be the same."

212

"I imagine so," replied Fane as he scooped up the last of his dinner against a piece of bread. "I don't think the programs are all determined here in Bucharest. The propaganda people in the US must have something to do with it."

"Whatever they do, it's interesting that the propaganda doesn't show through too boldly. Our propaganda isn't nearly as subtle or well done."

"Not exactly," agreed Fane feeling vaguely uncomfortable.

"I suppose," continued Leri, "that all they really need to do is show they are human and cultured. It's America, after all.I mean, everyone knows they have..." her voice trailed off.

"What's for dessert?" asked Fane.

"I made *gogosi*, doughnuts, for you. In celebration of the day we met!" Fane laughed with pleasure. "I'd forgotten," he admitted, "maybe because the weather is so nice today." They both laughed.

The new Director came and eventually things did change but not in a direction anyone, at least not Fane, had foreseen. Pamela, Pam as she liked to be called, had studied Romanian in Bucharest as a university student and, unlike most of the other people Fane had met from the US Embassy, spoke the language well. Fane found himself drawn increasingly into conversations with her, enjoying the intellectual exchange with an American though, of course, both stayed away from sensitive subjects. He also found he could help Pamela with the language, skillfully introducing new words and phrases until it became kind of a game for both of them. It didn't take Antonescu long to pick up on the new development.

"I hear you're becoming quite a friend with the new capitalist at the American Library," he said. Fane started in surprise. "No, it's not a problem at all," Antonescu said quickly, anticipating Fane's uneasiness. "I have to say it's not something I, we, foresaw but it's a great opportunity." He tapped his fingers on the desk, a bit dusty, Fane noted, in the office where they had first talked. "Let's think about how it might be useful..."

And thus it was that Fane found himself in a new role — the increasingly trusted and, it appeared, important liaison with the American Library. 'Not,' he thought to himself, 'that there aren't others or that I'm all that important, but still...'

The first time he and Leri were invited to a cocktail party at Pam's home, Leri spent several days fretting about what to wear. "Why don't you ask Rodica? How are they doing, anyway? I haven't seen them for some time."

"They're fine, I guess. I met Rodica just the other day. You know they had had some problems...but they seem to be over."

"That's great." Fane didn't want to be involved in his friends' personal lives — it didn't seem right — but he was glad that nothing serious was wrong. "You could ask Rodica," he repeated.

"No...I don't think so."

"Why not?"

"Going to...going to the American Library isn't something I want to talk too much about..." said Leri.

"Why worry? We have official permission," replied Fane.

"I guess then...I would like her opinion."

The next day Rodica stopped by after work and the two women spent an hour in deep and important discussion. Fane was amused and the evening of the party Leri was beautiful as he had known she would be.

Pamela lived in an apartment block dedicated to diplomats off Mihai Eminescu Street. As Fane told Antonescu a few days later, there were a mix of Americans diplomats and Romanians in the large but not enormous rooms, all trying to meet the visiting American author who was the occasion for the event. "Why do you think you were invited?" Antonescu asked.

"Probably because the American has written novels set in various periods of American history. I was able to talk a bit with him—I know the woman who translates at the Library through my dissertation..."

"We know who she is—an unreconstructed capitalist at heart in all likelihood, one of those old families, you know, but probably not a threat...but how do you know her?"

"The family had some prints that were of interest to me..."

"Of course. That makes sense. You know, I rather liked your thesis about Romania's being perceived as a European country. Not enough people realize our strong cultural ties...historical, of course..."

"I'm flattered you know of it...part of your work, I imagine."

"Well, yes, but it's also in an area which has intrigued me for a long time...the varying effect of indirect rule by the Turks, as here in Romania, and direct, as in Bulgaria. At the same time, it's hard to tell how much also comes from the indigenous population which..." The conversation drifted off course, both men forgetting for the moment their respective roles. Eventually they returned to a quick summary of who Fane had seen and what had been said. Noted among them, was Fane's conversations with several other American diplomats.

"Also with the interpreter?" Antonescu asked. "That Goga woman?"

"No...they do study Romanian and though most of them don't speak it very well, I've found that if I go slowly and use simple language, they can understand...and they seem very pleased to be able to use whatever skills they have."

"Probably get points with their superiors for being able to talk to a 'real' Romanian..." Both men laughed. As Fane walked back to the Institute of History along Calea Victoriei he thought about the conversation. 'I suppose,' he noted with some surprise, 'that Antonescu is becoming more than a...handler. Maybe a friend...I wish I could talk with Leri about it...' This wasn't the first time Fane had regretted keeping an increasingly important part of his life from his wife.

An outcome of both the party and Fane's conversation with Antonescu was more invitations from the Americans to events in their homes and permission to attend them from the Securitate. Leri went shopping. "I can't wear the same thing all the time," she said defensively after an afternoon spent combing the stores, "and it's gotten really hard to find anything nice. Maybe I'd better have something made...if I can find good material. I wish I knew how to sew!" Fane moved over and put his arms around her. "I like you in anything," he said, "and especially without anything..."

"Stop! Emil and Rodica are coming over, you know that!" Leri pulled away laughing and flew into the kitchen to prepare some snacks.

"Where did you find such good pastries?" asked Rodica after the four had sat down and coffee had been poured. "And excellent coffee!"

"There is a new cook at the shop in the *piata*," said Leri. "She's really good. And Fane brings the coffee — he gets it at work." The conversation turned, as it increasingly did now that it seemed harder and harder to find things in the market, to the merits of various canteens and what could be 'managed' from them at Fane's and Emil's workplaces.

"Are you going out of town again soon?" Fane turned to Emil. The hydrologist's work on inspections took him to various parts of the country and, like Fane and Leri, Emil and Rodica had become avid sightseers. Emil was particularly fond of hiking in the mountains, unlike the other three, so it wasn't surprising that he said he was going to an area near Cluj and that, since Rodica couldn't come, was planning to walk the Turda Gorges.

"Even though I don't share your enthusiasm for exercise," Fane said, "that's one place I'd like to see."

"It's strange that I haven't been there yet, but life does lead you along roads you don't foresee. This next summer, by the way, I may be working in the Carpathians, above Fagaras. There's some sort of project there."

"That's a good place to spend the hot months, but you shouldn't leave Rodica to sweat here in the city." Emil replied adding something about the seaside...but it was all far in the future. The conversation continued comfortably among the friends.

On a fine Sunday the following spring Fane was working in his small side garden. He was planting tall flowers in front, just behind the trash cans by the front fence, which would shield his small vegetable patch. It and the chickens he and Daniela downstairs had come together to agree to maintain in the back, provided fresh vegetables and eggs much of the year. It did mean that Mitica, Daniela's dog, was confined to the front yard except at night, which made that area under the trees even more unsightly but, Fane rationalized, it was a good trade off and they did need a watch dog.

"Hey, Fane," a familiar greeting came over the fence. Fane looked up, thinking he recognized the voice. Yes, it was Antonescu. Fane got up, feeling an unaccustomed twinge in his knee. 'I'm getting old,' he thought briefly. "Good morning!" he told Antonescu. "I'm surprised to see you here."

Surprised was perhaps less accurate than dismayed. Fane had kept Antonescu and their relationship so separate from the rest of his life that seeing him outside his own gate felt almost like a violation of some sort.

"I didn't expect to see you—I'd forgotten you live on this street," the other man almost rushed into saying. "I had heard there was asparagus at your piata and my wife wanted some...she loves it. It's a nice day and I decided to walk home."

"Where do you live?" asked Fane, most but not all of his suspicions allayed.

"Near the Television building," Antonescu said vaguely. Fane scanned a mental map and relaxed through his shoulders. Coming up Ady Endre was perfectly normal route, then. "Nice garden you are planting there," continued Antonescu. "I see you've put in tomatoes and eggplant and squash..."

"Do you know something about farming?" Fane asked curiously. "These plants are so small still..."

"I was raised in a village," Antonescu said shortly. "You must enjoy this work, being outside in the sun, creating something." "I do...and it's nice to have fresh things. Would you," Fane continued on impulse, "like to come up for a cup of coffee? I have a good source!" Both men laughed, since Antonescu was the "good source" for Fane's occasional packages of Viennese coffee.

"Certainly." Fane opened the gate and motioned Antonescu to precede him up the stairs. "Leri," Fane called ahead, "We have a guest." Leri came out of their room, obviously coming through from the kitchen, wiping her hands on her apron and taking the apron off in almost the same motion. "Excuse me," she said, "I was just doing some washing up."

"That's what we all do on Sunday, cleaning and shopping. I've been shopping for asparagus at your *piata*," Antonescu held up his woven plastic grocery bag, "and ran into Fane in his garden."

"Asparagus!" exclaimed Leri. "I had no idea...I must get some...Fane..." "Don't worry," said Fane, "I offered some coffee and I can make it." "I do hope you'll excuse me, but we haven't had..." "Of course, I understand perfectly..." In the flurry of excitement introductions were completely forgotten and when Leri returned, holding her bag aloft in triumph, Fane simply introduced Antonescu as a friend with a mutual interest in history.

And so the relationship moved onto another plane. Not, Fane realized, that Antonescu and his wife became visitors like, say Emil and Rodica, but there was a shared easiness with the man that went beyond what might be the normal interchange between someone like him and...Fane searched mentally for the right words, not client not boss...anyway, the normal relationship between a Securist and someone who was, not exactly spying, just helping out, keeping an eye out on behalf of the country, maybe.

And perhaps that was why Antonescu let some of his frustration with things show through his very professional façade on occasion. Much later, looking back, Fane thought perhaps it was when Ceausescu went to China in 1971 and came back with ideas about The Great Leap Forward and the role of culture and, of course, history, that things had begun to change but the changes in daily life had really began to be felt, to be perceived as long term and not temporary, around the time of Antonescu's chance visit and on into 1982. Fewer things in the shops, everyday necessities like coffee actually becoming a luxury and harder and harder to find, longer lines for more and more rationed food. And the jokes.

The first time he had told Pamela one of the jokes — a rather old and tired one ending "We pretend to work and they pretend to pay us," she showed her appreciation. 'Probably will report this and receive a pat on the back,' Fane thought cynically. After that Fane began to collect jokes going around among the Romanians and carefully rationed them out to the Americans he chatted with, tailoring their complexity to the diplomat's level of Romanian. It was another game, another way in which not to feel...inferior?...to these people who had so much and hardly seemed to realize it.

By the time Pamela left to a round of good-bye parties, socializing with the Americans and a few other foreign diplomats had become almost...routine. Fane shared gossip with Antonescu about them and about other Romanian guests but both of them knew it was just that, gossip. Fane never knew what Antonescu did with the information, if anything.

No one disappeared. People still worried, of course, since that was a part of life. As much a part of life as the increasing shortages in the stores and deciding where to go in August for your summer vacation.

The party was winding down and Fane realized it was time to go. There were only a few people circulating in the now-tired-looking rooms when he bid good-bye to his American host. As Fane took his coat and hat from the rack in the entryway, Dinu the film director joined him. They went out together.

"I've always liked this house," Dinu said. "It belonged to a boyar who built it for his mistress. Before."

"Really? I'd not heard that."

"Yes. I forget the family but see that," Dinu stopped and gestured upward toward the great fan over the entrance steps. Fane looked up at the wrought iron and yellow glass pattern dimly visible from the porch light. "What a wonderful conceit, the ability to create something like that, simply to shelter visitors from the rain as they came in. I'd love to film it."

"It is wonderful," said Fane, really thinking that it took a certain amount of idiocy to stand in the cold and admire something you could hardly see. "But we'd better hurry or we'll miss the last bus. Unusually chilly for this time of year, isn't it?"

The two men drew their coats in, put their heads down, and walked into the dark streets.

Part II

Ellen in Bucharest

Bucharest — August 1983. It's now two weeks since my arrival in Romania and I keep wondering about this city, Bucharest. Closed, silent, a blank wall for me. Empty. That's how it feels — closed, silent, empty. The long boulevards are lined with large buildings, at street level the shops have displays but their windows still seem empty. Above the shops are windows and balconies of apartments set in flat blind walls. The balconies are mostly closed in with glass or plastic or whatever. Sometimes you can see plants. On Bulevardul Republicii where I walk to work at least the buildings are older and some of the balconies have wrought iron, the windows have wonderful carved pediments and there are trees, but on Calea Mosilor there's only a dingy cement façade rising on both sides and stretching forever, a long wide urban canyon of nothing.

There are people but the city still seems uninhabited. Shadows walk and don't speak or, if they speak, almost whisper to one another. Cars don't honk and there aren't many of them. The trams clank and a rooster crows somewhere in the morning. The staff tells me that everyone has left since it is August but tomorrow is September first and it's still silent.

It's about fifteen, twenty minutes to walk to work from my temporary apartment near the Greek Church. The apartment is dark and bare in spite of the Welcome Kit, but it does look out on trees around a little park in the center of the traffic circle. There's sort of a park, that is, but I don't see many people in it, a few old men or women sitting on benches. They must talk but they seem silent, too. I have been stopping to buy the newspaper, Romania Libera, *from a small shop that sells papers and Romanian cigarettes and not much else, barely enough room for the woman behind the counter and she can reach everything without even getting up and the counter is actually open to the street, I wonder what she does in winter. She also has lottery tickets. The young woman is plump and drab but kind about my Romanian and we talk, with difficulty. Or, I talk with difficulty and listen, understanding only about half of her chat. Yesterday she said I should come visit her house for tea. I tried to tell her it might be difficult because I was an American, a diplomat. She said it wasn't a problem and the closed city walls had a crack in them. I had made a connection with a real person and it felt great.*

This morning when I stopped by the shop, she turned away from me and wouldn't speak, one imploring glance, then her soul fled from her face as she silently took my money and handed me the paper. Silence again.

Fane felt the creak and roll of the train through the night, half sleeping, half awake to be sure Leri was all right. Leri breathed quietly and Fane drifted in and out of slumber, thinking of their time in Bukovina, regretting as he had so often during recent years, the absence of Granny's screech. Granny had made the little house a home for so many years, passing on her stories and advice to Fane, her recipes and advice to Leri, her love to both. All the threads tying him to Bilca and Bukovina...and two of the strongest, Granny and Mihai, were gone...

The slowing rhythm of the train wheels on the track and bustling in the corridor woke Leri.

"Well, that was an easy trip," she said to Fane. "I hope you slept as well as I did."

"Of course," Fane replied, lying as usual in the small things, just to make her happy, keep her from worrying about him. Or about anything. That was what a man did for the woman he loved. He swung his feet onto the floor, stood up and touched her hair. "We're almost to Bucharest." "It will be good to be home. I love being in Bukovina, in Bilca, but coming home is always the best part." Fane agreed as he picked up their suitcase.

"It's a longer trip than to Horezu but the train schedules are so much better..." Leri said for the third or perhaps the seventh or seventeenth time.

The great North Station was busy as vacationers poured in from the north and west of the country. "Every time I come here I remember the first time, when Carol and Mihai and I arrived..." he said as he often did.

"I know. How is Carol, by the way? It seems like forever since we've seen him."

"It has been a long time. I'll give him a call and ask him by. He'll also be glad to hear news of his father."

"This would be a good time...we've brought half the country's produce with us." Fane laughed in pleasured response, feeling good about being able to provide favors and goods from the city to Bilca, and food for themselves and friends in Bucharest.

Carol answered the phone on the first ring. "Hey, Fane, you're back."

"Hay is for horses," replied Fane in the old joke shared with Carol and Mihai. "How are you? What's happening?"

"We're starting a new film and..." At an appropriate moment in the conversation, Fane mentioned that, being just back from Bilca, they were in a position to call some friends over, could Carol come on Sunday. "Are you going to Emil and Rodica's in the afternoon?" Carol asked. "Yes, probably," answered Fane, "but I haven't talked with them and I'm not sure they're back yet." "They went to the seaside, didn't they?" "Probably will come back with great tans, that's the only thing wrong with spending time in the north..." and so it went.

"I'm going downstairs to pick up the mail from Daniela," called Leri.

"Take her some of that sausage."

"Of course," Leri disappeared down the curving stairway into the dark entrance. Fane followed her to see

224

how his garden had fared during their absence. Daniela was supposed to water it if it didn't rain...yes, she had but she certainly hadn't bothered to pull any weeds, there was going to be a lot of work next Sunday and, perhaps, in the evenings after work. Even though September was around the corner evenings were still light...a neighbor passed and stopped at the gate..."You're back, I see, when did you come?"

Leri was already at the tiny dining room table when Fane came in, sorting the mail.

"Anything interesting?"

"Mostly bills, the monthly bulletin from the American Library — the movie this month is *Sophie's Choice*. I wonder if our...yes, here's our invitation to it and there's something else," Leri handed Fane an envelope, square, good quality paper, he noted. "Oh, good," continued Leri, "here's a letter from my mother!"

"How is she?" asked Fane.

"Give me a moment to read it...she's fine...Aunt Sanda had a good visit..." Leri's voice continued with small news. "I'm glad," said Fane, "she seems to be doing so well." "Perhaps she and your father really should come to live in Bucharest." "But where?" The conversation was the usual one and Fane absentmindedly tore open the square envelope from the American Embassy.

"Oh, look — here's an invitation to meet the new Director of the American Library. Ellen Pelletier...I wonder how the Americans pronounce the name, in a French style or like Pell-eh-tee-ur."

"Come now, they couldn't be so uncivilized."

"You never know. It's in two weeks."

"That will give you time to clear it." Leri still didn't know about Antonescu except as an acquaintance they occasionally met at the *piata* or on the street, but the whole world knew you couldn't just go to an American diplomat's house.

"Anything else of interest?"

"Let's see..." Leri continued looking through the stack of mail, the weekly literary paper, "Here is..." and the evening gave way to night and then to morning and the familiar path to the Institute.

It really was good to be home, Fane thought as he walked through the park to his place of work in the warm late summer sun. Bilca was...well...he loved the land and the smell of the air in Bukovina, he loved his memories but, he had to admit, the farm and house were seedier each year. Petru had, who could be surprised, continued to drink too much and had sold more land in spite of the money Fane sent every month. He'd aged badly, too, not like Uncle Vanya who was...Fane stopped in his tracks. He could remember both men when they were, what, nearly twenty years younger than he, Fane, was now. Shaking his head and continuing the last few steps to the Institute, Fane thought about the passage of time. Petru had been...his date of birth was never completely clear though, Fane mused, it could probably be found in some record, somewhere...but before World War I even in Bukovina records weren't always that accurate or well kept. No one, of course, had celebrated birthdays in those days, not peasants, at least. When they went to Transylvania, Petru must have been about thirty-one.

And now Fane was fifty-one. It didn't seem possible.

Later in the afternoon, after a day spent going through notices and papers and putting his notes from the summer in order, Fane thought again about Bilca. In fact, he mused, there wasn't much to fill the week they spent with Petru. He helped with the chores but Granny's beloved new cow was long gone, Petru's farming seemed to be limited to a scruffy garden and the fruit trees by the house and there simply wasn't that much for him to do. Leri worked harder, he admitted, cleaning and scrubbing and washing what seemed like a year's accumulation of dirty this and that. Someday Fane really needed to tackle the barn — maybe next summer.

Fane had spent most of his time with Carol's father. Granny had been a treasure trove of folklore; the former mayor was a similar source for the history of the area and he enjoyed talking about it with Fane. Probably because Carol wasn't that interested unless it was connected to a film he was making and, to be honest, Carol didn't have that much time to spend with his father. And he didn't want to be around his mother—something Fane could understand as he thought about Petru. Cojocariu was also a good source for current events in the countryside which weren't that good. Fane pushed the thought aside and considered Uncle Vanya and Aunt Anna. They had aged but were still vigorous, intelligent, well-informed people. The days with them were a pleasure of argument and fact leavened by theory and ideas. Fane also enjoyed meeting their friends, the older generation who had once seemed so knowledgeable and wise and interesting and who were now eager to hear his, Fane's, news and thoughts.

But the real pleasure of the summer, Fane thought as he turned into his gate, was being at Sucevita with Father Augustin. The monk had managed to remain in the great monastery in spite of political shifts and changes and even if you didn't believe in, well, weren't exactly a strict follower of organized religion because who really knew...anyway, Augustin offered a vision beyond...

"Fane," Leri interrupted his thoughts as he came into the house. "What are you thinking, lost so deeply in thought that you didn't even notice me standing here?"

Fane gave her a kiss. "I was thinking about Sucevita."

"A lovely place...I do so enjoy being there with you. Are you going to follow up on those documents Father Augustin said he thought would interest you?"

Fane assented and returned to the present. "Were you able to talk to Rodica?"

"Yes, they're back and had a wonderful time. We're going there next Sunday for the afternoon, then they'll come back here for dinner, just the four of us."

"Carol?"

"Did you call him? He's welcome, of course!"

"I forgot, got to thinking about other things," Fane admitted. "I'll talk to him tomorrow — there's plenty of time." It really was good to be back home.

Bucharest — September 1983. Today I discovered Avram's office. This American Library building is such a funny warren of stairs and doors and unexpected things. On the tour the day I arrived I met everyone in a confusing array of faces and facts and places and I still don't have them all straight. Pam had told me all about them in Washington — it seems so far away, sitting with her in that bookstore/coffee house near Dupont Circle. Another world. An easier one.

It also seems that there are two kinds of "libraries" in Bucharest, lending libraries — which we have here but it's only a part of what we do — and "Libraries" like us, the British and the French that have all kinds of programs. I wonder if there are any more "Libraries" — the word is said with a special emphasis, Biblioteca, *you can hear the capital B! It's confusing too because the word for 'bookstore' in Romanian is* librarie *anyway, I wonder if there are more besides us three, I need to ask someone.*

So our buildings must have been two houses belonging to the same family, I think, because they face one another. We, the American Embassy, built a connection that has the auditorium and the cloakroom in it. I can't believe we not only have 16 mm projectors but 35 mm as well. Then there is the library in the building opposite mine, the one with our offices and the exhibition space behind us, but there are other rooms and places like the Blue Room that has a kitchen and whose major function seems to be for staff parties. Pam liked blue. Now I've found Avram's office upstairs in the squinchy corner and there are other doors I haven't opened yet... At least it and the Embassy are places where I'm beginning to feel at home, beginning to feel three dimensions in this silent, two-dimensional city. It's sort of like that in every new post, new place, the map that is blank or meaningless is gradually filled in with your own history but here it's going to be harder...

Maybe something will come of that conversation last night at the party, the welcoming reception Peter held for me. The house is gorgeous, wrought iron fences, marble in the entryway, this lovely glass and wrought iron portico over the entrance steps, I wonder if I'll have such a beautiful house when I'm Public Affairs Officer somewhere, if I ever am. Three American officers in the Cultural section and all of us new – I wonder what led Washington to do that. Well, we can learn together and it saved the PAO money to hold only one welcoming reception. This man...Stefan I think, I must look him up as he's one of the regular Library contacts. He was really kind about my Romanian, easy to talk to. I think Pam told me about him. Maybe he really can help me find a place to ride... That might make a big difference, at least get me out of the usual diplomatic circles, they can be so insular.

Fane sat drumming his fingers lightly on his desk and wondering whether to call Antonescu about Ellen and the party and to follow up on his promise to her about riding. He heard someone clear his throat and looked up to see Hristu. "How are things going?" the visitor asked.

"Well, I think. And with you?" Fane responded to the Securitate agent. "How's your research?" he asked a bit meanly, knowing full well that Hristu's 'research' was static if it existed at all.

"All right, thanks. I've been asked to tell you that you have a meeting with our friend, the usual place, after work. I suppose it was about the party last night to welcome the new American diplomats. Anything interesting?"

"Well...have a seat," Fane gestured toward a chair and Hristu slid into it. Over the months and years Hristu and Fane had moved into an uneasy friendship. Fane, usually adept at finding out exactly what other people wanted and discerning thoughts they hadn't even formulated, found Hristu a bit of a puzzle. The researcher was assiduous in following up Fane's activities and tried to be friendly, to draw him out. He appeared to want to be warm and open but something was always a bit off, like a tomato that was red, ripe, and lovely but a bit too soft and on the cusp of rotting but Fane couldn't quite put his finger on the cause. And though Hristu tried to look busy, Fane suspected he was both lazy and underemployed. There was, after all, the matter of the books which should have been Hristu's business alone.

It hadn't been long after his second or third visit to the American Library that Hristu had come in to his office — Fane never tired of having his own space, a reward for his Senior Researcher status, but he kept the door open to show he wasn't setting himsef off — with a paper in his hand.

"It seems there is a book one of your colleagues wants to borrow from the American Library. Could you get it for him?" Fane took the paper and looked at the reference, some book called "Hard Times" whatever that meant, by a man named Studs Terkel. He looked at Hristu quizzically.

"So Teodorescu does the French Library and now I have the American Library?" Teodorescu was some sort of administrative assistant who ran errands. Hristu had the grace to look embarrassed. "They specifically asked for you to do it," he said. "I don't know why. I'd appreciate it if you would..."

"Anything to help, Comrade," Fane said, managing to sound sincere though he didn't believe any such thing. Almost as if he could read Hristu's mind, Fane knew that he was simply passing off work he didn't like but this couldn't be said so it happened that Fane applied for a library card and went by The American Library every week or two with a list of books. Occasionally he picked up one that Leri wanted — he had told her about this new 'duty' and they had both wondered what was going on, with some worry — and gradually, as a favor, added one or two novels for colleagues and their wives. All of it became easier when Hristu stopped collecting requests and simply asked for a list of the books taken out. Fane imagined that someone in the Library kept a list as well but as long as the extras were innocuous...people understood the need to help out with favors now and again...

Returning to the present, Fane turned his attention back to the man in front of him. "Not a great deal," he said, "but I was able to talk to the new American Library Director at some length. It seems she was raised on a farm."

"Really! Are there peasants in America?"

"I suppose so — they have agriculture."

"I..." Hristu started when the Director's secretary came through the door. "Dr. Dragomir would like to see you about the paper he is presenting tomorrow, I'm sorry to interrupt but..." Fane met Hristu's eyes and conveyed a helpless shrug and apology. Hristu nodded slightly and smiled. "We must talk some more about that matter at some point," he said and left. Fane picked up materials he needed and followed the secretary to Dragomir's office.

It was almost dark when he finally climbed the stairs to Antonescu's 'office'. "I'm sorry," Fane apologized as he entered, "but there was a long delay between busses this afternoon. It's usually very easy from Piata Victoriei but..."

"Don't worry about it," said Antonescu rising. The two men shook hands and sat down as one, smiling at their unthinking coordination. "You've probably guessed that I have been asked about last night's party."

"I thought that might be the case," Fane smiled. "Where do you want me to start. I did have an interesting conversation with Ellen Pelletier and think we may have someone there."

"An agent?" Antonescu was clearly startled.

"No, not that, at least not yet," Fane chose his words carefully, "but you know how, following The Leader's excellent ideas we have been trying to build influence in foreign countries, to demonstrate not just Romania's political importance but her historical and cultural importance, her position as a Latin island in a Slavic Sea, so that we have persons who are sympathetic..."

"Yes, of course," said Antonescu, perhaps slightly impatient. "Do you think this Pelletier person could be useful in that area?"

"It's clear that she is eager to like our nation. She apparently learned Romanian from someone who had her read Caragiale, Eminescu..."

"...but her Romanian must be good if she was reading those works!"

"It's not bad though she's not yet very comfortable with the language — doesn't have the background her predecessor did, I think — but she'll be all right."

"What do you advise us to do? Give her books?"

"That, the usual, but she had a specific request, a rather unusual one."

"Oh?"

"She apparently likes horses and wondered if there were a place she could ride in Bucharest."

"What in the...horses? She wants to ride horses? Does she ride like one of those, how do you say it, cowboys?"

Fane grinned. "I don't know but, get this, she said she'd stopped riding after college but started again in her last assignment, in the Lagos Polo Club!" "Lagos?!" "Can you believe it, Africa?" Both men laughed heartily at the thought of a Polo Club in Africa.

"But wait," said Antonescu a bit later. "Wasn't your cousin, um, Mihai, um Sirbu, Mihai Sirbu...wasn't he in Lagos?"

Fane froze. "I hadn't thought of that for years," he said honestly. "But you're right. I wonder..."

"So do I. Let me check. No, wait, it must have been before she was there if that was her last post...how fast the years pass. But where would she ride?"

"I don't know but I think I could find out."

"Remember, it can't possibly be at Dinamo, our club — I must take you there someday, come to think of it — or at the Army club...is there any place else? I must say I've never come across anything like this before...look, find out what you can and get back to me. We could use a bit of...success...at this point." Fane looked up in surprise. And stopped feeling good about the conversation.

"Success?" he repeated.

"We have a bit of a problem," Antonescu said, drumming his fingertips on the desk nervously. "It's not that they're unhappy with your work, exactly...you've managed to win the confidence of the Americans but...there's been a report that you, um, are a bit too fond of the Scotch served at parties and sometimes drink..."

Fane remained silent, half angry and half sick. 'It has to be Victor,' he thought.

"...and I've been told to advise you to watch it." Antonescu was clearly uncomfortable. "...but let's move on. I just needed to deliver that bit of advice. I'll find out if, in principle, this woman can ride her horses, if we can find a suitable place that is since it might lead to something else. I'll ask but if you have any leads, let me know."

"All right." The two men bid each other good-bye and Fane left, down the narrow stairway almost without breathing and out into the dark street. Street lamps on the back streets had been off for quite some time in order to save electricity which made negotiating the alley difficult but he hardly noticed it. Once he arrived in the dim light of the street he turned and walked quickly to the Bulevard. Usually he would have continued straight across the wide street to peruse the window of the *anticariat* facing the side of the University, "just in case," but tonight he was...late and... nervous. Home beckoned with at least an illusion of safety. Besides, Leri was waiting for him.

"I was beginning to worry," she said as Fane put his briefcase on the hall table. "I didn't know you'd be so late." She wiped her hands on the dishcloth and put it down.

Fane shrugged his light coat off and hung it on the coatrack. "I didn't know either, darling," he put an arm around her. "The...you know...they wanted to talk about the party."

"I thought that was probably it. And so do I, I want to know...you haven't told me a thing. I'm so sorry I couldn't go but...how was the new Library Director?" They walked through their bedroom into the tiny dining area and Fane began to give her a blow by blow description of the night before. Almost.

In the light of the next day the conversation with Antonescu didn't seem so menacing. Not at all. It really wasn't that bad, he just had to watch it at parties...damn. Such good Scotch they served. Well, two drinks...no one could complain about two drinks. He'd stick to that. He'd also watch out for Victor, it had to be him ratting.

The next thing was to get hold of Carol.

Carol was delighted. "You mean there's an American woman who wants to ride?" he asked with a grin. "Is she pretty?" "Pretty? Well, I guess so..."

"Come on, man, you need to be better than that. What does she look like?"

"She could be married for all you know...not that that seems to have much effect..." Fane's smile took the edge off his words.

"Is she?"

"I don't think so. No husband in evidence though she's certainly old enough...no," Fane grinned even wider," not decrepit. Nice looking, good figure but I don't," Fane thought a minute, "...you know, they're funny, these Americans. They introduce people by their first and last name and don't use Miss or Mrs. Or Mr., come to think of it, so you don't really know."

"They're still a bit wild, it comes from the Wild West. Can she ride? Does she use one of those cowboy saddles?"

Grinning to match Carol's smile, Fane almost told him that Antonescu had said the same thing, but caught himself in time. "I don't know...don't think so... I've talked with the, um, proper people and they've said they'll find out if it can be permitted but asked if I might be able to find out if there was a place. Her options are a bit limited..." Neither of them needed to go further. The best teams in every sport belonged to the military or the Securitate and would be off limits to a foreigner, especially a diplomat.

234

Carol thought a minute. "We've got horses for the movies, but not all the time and...no, I don't think that would work, but...there is a place. *Clubul* Olimpia!"

"Olimpia? Where's that? I never heard of it."

"It's off Mihai Bravu, near the Dimbovita River. There's a training facility there, I think it used to be for the Olympics, anyway there's a riding club... know the rider in charge, come to think of it, did him a favor once about a horse..."

"Great!"

"It's not as good as Steaua and Dinamo, no indoor riding ring, but I imagine she's not that serious. What I need to know, though, is something about how well she rides."

"Why?"

"To warn my friends, of course. Also, I'm curious. I want to meet this Miss Cowboy!"

"Can you clear it with your...?"

"I think it would be better if you did it for me. Keep everything in one channel so there won't be any miscommunication," he paused. "They'll tell our resident Securist anyway."

So it was that the following Monday Fane found himself climbing the narrow stairs to Antonescu's "office" again. "Come in," the familiar voice called when Fane knocked on the wooden door. As he entered, Antonescu turned away from the window and the last of the sunlight, filtering between the dirty walls of the old buildings. He was looking pleased, Fane noted.

"They're delighted to give their permission for your lady to ride!" Antonescu announced. "It seems that someone, I think perhaps," he lowered his voice, "well, it seems that one of our Arab friends asked for some horses from Mangalia, apparently there are rare bloodlines there, and now the Leader wants to promote Romanian horses." Antonescu's voice returned to a normal level, "you know, it's quite a coincidence but we've hit the right mark and the right time. They're searching for an appropriate place. This isn't exactly,

235

ah, on our list of target operations!" Both men laughed. "Have you found anything?"

"Yes," reported Fane, feeling good about it, "there's a club, the Olimpia Club, that's civilian, quite suitable I hear though I haven't been there, near the Dimbovita, off of Mihai Bravu."

"Good work. Your source? Your friend, Carol, I suppose." Fane was startled to hear Carol's name then thought, with some resignation, that of course They would know about him.

"Yes, it was Carol who thought this might be the best. He wants to meet Ellen and find out how well she rides."

"Why?"

"So," Fane thought quickly, "to be sure that she's mounted properly and won't be hurt. We wouldn't want her hurt..."

"Of course not, but can't the trainers at Olympia do that?"

Darn Carol, but Fane not only owed him on this, he was curious about what kind of relationship Carol and Ellen might develop and, who knew...perhaps... "Carol's used to mounting people who haven't been trained to ride properly," Fane ad-libbed, his nerves taut under his easy demeanor, drawing on past conversations with Carol and spinning them into plausibility. "...a lot of them in the movies, everywhere, most people, apparently talk about how well they ride but they really don't, so he's developed a sense of what they can really do. I'm not sure that whoever's in charge of training at Olympia has ever done that." Pretty good, Fane thought with some satisfaction, a satisfaction that only deepened when Antonescu agreed. Then he was caught off guard.

"...and, of course, you'll go out there and ride, too, to develop the friendship and monitor the situation. You can stay on a horse, I expect, growing up in the country?"

"No." Fane's refusal was instant and flat. "I don't want to have anything to do with horses." He expected Antonescu to be angry so the man's sympathy caught him off guard. "Did something bad happen?" he heard him saying and suddenly Fane, all the tension of the last days unwinding his armor into useless threads, found himself telling Antonescu about Haiduc, the trip into Transylvania, Petru's betrayal of the animal who had saved them and worked for them all his life, about Haiduc's ugly end. As the last words faded Fane realized the other man had turned from him and was looking through the window onto the wall opposite. Unexpectedly he heard Antonescu say in a muffled voice, "They killed our horses in '52 during the mechanization. I will never forget that day. I think it was the worst day of my life." Then Antonescu invisibly gathered himself and turned back to Fane. "I think Carol will do very well instead of you, especially since he's a real rider. Let the two of them tell you about what happens, but you need to make the introduction. Take them to lunch at Capsa. Give her some good food and wine, let Carol loose. Maybe..." The two men put the past behind them into that well of pain everyone wants to forget and smiled at a shared thought. Maybe they could snag another Western diplomat.

But the past wouldn't quite leave them alone, lingering in a shared shadow. "I'll walk with you toward the bus, I'm going home as well," Antonescu said shoving his chair back. It was the first time they had ever left the office together and Fane wondered if it was a breach of operating procedure but Antonescu seemed perfectly at ease. Until they were in a crowd of people on the Boulevard.

"I need to tell you about some things going on that might affect you...us..." he said in a voice that Fane could hear but too low to carry beyond him. "It's a warning...don't be alarmed but it does demand some...care. The Services are, um, divided about where primary loyalty should lie, to the Communist cause in general or the nation in particular. Maybe more than that, to who gets the most power...but Victor in the US Embassy and Hristu in your Institute are both on the other side, the side that a historian who knows

Romania's greatness would not be on, if you understand me."

"I think I understand perfectly," said Fane knowing both that he would be on the nationalist side even if it weren't for Antonescu but also that, at this point, it wouldn't matter since like it or not his future and perhaps his safety was tied to the man. Fane didn't mention that he already knew of this division between those in the secret services loyal to Russia and those who were primarily nationalists. From Mihai. There had been other hints and references over the years but it was hard to know what to believe, but Mihai... Fane's heart ached with loss both of Mihai and of the safety he had felt with Mr. Eichmann in the background.

"Hristu's an idiot but Victor is not," Antonescu continued. "I don't know what was behind the report we got last week," Fane knew it was based on his 'drinking', damn Victor, "but something may be going on. 'When the elephants fight, the mice are trampled'," he quoted.

"I understand. But what advice do you have for me?"

"At this point, nothing beyond watching your drinking and your back. And being observant of what they might be doing. Tell me if you see anything. But, um, maybe not when we're in the 'office' or a building..." 'God,' thought Fane sickly, 'I'd heard they spied on their own people but...what a world we live in...'

Two days later Fane and Carol went to the Olimpia Club together in Carol's little Trabant. Fane joked about the 'cardboard car' and once even asked why Carol didn't have a better vehicle. "Surely you could manage about anything you wanted," he told his film actor/director/famous friend.

"Yeah, I could," replied Carol, serious for once. "But the Studio has lots of fancy cars if I need one and I...I just prefer not to have a Dacia and being another copy of everyone else, faceless and nameless..." Typically, Carol changed the topic before Fane could respond. Now he turned the little yellow vehicle off a wide street onto a lane running downhill toward the Dimbovita. On either side were small, messy houses, children with uncombed hair and women in long Gypsy skirts. "Do you think we ought to show her this?" Fane asked. "It won't matter, people aren't dumb, they know there's stuff like this everywhere," Carol answered as they swung around one corner and then another only to be confronted by high solid metal gates decorated with a crude drawing of a horse's head.

"A testament to the neighbors," remarked Fane as Carol got out of his car and rapped on the solid obstruction. A tiny window opened in the metal, some words were exchanged with the face that peeked through, the gates creaked and swung back.

Inside was a different world, open and empty and stretching up to the wide street on the hill and a row of concrete apartment blocks beyond it. Turning before the entrance to a racetrack, the two visitors found themselves in a stable, a pile of dirty straw in one corner, clean lovely horse heads looking at them over the tops of stall doors. "Quite nice," said Fane.

"They have some decent horses. No budget to speak of but the guy in charge, Enache Florea, is a real operator and manages to hold his own against the big clubs."

After a short and satisfactory discussion in a dark, tiny 'office' Florea agreed to host a diplomat rider, not that he had much choice since he must already have been told it would happen, Fane thought cynically, but we're observing the forms of free choice. "Of course, gentlemen, we'll make the lady happy. It won't be the first time we've had diplomats ride here — Ambassador Harry, Harry Barnes...his daughter rode with us. Will she come with friends from the Embassy?" Fane and Carol looked at each other in surprise and with a bit of consternation. No one had thought of other diplomats besides Ellen riding. "We don't know, possibly," said Carol. "Never mind, we'll manage," said Florea. "Let me show you around." The two followed him out and through the stable yard to walk down a dusty, well-worn path by a high fence, high enough so that only the chimneys of the Gypsy houses and an occasional tree appeared over the top. At the end they turned to find themselves facing a fenced riding ring with bleachers at one end, professional looking jumps, and the race track stretching off parallel to the large street above them, "We use the hill for cross-country training," Florea pointed out. They all looked at the worn slope. The place looked as if there were everything a rider might need. Not bad at all.

Later, over a beer; Carol said, "You'll have to ask them about other diplomats riding, of course, but they can hardly refuse if we go ahead with Ellen. When do I meet her?"

"Let me clear things about the other diplomats. I'll give you a date."

"And where is this meeting likely to happen? At the American Library?"

"Capsa's, I think," said Fane. "You probably go there all the time."

"I've been...a couple of times. A bit stodgy but appropriate. Although I would have thought they would have used the Athenee Palace Hotel."

"Why?" asked Fane.

"Oh, just that it's...historic." Fane looked at Carol, who was clearly not answering the question.

"Of course, I haven't said anything to her yet." Fane decided it wasn't worth following up. "First I need to get an appointment with her."

"You'll have no trouble," Carol said with his usual optimism. And he was, as usual, right.

The secretary who had made the appointment was a bit nosier than she should have been. 'Part of her job, most likely,' Fane thought to himself as he walked into the Library courtyard. He had also thought that it was none of her business, so had evaded her questions politely saying only, "Madame Director asked about something and I've been able to find the information she wanted." 'Let them sweat a bit, it won't hurt, and they'll wonder exactly who I am...that's not bad...' his inner voice rambled on, making thoughts a bit more concrete and manageable as he climbed lion-flanked steps to the entrance.

"Come in, come in, you must be Mr. Vulcean," said a slim, pretty woman when Fane, after a moment's hesitation, had opened the massive doors into the Administrative wing of the Library. She pointed to an office on the left, "Please sit down. Ellen will be back from the Embassy in a minute. She's expecting you." It wasn't the secretary who had been on the phone, someone else. Glasses. Bright, intelligent eyes.

"Fane, please. Don't be so formal. What a splendid office you have," Fane remarked looking around. The pretty woman gazed at him levelly from under straight cut bangs. "It's pleasant to work in," she said. "Do I hear an Oltenian accent?" Fane asked, beginning to play his familiar game of identifying the other person, finding points of common interest, building bridges, learning as much as possible by appearing to be open. It was indeed a nice office, he thought, as they exchanged pleasantries, modern, warm...Western, perhaps. Nice color blue on the wall, obviously not Romanian paint...

"Oh, here she is," the secretary interrupted their easy conversation. "Just a minute, let me tell her you're here."

The Director's office was even more elegant, Fane thought appreciatively. Not European elegant, American... clean, nice posters on the walls, the wall behind a big desk same blue, really good looking furniture but it also looked as if work was done here. It wasn't a protocol room, but a real office. "...you, I'm so glad you came by," Ellen was saying. "Please sit down." She walked to a small seating area by the front windows and motioned Fane to a chair. 'Blue, of course, to match the carpet,' noted Fane. He smiled genially and asked how she was finding Bucharest.

"Very lovely but I feel as if the city is closed, somehow." Fane was startled at the unexpected answer.

"Why?" he asked with genuine curiosity. Bucharest was anything but closed.

"There are all these streets, all these apartment buildings, and it's not really unfriendly but I have the feeling I'll never be invited into any of them, never get to know what's behind the façade."

"Each of them really is inhabited by people, ordinary people, extraordinary people — you'll get to know much more, I hope. It seems you have a genuine interest in Romania."

"I do," answered Ellen, unconsciously brushing a lock of blond hair away from her face. "To be honest, this isn't a place I'd ever thought of living but now that I'm here, that I've studied the language, I'm finding I want to learn more."

"Well, I hope to help you in that and I'm coming with what I hope is good news." Ellen looked at him with a pleasant question in her eyes? "You said you wanted to ride while you were here."

"Yes!" she said eagerly, leaning forward ever so slightly. "Do you think it might be possible?" Fane allowed himself a broad smile. "I think we can manage," he said with a twinkle in his eye. "In Romania that's what we do, manage." Ellen laughed in delight.

The first step, as he explained, was to meet his friend Carol who was a horseman and could take her to the club to introduce her. Fane was pleased to see that Ellen was genuinely excited at the prospect.

"Is Carol a professional rider?" she asked.

"He's Carol Cojocariu," Fane explained. Ellen looked at him, puzzled. Fane mentally kicked himself. She wouldn't know. "Carol," he continued, "is a film actor, and now also a director, who is fairly famous in Romania but he's also a superb horseman with many connections and he can..." Fane let his voice trail off suggestively. Ellen, obviously working at understanding both the language and the meaning behind it, merely nodded. "When do we meet Carol, then?" she asked. 'Got her,' thought Fane.

It was Fane's first time in Capsa's restaurant even though it was only a block away from the Faculty of History and he'd passed it many times. As the two men waited in the small, wood-paneled entry he looked around and wondered why it was that some things simply weren't done, like have dinner at Capsa's...it wasn't beyond his means though it was expensive. But then, perhaps questions...Ellen came through the door and the men stood, ending Fane's ruminations. A flurry of introductions and they moved into the dining room, Carol nudging Fane in the ribs with his elbow and casting a look of approval, with a glance that lingered on her hips, toward the woman ahead of them as they entered. The table was ready, in more than one sense surmised Fane. Antonescu had made the arrangements and told him how to sign for the meal. Fane hadn't said anything to Carol but he assumed Carol knew that there was probably a microphone someplace, under the table or maybe in the flower vase... no, that would get it wet, probably under the table. The conversation began in earnest and left Fane behind in no time as his companions delightedly exchanged information about horses.

Bucharest—October 1983. This place to ride, maybe this will let me in on the real Romania. It's pretty scrungy. In the middle of the city so you can't ride out. Dingy, full of dirty straw and the facilities are fairly basic. But the horses looked good and well cared for and the people were friendly. I've found someone here, a woman in the Defense Attaché's Office, her name is Sandy, who also wants to ride though I'm not sure how much she knows, but it will help because I'm not supposed to be alone with Romanians — such a lot of rules! Apparently I've already broken them by going to the Club Olimpia with one, this Carol, who is a movie star of some sort, Stefan seemed to think he was important, in his car, a funny little vehicle hardly big enough for him with his long legs, let alone two of us. Strange car for someone who's supposed to be famous... they certainly treated him like royalty at the riding club.

The man who arranged everything, the one I met at Peter's party, Stefan...he's a historian, a regular contact of ours. I wonder if he's a spy. Probably. Maybe not. I'd rather think not but I'll have to be careful of him, this is going to be hard, making friends and being careful at the same time. I don't think he's ever been near a horse in fact I think he's scared of them, a real city person. He wouldn't go out to the club but he introduced me to Carol who really seems to know horses and seems much more...genuine? Maybe I'm being prejudiced because of the horses. He absolutely grilled me about my background and what I'd done and whether I could ride an English saddle which wasn't necessary for me, but I used to do the same when I worked in a riding club in the summer during college so I know how good he is at it. People lie so much about how well they ride... I must have passed the test because they gave me a really nice horse, Samurai, funny a Romanian horse having a Japanese name. We both rode for forty minutes – that seems to be the drill, forty minutes on the horse. I took Samurai over a few low jumps and people actually applauded. I hadn't realized before that they had been watching. Carol also jumped – a total natural with horses and seems as if he's part of his mount, a really beautiful rider. I think he has a magic feel for them. He's good looking, too, a bit older, must be in his late forties but absolutely fit. It's good that Sandy will go with me and lucky she got permission from the DAO. Otherwise I don't think they'd give me an okay on it. I'm going to have to work out something, I can't always have other Americans around when I'm with Romanians...I'm the only American in the Library, for God's sake, with a Romanian staff.

Guess I'll get to know Sandy well, she's my age, sort of 'other ranks' in the Embassy so she wouldn't normally be in my social circle. I like breaking out of these boxes. I wonder if Carol will grill her like he grilled me, but he found out I used to teach and take tourists out on trail rides, so maybe he'll just let me handle it. I don't know how much Sandy has ridden before. Have to find out.

It's going to be a long drive from my new apartment, my permanent quarters, my home – funny calling it that but it will become home – along the endless canyon boulevards, there are so many of them, all of them look alike except for Bulevardul Republicii. I'll miss my morning walk. The newspaper lady has gotten used to me and we talk a bit but now we both know we can't take it further. But I'll be able to settle down, get to know my new neighborhood, I can still walk to work but my car's coming, which is good, because winter's coming, too. And my HHE, my

244

Household Effects. It will be so nice to settle in, really settle in, invite some friends over, start some representational entertaining, get my own things again, start living my real life here instead of waiting in temporary quarters for life to begin.

Fane had a spring in his step as he went to meet Carol after the first riding expedition. He was eager to know how it went and savored the thought of being able to chat freely about the American. Waving to the waitress, he went into the small workmen's bar where they sometimes met. "How did she do?" he asked, almost before they'd greeted one another.

"Best woman rider I've seen," answered Carol with a grin. "I wish I had a leading lady that could sit a horse so well— good seat, good hands. Leans a bit too forward and rides with a shorter stirrup than..."

"Enough, enough," laughed Fane.

"You need this information," said Carol, dramatically pretending to be hurt. "It will be great fodder for your reporting!"

"Do you really think 'they' will be interested in how long her stirrups are?"

"Better that than anything important."

"Was there anything important?" Fane was serious at this point.

"No ...not. She's quite a looker. If she weren't American...I've always wondered if Americans were..." the waitress interrupted them but Carol didn't need to finish the sentence. "The one other thing," he continued, "that struck me, probably the only thing she said that wasn't about horses was when we were driving on Mihai Bravu how closed the city seemed and how much she wanted to get to know more about Romania, not just books and official events but real people."

It was one of the things that Fane reported to Antonescu. The other was to report, with a look that said, 'Do you have an explanation?' that one of his colleagues, Hristu, had left the Nicolae Iorga Institute of History. "Transferred to Arad,"

Fane said. "I understand that his family is there, his mother is very ill, a long-term illness, and he wanted to be near them. I didn't hear what he'd be doing there." Fane didn't mention that no one else knew what Hristu would be doing either though there were rumors of teaching secondary school. In a bad area.

"I had heard that," said Antonescu who kept up, it seemed, with most business at the Institute. The agent smiled with satisfaction, "But tell me about Ellen." Fane recounted the substance of what Carol had said, if not the entire flavor of the conversation and brought up the fact the she had talked about Bucharest being a closed city to both of them, as well as her casual mention of a woman in the 'DAO' office wanting to ride as well. "That's the Defense Attaché's Office," Fane said, letting his voice trail off suggestively.

"Excellent," Antonescu said with obvious satisfaction. "And I'm a bit ahead of you there." He smiled. "I asked permission for other diplomats to ride already. I pointed out that we wouldn't want to single Ellen out as a potential target, at least not to her own people no matter what we might think, and they also have some of the same rules we do— she won't be able to ride if she has to come alone. At least not at first—we'll see if that will slip with time. People do get careless...but her choice of a friend is excellent. In fact, outstanding. Oh, and something else. We think it would be good if you invited Ellen to your house for dinner some evening."

"You've got to be kidding. An American diplomat to my house?"

"Is anything wrong with your house? It looked nice to me."

"No, except of course for the entrance downstairs, but having an American come would be a good excuse...but what would we serve her? You know what things are like...would she like Romanian food?"

"I'm sure she'd like Romanian food or at least pretend to. It would be easier for her than pretending to eat grasshoppers or whatever they serve guests in Africa..." Both men chuckled and grimaced at the thought. "If she really wants to get, how did she put it, get 'behind blank walls?' this might be a good thing, though don't invite her until I am sure it's approved. Now let's talk about Hristu's position." Fane sat up. He hadn't expected this after the digression into Ellen's eating habits. "It's been decided," Antonescu went on, "that the Iorga Institute is too important to the cause to be left in the hands of someone who's not," Antonescu looked over Fane's shoulder a minute at an invisible point, "who's not a first rate intellect as shown by real accomplishment. I have been directed to ask you to take his place."

Fane was dumbfounded. Helping out with the American Library was one thing. Being the Institute's resident Securist, feared and...despised? Probably. Maybe he could overcome that... "There would be considerable benefits to you," Antonescu continued, obviously sensing Fane's discomfort, 'He knows me so well,' thought Fane, "but the main objective is service to the nation."

"I am...honored..." stammered Fane thinking quickly. "Honored that you have so much confidence in me. I... hesitate to take time from my research which, as you know, also serves the nation. It is a hard choice."

"I agree, a difficult choice," said Antonescu with a gesture and a look that told Fane quite clearly that it wasn't a hard choice at all.

"But...on reflection," Fane continued, glaring at Antonescu who shrugged as if helpless, "I can only say I have no choice when it comes to the glory of Romania and her people. Whatever is believed I can do, I can only attempt to perform that task to the best of my ability."

"I think you will find it a useful and interesting service to perform. You're very good at picking up things from people and they confide in you. We wouldn't, of course, be asking you to...do anything against your conscience, simply to help people should they run into difficulties and, of course, to safeguard the interests of our nation." Fane didn't believe this for a minute — he'd seen too much — but if it was his neck or someone else's or, more importantly, Leri's neck or someone else's there wasn't much... Antonescu's next words interrupted his thought and Fane realized that he was being given instructions about his new post.

Walking toward the bus stop Fane felt angry and cheated, robbed, his comfortable existence yanked from under his feet. All right, there would be a few more privileges here and there that would be nice, and perhaps power, well...maybe...but it would take time away from his real work. People would come to look at him differently. At least he was a legitimate scholar, had a reputation, not a pretender like that Hristu. Maybe people wouldn't know.

But they did know, almost from the next day. Requests for books from foreign libraries had to be approved by Fane which meant he had to look at them, as opposed to handing a list to the Reference Librarian at the American Library. Now he had the French Library as well and invitations to events involving foreigners or even, to Fane's surprise, some Romanian functions, went through him. This happened almost automatically with Fane's old acquaintance, the porter at the door, bringing them. Fane's barely concealed start of surprise the first day was met by deference and a silent indication that the elderly man was pleased at the change. 'He must work for them, too,' thought Fane and was glad that he had been friendly all these years. Some things, at least, paid off.

At least the extra work was almost interesting. The activities of Fane's colleagues were more varied than he realized and he enjoyed seeing the titles of books they requested, having them open windows into new avenues of research, ones he didn't personally wish to pursue at that time but that might have attractions later. He worked with a dictionary but that, too, was interesting as he put together English and French.

248

And the knowledge gave him a feeling of power. He felt bigger. More...more something, important...

The first time Fane went to talk with Dr. Dragomir after his new 'appointment' had been a dreaded trial. He didn't want Dragomir's bad opinion but at the same time saying what he felt would be impossible...even if he knew exactly how he felt.

At first the conversation seemed absolutely normal, a discussion of possible sources for Gavriil Uric's 1429 manuscript, Byzantine or perhaps Romanian. It was only when they had mutually decided they couldn't come to a conclusion that Dragomir shifted his great bulk in his massive chair and looked at Fane, raising an eyebrow. Fane looked down at his hands, his usual pleasure at the wellmanicured nails, the lack of callouses except where he held his pen, at war with the butterflies in his stomach. 'I feel like a child,' he thought resentfully.

"I heard an American saying once," Dragomir said into the silence. "It was, let's see, 'There's no free lunch.' Have you come across this saying at the American Library?"

"No," replied Fane, "but it is, perhaps, universally applicable."

Dragomir grunted and shifted again in his chair. "Your work on those Moldovan manuscripts has been excellent and your interpretations of Romania's place in history much appreciated. I think you will find that, in the long run, this is what is important." Fane lifted his eyes and the two men looked at one another. "Thank you," Fane said gratefully, but it was Dragomir who looked down first. A sense of triumph shot through Fane, as pleasurable as sex, followed by shame. "Thank you," he said again quietly and pushed his chair back, leaving without saying good-bye.

It was to Carol that Fane expressed his greatest fear. "What will I do if Leri finds out?" he asked as they walked along. "What will she think?"

Carol scuffed the leaves in front him, few and dry in the beginning of winter, much as Mihai used to do in Radauti.

"How much does she know?" he asked.

"Nothing."

"It will be when she finds out, not if, and you'd better give her your version before she hears someone else's. Word has already gotten around. It won't be long before someone says something to her." Fane considered this. "Thanks," he said, only half ironically.

But it did seem like the best idea, maybe. He wasn't supposed to tell anyone, what a farce since everyone at the Institute knew or thought they knew, but Leri wasn't just anyone. Fane returned from his talk with Carol, dragging his feet up their endless narrow stairs, watching how the staircase curved back on itself in the small space, counting them as he had done so often, feeling the staircase was longer than his tired body could manage. Leri greeted him from the kitchen as he took off his coat in the hall, Fane was unusually silent through dinner but made love to his wife, almost savagely, afterward. Fortunately, she liked it. Fane woke during the middle of the night and felt her breathing close beside him in the same small bed they had continued to share since they had moved in this place. Fane thought about his past dreams of a square, clean apartment in one of the new high rises and then realized he was grateful they had never come to pass. Not only was he used to this place, this neighborhood, but with their stove that would burn wood or coal they had some control over their heat. Important nowadays that the Government turned the Central Heating down so often, so much. His heart squeezing in pain, Fane thought what losing all this might mean and how, however, could he keep it safe? All of his fears, present but pushed out of sight for months and long years, resurfaced and were determinedly pushed aside again. 'We'll manage,' Fane told himself, half believing it.

Day finally came and with it the morning routine, almost normal. Maybe he could just forget it and...no..."Let's leave a bit early so you can walk with me to the Institute and take the bus from there," Fane suggested, grasping his doubts and pushing them roughly aside. Leri looked at him in surprise — the request was nothing new since they often shared the extra time together, but usually the weather was better. She glanced outside at the gray skies and back at Fane, seeing something in his face. "All right, it doesn't look as if it will rain for a while."

Together they left the gate. Right or left? The distance was almost the same around the lopsided triangle of their long block. Fane made the decision by himself, turning right and taking Leri with him. They walked in front of the neighbors' houses, passed the villa where Rodica and Emil lived, came to the wall of the garden of the house that once belonged to Ana Pauker. There at the end of the block Leri knew something was wrong when Fane continued north instead of turning toward the Institute. She tucked her hand under his elbow and he pulled it against his side. "I love you," Leri said softly, too low for anyone but Fane to hear although no one was in sight.

"I have something to tell you..." Fane started. "I don't know how to say it."

"Just try." And he did try. He told her of how they had first gotten their invitations to the American Library, how that led into more activities and, finally, how he had been cornered into becoming the informer to the Securitate for all of the Nicolae Iorga Institute. His hopes, his fears, the war between his sometime belief that he might be helping their beloved country and his realization that things weren't going well in that country. Fane talked of Antonescu, their growing friendship, and said aloud for the first time his feeling that even Antonescu didn't believe in what he was doing sometimes. "And, I guess, my work at the Institute...what I'm doing isn't for Them, it's for my colleagues, to protect them from the...consequences of...of not doing... doing something they shouldn't." Fane's voice trailed off and they walked in silence, his heart aching with every anguished beat.

"I love you," Leri said again and held his arm tightly against her breast. "I love you more than I love my own life.

And I believe in you. I believe you didn't do, won't do, anything wrong. I don't...like Them...but you didn't have a choice, did you?"

"No, I didn't. No, not really."

"You're a good person. We'll come through this. And you're right, you're helping people at the Institute, you're protecting them even if you have to work with..." Leri's voice trailed off as Fane's relief at her words lifted his feet and spirits. Even if he did wonder if he were as good as Leri believed.

"Oh, I forgot. I think we're going to have to invite Ellen, the American Library Director, to dinner." Fane broke their now comfortable silence as they approached the Institute.

"What?! You have to be joking! With food the way it is? We can't! She's an American!" The ensuing flurry of discussion erased the previous conversation and made them both late to work although in Fane's case it didn't matter.

Bucharest — February 1984. I am so tired of this winter, the snow, the cold...it's not that much colder than Iowa but the streets aren't cleared and are icy, the city dark. It's depressing, silent crowds of people huddled inside enormous coats. Of course, I have one too, now, my lovely sheepskin cojoc *with its furry cuffs and hem that I just walked in the Hotel Dorobanti and bought out of the shop on impulse one day because I was so cold. It was a good investment. At least the Library and the Embassy are warm and welcoming and I'm making friends, both Romanian and American. The Americans... Sandy from the DAO office who rides with me. Roger the Regional Security Officer who also rides and he isn't a really close friend, but I have come to an understanding with him about reporting contacts. I can thank the afternoons at Olimpia for that, I guess, so now I can go riding by myself and meet Romanians and don't have to report unless there's something special or...well, whatever I think needs to be said. I don't like it but I do guess it's necessary. But it's hard to think of Romania as a hostile country.*

Then my boss, Scott and his wife, they're nice. So are the Mellons. Dave in the Political Section...we all seem to meet in Mom's at lunch, funny place Mom's, kind of half underground and

252

warm and smelling of food, how could it not since the counter and kitchen are right there in the dining room if it could be called a dining room. The Romanians complain about the prices but I see them there most days.

And the villa at Sinaia is a treat, a great getaway place. I like Sinaia in those beautiful mountains, the great trees, the hodge-podge of chalets and houses and Germanic and Romanian fanciful architecture. Romania is such a lovely country – I remember the time a bunch of us went up to that Dacian archaeological dig with the Fulbright archeologist...I should remember his name but Jim deals with the Fulbrighters and there are so many names to remember.I saw grapes hanging down from a trellis over a courtyard in the village and took a Polaroid picture.The old couple who owned the house were delighted and insisted we drink some of their homemade wine. It was wonderful, sitting in sun dappled by the vines on that warm afternoon, drinking wine...what a glorious country this could be. I suppose it will get warm again in the spring, it's just hard to wait.

The last of the spring light filtered through the trees and lit the floor behind the four musicians. They finished the Adagio in D minor from Beethoven's *String Quartet in F major* and the small audience sat quiet a minute before clapping, softly but enthusiastically. Fane later complimented Emil on his playing, "Though," he added, "I actually like Mozart and the older composers better. Emil looked at his friend in surprise. "Really?" he exclaimed. "I love them, of course, but Beethoven has so much more depth, greater darkness, complexity, at times musical surprises..."

"That may be why I prefer the older composers," Fane said thoughtfully. "There's so much we don't control in life, so much darkness, so many surprises that the very predictability, measured rhythm..." At this point they were interrupted by Rodica with a glass in her hand and a tray of puff pastry..."I'm sorry we can't offer you anything better..." "No such thing..." and the conversation moved into news of families in the country and back into expressions of appreciation for the music, the afternoon, the glorious spring weather and one another's progress.

"Where are you thinking about for your vacation in August? I know it's early but..." someone asked Emil.

"I'm not sure. There's that hydrological project in the Carpathians they talked about last year. I need to look at it and since the working season is short, it's apparently up high, I may not be able to take my regular leave."

"What a shame. We're debating whether to return to Mamaia — a bit scruffy but so interesting with the artists — or to take the waters at Calimanesti..." The voice trailed off as Fane turned to another friend in the small group and listened to a request for a good word at the housing central office. 'I seem to be everyone's 'go-to' person,' Fane thought comfortably, knowing that his help here would be returned there though this tendency of some people to give him information about others wasn't..." "Fane, Fane!" It was Leri. "Have you forgotten Carol's meeting us..." Good-byes said, the couple left, another nice Sunday afternoon, another few hours they could leave cares aside...but the worries always returned.

Today they were about Daniela downstairs. "She's getting old," Leri had pointed out, "and she always was a bit off, but she's becoming battier and battier and even less careful about her, uh, dare we even call it housekeeping?"

"It's too bad she doesn't have children to take care of her."

"I know...oh, look, Carol's waiting for us at the gate! I wonder if I made a mistake about the time." Carol didn't smile, he had a sympathetic look on his handsome face. 'Lucky bastard,' thought Fane, 'he hasn't put on the weight I have and looks ten years younger...' "Fane, Leri, I hope you'll forgive my coming early but," Carol turned to Fane, "Father was trying to reach you and no one answered, so he called me."

"Why, is something wrong?"

"Yes, yes...I'm afraid there is. Let's go inside."

"Tell me now, please."

"It's your father," Carol began, slowly so that Fane could prepare himself. "Your father...he's..." Carol hesitated.

"Are you trying to tell me he's dead?" Fane interrupted, impatient to have this over with, to know the worst.

"Yes." Carol moved forward and the two men embraced silently, then pulled apart. Leri moved close to Fane and he put his arm around her, drawing her close for comfort. "Let's go upstairs," he said.

Fane's thoughts raced ahead of his heavy steps, he'd need to go to Bukovina, he'd have to cancel this meeting and... The two men unconsciously turned into the little dining room and sat at the tiny table, each one a bit too big for the space, while Leri put on water for tea in the kitchen. "Maybe we need something stronger," Fane suggested. "Of course," she answered, "but also drink this herb tea. It will help." Fane shrugged his shoulders and mouthed 'women' at Carol forgetting, for a split second, what he had just learned. Carol's words brought him back.

"Father said Petru died of a stroke on the road to your house. It looks to have been very quick—he staggered a few steps and fell. Your neighbor, Tante Elise—do you remember her?" Fane nodded, of course, she must be a hundred and ten by now, "she had just come out of her gate, you know how it faces the lane just at the corner and she can see down it..."

"...and has used that to know what her neighbors were doing all my life..."

"Well, she saw him and ran to help but it was too late. He didn't suffer."

"That's a blessing." Fane pushed his chair back and rose to pace the floor, realized that of course there was no room to pace, and sat down again. "I need to go to Bukovina."

"Yes, you do. And that's...that's not the end of the bad news."

"What more could there be? What will I do with the house? The land? Not that there's much left..."

Carol looked at his friend with enormous sympathy.

"That won't be a problem, I'm afraid."

"What...? What else is there?"

"Petru sold the house. Father didn't know until just now or he would have done...well, something." Fane sat silent, dumbfounded. Carol continued, as much to fill the silence as to provide information. "He sold the house with some sort of agreement about his living there. The man who bought it, he has papers, says the deal included the house and everything on the farm. We might be able to fight it but Father says..." Fane glanced up at the little green and yellow plate on the wall. Was this all of Bukovina that remained to him?

Carol interrupted his thoughts. "I've arranged for train tickets for tonight," he began. Fane looked at him wondering what miracle next. "You'd better pack. It might take us a few days to settle everything." Fane looked wordlessly at Leri. "I'll come if you want," she began, "but..." "No," Fane heard himself say. "You have school and...I don't know..." he floundered for words, not wanting to reject Leri, not wanting to what...share this last bit of his childhood with an outsider, how could Leri be an outsider...where was Mihai, how could he tell him...But Mihai's father already...

'I understand,' she said wordlessly with her eyes, then stepped forward and took him in her arms. "I love you," she said aloud, the most comforting words he could have. "I'm here. I'll wait for you."

The journey was long, the night spent in tossing from side to narrow side in the berth, listening to the wheels of the train clacking endlessly north. 'I have no father, I have no home,' Fane repeated to himself over and over almost in wonder. 'What does this mean? Who am I without part of Bilca in me and part of me in Bilca, without Bukovina?' By the time they reached Radauti Fane was groggy with fatigue as they climbed down onto the platform at Radauti and stunned when he saw a virtual welcoming committee, Uncle Vanya, Aunt Anna, Professor Brebean, Carol's father, two or three friends from his childhood and many trips. The men embraced each other wordlessly or with murmured words so soft and trite they were background noise, then arranged to move off the platform together, low voices humming continued condolences. 'I wonder if they understand that it isn't the loss of my father, it's the loss of my life,' Fane said to himself. He must have said it aloud as well for Aunt Anna took his arm and moved closer. "Mourn all that is past," she said. "But it's not gone. It will live as long as you remember it."

Those words gave Fane solace through the next days. Memories. There was little enough left in the small house to take but he had memories as he picked up objects, looked at them and set them down again. Aunt Anna had come to help and under her guidance Fane gave some things to friends or set them aside for the poor, the carpet from the wall would go with him though where they would put it in Bucharest he had no idea. The tools and farm implements were to go with the land, he understood that and it wasn't a loss to him personally except perhaps for one of the scythes he remembered swinging at a young age, cutting a few wisps of hay for Haiduc. Fane slept in his father's bed, his parents' bed, looking at the handloomed, coarse sheets and thinking how worn, how old, how many memories were woven into them, memories that came alive and infused his dreams with the past through restless nights.

When he sorted through things in the kitchen with Aunt Anna she put different objects into his hands. There was the great wooden trough Mother and Granny had made bread in, polished smooth from years of handling dough, a large wooden scoop for flour, a small one for sugar, a little wooden spoon with a carved handle. Fane held it up and looked at it, eyes misting over yet again. "Keep these," said Aunt Anna. "Keep them. They have been used for generations and will disappear along with our heritage if we don't treasure them." Fane looked at her, questioning. "Haven't you seen the bakeries, the metal utensils in stores?" asked Aunt Anna. Fane nodded and put them aside feeling as if he were approaching the end of more than his father's life.

Finally things were over. It had taken two full days to clean out the little farm and two more to visit with all the people who wanted to share their condolences and own a part of their village son who had gone to Bucharest. Fane subtley assured them that he was still a part of Bilca, still available to them, and was given both flattery and real warmth in return. His last conversation was with Ion Cojocariu who took him to the station driving, Fane noted as he had before with amusement, a Trabant like his son. Carol had left after he had seen that Aunt Anna was a pillar for Fane and knowing his father was there in the background.

"The car isn't the strongest," the former Mayor, now grizzled and a bit bent but still powerful in his bearing and gaze, explained, "but it's become a...joke with Carol and me. He's been coming more often now he has a car to drive." Fane nodded, murmuring something appropriate. Both men knew that Carol's visits became more regular when his mother finally died. "I'm sorry things turned out as they did. I hadn't known..." Cojocariu continued, his eyes leaving the road to meet Fane's, bright blue under bushy gray brows.

"I know that," Fane assured him."Maybe you can find me some old paper for me to practice writing again..." he joked. Cojocariu smiled. "We did some good things," he replied. "And my house is yours, always will be, when you want to come home." The words were genuine and oddly comforting. There still was a place to call home. "You know...wait," said Fane suddenly. "Don't drop me at the station, take me to the bus stand. I want to go to Sucevita, the Monastery...there's, uh, there's something there I've been meaning to consult and it would be...while I'm here..." His voice trailed off. Ion Cojocariu looked at him and smiled. "Sometimes the old ways are best," was all he said as he turned the car.

Bucharest — May 1984. I don't think I'm going to eat again in my life. Scott and Norma feel the same way. Imagine, being overfed in this country where there's nothing in the shops, the markets, where there are lines for bread.

At least we got to see a real Romanian home and Valeria, Stefan's wife, is an absolute darling, a teacher, Romanian literature I think but she didn't really say, just something about secondary school. She seemed a little nervous at first and apologetic about her house and it is tiny and crowded, but really nice. Imagine, right behind the Ambassador's residence and I had no idea that little island of charming houses – rundown, of course, but charming – and their cobblestone streets was even there. It seemed as if there were nothing but endless apartment blocks and the funny wonderful roofs I see out my window though there must be houses below them, too.What I see is only the roofs and dirty tops of walls...but no...this seemed like a real neighborhood. The kind of thing you should have in Europe, a European city...

The entrance is down the side of the building, by what is obviously a lovely little strip of garden in the summer, I wonder who keeps it so neat, a loving hand, and why the little garden in front of the house is so messy. The entrances to a lot of Romanian houses are at the side, something to do with taxes in the old days I heard but forgot, who was it that told me? The apartment, upstairs, a small, dark stairway winding up, was full of books and we sat and ate in the same room, warm and cozy...I wonder what the rest of the their apartment looks like. But the food...I still can't believe it. If only we hadn't thought the 'Cold Appetizer' was the meal we would have been all right. No, there was still too much food, a hearty soup, then that cold beef in jelly thing, they called it piftie, a word I hadn't known before, and it was surprisingly good because the thought is pretty revolting, and THEN the 'main course' and two desserts. I thought we'd die, we kept looking at one another and wondering how we'd manage to be polite and keep eating but Stefan and Valeria were so hospitable, so warm though I once wondered if Stefan was enjoying our discomfort. He is probably Securitate, Scott thinks so and I guess I have to agree because otherwise why would he, not speaking English, be at everything at the Library. Valeria was in the kitchen a lot but surely Stefan noticed we were overstuffed. He does make it easy to speak Romanian, somehow I don't feel bad about making mistakes and he's always talking even though I miss a lot. Scott's Romanian isn't very good and Norma doesn't speak any at all so I had to keep translating and felt pretty good about myself. Bit by bit I'm finding cracks in those endless walls.

Spring has really come and the roses are blooming in the long May evenings. Bucharest is lovely this time of year. I found a book in an old anticariat, a used book shop, down near the Curtea Veche. There's a man there, Andrei, who is really nice and suggests things that might interest me. This one is called "Bucharest Weekend" and has seven journeys, day trips, around Bucharest. Sandy and I have been doing them one by one on Sundays after church. She also enjoys getting out of the Embassy, so few do, and we've even visited a functioning monastery. They were surprised to see us but invited us to lunch – they seem to eat nothing but fish. One of the monks explained some of the differences between Orthodox and Western Christianity and seemed really glad to find someone interested in such things.

I'm a bit surprised that I am interested in them in fact. I've never been very religious, yet somehow I've started going to church, to the little redbrick Victorian church attended by Queen Marie. There's another interesting piece of Romanian history, Dave in the Political Section gave me Hannah Pakula's biography of her, he's becoming a friend. Single but I think he's gay. Anyway, that doesn't matter. I understand there's a better biography of Queen Marie by someone else but this is certainly interesting. There's nothing in the bookstores in Romanian about the Royal Family, of course, since the Communists don't want anyone to know about them or, maybe more accurately, remember them and how things used to be I guess. Andrei in the Anticariat though, did show me some prints of a parade that apparently was in honor of the King. All the guilds had sort of floats illustrating what they did and I bought one of them, the Baker's Guild. It's too bad things are so expensive. If we can't pay for them in Kent cigarettes, that is, our "other" currency. I'm going to buy a saddle with Kents if Enache can manage one.

So things are beginning to unfold, I'm beginning to make some Romanian friends or acquaintances. The only problem is the riding club. Sandy and Roger and I – the three of us who go most *regularly — were looking forward to good weather. Then we found out that it's horseshow season and all the best horses are in training or being taken to the shows. I talked to Carol about it and he might be able to do something. That's a friend I've made, Carol. Attractive, too, even if he's older but, then, he's Romanian and off limits. I wish there were more single men in the Embassy. I'm lucky to have great colleagues and some good friends, but most of them are married, like Scott and he's my boss anyway. I like Norma, too, which is nice, but a life with no men in it...*

"Fane," Carol said a week or two after Fane had returned to Bucharest, "I need you to get clearance for something." He leaned back against the high booth in the restaurant they had chosen for lunch.

"Huh?"

"You know, permission from your friends."

"They're not exactly friends," Fane said ironically as he picked up his fork. The food looked great — Carol always seemed to have inside information about where to find good meals. "What do you need."

"Um, a horse." Carol grinned disarmingly but, Fane thought, a bit tense underneath.

"You have access to plenty of horses," Fane said. "What's up."

"Let me explain. It involves Ellen." Carol went on to describe the situation with horses being gone from the riding club for shows during the spring, summer and early autumn, "...which affects me, too, as I don't have a decent animal to ride half the time."

"How often do you go?" Fane asked, realizing he should have kept better tabs on this activity. "You only go when Ellen's there, I imagine," he added.

"Well, no..." Carol looked a bit abashed, if that's the word, Fane thought. "You see I've been, um, taking riding lessons." Fane froze in astonishment, fork with food in midair. "You what?" he exclaimed. "You? Riding lessons?"

"Riding lessons. There's a Col. Molnar there, a Dressage master, Balkan Championship and all that. I've been riding his horse, Bufon, and learning things that I didn't know were possible or...important. I've done some of it all my life, of course, lateral work, but the balance and precision required..." Carol's voice trailed off as he realized that Fane, as usual, was retreating into boredom or some other state not having to do with horses. "King Carol liked horses," he added wickedly, bringing Fane's attention back into being.

"Which King Carol?"

"Both, probably. Mainly Queen Marie. Listen, that's not important. What is important is that I want to get myself a young horse to train and thought we might manage to get Ellen a horse at the same time. She doesn't know about this yet, of course, because, well, you know. But she and that friend of hers both ride fairly well, Ellen's really good, actually, and could handle a proper jumper that she could work with regularly. And it would keep them coming to the Club regularly."

"Is that important?"

"Well," Carol said, "it could be because they are making friends, particularly Sandy, that's the girl in the Defense Attaché's office..." His voice trailed off. Fane's ears tingled. How much did Carol know? "Defense Attaché?" Fane said mildly. "He's got quite a reputation, the Defense Attaché. What does this Sandy do?"

"I'm not sure...some sort of clerical work, I think. What about the Defense Attaché?"

"Oh, nothing, well...it seems he's apparently been gathering information on the railroads," Fane smiled, "he's actually been prowling through railroad yards at night and once when he was stopped and asked what he was doing, he said he was hunting pheasants!" Both men laughed...an American with a sense of humor! After a pause, Fane asked, "Is all of this about this woman true or are you making it up to get another horse you can ride?"

Carol drew back and laughed again, slapping Fane on the back. "I can get horses to ride if I want, but Ellen's a really good rider and I want her to have a good horse. And I want a horse I can train. And the part about the friend, Sandy, you know she works in the Defense Attaché's office so that should provide your friends some motivation."

"They aren't my friends," said Fane automatically but he knew he was lying. By this time Antonescu really was a friend. "All right, I'll see what I can do." The conversation moved on to the quality of the food and where to find auto parts. Carol, as usual, had a connection that could help Leri's cousin's third whatever...

..."That's an interesting idea," said Antonescu, leaning back in his chair. The air in the 'office' was slightly stale, as usual, and the desk was clear of any papers or signs of life. Fane looked past Antonescu's head at the wall outside the window. "Getting a horse. It just might work. You said that Carol mentioned Jegalia, that's a place where they raise horses?"

"It's near Bucharest, near Calarasi, they raise sport horses, jumpers and so forth."

"Let me ask. It's an interesting idea. Could give us..." Antonescu's voice trailed off then came back to normal. "On another topic, I have a favor if it's possible?" Fane braced himself for something unpleasant, especially as Antonescu was, unusually for him, playing with a pencil and fidgeting. "It's my wife," the Securitate agent continued. "And my daughter...I made a mistake and mentioned in passing that a friend knew Carol Cojocariu and now they want, well, they want to meet him. Perhaps get a picture... you know..." Antonescu's voice trailed off and he coughed.

"Of course, I can arrange something. I'd be glad to!" Fane found he meant it. It wouldn't be hard and he liked Antonescu.

And it would be a little debt, just a little one, but a favor owed was always useful.

So it was that meetings and photo opportunities were planned and happened and two weeks later Fane found himself crammed uncomfortably in the back seat of Carol's little Trabant, listening while Carol and Ellen chatted about horses. After rattling over a long series of neglected streets through Bucharest they were finally on the similarly neglected highway to Calarasi. 'If we're so great, why can't we have better roads, like they have in Western films?' thought Fane rebelliously as he felt a headache creeping up from his neck. The flat Danube plain stretched out endlessly, broken by patches of woods, and small villages with unrealistically slow speed limits which had to be observed because otherwise the local militia would have a field day. Finally, interminably later, they arrived at the horse farm — "So soon," exclaimed Ellen — where they were met with smiles and obsequious bows and then genuine pleasure as people recognized Carol's well-known face. Before long they found themselves in the Director's office sharing a glass of *tzuica*. 'They probably don't have any coffee,' Fane thought to himself, still in a bad mood as he studiously ignored a lively discussion of horses, breeds, breeding stock and Ellen's endless questions about them all. It seemed an age before the man who had been introduced as the veterinarian came through the door, bowed to Ellen, and said in perfect English, "Madame, your coach and four are waiting." Ellen's face lit with pleasure and she turned first to the Director then back to the other man excitedly. "Really? How wonderful! I'm so sorry Sandy couldn't come!"

It was, Fane had to admit to everyone a few minutes later, rather nice, having a large, comfortable coach, a driver and four beautiful horses take them around the farm. It was, he also admitted himself, nice to be treated like a VIP. When they descended from the coach he went up to the horses, put a hand on the inquiring nose of one, and looked at the harness. So light, so lovely. He fingered the soft reins and examined the hames. The coachman came up and Fane asked him about braking and how well it worked. When he

264

finished the conversation and turned away, Ellen was looking at him curiously.

"I thought you were a city person and didn't know anything about horses," she said. Fane felt caught out. "No, I was raised in the country, on a farm. Remember?"

"Oh," she started, then Carol called and they went to look at the animals they might be able to lease.

It had been, Fane explained to Carol when they planned the day, the only option for Ellen. It wasn't clear why the Government didn't want foreigners to buy horses but they didn't, so she and Sandy could lease a horse, for a fairly steep price, then pay to keep it at the Club. "They probably want to make money off the foreigners," said Carol sardonically. He was probably right. Carol, however, could have a horse assigned to him at no cost though it might cost another photo opportunity. Or two. The two men had laughed together at this.

Finally, after Ellen and Carol had tried several, two horses had been chosen, both five years old, both lovely. Watching on the sidelines, the Director said softly to Fane, "She's really good. I wonder if they train diplomats to ride as part of their education."

"I don't know," was all Fane could reply. "Perhaps." To himself he said, 'I wonder if she realizes how lucky she's been, to have had horses just to ride...not to be worked to old age and a salami factory...' He shut his thoughts off with a snap.

The deal was sealed with another *tzuica* — Carol abstaining, of course, as he was driving — and as the case may be, several more *tzuicas* between Fane and the Director and they parted company cheerfully. Fane slept during the drive home, dreaming of Haiduc sailing over jumps of impossible height, and woke uncomfortably as they bounced into Bucharest.

"What was it like?" Leri asked when he had settled into his chair at their tiny, comfortable dining table and sighed.

"It was," Fane began and paused, trying to describe how it was and how he had felt, "it was like another world, two or three worlds meeting. First there was the *herghelie*, the horse breeding farm. They breed dozens of beautiful, beautiful horses and I'm not sure why, except they do use the stallions that aren't so good for mounting mares in the countryside." As he said this Fane suddenly realized that Haiduc probably had been the product of some such program with his fine head and beautiful proportions. He hadn't been imagining that he was a good horse, maybe he really hadn't been just imagining... "Then there was Ellen. She's a really good rider — I hadn't realized that before even though Carol had said she was. They were impressed at the farm. Then there was Carol, the center of adulation although they had to pay a lot of attention to the American diplomat, of course."

"And you were like a fly on the wall?"

"No," Fane said slowly. "I had a good time there, I did. In the end, I have to say that. The Director is an intelligent, thoughtful man and we had a good discussion. I learned a lot..." "Are you going to start riding then?"

"No!" And Fane changed the subject.

But the visit stayed with him. There was perhaps another aspect to it, the breeding farm was lovely. It was well kept, the people working there obviously liked their jobs and were proud of what they did. And it was totally hidden away from the rest of the world. He raised this with Antonescu one afternoon when they had met outside for a beer.

"Hidden away? Maybe," Antonescu said cynically. "Remember, there are members of The Family who like horses..."

Fane put his glass on the table, perhaps a bit too forcefully. He didn't want his dreams shattered. Again.

"We need to plan the next step in our campaign," Antonescu continued. Now..." The two sat, talking into the warm evening.

Bucharest—July 1984. We heard today that the Romanian government is taking away the Embassy villa at Sinaia. They say there will be another, someplace else. What a pity, it was a lovely place and we've had such fun there. I'll always remember the first time I won the lottery to choose weekends and it was Presidents' Day. There was snow on all the funny roofs of the town and on the great fir trees, a winter picture postcard – this country can be so lovely. The rumor is because it's too close to Peles, where Ceausescu sometimes stays. What a pity.

I hope they don't stop us going to the riding club but it's probably too shabby for Ceausescu to be interested in. Anyway, they wouldn't have let me lease Ropot if they were going to keep me from riding him, at least I think not. He's such a lovely jumper, a little full of life but that's great. And they've let the Austrian Commercial Attaché – what IS his name I always forget – lease a horse, too, that beautiful gray that's too much for him to handle properly. I think he's scared but he still gets out and rides.

Part of the problem for some is that almost all the horses are stallions, just Igor, the other Dressage horse from Bufon, is a gelding and Enache said Igor was gelded after he had killed someone. Carol takes lessons on him now that Col. Molnar is taking Bufon to shows. Carol and Enache are the only people Igor doesn't buck off... he has such a beautiful seat, Carol does.

We almost always sit in the Clubhouse after we ride on Saturdays. That's the only day because if I can get out there early on a weekday morning I have to leave for work as soon as I finish. What luxury to be able to hand the reins to someone and know the horse will be cared for. On Saturday afternoons when we finish we drink tzuica, the plum brandy, together. The Romanians are all so pleased that we Americans like it but we still bring a bottle of Scotch most weeks and always some food. They usually have food, too, and we share. Saturdays, unless there is something on, which doesn't usually happen since we always seem to do our socializing/work on weeknights, sitting there at the Club I eat and drink so much I don't want dinner when I get home. They're so generous with what they have and I know it isn't much. And we talk about Enache's adventures when he was an ambulance driver and this and that, they talk and we try to understand but we do okay – amazing how Roger's Romanian is so much better. They told him in Washington he couldn't learn languages but put him on a horse or in the club and he does all right, and Sandy is really doing well, too. She and Enache chat on about nothing though I'm not really sure they understand each other. Perhaps we should get everyone in the Embassy out to ride and practice their language skills – they study so hard in Washington then they get in the Embassy and forget everything because they don't use it. I'm all right since I'm alone in the Library and some of the Romanian staff doesn't speak English and then there are the people who come in with letters for the President, VOA, and, of course, the VOA monthly program so I'm talking and trying to understand all the time. I hate recording the VOA program and always stumble even though it's all written down in Romanian translation for me and we practice but I suppose it's good...I wonder if anyone ever listens to it.

Fane stepped down from the bus and crossed the May 1 Boulevard, thinking fleetingly of dipping into the market to see if there was anything of interest then pushing the thought aside. The day was lovely, warm with only a hint of autumn, and his news was good. Before he'd gone to the University Library, Director Dragomir had called him into his office with some startling information.

"What do you know about Gregory Tamblac?" he asked as Fane walked in. "Sit down and tell me."

Fane eased himself into a chair. "An emissary from Constantinople to Moldova or, more specifically, Suceava to asses the church there and report to Constantinople. The report was favorable so the Metropolitanate of Suceava was officially recognized. I believe..." Fane hesitated a moment, mentally riffling through pages of history, "he remained in Moldova to lecture and teach then...he went to Kiev..."

"...but retained his ties with Moldova." Dragomir finished for him, "and participated in the Council of Constance. Where was he born?"

268

"Um...if I remember correctly, there is some controversy about that. The Bulgarians claim him, he was, er, possibly from Serbia or perhaps Macedo..."

"Macedonia," Dragomir cut in, uncharacteristically. The Director heaved his great bulk forward. "And our friend Father Augustin at Sucevita has just informed me that he has been brought scraps of a manuscript which he believes was written by Gregory Tamblac and in which he refers to his Aroman heritage as linking him particularly closely with Romania!"

Fane, too, leaned forward in excitement. This would be groundbreaking and well...really, very...well received in the highest quarters though maybe because it was religious, but still the historical validation... The two men talked excitedly for some time and Fane left with instructions to get himself to Suceavita as quickly as possible.

Leri wouldn't be able to go, which was a shame, Fane thought as he turned into Ady Endre, because she enjoyed Sucevita and Father Augustin as much as he did, and they probably would be able to see Uncle Vanya and Aunt Anna and perhaps even go to Bilca. And here in town he might miss the first autumn gathering at Emil's. That was really too bad, he'd missed Emil, away in the Carpathians all summer, and Fane enjoyed both the music and the atmosphere of those gatherings. He also, he thought, enjoyed talking to Emil, one of the few people he could really discuss ideas with, chew things over with now that Mihai...but this opportunity, if Gregory Tamblac were really of Romanian origin... Fane unlatched the gate and admired the last of his garden before he glanced up to the bathroom window to see if Leri were looking out, waiting for him as she sometimes did.

Instead Leri was at the head of their stairs standing in the open doorway crying. "I heard the gate," she said between sobs then fell into Fane's arms. Alarmed he held her tightly and put his face against her hair. "What's wrong?" He felt her tense and grip him even more tightly.

"Emil has been killed," Leri said in a flat tone which told Fane of the effort she was making to speak.

"I was with Rodica when she had the telephone call this afternoon. There was an accident. I tried to call you at the Institute but you weren't there."

"I was at the University Library," Fane said mechanically, thinking he should have been at home or at least in the Library of the Metropolinate of the Orthodox Church which would have been more...he brought his thoughts into greater order. "Do we know what happened?" he asked. "What kind of accident?"

"It wasn't clear. He was in the mountains and there was a landslide where they were excavating for a pipeline or something, not a bad one but he slipped and fell and hit his head. At least, that's what I understood. Rodica was hysterical when she got off the phone and told me."

"Where is she now? Is someone with her?"

"Emil's parents were at home, and his brother came..." Leri's voice trailed off.

"We should go see what we can do..." Fane remembered that he had to leave in the morning for Suceava and Sucevita. Oh, my God, he thought.

The next day on the train rumbling north he tried to put his thoughts in order. It was the second time he had gone north recently with a death on his mind, he noted to himself, and the first was devastating but so was this...Emil wasn't a relative...but a good friend...maybe it was because he was Fane's age, not an older person but...Fane sat up and for the second time in his life saw himself in perspective. He, too, was getting old.

The surprise of this realization stayed with him until Radauti and was reinforced by the frailty of Uncle Vanya though Aunt Anna seemed as energetic as usual. But Vanya's mind was as incisive as ever and his words, his ability to take something like death and put it out on the table in front of them to be examined from different angles was comforting as nothing else could have been.

Fane spent the night in Radauti then found a car and driver to take him to Sucevita. He'd become a bit old for the bus, he thought as he sat beside the young chauffeur; those days were past.

Father Augustin came as soon as the man at the gate sent word that Fane had arrived. The two men embraced then Augustin drew back. "Something is troubling you, what is it?" he said, the naked question jolting Fane almost into tears. Augustin took him by the elbow and steered him into his office. "Sit here and tell me."

Relating the sad story of Emil's accident — it wasn't necessary to ask Augustin to pray for his soul — made Fane feel better and after the normal condolences they were able to move on to Augustin's discovery. The monk opened a drawer and drew out a folder containing pieces of an ancient and very dirty manuscript. "You see, look here, it says...but I'm not sure..."

Fane remained at the Monastery two full days working with Augustin, poring over the ancient texts, fragmented and almost indecipherable but by the end of the second afternoon both were convinced that, without doubt, Gregory had written of his Aroman heritage. "This is a great discovery!" Fane said as Augustin closed the folder for the last time and both men stood, "A great discovery!" he repeated.

"I agree. God has given us a magnificent gift in this, through the person of a poor peasant." Augustin had told Fane of the man who came to the Monastery with the folder, how he wouldn't accept payment but only asked for prayers. "We must celebrate tonight," Augustin continued, "and I have a wonderful bottle of wine I've saved for just such an occasion. First, though, I would like to stretch these old aching legs since we've been sitting all day. Would you come with me?"

The two men talked casually as they left the monastery and turned into the woods on the hill behind it. A small path led, as Fane knew, past the hidden forest strawberry patch then up to a meadow at the top if they felt energetic enough to get there. Augustin, however, took another small path off to the left about halfway up, one that Fane didn't know. It led to an open space looking out over the valley to the Carpathians beyond. The late summer sun was low in the west, bathing them in its warmth and casting a red-gold haze about them.

"Isn't God's creation wonderful?" said Father Augustin unconsciously. Just as unconsciously Fane agreed.

"Let's sit on these rocks a minute," continued Augustin. "I have a duty, a burden that I must share with you." Fane wondered at the use of the word '*sarcina*' — it seemed heavy and out of place on this day.

"There are a few men like you," Augustin said, "who come to me as a friend and seeking, perhaps, God or at least some meaning greater than is found in everyday life." Fane nodded his head, inexplicably jealous about sharing this special relationship...but nothing could be like their relationship. Augustin continued. "One of these was the man who was, I'm infinitely saddened by that word, 'was', also your friend, Emil. In fact I think you met him here..."

"You knew, didn't you. That Emil had died. Before I told you." Augustin nodded. "How did you know?"

"Word moves quickly at times," he replied unhelpfully, "but how I knew isn't important. It's what I know and that I must now share with you."

"What exactly...?"

Augustin shifted to a more comfortable position on the rock and Fane settled in for a longish talk as he knew Father Augustin's way of going around information before he came to the heart of it. This time, however, he was surprised. And shocked.

"Emil didn't die in an accident, he was killed," the monk said bluntly. "He was killed because he knew too much. The first sentence I know is true because a trusted source told me. The second is true because I know what Emil knew and why that made them kill him." Fane froze. "Don't be afraid...or,

272

rather, do be afraid. I am sorry to do this to you but I must pass on this information as it is too important to stay with me and someone must know who can help us be sure worse things, very bad things won't happen.

"The 'hydrology' project that Emil was called to work on was a project to develop a nuclear bomb. They needed a hydrologist to deal with the water involved — I don't know the science but apparently nuclear weapons require, in some way or another, quantities of water. It didn't take long for Emil to realize what was happening but he couldn't say anything or do anything about it. You know how it is." Fane nodded. He knew how it was.

"Emil pretended he had no understanding of what was going on and continued his work. It was probably the will of God that his wife's mother died in late July and during Emil's trip to Bucharest for the funeral, Mrs. Rodica insisted that they come here so I could conduct a service for her. While they were here, Emil asked to confess to me absolutely privately. I thought perhaps he had sinned, being away from Rodica all summer in the mountains, and in the face of his mother-in-law's death wanted to be told God still loved him but it was nothing so trivial." Augustin's voice had become hard and bitter. "It was this enormous matter of possible death for many, this weapon which, in the wrong hands, could ruin vast swathes of God's creation and all God's creatures within it. And now, because of his knowledge, a good man, a good friend, is dead."

"What can..." Fane began after a period of heavy silence but Augustin raised his hand. "I'm not finished," he said. Fane nodded and resumed listening.

"Part of what Emil told me meant nothing, but he asked me to memorize it. My years of study and memorizing sacred texts helped me in this and I hope that you will be able to remember what I am now going to tell you." Fane nodded and Augustin went on, reciting a series of words and letters and numbers some of which made sense some of which didn't, and the whole of which was totally out of Fane's reach. He asked Fane to recite them after him, first in pieces, then in the whole. Augustin had formed them into a chant, which helped Fane remember. Finally, satisfied that the other man would retain the information, Augustin stopped, his face suddenly gray with fatigue.

"What can..." Fane began again. Once again the monk cut him short.

"I am not asking, not suggesting, you do anything. God will lead you to what you will and must do. I am burdening you because of all people, you are the only one I know with the intelligence, the honesty, the strength to, by the grace of God, possibly do something to prevent..."Augustin's voice trailed off into a prayer and Fane realized what an enormous burden this was also for the monk, now for both of them.

"Forgive me, my friend. I prayed long and hard before I decided to call you and share this with you."

"But the manuscript? That was a stroke of good fortune that it came at this time or...it is real, isn't it?" Fane was anxious, afraid that the vagaries of the outside world in all its harsh reality would catch him in a series of unwelcome lies.

"Absolutely. It's very real and absolutely authentic. But it didn't come at this moment. I have had it for some time, waiting for the right...occasion," Augustin rose, a bit stiffly, and took his walking stick, "God once again gave me a gift and let me use it as I hope He wanted it used. Let's return. We both need that wine."

The next day Fane looked out the Dacia window as they passed through Marginea, remembering buying black pottery with Leri that time so long ago when things were simple, wanting to forget everything that had happened in the last days or, better yet, have them not have happened at all, and repeating the formulas and numbers and words to himself to the tune of the chant in his head in spite of everything. It was like a Sufi prayer to God, breathe in and say the name of God or, as in this case, a string of sounds, breathe out and say the name of God or another string of sounds, a continuity of devotion that formed a background to all the rest of the world.

The train left in the late afternoon for Suceava and the sleeper to Bucharest so Fane had time to lunch with Uncle Vanya. The older man had invited Professor Brebean and his wife to lunch as well—it was, Fane realized belatedly, Sunday, and a normal day for visiting. Normal! Anna's food was, as always, excellent, and Fane complimented her on being able to present such a lovely meal.

"It's getting more difficult but we're fortunate—Vanya's old patients now take care of us!" Anna pushed compliments aside, again as always. Fane could almost relax into the familiar atmosphere, perhaps into the past, in spite of the Sufi nuclear chant in his head. Then the conversation pulled him back.

"...and I hear they want to continue systematization with Radauti, tearing down the Synagogue..."

"...those apartment blocks they've been building are bad enough..."

"...Fane, what's happening in Bucharest? What HAVE you historians been doing?" Fane turned to Aunt Anna. "We've had a number of seminars and made representations..." he began, knowing full well that nothing had or would come of them and he had avoided thinking about them for that very reason. "...and...well, the plans we are hearing rumors about are really frightening. There is even talk about Mihai Voda Monastery's being torn down, also Vacaresti Monastery..." "No!" "That can't be!" "Those are architectural treasures, not just for Romania but for the world!" "Yes! For the world! What is this country coming to!"

'What, indeed,' thought Fane, weariness aching in his bones and being, 'is the country coming to?'

Bucharest—October 1984. What a lovely weekend, what a lovely day this has been! It was Scott's turn at the villa and he invited both me and Dave to share it with their family. It's still the

Sinaia villa but this is the last year, they say, we'll have it. It's so important to have a place to get away to, out of the city, especially for the staff who don't get to travel because of their jobs. And the hotels here are so bad and expensive, imagine over a hundred dollars a night for an unheated room and dirty sheets!

It's always great fun hunting food in the villages along the road when we travel. The villages are so picturesque and the architecture of the little houses changes so much as you go up into the mountains. People set out what they have to sell even though they say it's illegal. This time we were looking for pumpkins for Hallowe'en. We found some smoked cheese high in the mountains, near Rucar on a road I've never traveled before. Great rounds of yellow hard cheese, and there was white cheese wrapped in bark! Then we came down a long valley in the late afternoon I guess in the foothills of the mountains. We had seen pumpkins up against the shocks of hay — the hay has a different shape than in Hallowe'en pictures at home but it's still like the Hallowe'en pictures I drew as a kid... Then we got to a village were there were pumpkins in the yards but none for sale. Finally we just stopped at one house and asked. The old woman was delighted to meet us, invited us into the kitchen in the back of the house — imagine, no running water — and sold us two kinds of mushrooms, tzuica, quince jam — such a funny guttural word, 'gutui' for quince, it must be Slavic — and also some sausages she had made, then she just led us out and gave us a pumpkin. She wouldn't take any money for the pumpkin, said it was for the children, but we had some candy bars which we gave her in exchange and she was so pleased, saying she'd give them to her granddaughter. I guess the kids in the villages don't get much chocolate.

Then at home we cooked the sausages and I battered and friend the mushrooms and we ate the jam and cheesewith bread for a wonderful meal, along with the tzuica of course. Such a good feeling in the autumn, to have produce from the land. I hadn't realized how much I missed it until now.

And my new house is much nicer than the apartment on Mihai Eminescu. It's further from the Embassy — and the riding club, though not much — but the neighborhood is old and beautiful and filled with nice houses and gardens. I have the upstairs of a big villa *and a Consular officer, quite young with small children, is downstairs. The street, Paris Street, is tree-lined and quiet except for the rooster opposite. He's behind a high wall but I can hear him and I wonder if I'll ever see him or his hens. Such a change from the rather grim set of apartments we were in with other diplomats. It was because of the Libyans, whose kids had been beating up the Gunnery Sergeant's son and exposing themselves to the American girls. Probably to the Romanian girls too, I guess. That's why we were moved. I heard one mother went to the Libyan mother and complained, but the Libyan mother said it was natural behavior all boys did that! Anyway, Roger and his guys decided it would be safer for all the Americans to leave. I wonder what's going on with Libya? Odd how things happening in North Africa can change my life in Bucharest...I'm yawning...a wonderful day...Romania is so lovely and people are really friendly...this bed is so comfortable...*

Antonescu slipped a small packet into Fane's hand as they walked through the Lipscani toward the Hanul Manuc and Fane slid it unobtrusively into his pocket. "It's not much, harder and harder to get, I'm sorry." Fane was grateful anyway...all that was available in the market now was "coffee with substitutes," burned oats most likely.

"I thought it would be good to stretch our legs a bit," Antonescu continued, looking at the façade of the National Library, ornate and dirty, before they turned right into a small street. "Besides, the office is a bit chilly these days." He hadn't needed to add that, Fane thought, striding at Antonescu's side in the road. Everywhere is cold, these days. Almost everywhere, he amended, thinking gratefully of the stove Leri had insisted on keeping and the fact that it burned wood as well as coal. And the villager who had brought him wood in return for, what was it? a referral to some doctor or bureaucratic office.

"At least there isn't much traffic," continued Antonescu as the two men walked in the cobblestone street. Private cars had been banned from being driven again this winter and a sidewalk was almost irrelevant on these quiet back streets in

277

the city. Besides, with the gas rationing no one drove if he could avoid it anyway.

"I'm being pressured to bring in some results," said Antonescu almost noncommittally. He paused and the words hung in the cold air between them.

"What kind?" asked Fane.

"They'd like all the plans for the American military and their best equipment...more seriously, I don't know. Probably anything that makes it look as if we're progressing, makes them look good." He paused again, then continued. "I've also just learned that they have a person inside that riding club, Olimpia, who's giving them information. I don't think there's anything of importance but we haven't been feeding them much. I don't suppose...your friend Carol...he sees Ellen a lot..."

"Not willingly," said Fane, thinking of Carol's often expressed opinion of the whole Security apparatus.

"That's the end of that, then," said Antonescu candidly. "He has friends in too many circles for people like us to bring any pressure." He paused again as they negotiated the open thoroughfare through the Hanul cu Tei then resumed when they emerged onto Lipscani Street itself. As always, the historian Fane thought briefly of the time when great caravans of goods came from Poland and Turkey to the inn behind them and...Antonescu's next words brought him back to the present. "They are pleased, I understand, with our effort to ensure that Ellen meets Romanians and appreciates Romanian culture. They're still pursuing the idea that the 'nation' as well as the Government needs friends. Maybe we could do something in this area...how about...well, maybe Winter Festival celebrations in a village. Like your Bilca." The two men entered the coffee house at the end of Covaci near the Hanul Manuc. It was dark inside but there was real if not very good coffee being served. "You know... maybe you don't know..." Fane hesitated and caught his breath. "I don't have a house in Bilca any more."

Antonescu was surprised. "What happened? I knew your Father had died but I assumed you inherited the house..." Fane was oddly pleased that something had slipped through the system, painful as the loss of his home still was.

"My father had sold it, without my knowledge and that's the end of that..." he began slowly "...but there may be something else we could manage." He thought of Ion Cojocariu's offer. What would he think about hosting an American? If Fane knew the man at all, he'd be delighted especially if there were an opportunity to talk a bit about the history of the area...

Walking on to the Hanul Manuc after they had decided to explore this topic, Fane thought about practicalities. They'd have to get permission...Antonescu would take care of that. Should he invite Carol as well? Might be dangerous for Carol if he...let's not think about that...he could hardly not be invited. There would be food, funds...Antonescu would have to come up with some of that. Well, the first step would be to see if there was approval of the plan then they could move on the other fronts. It would be fun to show an American Bukovina and the Winter Festival. It might be useful to teach an American the history of that beautiful land torn apart by the Russians...this idea of making friends for the '*neam*', for the Romanian people and their heritage might not be a bad idea after all though it was a long-term proposition. Never mind, if it would help him and Leri and...Antonescu too...Fane turned at the Hanul Manuc, not wanting to see the empty lot where the historic Brancovanesc Hospital had stood. Damn this regime and the wanton, useless destruction it was bringing about. Fane stopped himself from thinking about it since he couldn't do anything anyway and stepped inside the Curtea Veche Anticariat to find Andrei sorting books, dressed in a coat and muffler.

"I see it isn't any warmer here than in my office," said Fane.

"Come off it," replied Andrei. "I know you have heat in the Institute."

"Not much. Do you happen to have some *tzuica* in the back?"

"Not much...how do you think we keep warm? It's only November — I wonder what it's going to be like in February! I hear they're going to cut the hot water in the apartment blocks from five days a week to three and..." Andrei opened the door into the back room after hanging a sign on the door saying the Anticariat was closed for inventory. "There's no one buying books anyway," he remarked. "Come on in." The two settled into their normal chairs and Andrei poured them both a drink.

"Health. Where's your boss?"

"Health. Up at the Centrala getting some more books, I think, though we really need to sell some before we get more in stock."

"Not many people buying books these days? Do you have anything I might be interested in?"

"Not much," said Andrei candidly, "though I think there may be a collection that's very interesting with some things for sale. But you have a magnificent library already...there's not much that you haven't seen or acquired."

"I'm always looking."

"There's something else that's interesting, though. There's an American who has an interest in Romanian history, two of them come, but one is more of a bibliophile."

Fane's ears tingled. "Who are they?" he asked, taking another sip of *tzuica* and hoping he could hide his reaction. Andrei didn't, at least he thought he didn't, know about Fane's 'other' role though he did, come to think of it, know that he went to the American Library.

"His name is Dave. I have his last name around someplace as he gave me his card. I put it away because I'm not sure whether I want to report the visits." At this Fane made a mental note that he'd have to protect Andrei in this, one way or another. Maybe he'd report him to Antonescu as having been 'recruited' but only if... Andrei continued talking, "He's in the American Embassy and comes with a woman, I don't think she's his wife, I don't think he's married. In fact, you may know her since you go to some functions at the American Library. Her name is Ellen."

Bucharest — November 1984. We NEVER had anything like this in Lagos. Imagine Hal Holbrook coming here and giving talks and a performance. He was so very good as Mark Twain and the Romanians truly appreciated him. The real surprise, though, was that Carol came to the dinner for Holbrook in the Public Affairs Officer's house. The Mellons' residence is so beautiful with all the marble in the entryway and the spacious rooms...I heard it was built by a rich Romanian for his mistress. I'd love to have a tour someday but it isn't something I can ask about I suppose.

Seeing Carol there was a shock though as Romania's leading actor I suppose it made sense but still...at the Club I'm used to his being around and can keep a bit of distance to myself but here when our eyes met...I hope no one noticed. I think he felt the same! I hadn't known he spoke English. Johnny Raducanu, "Mr. Jazz of Romania", what a nice man, introduced us. 'We've met before, I believe, haven't we, Miss Pelletier?' said Carol, his blue eyes...oh, bother. He's Romanian and I can't think of him that way.

I'll think about Thanksgiving. The Library staff is looking forward to it and I've gotten two turkeys, so there should be plenty. We'll have to cook one in the microwave — I wonder how well that will work. Emilia is making pies — she's such a good cook but she really can't do a pie crust well, she wants it to look nice and you need a light hand. My grandmother had such a good hand with pastry, you can't work it too much. Then I'll have peas and salad — I saved lettuce from the last Support Flight and have frozen peas. Mashed potatoes and gravy, of course, I can get the potatoes from the diplomatic store, and bread and butter... I hadn't known Carol could speak English, it's so sweet to hear his mistakes because he's always so self-assured. Even when he makes the mistakes he is perfectly self-assured. I wonder what his background is to make him that way, where he grew up. We've never talked about it, I've asked but he always changes the subject, I only know he's from the Northern part of the country. I need to go there, I hear the monasteries are beautiful and the countryside is lovely. Some day.

A woman stopped me today on the way back from the Diplomatic Shop and asked where I had gotten the eggs. She thought I was Romanian. I do blend in here on the street with my new caciula*, my wonderful fur hat, they said it's fox but it's probably rabbit, I hope it's not cat, it wasn't nice of Dave to suggest that...but no one asks me to change money any more. People just can't get supplies easily and there are always lines at the shop on the corner by the Embassy, even when it's open which seems to be only part of the time.*

Johnny Raducanu played the piano again later in the evening. He's great and I think Holbrook really liked it. Imagine, I get paid to do this.

What I don't understand is why Washington wants me to give this message – Ellen, sitting in the Chancery, looked at the classified cable in her hand, the reason she had let her thoughts wander while she absorbed its contents – *why they want me to give this message to Stefan Vulcean of all people.*

After the embraces and greetings had flurried themselves into a moment of quiet, Fane sat back in Aunt Anna's comfortable chair and looked around the cozy living room. He really needed to talk to them, to Uncle Vanya. "It all seemed so promising in the beginning, or perhaps I wasn't paying enough attention..." His eye caught Aunt Anna shaking her head and pointing to the telephone. Not here, not here as well. "...but the manuscripts we thought would provide a link between Putna Monastery and Emperor Constantin turned out in the end to be forgeries." Aunt Anna smiled gratefully and shrugged in apology. Later, after a lively discussion of up and coming novelists in the area Fane and Vanya left for the market. "It's good to have a young person to carry things," remarked Vanya as they left.

"We don't know really whether our telephone is tapped," said Uncle Vanya as they walked through the crisp afternoon toward the market. "But I am an Old Communist, I know a lot of people, and...everyone wonders these days."

"It's worse than it ever was..." started Fane when Vanya interrupted him. "No. No it isn't. You don't know, you were at University and starting your career, you didn't know people, you were protected, most of all you three were protected." Fane fell silent, feeling like a schoolboy again, a bit resentful. Vanya's voice calmed. "In those days so many, so very many, went to prison, never emerged or came out broken, entirely broken, through torture, starvation. These days are hard and dangerous but...no, it's not as bad."

"But it's not good. Look at this shop window...there's nothing...what, by the way, are we looking for?"

"Some peace," Vanya smiled. "The meaning of life. What is the reason for my life? I wonder. Have I accomplished anything?" The smile had vanished. "The hopes I'd had, nourished even through the bad days of the Soviet occupation and Gheorghiu-Dej who, mind you, may not be judged quite so harshly in the end because...never mind. Those hopes were useless. Perhaps I contributed to the suffering endured by our people, to the state of the country today. Imagine, not enough food to feed our people, ROMANIA the breadbasket of Europe! Perhaps...but who could have stopped the Russians."

"If the Americans hadn't given us away at Yalta. It's their fault," said Fane. Everybody knew that.

"No," said Vanya, wiping his mouth with the back of his sleeve. He had been so excited, Fane realized, he had literally spat out his words...he was getting old. Fane felt old himself. "No, it wasn't the Americans," Vanya continued. "Look at it logically. The Russians had Poland, Hungary, Yugoslavia, Bulgaria...we were surrounded. Our geography betrayed us as it so often has. Also, you're a student of history, the Americans were fighting on two fronts at the time and Roosevelt was ill. Now if Chamberlain..." and the conversation continued into an analysis of Bukovina's position and how the world might have been different. Fane wanted to talk to Vanya about Emil and his death and why he had died but...it would put this dear old man into danger.

There was no one he dared tell. Why did this have to happen to him?

On the way home, a sack of potatoes from one of the doctor's patients in Fane's hand, Vanya came back again to the topic of what his life had been worth. Fane had asked him if he still practiced medicine, hoisting the bag he held as an illustration of his words. "Just a bit. Enough to keep my hand in and take care of my old patients." Fane looked at him quizzically, for the potatoes had come from a young man. "And a few new ones, mostly children I delivered...but this...if anything, anything at all that I have done is good, has helped make this a better world, it has been the medicine. I am grateful for this, at least."

Fane nodded and said something and wondered what he would say in another twenty years. What good would he have done? Articles on Romania's greatness? On Gregory Tamblac?

Ion Cojocariu picked Fane up the following day. "I've got extra gas rations for this venture of yours and have to thank you," he grinned, still the imposing figure Fane had always known even in old age. He must be...in his late seventies? "Now when do our guests arrive and how many are there?"

"They're driving up tomorrow and probably will arrive near dusk," Fane replied, and mentally counted, "and there are, let's see, six. One woman, one man, they're not married, and a couple with two young children."

Ellen had been delighted with the invitation and had almost accepted immediately. She would, Fane was sure, have to ask permission from the American Securitate which was why she said she'd get back to him as soon as she checked her calendar. When she did return his call she said that some person named Dave and the Cultural Attaché, Scott MacPherson, wife and two children would also come. Two problems, Fane put in his mental file. Well, three if you counted each child — Fane had said to bring as many friends as she liked, but they hadn't thought about activities for kids. The more important one was that the woman from the

Defense Attaché's office couldn't come. Forging cultural ties was all well and good but this one might provide hard information. Carol was busy with some party given by someone he couldn't refuse and had to regret as well which might be easier. But this Dave might hold some promise.

As they drove Cojocariu went over the arrangements. Permission had been given to take a pig from the collective farm and slaughter it for the guests, "As if we couldn't have supplied our own," laughed Cojocariu as they drove, "but who's going to refuse a pig?" and other supplies, cheese, milk, sugar, coffee, all had been managed. The diplomats would see how good life was in the country, how rich and full and fun and...Cojocariu broke into Fane's thoughts again.

"I've had my neighbor move out of her house for a few days, and we've fixed it up for the guests. The only thing is that there isn't any indoor plumbing."

"Ellen comes from the country in the US, so she's probably used to outhouses. And the others, if they're city people, they probably have had rural visits too. I think I remember the house, it's the one just to the west of yours? You have a common fence?"

"That's right. A very traditional house, well-kept and beautifully decorated, nice courtyard, chickens and all that, a pig or two, cow in the barn..."

"Your neighbor is well off?"

"She had a little help with the cow from my own barn!" The two men laughed as they turned into the Cojocariu courtyard. The next sentence broke into Fane's thoughts, "It's a pity you don't still have your old house, it's one of the nicest examples of traditional architecture in the village." Fane remained silent for a moment, absorbing this. He'd never thought of his home in those terms. Then he put the stab of pain the thought brought him aside and replied, "I need to take them to see the border and our lane is a good way to go but perhaps you know a better one."

Bukovina — December 1984. I wish I hadn't forgotten my camera, this road is so interesting. I particularly like the wells and the way they've changed as we've gone north. In the Dobrogea and the south there were ordinary 'Hansel and Gretel' wells, but also some sweep wells. It must be such a lot of work, getting water up in a bucket on the end of those long poles but they look so picturesque silhouetted against the sky. Further north, though, the wells become more elaborate, not just the well and a little roof but also a lot of carving and some have little platforms. I could have made a photographic chronicle of them, but then we'd be even later. Too bad we got such a late start.

We stopped at one well to eat the lunch we'd brought and found a tin cup we could drink out of. Scott and his wife didn't want to do it or let the children take the cup hanging on a chain to use — they wouldn't even drink the water — but Dave and I had fun pulling the bucket up. The kids were entranced. I hope they'll enjoy this trip, taking young children along can be so difficult, but we could hardly refuse, especially after they were so hospitable at Christmas, inviting us over for dinner.

It was a good Christmas, I loved the service of Lessons and Carols at the Anglican Church, but the part that will stay with me forever is the colinde *at our Christmas Carol concert. What a shame that the Romanians aren't even allowed to sing their own Christmas Carols or, for that matter, even have Christmas simply because it's religious and the Communists don't like religion. I didn't either but there isn't anything like persecution to bring one Faith, I guess, maybe I'm becoming a believer.*

Anyway, since Christmas is pretty much forbidden, a regular working day and I understand that the markets are kept empty until after December 25 so people will only celebrate the New Year, we do it up big at the Library. We got an enormous Christmas tree that we put in the stairwell on the library side and we had a great time decorating it, then we had an exhibit of Christmas paper shopping bags! They wondered at the Embassy about it but it was lovely and has been a great hit with the Romanians though I suspect some of them come to the receptions mainly for the food and drink, I have to find a way to stretch the Representation budget, but the best was the Christmas Caroling. A bunch of us got up on the

286

auditorium stage and sang American Christmas carols. We passed out music and a few people sang with us but, at the end, we sang several Romanian colinde, *"Mos Craciun" and "Steaua sus rasare" and some others. Imagine, I had to teach them to some of the staff, because they'd never learned. Others knew them but pretended they didn't. What a strange country and regime, when a holiday is so political you can't celebrate it!*

But at the performance the audience loved the Romanian carols and kept asking for more. Fortunately, I had found a book of carols in the Anticariat on May 1 Boulevard. I don't think the lady meant me to see them but she took the money and a little gift anyway, so I have them. So the pianist was able to play almost everything and the concert went on much longer than we had planned. And afterward an old woman came up and said, "Thank you for allowing us to sing our own Christmas carols." I still get teary-eyed thinking of it.

And now the New Year's festival. It's exciting to be able to come to the countryside for it and to see the painted monasteries at last. I hope the MacPherson kids behave.

Fane waited with Cojocariu at the intersection where the road from Radauti met the main road through Bilca. It was getting dark and bitterly cold and the two men weighed the relative benefits of a warm car and saving gas. Saving gas won out so they walked up and down and talked, hoping to ignore the cold. Finally two cars, clearly not Romanian Dacias even from their headlights, approached and slowed to a halt. Ellen got out of the driver's seat and looked at the muffled figures. "Stefan?" she asked, tentatively.

Fane smiled broadly and approached her, hand held out. "You don't recognize me, hidden under my coat and hat!" he said, slightly accusing. "Oh, it's so good to see you!" Ellen replied, "I'm sorry we're late, the road..." She was joined by a man from her car and the driver of the second car. "This is my friend, Dave, and my boss..." Introductions were quickly made, dispensed with, the visitors seated back in their vehicles and the little caravan set out through the village.

Before he went to sleep that night, Fane reviewed the evening contentedly. The visitors had been charmed with the little house they were to stay in, "It is being made into a museum by the village," Cojocariu had told them, Ellen translating for the others while Fane restrained his laughter, and they didn't seem to mind the outhouse at all. Probably there were more outhouses in the US than he realized. After all, even on the outskirts of Bucharest...probably in American cities, too. Maybe? At any rate, Cojocariu had arranged for a good meal, lots of food, Moldovan cheese cake for dessert which Fane had talked about at length, telling the Americans the difference between this and the same dish in the South, lots of *tzuica* and wine. As a matter of fact...Fane was on the brink of sleep...he'd really had quite a lot of *tzuica* and wine but it's necessary...he yawned and the events of the day drifted into half reality...it's necessary to make guests... Fane slept.

The program had been carefully arranged which, Fane thought the next morning, was a good thing given his headache. They toured the village in the morning, going up to the no man's land next to the border of the Ukrainian Soviet Socialist Republic, where Fane explained what had happened to the village in World War II. The Americans were horrified and stared at the open, empty countryside on the other side of the wire mesh fence, Fane thought, as if it were full of land mines. Which it probably was, but that was beside the point, the important thing was that they were impressed with the way the Russians had attacked the Romanians and taken their land. Fane wasn't sure this was on the Government agenda as he told them about the other half of the lost Bukovina, but it was on his.

After visiting the border the group piled into cars and went to a series of monasteries beginning with Sucevita. They'd do Putna tomorrow, Fane thought, since today it made sense to do a round through Moldovita where the few nuns there would provide lunch and they would visit a woman who decorated eggs, Voronet, Humor and end up in

Radauti for dinner at a restaurant. The restaurant had been advised of the party and food had been arranged there as well. It was too bad the day was gray and cold but, Fane thought, this was winter.

And it was winter even if it wasn't actually snowing, and bitter cold. By the time they reached Voronet it was almost dusk and Fane realized they wouldn't be able to do Humor as well. He hoped Bucharest wouldn't make a fuss about that but they had illustrated very well how much the Romanian State cared about and maintained its historical monuments. As the group admired the splendid blue west façade of the church, blowing on their hands and stomping feet, Ellen came next to Fane and said, "Stefan, could I talk privately to you a minute?"

I hope there isn't some problem with the kids or something, Fane thought angrily but he was all affability as he assented and they wandered off to look at a side chapel.

"I have a message for you from Washington," Ellen said. Fane could hardly hide his surprise. "It's that Haiduc is in Munich with a friend and his feet are in great condition. And please don't ask me about it, because that's all and I don't really know what it means, but I suppose you do."

"Does anyone else know about this message?" Fane asked before he could stop himself.

"No...yes...I mean, of course, since Washington sent it to me, but no Romanians do if that's what you mean."

"Thank you, it's very unexpected."

"I hope it's a good message for you," said Ellen sympathetically, angering Fane enormously...her stupid sympathy, how could she know, these Americans were so naïve! He reined in his emotion knowing it was unfair to direct it against this woman, however stupid she might be about things, and thanked her. "Now we'd better get people together," he said. "It's getting late."

It was late, indeed, before the group returned to Bilca, especially as they had to find a petrol station that was open and had gas. The children, who had been good most of the day, were whiny with cold and fatigue, their parents were irritated, and it was with relief that people piled into the little house where they were staying even if they did have to go outside to the outhouse in turns with a flashlight.

"You'd better scale back what you're planning for today," warned Cojocariu the next morning as the two men appreciated their hot coffee before they joined the Americans for breakfast. The village women had been pressed into service to provide 'typical' meals and both men looked forward to a large array of salamis and cheeses and fresh bread.

"I think it will be okay," said Fane. We'll go to Putna in the morning as we planned. You've arranged for lunch at a house in the village there?" Cojocariu nodded. "Excellent. Then I thought we'd go to Brodina in the afternoon before coming back here for the New Year's Eve feast."

Cojocariu raised his eyebrows. Brodina? I thought you were going to show them Radauti and the glass factory in Dorohoi."

"It seems that the glass factory isn't working right now," Fane replied. "At least, not the way it should, and the extra driving is probably too much. Besides, Ellen loves horses and she actually has a Gidran horse leased at this club where she rides." Fane could see the older man putting things together in his mind.

"That's where Carol has a horse," he started. Fane nodded. "I wondered about...Carol's not chasing this American, is he?"

"I don't think so," replied Fane.

"You don't sound very certain," said Carol's father. "Americans are dangerous, especially diplomats."

"I've warned him," replied Fane, "but I'll do it again."

"Horses and women...it's a weakness in our family..."

"I didn't know you liked horses!" joshed Fane and the two men laughed, putting the matter aside.

Fane woke up the next morning wondering, uncharacteristically, where he was for a moment before he looked around his room at the big wardrobe, the desk, the early winter light beginning to bring the outside world into soft focus in gray and the beginning of blue. He knew this room. He had spent many hot summer days in its cool shadows, copying land records, talking with Carol's father. Now it was still cool but not cold, the lingering heat of the great tile stove in the corner taking the chill off the early winter morning. "Haiduc is in Munich with a friend and his feet are in great condition." Mihai...at Radio Free Europe...with... Pyotr? Probably. Relief and loss and fear coalesced into anger. How dare he?

The day went better at the beginning. The children played in the park in front of the Putna Monastery, their mother staying with them willingly — probably not interested in culture, thought Fane, or history — while the others wandered through the great buildings and the ice cold museum. With a bit of pushing Fane managed to get cases open so the guests could feel the sumputuous centuries' old cloth, "I don't think we should touch it," said Ellen but Fane overrode her silly fears. It wouldn't hurt a thing.

Then the road to Brodina, bringing memories of two boys and a family and a horse and days lost forever. "Tell me about the horse farm," said Ellen and Fane, irritated still by the message, the smug tone of Mihai's telling him he was safe and happy, how could he be, this woman who just wouldn't shut up, answered, "You will see Maria Theresa architecture in the stables. The stud was built in..." like a bloody fool guide.

Fane half expected to see a half remembered Cousin Fane at the stud but the manager wasn't there and the stable men were people he didn't know. The manager's absence was inexcusable, he had had a day's notice that visitors were coming. Fane's mood improved marginally with one *tzuica* and then another. Horses were brought out and admired, the architecture appreciated. Suddenly it seemed appropriate that Ellen ride one of these beautiful animals.

"Bring a horse for our guest to ride," Fane ordered the stable boy. "She's an excellent rider."

"Comrade, the horses are for breeding, we don't have any riding horses."

"There must be at least one, bring one out or you'll hear about this."

"But Comrade..."

"No 'But Comrades' boy, bring a horse!" With much grumbling and some delays along with Ellen protesting that she didn't need to ride, a saddle and bridle were found and put on a stallion. The stallion was dancing and half rearing through the unfamiliar process, Ellen protested, Fane insisted, pushed forward by some malign god inhabiting his gut and taking over his reason. Ellen swung up on the horse who reared, the stable boy hanging on to the reins. "Don't let him go," she said softly to the stable boy. "I won't, Ma'am, he's not a riding horse. Be careful," the young man answered, gripping the reins. "Let him go, let her ride," insisted Fane.

"What in hell are you doing!" The voice, strong, authoritative, familiar, rang out from the entrance to the stable yard. "Ellen, get off that horse. Fane, what's going on?"

With relief, Ellen vaulted off and stepped away from the stallion. The stable boy spoke to him softly, and he calmed as he was rubbed under the chin but still moved nervously about. "Ellen, are you all right?" Carol asked.

Ellen, embarrassed and red, ashamed of being bullied on to the horse, ashamed of not being able to ride even this stallion, nodded, speechless. Carol moved toward her and stopped, then turned to Fane. "We'd better go," he said. "Father said you'd be here. The pig has been killed and he'd like them to be there for the festivities."

Good-byes and thanks were made as if nothing except a totally normal visit had happened, everyone eager to forget that there may have been unpleasantness, even if not everyone understood the nuances. The Americans rode together in their cars, Fane with Carol.

"Those horses aren't riding horses. You know that," Carol said biting his words off one by one. "She could have been hurt."

"I can't explain, not right now," Fane replied, motioning to the car and indicating he had something further to say, where there wasn't a chance of being overheard. "I don't know exactly what came over me."

The group arrived in Bilca to find a great flurry of activity in the Cojocariu kitchen. "You've just missed the killing of the pig," Ion said. Scott expressed regrets in limping Romanian while Norma quietly expressed relief to Ellen. "There's some cultural things the kids don't need to see. I don't need to see them either, come to think of it." She looked meaningfully toward the place where it appeared the pig might have been killed and Ellen agreed, falling back into the role of translator and general go-between, helped by Carol. Several village women were cutting and cooking and grinding and doing a dozen things with heaps of meat while Cojocariu was pouring a celebratory *tzuica*. It looked to be a long evening.

"Maybe the children would like to go gather the eggs," said one of the women to Carol. "I don't think anyone's had time to do it." Carol turned and asked them in English to their great delight. Dave intervened with a question. "I thought you gathered eggs in the morning, I seem to remember this from kid's books."

"No," remarked Ellen. "During the day or evening is best since the hens lay during the day. If you leave them overnight some sort of varmint is apt to get them." Dave laughed at the word 'varmint' and Carol stopped translating for the ladies to ask about it.

"Oh, that's a colloquialism, a word we just use that's not really correct, maybe from the American South, for animals which are pests. The kind that steal eggs." When this was explained to the Romanian ladies they laughed approvingly and remarked that Ellen must have grown up on a farm. "Do you," asked one of them, "*smulgetivacile*"...Ellen couldn't make out the question and looked at Carol. "...um... take milk from cows?" he translated haltingly. Ellen's face lit with understanding and she turned toward the women, moving her hands as if she were milking a cow. The women laughed merrily.

"I did grow up on a farm," she explained to them and the questions came from all sides about a subject they all could understand, common ground bringing them together. Carol beamed and Fane jostled him. "Let's go out." Soon Carol and Fane were inspecting the barn and fields, away from prying ears. "So what happened?" asked Carol. Fane, his usual affable unflappable demeanour back in place hesitated only a bit. "Ellen gave me a message that was...a problem," he said. "I think it made me a bit crazy."

"What exactly?"

"That Haiduc was in Munich with a friend and his feet were in great condition."

"Oh, my God. No wonder you were upset." The big blond man paced ahead across the uneven winter furrows of the field. "Maybe we'll see some rabbits, what do you think?"

"At this time of year?"

"Who knows? Mihai, huh? And the friend..."

"Pyotr, most likely. The feet?"

"Smokescreen for everything's fine, I'd guess."

"That's what I thought." Fane looked at the last of the sunlight fading over the distant mountains. "We'd better go back."

"Munich?" Carol was still musing. "So he's moved from Voice of America to Radio Free Europe?"

"That's what I thought."

"It won't help either of us when They find out."

"That's also what I thought."

"Well, we'll manage. I wish he hadn't sent the message."

"Me too. Except perhaps he felt he needed to warn us, not to take us by surprise." Fane turned toward the buildings behind them, realizing he now had another secret he didn't want. Should he tell Carol about the nuclear bomb in the

294

Carpathians? The one that had had Emil killed? He hadn't had a chance to say more than the usual friendly formalities to Father Augustin when the passed through Suceava and he felt lonelier than ever, isolated by this burden of knowledge. And that, he thought, was the way it would have to stay. Maybe some time.

"Who's this Dave person?" Carol asked as they returned.

Fane kicked a clod of dirt and regretted getting his boots dirty. Dirtier, that is. The courtyard of the breeding farm stables hadn't been exactly pristine. "Some man in the Economics Section of the Embassy, I gather. Keen interest in Romania, understands a lot of Romanian, speaks it badly."

"I mean, is he Ellen's boyfriend? No, I don't think so." Carol corrected himself without waiting for Fane.

"Why not?" Fane asked, curious that he'd come to that conclusion so quickly but feeling the same without quite knowing why.

"Because he's a fag. Surely you see it." Fane received this information with surprise, then dismay — not, this time, at the fact of someone being homosexual but because once again he hadn't perceived it. Carol was so fast at these things.

"Why did you want to know?" Fane countered. "Is it important to you?" Carol stopped. "No. Perhaps...no..."

"This isn't someone you should get involved with. Not unless..."

"Don't warn me. I know. The one woman I've wanted in my life and I can't have her," he said savagely. They walked on a few steps then, in spite of himself, Fane said, "You could, you know. You could have her." Carol stopped and faced him.

"I know exactly what you're getting at and that's precisely why I can't, won't, pursue this. Shit. Don't ever say anything like that again." This said ferociously, then in a low voice dripping with menace, "And don't ever, ever, involve her in your dirty plans." Fane stepped back in dismay, then turned and walked away. Carol joined him and they were side by side again. The men reached the courtyard of Carol's family home along with the dark. They wiped their boots carefully at the door, then entered.

Bucharest — January 1985. That was a really strange trip, nice, the long road north lined with those wonderful wells, I must go back with a camera some time, the great food, the beautiful monasteries. But a lot of subtexts. And I've never been so cold in my life as traipsing around those monasteries admiring the paintings or trying to admire them. Maybe I could appreciate them better in summer. I feel bad that I don't know enough about them, the stories and everything and I tried to understand Fane, especially to help the others, but it was hard. He just talks on, saying interesting things in that nice voice of his that you always feel has something underneath it, something you can't quite get.

What I really don't understand was that scene at the breeding farm. Why did he insist that I ride that horse? Was it to humiliate me in front of everyone? Surely they could all see it wasn't a riding horse, that...oh, I don't know. I'm so grateful Carol came when he did. Everything was all right as soon as he got there and took charge, thank God he took charge. I think I would have gotten off the horse even if he hadn't come but...I guess I did want to prove I can ride. Scott has heard so much about the riding from me and puts up with my coming a bit late to work if I need to work Ropot... Sandy doesn't really ride him much, I think she's a bit scared of him, so it's mostly me and the people at the Club sort of understand and just give her another horse to ride without charging her for it. Of course, Enache expects to have Ropot as the club horse and win a lot of shows with him when I leave, he told Carol that was part of the deal and Carol told me. Carol's been riding Robespierre in the morning with me...he's so beautiful on a horse. And Robespierre is gorgeous. He's better behaved than Ropot. Funny, I should have the wilder horse when Carol is the better rider.

But the incident with the stallion...maybe the message upset Stefan. I think he was drunk. I'm sure he must be working for the Securitate, otherwise how could he invite a group of Americans to visit like that? He says he isn't, he's always referring to how he's getting away with things and then there was the time, outside which monastery? that he said we were being followed by a local

Securitate car but not to notice. But he made the visit a good one, stopping at Marginea so we could buy pottery, taking us to the naïve artist where I bought the scene of a winter pig killing, kind of like the one we didn't see in Bilca. It was at Marginea I asked Stefan why his wife didn't come or, rather, expressed regret that she wasn't there with a question mark in my voice. He was so nice then, not like at the stud farm at all, telling me she had gone to see her parents, who are old and ill, during her school vacation, then telling me how she had fallen in love with the black pottery on her first visit there. I think he really loves his wife.

The shop also had the black and white plaid bags that they make in this area. I asked because Stefan had presented us with some, saying they were very hard to get and making a big deal of it. I wonder why he did that? It was nice of him to give us anything, he didn't need to do that – I mean, give us anything, but also then to lie about it. He's a strange man. I wonder what the message really meant. I didn't ask if he wanted to send a message back and he didn't ask if he could.

If he's a Securist, why is Washington sending him a message about Munich – it's got to have something to do with Radio Free Europe. Perhaps...he couldn't love the Russians, not after what they did to his village. But it had to be the Communists who helped him go to school, to the University, so he'd benefitted from the system. I wonder where his heart lies? If he has a heart. But maybe it wasn't the Communists – certainly the Cojocariu house was nice, good old furniture.

That was another funny thing. Fane invited us but he never took us to a house he said was his. Maybe it was the house we stayed in, but I don't think so. He didn't seem to know where things were when he took us over. It's all so puzzling. I wish I knew what was going on.

We ate so very much, the food was great. Romanians certainly eat a lot of meat. I'm sure that our host, besides Stefan, was Carol's father. Domnul Cojocariu, of course he is. Why wasn't he introduced as Carol's father? But the others don't know, well, didn't know Carol. Carol did tell him about my riding...I remember that...he seemed proud of me. Domnul Cojocariu looked a bit familiar when I met him but when Carol was there it was obvious.

No one was very precise, though, maybe they thought we knew. I'm pretty sure, well, he had to be Carol's father because it seemed like Carol's house. There is so much swirling around in my head it's hard to get it all straight. Maybe someone said something I didn't catch there was such a hullabaloo with the cooking and the meal and all the people and drink and everyone getting drunk. Now I do know more about Carol's background and it's nice, not too different from mine. I guess he grew up in that village, went to the school there. I wonder if there is a high school there, too? It must have been a peaceful, pleasant childhood.

And we really saw village life, the pig, the animals, no indoor plumbing. I'm glad everyone thought that was an adventure, even the kids. They were really well behaved, I'm not sure how old they are but I think eight and ten, nice ages really. They loved getting eggs from the hens, they were so proud, so very proud of themselves and they seemed to chat along with the woman who took them out in spite of language differences. People who get along with kids well have that ability, I think. The ladies were pleased that I knew something about farming as well...how could I even begin to explain to them how different things are? I wonder if they think we have outhouses on farms, too. We used to, I remember my grandmother's farm, before she had to sell it and move in town. But...I wonder if there are still any houses in the US now without indoor plumbing. I don't think so. It was so nice seeing Carol.

Fane drove back with Carol, turning in his train tickets at Radauti. It was a comfortable trip. The incident at the stud farm aside, they both knew that the visit had been a success for the Americans. Bilca would be talking for months, if not years, about the Americans who came and how this person looked and how that person did that, fodder for the old ladies'conversations...Fane could imagine it now, ten years hence, two of the ladies sitting on a bench by the road just outside their courtyard, chatting. "Do you remember when..."

Carol's voice interrupted his thoughts. "...and I think they'll start the new movie in the middle of the month, the leading lady..." Fane listened with half an ear. Leri loved these details of Carol's life. It was her brush with fame and gave her something to talk about at school. Then he turned his thoughts to the list of favors he'd been asked, sorting them into various groups. That was the only trouble with these trips but then there was also the car, loaded with meat and potatoes and apples held in cellars after the fall harvest as well as several bottles of *tzuica*. And some cheese...

Leri was already back from her trip by the time Carol drove up to the front of Ady Endre 16 as the light in the window of the front room was on. I wonder what she's doing there, Fane thought. Carol helped him take bundles and packets upstairs and they found Leri with Rodica Toma, sitting comfortably over a cup of tea.

"I didn't think you'd be back until tomorrow," Leri said, rising. "The train..." Fane came in the door of the warm room, reacting automatically with unthought pleasure at its feeling of hospitality and comfort, books and a few pieces of art, so different from Bilca, at least from the tiny house he grew up in. "Carol brought me home," he said, the actor following him in.

"Carol! It's been so long," said Rodica. "Carol, come in and sit down," said Leri. The women shifted chairs and Leri went into the kitchen, overriding Carol's polite protests with an offer of wine. When the four of them were settled, the conversation resumed. The two men comfortably described the trip, this amusing incident, that meal, the tour. At the mention of the monasteries and Sucevita a shadow crossed Rodica's face.

"Is something wrong?" asked Carol.

"Oh, no. It's just that...you know, Leri and I met there and discovered we lived on the same street in Bucharest and we've become friends."

"Very good friends," said Leri.

"Do you go to monasteries often?" asked Carol politely.

"Not really. My husband had a special..." Rodica's voice faltered and her lower lip worked as she stared beyond Carol's shoulder. "I...my husband..." she couldn't say more and Leri put her arm about the woman's shoulders to help her through this moment.

"Rodica's husband was killed in an accident in the mountains," Leri explained to Carol. "Last summer." Carol looking sympathetic and embarrassed, murmured appropriate banalities. He caught Fane's eye with a look communicating helplessness in the face of sorrow, holding the glance for an understanding moment between two men, and Fane felt again the anguish of his solitary knowledge.

In a few moments, however, the evening revived and ended well with the four enjoying the bounty of a remembered village.

Settling back into his routine at the Institute provided Fane further comfort. The article on Gregory of Tamblac, co-authored with Director Dragomir, had been well-received, very well-received indeed, thought Fane. So well-received that the Institute had been given enough funds to fill the vacant Deputy Director position.

"It was a real coup," said Dragomir to Fane over a cup of hot tea, welcome warmth in the chilly office. "Making that connection for us, for Romania...it was truly important. So much so that I have heard, well," Dragomir was uncharacteristically reticent, "that it may result in a new member of the Romanian Academy. No...no congratulations, at least not yet. I haven't said anything to the rest of the Institute but..." Fane smiled with genuine pleasure. Dragomir had been good to him over the years.

"You know," the older man continued, "that I am not growing younger." Fane demurred, saying obligatory niceties about health though he wondered, as he often did, how his Director's health could be, given his truly vast overweight body. "...and the Deputy Director position is now to be filled..." Fane kicked himself for not being totally attentive.

"Excuse me," he said, pretending to feign a lack of understanding to hide the very real gap in his attention.

"I am hinting," said Dragomir with a touch of asperity, "I am...touching on the subject of the Deputy Director position. You needn't be polite, not with me, and pretend you don't know I am going to put your name forward for it." He smiled and relaxed back in his chair with genuine pleasure at being able to give this news and Fane smiled in return with equally genuine pleasure.

"We can fill your position with a younger researcher, there are several gaps in our historical coverage, perhaps even get a new position and increase our staff and..." the Director went on with Fane paying real attention and entering into the discussion, almost as an equal, for the next half hour.

Antonescu wasn't in quite as good a mood that afternoon. "Excellent work," he kept saying of the report Fane had given him. It had been easy to play up the genuine enjoyment of the Americans, the propagation of the importance of Romanian culture, the visit to the border — "Important to the highest levels," Antonescu had said, "to underscore our independence as a Socialist state" — and a few details about Dave and his position in the Economics Section of the Embassy would be very well-received, especially the favorable report on conditions in the Romanian countryside that was likely to be put forward.

"Well done," Antonescu had said as Fane wrapped up the visit and his gleanings, handing Antonescu a written sheaf of documentation but the man behind the desk still didn't seem very happy. Finally, Fane took the initiative and said, "You know, I may be catching a virus because I feel very cold. May I invite you for a cup of tea?" Antonescu accepted with alacrity and the two men stepped out and walked down the street, choosing one of the small anonymous coffee shops they occasionally patronized.

"At least it's hot," Fane said, warming his hands on the steaming cup of herbal tea.

"At least plants still grow in our forests that people can gather for hot tea," replied Antonescu.

"Is...something bothering you?"

Antonescu turned slightly to look around the small room, empty except for the waiter who was listening to a vapid popular song on the radio. "I have learned that they plan to demolish the Mihai Voda Monastery," he said abruptly. "And, you probably know, they are acutally tearing down the Vacaresti Monastery." Fane stiffened. The news wasn't new, but this was official confirmation. Just as bad, it was Antonescu who was telling him this. What was behind it? Was there a trap? What...?

"I had heard a rumor about Vacaresti — it's been a prison for the past, how many years? But I hadn't heard anything about Mihai Voda...yet," he said cautiously, feeling sick with dread, with the destruction, with the possible danger. He liked Antonescu, but you couldn't trust people, not at this level.

"I don't know..." the other man started, then continued in what appeared to be a different direction. "Our country is a small one, but it has had great moments and it has some great art. Our monasteries..." he hesitated again then continued, "our monasteries may be remnants of a pre-bourgeois culture which may need to be erased," Fane noted the use of the qualifying term 'may', "but as art, as expressions of the Romanian heritage, they shouldn't be lost. The Brancoveanu Hospital...how many countries in this region HAD a hospital at the date it was built? How many countries HAD such beauty...I know, I know, Rila Monastery with its stripes and Tirnovo and some...but WE, we ROMANIANS..." Antonescu lowered his voice. "Excuse me. I'm not acting and I ask you to believe me. And I'm not alone... there are people like me, people at higher levels, who want to save our heritage."

"But what...?" asked Fane.

"You could...drop a word into the ears of the Americans..."

"But what can they do?"

"I don't know. Perhaps something, perhaps, we think that, maybe, international publicity, something might help. I just don't know but how can we sit by and do nothing?"

How can we sit by and do nothing, indeed? thought Fane on the way home. We've been sitting by and doing nothing for over thirty years, 'The man who puts his head up gets it cut off'. What was that someone had said to him once, 'There are no Romanian martyrs'? I don't want to be the first Romanian martyr. But that's not true. The Church might not recognize them, but there have been martyrs...Nevertheless, he had his instructions.

"Look," Antonescu had said. "You will be on the list for the US Ambassador's next reception." Fane started, almost pleased. This would be the first time he had been invited to the US Ambassador's Residence...Ana Pauker's house!...at the end of his own street. "It makes sense," said Antonescu, "as there will be a speaker on US history and you are going to be the Deputy Director of the Institute of History." How did he know this? Fane wondered, then realized that, of course, it would all have been cleared with...authorities... and then communicated to Antonescu. "In fact, the speaker is going to visit the Institue. The Americans," he added, "have been trying to get into it for some time, God knows why but that Cultural Attaché, MacPherson, has a doctorate, seems to be an intellectual, wants to visit all our research institutes though it may be a cover for something else." Fane nodded, thinking that he hadn't known all this, who else provided information...of course, They weren't going to rely on only one man... "Hard to think of Americans as valuing history. Anyway, you will have met the visitor then, a Professor Hunter, so the reception will be quite natural."

"Why is the reception being held at the Ambassador's residence? A historian hardly seems important enough..."

"Our information is that this Hunter is quite important, a professor of the American President years ago and has maintained relations..." Antonescu didn't need to say more.

"During the reception it is only natural that you talk with the Pelletier woman, after your visit and all. During that conversation, at a good moment, tell her she absolutely must visit Vacaresti, it's being torn down. Go on a bit about its importance, all that. Suggest she go out in the next few days or there won't be anything to see. The Americans do have an interest in this, only they haven't done anything. Also..." Antonescu hesitated, "There's Professor Constantin. You surely know him." Fane, of course, did, though not well. The famous historian, son of a famous historian, grandson of a famous historian, not a friend but an acquaintance. Someone you wanted to be close friends with but it somehow hadn't come about though Fane had tried. "Put Ms. Pelletier together with him after dropping a word into her ear. He's concerned about the subject and will do your work, our work, for us."

Carrying another message, Fane thought...but this didn't seem too bad...he was just following orders, wasn't he? He couldn't get in trouble for that, could he? Possibly, but there wasn't much choice, calling Antonescu a liar on the one hand against passing a message on the other. Was there? Besides...the Vacaresti Monastery should be a national monument, not a prison...

"You know where the microphones are at Mellon's residence," Antonescu continued. Fane nodded. He had manoeuvred an unsuspecting American into what he hoped was their range often enough for conversations. "In the Residence, these are the places to avoid. Under the arch between the main reception room and the library at the side. Any place in the library the Ambassador uses as an office..."

Home seemed especially dear to Fane that evening. Leri had cooked a fresh pork stew made from the bounty of the Bilca trip and the old stove kept the kitchen and tiny dining room warm. Leri was smiling and pleased with her classes. She was even more pleased at the news from the Institute and they celebrated with a bottle of wine Fane had put away for a special occasion...like this. After dinner he pulled Leri away from the sink, against her protests, nibbling the spot on her neck that had become a signal between the two of them and moved her, almost unprotesting, to the bedroom. For a bit Fane put cares aside and sank back into the Bucharest life he loved so much.

Bucharest – February 1985. I'm almost home now, driving through the endless boulevard canyons, it's dark but there isn't any traffic since they stopped private cars from being driven in winter. I think this killed Alina, our head librarian. She wasn't old, maybe in her thirties? And lovely, so pretty, and she died because there wasn't a taxi to get her to the hospital though I've heard conditions in the hospitals are bad, too. I don't know whether Washington would have approved of our lending the Library van to be her hearse because they couldn't find one, but Scott agreed and we didn't ask and I'm glad though I'll never forget, never EVER forget Alina's body laid out on the dining room table, I think her parents were Communists and not allowed to have a church service so the priest came to the house. Never forget the procession to the cemetery with Alina's coffin in the Library van, other Embassy cars behind crammed with staff and family, stopping at each crossroads and getting out for a prayer. Never forget her mother trying to throw herself into the grave as the first shovel of dirt hit the coffin, snow all around, snowing into the mud of the grave, the cemetery deserted, grim. They say that this naked expression of grief can be a way to exorcise sorrow but I don't believe it, I almost cry every time I think of it, maybe it's better to shove things out of sight the way we do at home.

There's so much here I won't forget. The sight of the painted ceiling of the Vacaresti church against the bright blue sky, snow drifting across the floor, the big machine with the wrecking ball. After I talked to Scott and Peter about what I'd been told, we all three went out to see what was happening. It was like a film, something Carol would be in perhaps. We decided to spread out so they couldn't stop all of us. A man stood in front of me on the snow-covered hill and told me not to take another step or he'd hit me. I asked if that was what Romanian men did, hit women diplomats, then walked on and he stepped aside. I don't think any of these people want their churches destroyed...Oh! I nearly ran into that person, all in dark clothing and stepping in front of me on this dark street, he must be crazy.

Look at the people waiting for the tram, or maybe it's the trolley I can't figure when to use which one or whether the Romanian translates into the same words in English, **tramvai** *and* **troleu***, at least I think that's what it is, the tram he's waiting for. This has got to be the coldest winter ever, and Ceausescu has turned the heat down. It's freezing in our houses. I turn on the dryer and I've vented it into the kitchen, which warms it a bit. I hear women have to get up at two and three in the morning to cook for the day because that's the only time there's gas. We diplomats have electric heaters, but they say that they are forbidden to the Romanians and they say there are only forty watt lightbulbs, one to a room, allowed and that police look for too much light coming out from behind curtains. What an awful regime this is, starving its people. And even our office...the Library is cold though it's warmer than people's houses. Odd that the Cultural Affairs Officer's house, Scott's home, has heat. Apparently it's on some line that also brings gas to the highest Party members, but it's on Plantelor, over by the Firemen's Tower, and I thought the Party members all lived in that area we aren't allowed to drive in, near Herastrau. There's so much I don't know. So much mystery.*

Imagine that this seemed like a quiet assignment when I first came...but then, it always seems quiet until you get into things, I guess. Professor Hunter's visit was successful! Scott got sick so I had to take him around, to the Institute of History — Scott really hated not being able to go there, he'd arranged it specially, he has such an interest in seeing Communist institutions. He says it's because he loves knowledge and history but it's really curiosity. The true history buff is Dave. There wasn't much to see anyway, the outside of the building, a sort of hall, empty and dark, then the little room to the left, the 'Protocol Room'. I wonder if they recorded the whole conversation. Not much was said. Stefan and the Director, a man named Dragomir, and someone else were the Romanians. We were three, the two Americans and our interpreter, Mrs. Goga. She's so good. I had the feeling she knew Stefan — but they often come to the same Library events so it would be natural.

306

Then there was the reception at the Ambassador's.We get such a lot of business done at receptions, under the hum of multiple conversations. Stefan told me about the Vacaresti Monastery and sked us to help save it. I guess because he's a historian. I don't know what we can do. I didn't tell him that Sandy and I already visited the Monastery, when they first talked of demolishing it and that I already knew Professor Constantin. That was the first rule Pam taught me, never talk to any Romanian about any other Romanian. Sandy and I went to Vacaresti and talked our way in and met with the former director of the prison or something like that. He actually gave us tzuica – two women are so innocuous, so unthreatening. We get away with a lot more than men can. The Monastery was in shambles. I found a piece of white tile, part of a horse and a hunting dog on it, I guess it had been part of a great decorated tile stove. I asked if I could have it as a souvenir. "Why not," said the director. I have it in my office. I don't think anyone notices.

It was cold, even at the Ambassador's. I'm so tired of being cold. At least the room beside the office at the riding club where we sit around the table which barely has enough room for all of us, benches on the sides and a bed, a cot, at the far end someone must sleep there, at least it's warm becaue of the wood stove. Carol is usually there at the end of the week. For a while he was coming in the morning when I ride before work, when the weather is all right, but when the man started to appear in the little woods by the ring, about that time Carol said he'd have to be absent a bit, because of a movie. He's at the club most Saturdays and Sundays though, working with Robespierre, Ropot's brother. Well, half brother. Carol's studying Dressage with Colonel Molnar and I think I could get lessons too. I wonder... Enache is happy to have him around and has been saying something about his riding in shows. I wonder if I could ride for them... I'm good enough, but... I wonder why Carol comes to the club, he must have access to better facilities, there must be better facilities somewhere...don't know but it's nice...he's such good company...here I am, Piata Dorobanti and around the wolf, the copy of the Roman she-wolf with the babies, in the little park, down my street, up the stairs, I wonder what I'll fix for dinner, but we had some stuff we brought to the Club and I'm not really very hungry, I guess. It's good to be home.

Fane ran into Carol at a small shop that sold *martsishor* on the Piata Rosetti. He was fingering the red and white string of one and looking at its little charm, this one of glass and perhaps nicer than the metal frivolity on that one... Fane sometimes thought that after so many years of marriage this custom could be put aside, but Leri loved getting something from him. Her students brought her dozens, he pointed out, "But it's not the same!" she'd say and kiss him. Besides, he needed to get others, mustn't forget any of the women at the Institute and then...a hand rested on his shoulder and he turned to see Carol behind him.

"What brings you here?" Fane asked. Outside the first signs of a welcome spring were beginning to show, pussy willow for sale on the corners, a few bare heads on passers-by, clouds finally being chased across an increasingly blue sky by a wind that was chilly but only...chilly. Not freezing.

"The same thing as you, except for me there are dozens of women," replied Carol with an easy grin. "All the damsels of Bucharest who will be distraught if I don't bring them a *martsishor*. And how many are you getting?"

"Let's see. I need...oh, I don't know. I always forget someone. Right now I'm looking for something for Leri, and since we're close by I'll buy a few to give to the women at the American Library."

"What's new there?" asked Carol with seemingly genuine interest.

"You should know, you're still seeing Ellen at the Club every week, aren't you?"

Carol replied easily. "Yes, of course, but we really only talk about horses." It was, by and large, true. Other conversation was full of minefields.

"Safer, that way, I suppose though intolerably dull. Speaking of horses, do you," the two men were outside and walking together across Piata Rosetti, "or, rather, have you heard anything back about our Haiduc?"

"No. Have you?"

"No. I've wondered...why not. They must know."

308

"Perhaps they know as well that we haven't any contact with him." Fane agreed and they walked on. At the next corner, where Fane turned up to the American Library, they paused and Fane felt this was the time to tell Carol about Emil. He was strong and could...help...perhaps. They faced one another and Fane started to say, "Come, let's go on a bit further, there's something..." when a young woman came up and accosted the movie star. The spell was broken and they parted with a promise to get together soon.

A short block later Fane turned through the open wrought-iron gate of the American Library and climbed the now-familiar steps to Ellen's office. When he opened the door he turned left to her assistant's office to exchange a few words and present his small charm only to see a stranger. He stopped in his tracks.

"Good morning," the woman said. "May I help you?" She didn't look friendly but at least she was polite.

"Good morning," Fane replied. "I'm Stefan Vulcean and I brought a *martsishor* for Ellen. I had also brought one for Georgiana..."

The young woman smiled and brushed her brown hair back from her eyes. "Georgiana isn't here any longer," she said without further explanation. "I think Miss Pelletier is in but I don't know if she's able to see you, let me ask." Feeling uneasy without knowing why, Fane nodded with a genial smile, communicating a warmth and friendliness he didn't feel underneath. Ellen it seemed was in and the woman, who introduced herself as Ruxandra, ushered Fane into the blue and white office.

"Hello Fane! Please have a seat." Ellen was the same as usual, friendly, open...naïve perhaps. Fane sat and they exchanged small talk after Ellen had exclaimed her pleasure over the small red and white string bracelet with a tiny china flower dangling from the middle.

"Have you heard about the seven old women and the first days of March?" Fane asked. Ellen laughed. "Yes, and how the day you choose and the weather determines your year? I hope mine is sunny!" They both laughed. Finally Fane brought the conversation around to Georgiana.

"I brought a *martsishor* for Georgiana. I hope she's well." Ellen's open expression closed ever so slightly. "She's fine," the American replied. "But she's not here now. She's out of the country." Then the subject was changed.

Antonescu explained a few days later. "The Assistant at the Library, yes...she's finally emigrated. As you know..." he didn't say 'reported' but the word hung between them, "she had a boyfriend in Sweden who had left here last year. Some people..." 'have all the luck' was also left unsaid. "It was very fast, the emigration, once she applied. As you also know, with a high level father she didn't have to help us and she made it clear she didn't want to. No loss there. It may," Antonescu added, "have helped her get the exit visa for all I know. Of course, we also don't want to, uh, damage our relationship with the Americans or seem as if we don't have free movement in the country..."

"The new assistant, Ruxandra Onesti," Antonescu leaned back and drummed his fingers on the empty desk, "is, um, one of us and will be much more cooperative. She's quite a friend of Victor, you know, the PAO chauffeur who tends bar at all the functions Mellon holds. Sometimes for the Ambassador or other Embassy officers as well. They pay him in Kents, of course..." Both men smiled, but Fane felt a tightening in his neck and jaw and Antonescu caught his eye, communicating caution. An unwelcome world was closing in around him. Maybe around both of them.

Bucharest — March 1985. U*rzici, that's the word for nettles, it sounds so nice,* u*rzici. Emilia made me some last night. They seem to be the first green fresh vegetable in spring. They make a sort of soup of them, very bright green, I'm not quite sure how much I liked it but it felt full of vitamins. If we didn't have the bimonthly support flights and didn't have any fresh, not even frozen, vegetables all winter it would be so welcome. Georgiana asked me to dinner once at her apartment when Bebe was still here — when*

310

they both were here, how I'll miss her! – no, I miss her already. Anyway we sat in their little basement apartment and we had zakuska, a canned tomato and pepper and eggplant sort of relish, so good but still...it wouldn't be fresh vegetables. I must get the recipe...but she's gone. Her replacement that ODCD sent – I did get to interview several women but most were like the one who came in a ski suit and stretched, waggling her breasts at me, and said in a sultry voice when I asked her about her qualifications that she was a friend of the Foreign Minister... Did she think I was male? Or interested in women? Maybe it was a test of some sort. Anyway, Ruxandra seemed like the best and she's good but I just don't know...someone has been looking at my typewriter ribbon. I should take it out and lock it up at night but sometimes I forget. But if I forget, I always check in the morning. I type a bit then look and can tell if there's a gap between the last letters and the next ones, an uneven gap. Imagine, they must go blind trying to read that ribbon...but I've got to tell Roger about it. That's something our security guys need to know, that someone's doing that. Lucky I never do classified stuff on that typewriter, of course I wouldn't, we're so vulnerable at the Library, but still...could it be Ruxandra? I don't remember it happening before. It makes me even more nervous about leaving my purse anywhere, even if I just go across to the library. I need a safe that locks. All those people who slip in the door and my office and have a letter for VOA or the US President. I don't take any personal letters, of course, but we can forward the others. Poor people – that man who was given a prescription for his heart and couldn't get the medicine and when I asked the Health Unit it turned out to be Vitamin C, maybe just to make the man think he was getting something useful. We gave him some. I'm glad I've worked out giving outdated medicines to the clinic in Moldova, even if we aren't supposed to.

But the typewriter ribbon – I wonder what else. I suppose 'they' are unhappy with me. Ever since Professor Constantin told me about Mihai Voda I've been going to see the progress of the demolition, daily. I took Donald Barrier from the New York Times once, the Spanish Ambassador, various people from our Embassy, even the Father William from the Anglican Church. Poor Father William. They didn't heat the church at all in the winter, or at least not much, and he lives in that little room at the side. A room that, under normal circumstances, would be a Sunday school or a store room or something. I don't know whether it's because there isn't enough money, but I think I heard it's because they wouldn't allow him to live elsewhere, it's sort of a concession that we have a priest living here at all.

But we may be successful in saving something. The Monastery is gone, such a pity, they are destroying their own history – I found a picture of it by an artist named Luigi Mayer at the Curtea Veche Anticariat. That man there, Andrei, is so nice and ever since Dave found that his boss, the old bookseller who's only there part of the time, likes Scotch we've had some roaring times in the back room. I hadn't even known there was a back room. There are so many interesting things there. They won't sell us some of the books there, say it's the old guy's personal collection, but other things we do get to buy. I like the prints and pictures best, Dave's the real book collector. At least it's warmer there, or maybe it was the whisky.

I'm sorry, Ropot, I haven't been paying attention to you. Let's do some circles and then we'll jump. Not too much today, but I think you'd enjoy a few exercises and changes of pace. At least that man who pretended to be bird watching, or taking a leak, or exercising – he must have been so cold in January – over there in the woods is gone. Ever since Carol stopped riding with me. That's a vote of confidence in Carol, isn't it. His hand brushes mine when we're sitting together at the Club, I think it's on purpose, but he doesn't take it, take my hand, that is. Of course not, that's in public. Maybe another vote of confidence. But why then would they allow him to spend time here, maybe it's for the riding? He's really good at Dressage. Romania hasn't had a Balkan championship in Dressage since Col. Molnar won it and that was some years ago. Come on, Ropot, pay attention Ellen. Stay straight, boy, measured pace between jumps, two more strides, I'm letting you go, UP...

Fane and Antonescu were walking as they seemed to do more and more often, leaving the little, bare office behind after enough of a meeting to satisfy whoever might be listening. Fane sometimes wondered if anyone actually did listen. Everyone he knew thought he or she was being recorded most of the time — it was almost a status symbol to have the Securitate listening to you. Well, he amended the thought, not everybody, not the market lady or the man who swept the streets or probably most of the peasants or...but certainly anyone who was anybody. So, if that were the case, how many hours had to be spent listening...he turned his attention back to Antonescu.

"Good news," the other man said. "I heard through, uh, channels that they will move the Mihai Voda church, but not destroy it. Not," he continued bitterly, "that this preserves Romanian heritage in the way it should be saved."

"Is it the Russians?" Fane asked almost idly knowing it wasn't but wondering if Antonescu would actually say what he believed. He did. "No," Antonescu was serious in his reply, "it's our Leader. He wants Romania to be modern, he wants to build the largest building in the world on the site, to imitate Paris to build a great boulevard stretching for miles. But you know this, I'm sure." Antonescu wasn't clueless, he was really quick, that needed remembering, Fane noted. It wouldn't do to get careless, no matter how close they might feel.

"I heard that it was She who wanted all this, who put gold faucets in the Cotroceni bathrooms," Fane remarked.

"Rumors. True, I think. I heard that from a friend who had talked to one of the plumbers who installed them." Fane just nodded. It was true, in fact. The plumber in question was from Slatioara and one of Leri's family's acquaintances who had needed some help with some paperwork, but no need to tell Antonescu that.

"Now," continued Antonescu, "there is talk of tearing down villages and putting peasants in apartment blocks."

"No!" Fane stopped in his tracks, stunned. "Don't tell me...how can peasants...there could be another revolt... they've given up so much, now to take their courtyards... besides, they produce so much on their plots."

"That's one of the problems. It doesn't 'look good'...

but I've got something else I need to tell you. You know Andrei Roveanu, don't you?"

"Yes." It had long since been established between the two men that they both collected books, though Fane had learned that Antonescu's passion was Romanian folk art in spite of his history degree.

"You'd better say something to him. His boss and Andrei himself have gotten altogether too friendly to the Americans and some other foreigners. The old man has been selling them books out of the back room." This was the first time Antonescu had admitted to knowing about the back room, one which most *anticariats* had but few of which had such a rich collection...except maybe the shop near Fane's house... "And it's gotten out of proportion."

"How am I going to say anything without..." Fane's words hung in the air, the rest of the sentence not needing to be completed.

"Think of a way," the two men had arrived at Cismigiu Garden. "Let's go in, the daffodils must be in bloom. I can hardly warn them," what he meant, Fane thought, was that it would be a greater breach of security and greater punishment if he were caught, "and they're likely to get in trouble."

"What would happen? Prison?"

"Oh, probably not. Nowadays if they simply let people go from the workplace and the people don't 'find' another job, they can lose ration cards, apartment allotments...but they need to back off from sitting and getting drunk with Americans."

So Fane found himself carrying yet another message. It was certainly easy enough to find an excuse to visit the *anticariat*. The bell rang as Fane opened the door and Andrei turned to him with a smile, putting down the books he always seemed to have in his hand.

"Fane! So good to see you — it's been a long time!"

"Since January, I think...things have been busy."

314

"Come on back, I have some stuff I want to show you." Curiosity overcame caution and Fane assented readily. "Look," said Andrei, picking up a book from a table piled with them just as soon as the door had shut behind them, "here's the Transylvanian series of the *Bulletin of the Commission for Historical Monuments*! It's complete!" Fane's eyes lit up and he reached for the volumes, only a few, automatically. "This is great, the last missing pieces in my collection except for that one issue during the War that..."

Finally, bringing himself back to his original purpose, Fane proposed that they celebrate his acquisition with a *tzuica*. The two went down the stairs into a cellar bar across the street and chatted idly over a drink. When they came out, Fane asked Andrei to walk to the bus stop with him.

"I've...found something out..." Fane began awkwardly. "I have a friend, sort of a friend, from my village actually," the lies began to come more easily, "who's," Fane moved his hand to his shoulder, patted it a couple of times in the well understood sign for Securitate, then straightened his collar. Andrei, sharp eyed under the circumstances, nodded slightly, and Fane continued. "He's a book lover, apparently some of Them are. He told me that you are entertaining some diplomats in the anticariat and you need to stop."

"Why...why," Andrei was confused and obviously unsettled. "How...?"

"Who knows?" said Fane. "I try to stay away from those people myself, not the diplomats, the others. I've gotten to the place," his voice gained confidence, "where everyone thinks I'm connected with them because I go everywhere, but it's a smokescreen." The lie didn't bother him any more at all, if it ever really had. Whatever it took. Besides, he was doing Andrei a favor. "But I do know some people who are and some of them are educated and...not all bad. Be careful. You need to be friendly to the diplomats, or course, but watch what you say and...do."

The two men parted and Fane continued across the boulevard to catch a bus toward home, feeling good that he had helped a friend.

Oradea – May, 1985. We're almost back to Oradea, I'm so glad there are diplomatic lanes at the Hungarian border. Trust the Communists to know how to treat an elite! It's been a long day, kind of difficult in a way, also fun. I've been driving, too, as Scott doesn't really like to drive. I guess his wife normally drives when they go out as a family, come to think of it, she drove most of the time in Bukovina. Funny, an American man not liking to drive very much but I'm happy to do it though it's tiring, especially in a foreign country. Look at that, I'm thinking of Hungary as a foreign country – maybe I've been here too long. Things in Romania begin to seem normal until you get 'out' and look back and think, 'That's a really strange place.' Like today...it was a good idea, Scott had, to buy the salami and cheese and wine and stuff for the reception at the Oradea Museum in Debrecen, across the border because it really showed how Romania is, well, different, I mean, think of our reactions when we came into town and saw that butcher shop, full of things to buy, no empty shelves. We looked at one another and Scott said we should go in and buy the stuff we needed. I said we had planned to do some sightseeing and it was a warm day and the food might spoil in the car. "But what if it isn't there when we get back?" Scott asked. It was a valid point. We looked around, there weren't any lines that we could see, we went in the butcher shop and looked around some more, then we finally decided it would probably be all right to do some sightseeing first. And it was alright, the salami was still there. We bought a lot, cases of wine as well as meat and cheese to take home. I hope it will keep. We'll have plenty for the Houser-Namingha reception tomorrow night, too. What great artists, I know the Romanians will love them. The Romanians have this thing about American Indians, but it's really, really good art, too. Carol loved it when I took him around this morning – what a surprise, seeing him in the hotel dining room last night but I guess there's only one hotel people stay at in Oradea. He's looking for a location for his next movie but said he didn't find it, he joined Scott and me for dinner and I'm just thinking of all of these details because I don't want to think about him kissing me. He saw me to my room. I unlocked the door, then turned and faced him to say goodnight and he just took me in those wonderful strong arms and held me and kissed me. I felt his body all along mine and I wanted it there, I wanted...I wanted that moment forever and more, so much more. Then he just looked at me and said, "No, we can't. My love..." and he left. I haven't felt this way since I was thirteen, maybe never, not even with Bill. I don't know what to think. I certainly don't want to think about Bill, that's in the past. I'm not going to report this to Roger, nothing happened. The hotel room is probably bugged anyway so nothing could have happened, we wouldn't have dared.I hope the hall wasn't bugged.I don't think anyone saw us. Oh shit. What a mess.I don't think I've ever felt this way about a man. Is it just because I can't have him?

The party swirled into the garden of the Mellon residence, fragments of lingering May dusk complementing the lights set around the terrace and walls. Climbing red roses were fragrant in the warm air and Leri was under them, talking to one of her former professors from the University, her face framed against the flowers. The guest of honor, an American poet, had given a dull talk and duller reading but the Romanian guests exclaimed politely about the depth of meaning he had conveyed. Fane didn't understand everything they were saying as he listened with half an ear; he had been making a quiet effort to learn English and was able to catch some of the conversation. Not that it was important.

"Stefan, chay mai fatchits?" Peter Mellon's Romanian hadn't improved, but Fane had learned that the diplomat had a good grasp of literature as well as art and was worth the effort it took to communicate anything back and forth. They stood for a while, drinks in hand. Music played softly in the background, the Scotch was excellent and the food being handed around even better. This American pizza, for instance, Fane thought as he took a bite, was quite nice. Someone came up to Mellon and led him off, talking about an introduction so Fane wandered over to the bar to replenish his drink.

"Still at it," said Victor and looked disapproving as usual, but Fane thought he saw another emotion, perhaps one of...triumph? Was he imagining that? Fane shifted uneasily, smiling at Victor and bantering to hide his discomfort. After a minute Victor filled his glass, grudgingly or maybe with an agenda, Fane wondered? and Fane thanked him before turning back to the party. Fane continued to chat with this person and that but the pleasure of the May evening had receded, carried on a tide of unease that seeped into the nooks and crannies of his mind bringing with it the churning in his stomach that seemed to have become as regular a companion as the shopping bag Fane always carried. The shopping bag was for the unexpected find, toothpaste, soap. What was the parallel for the churning in his stomach? What was..."Stefan!" He turned to see Ellen, smiling, apparently genuinely glad to see him.

"Stefan — I haven't seen you in a long time, have you been traveling?" He once had told the Library Director that he occasionally traveled for his historical research and as she was always interested in places for weekend trips he had made several suggestions. They talked a bit, strolling into the garden, then she asked about a print she had just bought, a picture of the Dimbovita by an artist named Preziosi.

"Yes, Amedeo Preziosi, he came in 1868 and then returned — there was a famous..." Fane continued to elaborate a bit about the prints he had done.

"Wasn't that at the time of Carol the First?" Ellen asked. Fane was surprised that she knew. "Yes," she responded to his question, "my friend in the Embassy — you know him, he came with us to Bilca — Dave, he's very interested in Romanian history and he's gotten me interested as well. I...well, it's too bad there isn't more information about the royal family and what they did for Romania but also so many of the things since then, it's so hard to find out what happened...in the Second World War, for example. Why one time..." Ellen checked herself and then said, "...but I guess that isn't something we can talk about."

"There are many things we can't talk about," Fane said bitterly. "I can't talk about my friend who was killed because he knew too much. But perhaps I can tell you." Fane didn't quite know where his head was, he sipped the Scotch automatically, buzzing in his ears, heart thumping, his mind leaping here and there but he continued apparently calmly, trying to look absolutely casual and as said, "He knew that they are building a nuclear weapon in the Carpathians. Above Fagaras. You know, I could be put in prison for telling you this."

Ellen smiled casually but the lines around her eyes deepened. "I don't deal with this but I know people who do."

"I can't meet them."

"Can you tell me something specific that will prove to them this isn't simply a rumor." Fane felt new respect for the woman and the buzzing receded slightly. "Yes, can you remember this?" He repeated two lines of the chant Father Augustin had taught him, a chant which had run as a constant background to his everyday thoughts for months, an eternity.

"I hope so, Oh, Hello Greta, how are you?" The other woman exchanged enchanted pleasantries and moved on, leaving the two alone.

"Try setting them to music. Fane hummed the chant quietly, it was easy to pick up. "That helps," said Ellen. Fane repeated the words and Ellen thought them silently over a few times. "I've got it."

"Then let's celebrate!" Fane raised his glass and they toasted one another.

"What's the occasion?" Peter Mellon had returned, unnoticed.

"I was teaching Ellen a Romanian religious chant and she caught the music right away," replied Fane quickly. Mellon looked confused. Ellen repeated it in English and Mellon smiled. "She's quite musical, our Library Director," he said and the three moved into inconsequential conversation.

What have I done? Fane asked himself a dozen times on the way home, chatting with Leri all the while. Leri had met a school friend who...Fane let his thoughts wander and was saved by the arrival of the bus. This late there was no problem finding a seat and the two sat down together. Fane took Leri's hand and received a grateful warm squeeze of his fingers. They continued to hold hands as the bus turned on to Magheru and Fane watched the darkened buildings of his city roll by, the Nottara Theater where Georgiana's father was the Director — I wonder, he thought in passing, how she likes Sweden, must be cold but they probably have wellheated houses — the Gradinita Restaurant, the Piata Romana with the Academy of Economic Science, the grand houses along Ana Ipatescu, the Foreign Ministry in the Piata Victoriei, the apartment blocks and small buildings along May 1 Boulevard, the funny tower of their own marketplace. Here they got off and walked into the lovely old quarter where they lived, Leri holding his arm as they crossed the cobblestone street, her high heels as always a hazard. How long will I live to see this? Fane thought, 'What have I done? I could pretend nothing happened, that I didn't say anything, maybe they won't be interested, maybe they won't believe me.' The two continued, still hand in hand, and turned in their gate, the familiar creak bringing another pang to Fane's knotted, churning stomach. What if Leri wants to make love, tonight, I don't think I could do it, what in hell? I could say I have a headache. He snickered at the thought and Leri said, "Fane, what's going on?"

"Oh, nothing, really, but I have a bit of a headache." Leri murmured sympathetically and urged him to go to bed and get a good night's sleep. Surprisingly enough, he did.

The next day Fane walked to work as usual. He greeted the gateman and exchanged a few words and entered the Institute. Today he needed to look at articles by various staff members proposed for publication, one on Dacian coins, another on Cucuteni pottery. How much should they push back against the order to relabel Mircea the Old so that he became Mircea the Great—it seemed the Leader of the country didn't like the word 'old' applied to rulers... then there was a meeting with the editor of *Magazin istoric*. Perhaps he should stop by the Romanian Academy on the way back and meet a few people since it was a lovely day and he could easily walk the distance...the nuclear chant continued in the back of his mind, not interfering with his conscious thoughts, not going away but stronger, more insistent than ever.

Leaving the *Magazin istoric* offices after a satisfactory conversation Fane decided there wasn't time to walk and went, instead, to the bus stop. On the corner of the street was a church and he could hear chanting, like the chanting in his head but in beautiful deep voices — he looked around, saw no one he knew and went in. Stepping against an interior wall he bowed his head, "God, if you exist, help me. Help me. Show me the path. I..." An elderly woman fervently crossing herself jostled him as she went to kiss an icon and broke his mood. Slightly ashamed and hoping no one had seen him, Fane left.

When he arrived at the Institute there was a message for him. Carol had rung, suggesting they meet for coffee. "How is he, Comrade? What is he like?" The secretary had been there just long enough to be able to ask about the movie star and Fane obligingly gave her some inconsequential details she could take home to husband or mother or whoever else shared her life.

This time the coffee shop was a new one but they didn't remain long and they had a *tzuica* rather than coffee. Carol talked about his father and a letter he'd recently had..."He's fine, but his knee is bothering him"...they talked about growing old, about Fane's book collection. "If anything ever happens to me," Fane said, "you take my books." Carol started and looked at him strangely.

"I'm hardly a good candidate," he said.

"But you would know their importance," Fane replied.

"Yes...I know that. Speaking of importance, I need to get some medications for my father. Want to walk with me?" Fane assented, realizing there was something else to the meeting. As they strolled through back streets to a pharmacy Carol knew, Fane thought of how many times he had had important conversations while walking, with Leri, Carol, Mihai, Antonescu, Brother Augustin, countless others that were perhaps not quite so important but made the speakers nervous, requests for intervention with the authorities, requests for a doctor who might...help...a woman who was pregnant. Request, confidences, all at a measured pace through the city or the woods or someplace other than a living room, an office, a place where other ears might be interested. What would it be like to live in a country where a man could sit in his home and talk freely about anything? Was there such a country? Why hadn't he thought of this before?

"Fane," said Carol at an appropriate time. "I have a problem. It's a woman."

"That's nothing unusual." They both smiled at each other then Carol looked away.

"This woman is...It's Ellen." Fane stopped and grasped Carol's arm. "No, don't tell me. I don't want to know."

"There's nothing to know. Nothing has happened. Except maybe that I've finally fallen in love."

"You said that before, more or less."

"Yes, I have." Carol walked on. "And there's nothing to be done, is there? Nothing has happened between us," he repeated, "except I kissed her."

"Did anyone see?" was Fane's first response. "What difference would it make? A man kisses a woman! For God's sake!"

"She isn't a woman. She's an American diplomat."

"At least you aren't suggesting that I follow up and recruit her...but I don't think I could if I wanted to, it's out of the question."

"You already told me that, too."

"I did, but I told you that I wasn't willing. It's also because she isn't...I don't think she would betray her country...I don't think she'd betray anything or anybody if she had a choice. She's so clean...so wholesome...I've learned that this is a word they use about people from that part of the United States, the place she comes from, 'wholesome'. It's a funny way to describe a human being — healthy, good for you, good, maybe — but that's what she is."

"So why are you telling me this?" Fane asked, suddenly curious.

"I need to tell someone. I want to tell the whole world and I can't, so I have you." Carol shoved an elbow in Fane's ribs and smiled. "Let's go get drunk. By the way, I've been asked if I've had any contact with Mihai." "So have I," said Fane. "I haven't, you haven't..." "That's right, they knew that." "Good. That's another good reason for a toast." The two turned into yet another small anonymous bar.

Bucharest — June 1985. I couldn't believe Stefan was really telling me about a nuclear installation, I thought it was...I just couldn't believe it but it really seems to have 'substance' according to the guys in the 'Other Agency'. Since we're the US Information Agency in Washington, they are the 'other' agency. Funny we call them that — we never say CIA, I'm even a bit uncomfortable thinking the words. We do keep things secret as if people couldn't figure it out, "other agency". And 'substance,' a funny way to say something might be useful, but I guess the word is useful. Useful. Substance. Anyway, they'll get back to me. It's the first time they've wanted to have anything to do with me. I'm not sure how I feel about that. I mean, we see each other at Mom's and I know Rick plays tennis because he talks about it a lot and I know their wives...but our work doesn't bring us together. Much. Except for that message. I guess it's the second time they've wanted to have anything to do with me. But whatever the things I memorized mean, they were interested. I guess I could look them up and figure it out myself...but I don't want to know.

I wonder if I'll see Carol tomorrow at the Club. I've neglected Ropot, I've only ridden a couple of times this week. He'll be impossible. If the horses were turned out they could work off some of their energy, but they aren't. I wonder why? I'd better lunge him tomorrow and let him get some of the zip out of his system so we can work properly and he doesn't just want to run. I wish I could be in two places at once. I want to travel more and I want to ride...I think Sandy and I have explored everything within a day's drive of Bucharest, on this wide flat plain. Now, of course, we're going to go regularly to Balteni, where that little Brancoveanu church is that they say Ceausescu wants to demolish because it's just across the lake from his hunting lodge. Dave even found an article about it in the Bulletin of the Commission for Historical Monuments, *in one of the first issues, 1908 or something like that. He brought the article along with us the first time we visited. The priest was delighted to see it and they went over the church with the magazine in hand. I thought it was pretty boring but the day was lovely and there were lilacs by the priest's house. His daughter is studying the flute and she played for us, Mozart I think. It was a timeless moment. This is, could be, such a lovely country.*

I'll be back at the Library in a moment. I've gotten to know this walk well, between the Library and the Embassy at the back of the National Theater. Uh-oh, there's that crazy woman who follows me around and always wants to talk...they just recently let them out of the hospitals onto the streets I heard but she's been around a long time. Funny, she speaks good English, is obviously educated. She's given me long letters full of beautifully written gibberish. Now, I'll just duck in the gate, up the steps on the Library side and through the door and, good, Liliana will stop her and I'll get away through the upstairs...good to have learned all the nooks and crannies of this wonderful building. Oh, there's Emil, I need to talk to him...

Fane got the phone call about an hour after he had gotten to the Institute. Leri, on the other end of the line, was sobbing and gasping and trying to talk. Gradually she calmed enough to tell Fane that her parents had both passed away. Fane caught his breath in shock.

"But...your mother...she went in for an operation, but..."

324

"Aunt Sanda called. She said the doctors had found cancer, Mother didn't survive the operation, it was too far advanced. Father sat beside her and had a heart attack. He couldn't live without her..." Leri's voice dissolved in sobs again.

"We have to go to Slatioara, obviously, do you want me to pick you up at school — I'll get a car from the Institute...I think the Director will help us out or Carol..." When Fane told him, Dragomir was shaken by Fane's news — the loss of both parents at once, unexpectedly...he offered the use of an Institute car and driver before Fane could bring up the subject himself. Shortly after noon the two and Florin, one of the Institute drivers, were on their way west on the long modern highway to Pitesti. Once through that city they climbed up and down the foothills of the southern Carpathians, crossed the mighty Olt River and wound their way to Horezu and through it to Slatioara, talking, Leri crying from time to time then drying her tears, Fane holding her hand in silence. As they finally turned on to the dirt road that climbed up to his in-laws' house Fane thought, as he usually did at this point, about their decision to live in such a remote place.

"Why don't you come to Bucharest and be near us?" he had asked several times. "Leri would love to have you near and...we could manage the paperwork." But they had both thanked him and refused quite firmly. "We have friends, ties..." "Well, then, why not Horezu? There are facilities there..." Fane meant a hospital but there were also stores.

"We thought of that," Leri's father had replied, "But we have found a house we both like, with good neighbors, actually sort of cousins to us, and the forest just above us...I want the peace and quiet of country life. It's why," he added, "I became a veterinarian in the first place, loving animals but also loving to be in nature, away from the city." And why, Fane thought, he had chosen to be in a poor, uncollectivized mountain area as well, no doubt. Understandable, Fane reflected now, but it must have been hard in winter and

325

when they became more advanced in age, less able...but that wouldn't be a problem now, would it?

The funeral was large and well-attended as Dr. Matei had done more than one good deed in the course of his life. Even his work, Fane reflected, was a good deed...perhaps a bit like Uncle Vanya's. Pity the two men never met...and the needs of the moment pushed away the pressures of Bucharest giving Fane more peace than he had felt for months. It wasn't until Fane and Leri ran into Ellen that they surfaced again.

The occasion was the annual Ceramics Fair at Horezu and Antonescu was the reason they were there. Fane had called to cancel a meeting as he tied up various pieces of business before leaving Bucharest for what could easily turn into a week's absence.

"I'm so sorry," Antonescu was genuinely sympathetic, "and please give your wife my profoundest regrets. This is terrible news." The conversation went on in a similar, predictable vein then Antonescu changed the subject.

"This is something I hardly...it isn't the time...and it's entirely personal, but I had hoped to get to Horezu this coming Sunday myself." Fane expressed genuine surprise and tried to convey a mixture of pleasure and enquiry in his voice. "Yes," continued Antonescu, "it's the annual Ceramics Fair and I undertand that a potter from Arad, one Betea Dumitru, is to be there. I've heard of his pieces but I've never seen them and haven't had a chance to...but it's too much to ask."

"As you can understand," Fane demurred, "under the circumstances...I don't have any objection but Leri...if it's possible..." As it happened, after three full days of mourning and sadness Leri herself suggested they stop. "Just for a bit...I haven't been here at the Ceramics Fair for years and I do love..."

"We don't have any room, dear..." cautioned Fane.

"I know but still..." "I'm glad to stop, sir," said Florin from the front seat. "My wife likes these things." "In that case," Fane seized on this very good reason, doing a favor for the man who had been helping them, not that he hadn't had three days of good food and little work but still...

The fairground was slightly muddy and they picked their way carefully through the lines of stalls. Leri picked up various pieces and exclaiming about them while Fane made enquiries about the potter from Arad. They were standing talking to the Arad potter, in fact, when Ellen came up.

"Stefan! Valeria! What a pleasant surprise!"

After a round of exclamations and explanations and introductions since Ellen had come with Sandy and Dave, Fane walked with Ellen while Leri explained the fine points of various pieces to Dave and Sandy.

"Stefan," began Ellen, "I did talk to the appropriate people about what you told me and they are interested. They particularly want to know if you have the exact coordinates of the site."

"I do," replied Fane, the churning surfacing in his stomach and spreading through his body. "But..."

"The question is how and...I guess," Ellen was clearly uncomfortable..."Well, there are two things. How you are rewarded for this information and how we can keep you safe."

Fane recoiled. "Rewarded? Compensated?" He should have thought of this but the idea of money...Ellen touched his arm. "I told them you weren't that kind of person," she said and Fane remembered Carol's description of this woman. "Wholesome." Did one think of wholesome and sex at the same time...? He put the thought aside, "...so they have come up with a proposal," Ellen continued. "If we can find a way to get you and your wife out of the country, we'll provide for you in the United States — give you English lessons, a place to live, work out support..." Fane was dumbfounded.

"Leave Romania?" Ellen nodded just as a small, round man buzzed up. "Fane! And you are Ellen, aren't you?" "Hello, Dan! Ellen, may I present..." The three exchanged pleasantries, Ellen learned Dan was a writer and theater director, "But I should know you..." she said. "You should!" he answered. "And now you do!" and chatted about Bucharest. "Have you come here for the fair?" asked Ellen, Fane's stomach continued churning, "Not entirely," Dan replied, "since I'm from Slatioara, that's the village after Marasesti, and have a house there..." Fane wished he'd leave, "...and, Fane, I'm so sorry to hear..." After an eternity Leri arrived and embraced Dan, there were more exclamations, condolences, introductions, more buzzing in Fane's head, and finally he was able to turn to Leri and say, "This is marvelous, but we really need to be on the road if we want to arrive in Bucharest before dark." "Oh, yes," said Ellen, "we must also..." and the party broke apart and fell into its separate pieces as each car left the grounds. Fane leaned back against the seat of the Institute Dacia, almost nauseous. "Don't you feel well?" asked Leri solicitously. "Too much rich food," she answered for him.

"Probably and...I can hardly say I'm upset about your parents, sitting next to you while you are living with your loss, but they were very good to me..." and indeed, thought Fane, they were. They had accepted him as their son, not even as their son-in-law. He and Leri had spent many happy hours in their house and now that would be gone. Fane looked at the mountains to the north, thought of his beloved Bukovina. Would that all be gone for him, too? What would he say to Leri?

Bucharest — June 1985. How strange but what good luck to run into Stefan where we could talk. If only we'd had more time before that man discovered us, though he certainly is interesting. I asked Ruxandra about him and it seems he's very important, I think she meant high in the Party but I'm not sure, but he also has a reputation as a dissident. Could the two things happen at the same time? But I wish I'd had more time to talk to Stefan. I told the guys from the Other Agency that I'd relayed their message and they said they'd work on it. I think they're nervous. It must be a big decision, they're offering a lot of money in that plan. Take them to the US, take care of them there, I wonder what exactly that means? What it means, I guess, is that if the information isn't worth much they're in trouble. But also what does 'take care of' mean? I suppose I'll have to ask because Stefan will want to know. I don't like asking them much, they're not very...oh, time to stand up and sing a hymn...this is such a lovely little church and I do like Father William. I wonder if I could talk to him and ask his advice on this...you're supposed to be able to talk to a priest about anything and they don't tell. It would be such a comfort, to talk to someone I respect and could trust. I'm asking Stefan and Valeria to leave their country, though enough people really want to get out...but I'm sure that's not why he told me what he did. It's 10:30 and the sermon will last at least fifteen minutes then communion...I wonder if Stefan could be a double agent.

I mustn't think of Carol.

What would it be like to leave my country forever? Not to be able to go back? But this regime can't last forever, I just don't think it can, things are so bad. How much will Romanians put up with? A lot, I guess.

The trip to the village of Vaideeni, near Horezu, was lovely. I'm so glad that Dave met that family who invited us to come and camp on their land. It was so funny when the police came and arrested Dave...they looked at Sandy and me and took him because he was a man. There is an advantage to male chauvinism sometimes. When they found he was a diplomat they let him go. Dave said they made some phone calls then apologized and let him go. I hope the family doesn't get in trouble — they were such good hosts and it was fun sitting around the camp fire at night and singing our folk songs for one another. Dave won't sing but Sandy and I do really well together. We even harmonized a bit on Shenandoah *and* Jamaica Farewell *and some other songs we both knew. The Romanian songs were lovely, some so sad. The way that Cristi sat with his hands on his knees, palms up, eyes closed, his face outlined by the fire, singing that one song, a* 'doina' *he called it, so absolutely still and yet such emotion...it brought shivers down my spine. I think Dave gave the police some Kents, a couple of packets, not enough to be a bribe but now I'm sure they reported everything to Bucharest.*

Maybe that's all they had to do, I don't know but I will ask Dave about it.

I wonder how Stefan and Valeria could get out of the country. If they want to go...oh, wait, time to stand, "I believe in God, the Father Almighty, maker of heaven and earth..."

When Fane returned to the Institute Monday morning he brought *coliva* with him, a heady mixture of walnuts and wheat and spices, to share both the food and his emotions with his colleagues. It was, he thought as various people expressed their sympathy and genuine feelings, a comfort to have a group like this, your own collective, people who cared for you while you cared for them.

This mind set was broken when he went in to see Popescu.

The Accountant sat at his usual desk in his usual chair but, unlike Dragomir, Popescu seemed to have shrunk. For the first time Fane realized that Popescu, too, had been getting older, much older. The man stood, steadying himself slightly with a hand on his desk as he rose, and moved forward to embrace Fane in sympathy, Fane offered *coliva*, and the two sat down again.

"I've taken care of your most recent trip," the older man said with a smile, but the smile vanished with uncharacteristic swiftness. "It will be all right," Fane realized he meant the trip to Horezu, "but I had to do a bit of, um, paperwork. They're getting more watchful about expenses." Fane knew he didn't mean Dragomir.

"I would be glad to, uh, reimburse..."

"Not a question," Popescu waved his hand in dismissal. "It's taken care of but I do want to tell you," he lowered his voice, "that there have been some enquiries in more general terms about you through the Party. Do you have, uh...is there someone..." Fane could complete the sentence himself so he nodded in understanding and Popescu left the words themselves unsaid. Popescu went on about a new regulation for reporting expenditures but it was clear. Popescu had warned Fane that someone—perhaps some people—were looking at him. In an unfriendly way.

The meeting with Antonescu was no more reassuring. The Securitate officer was delighted with the two pots Fane— well, Leri—had chosen for him and reached for his wallet. "No, no question," said Fane. "I must, I asked..." "I was glad and it was nothing but..." After the pro forma exchange was finished, however, Antonescu became perfunctory, not the usual genial conversationalist Fane had come to know over the years between them. No matter how unimportant, Antonescu had always been interested in whatever Fane had to say, drawing him out and communicating the importance of the information. Today he seemed totally uninterested. When the meeting ended both men stood up, shook hands, then walked out together. Once on the steet there was a subtle relaxation and they walked side by side.

"Is something wrong?" asked Fane.

"No more than usual, I suppose," Antonescu replied. "The pro-Soviet faction in the service hate us and are watching both you and me, though we're small fish and we're certainly not the only ones they're watching. Our only importance to them is that they could use us to get at our superiors. Our superiors are doing the same to them. We stay out of the way as much as possible..." When elephants fight, the mice..."

"I wondered if something was going on...I've received signals from some other friends," Fane said.

"Don't worry too much, but watch your back. That Victor...for some reason he's taken a real dislike to you. Have you done anything to him?" Fane riffled through his mental files. "No...I can't think of anything." "Some people are simply vicious by nature. Or jealous." The two walked on, threading as they often did, the labyrinth of back streets in the old merchants' quarter.

"There's one thing," began Fane hesitantly then his thoughts, formulated over a long period of time, finally surfaced. "I've wondered about...because...well, I don't think I give you much of value. I come and report and tell you this and that, but there's nothing very..."

"...'important'...was that what you wanted to say?"

"Probably. Exciting. Maybe it's all interesting if you like gossip but I haven't found anything that would be dangerous to Romania or the Party, nothing that I can think of. I give you this detail. That detail. In the beginning I...thought that's all I would do because I didn't want to get anyone in trouble," he paused and Antoescu nodded, "but over time that's all there was. Nothing else."

"The details can add up, but probably no one cares all that much." Antonescu was uncharacteristically cynical. "I get paid on the number of informants I recruit, the number of reports I file. The man above me gets paid for putting things together and filing more reports. I'm not sure how many people look at the reports in fact." Antonescu wiped sweat off his face. "It's warm today, a real heat wave."

"Early in the season, but it feels good after the cold winter."

"I guess we can't complain. Next week, the usual time?"

"All right."

They bid each other good-bye and went their opposite ways, Antonescu toward the trolley stop at University Place, Fane toward the bookshop at the Curtea Veche, uneasy as he walked, wondering if he had said too much, wondering why he said anything, wondering if Antonescu was sincere or leading him on, the tightness in his stomach worse than ever.

Andrei had the door of the *anticariat* open and a fan positioned to bring in a breath of air. "Soon it'll be cooler, but right now...but let's not talk about the heat. I have a book that might interest you." The two walked back into the windowless second room and Andrei handed Fane an old volume. "Take a look — it's too hot to close the front door so I need to stay out in the shop, we're behind on our quota of sales." Fane sat down behind the little table, enjoying the peace and solitude, the wonderful smell of many books kept together, and examined the volume in his hand. It was in French, published in Bucharest in 1944, *La Roumanie vue par les étrangers* by one Cioranescu and it had plates by many of the artists Fane had included in his dissertation.

"Cioranescu left the country in the forties..." Andrei's voice startled Fane out of his reverie. "That's why this isn't easily available."

"I thought I'd seen everything...it's something, isn't it, published in 1944...in that terrible time we still published books."

"Not much keeps the Romanians down..." Andrei's voice trailed off. Fane turned to another plate.

"These are quite wonderful."

"Unfortunately, the book isn't cheap. You know, these books that don't come in through the normal means..." Fane did know. It would be a wonderful addition to his collection. "Of course, I've never known you to be stopped by small concerns like money when..." Andrei's voice continued. Fane continued to leaf through the volume.

"Look, two plates together of the *Dorobanti*, one by Bouquet and one by Duverger...this is a treasure."

"Would you like me to keep it for you?" asked Andrei.

"Of course, I'll let you know...no," Fane hesitated. Why should he buy this book for a collection he might leave behind, never to see again...but if he didn't buy it, it would be out of character and if he were being watched, if Andrei were reporting to someone...no, he wouldn't...but still. "I'll come back for it next week or before," Fane said decisively. How could he go against the habits of a lifetime? And the book was a find...

"Take it now," said Andrei. "I can trust you with it."

Bucharest—July 1, 1985. How I've come to hate the Fourth of July, all the people who want invitations to the Ambassador's reception, these endless boring awful meetings. Everyone fights about which section gets to invite which persons, each one says its contacts are more important than anyone else's. I wish Peter would take care of it but the Library contact list is so long and has so many important people on it, and he doesn't know them all. I think the Political Section hates us — we know so many people. But we have things people want, movie tickets, books to lend, trips to the US, invitations to this and that. The Fourth of July reception is one of the only things the other sections really have to hand out — but they could give me lists of people to invite to our events. They don't. I wonder why not? I have suggested it several times but they don't.

In Nigeria we moved the Fourth of July to February because of the rainy season. That was strange but the Brits do the same thing with the Queen's birthday. In fact, I know when the Queen's birthday party is but come to think of it, I don't know the day she was actually born. There we worried that important people wouldn't come, whether enough people would come to be respectable. Here, it's the opposite — everyone wants that invitation and they want it for their wives and kids and relatives and friends...I start getting calls weeks ahead of time. If it weren't so annoying it would be amusing. The first calls usually start with some other subject, a theater performance they want me to attend, a book they'd like to give me, then they come around to the July 4 party. 'I imagine it will be good weather, I do so much enjoy...' These calls aren't so bad because I don't really have to say anything since the list isn't made up and a lot of those people are going to be invited anyway.

Closer in people are more direct and it's less pleasant. 'I haven't gotten my invitation yet and wonder if it's been lost in the mail somewhere...' 'Why haven't I gotten an invitation? I'm ALWAYS invited on the 4th.' 'You can't invite the director of Theater A and not invite me the Director of Theater B' and on and on...I never know quite what to say. And then there are the ones who come with gifts and wait expectantly. Everyone brings gifts, all the time — I see Ruxandra gets lots of flowers and I wonder what else, but she gives out tickets to the public movie performances. That's okay — all our employees have a couple of tickets to give out to the public performances but sometimes I wonder how many Ruxandra takes before people line up for them. But all we do for the July 4 is submit a list and give it to Peter who... I wonder why it's so important to people? It isn't as if the food's great though these days people scarf *up anything. That's another thing I hate, the whole representation allowance and how not to spend so much on this event...last year it was so embarrassing when they cut the hot dogs in half. I hope it will be better this year.*

Thank goodness, it's ending. I can get back to doing something useful. About the only good thing is that Carol will be invited this year – as well, of course, as Stefan and Valeria. I'm glad they decided they'd invite wives, too, since people will come with them anyway and it's embarrassing to turn them away. There are always some gate-crashers, I hear. There were last year. Ah, it's good to stand up and stretch, even if invisibly...I'd better go up and see what plans have been made about Stefan and whether I am supposed to talk to them about it.

Fane took the book with him, promising to bring Andrei the money in a few days. This was too precious to let go, even if...he walked past the Museum of the History of the City of Bucharest and looked across at the new National Theater. This was one building he wouldn't be sad to leave. Nor the Intercontinental Hotel where, he had heard, they were no longer allowing Romanians to go in. Probably didn't want people to see how much food they would give foreigners who paid in foreign exchange.

Leri had just finished washing her hair when he arrived. "It's so hot," she explained, pinning it up, "I couldn't stand it." Fane looked down at himself, almost wet with sweat from the heat, maybe from nerves. He had decided on the way home he had to tell Leri.

"Is it too wet to go out?" he asked. "It's so hot...I thought it would be nice to walk in the park."

"What a good idea," Leri's voice was muffled through the pins in her mouth. "Give me a moment...there. Does it look all right?" Her hair, still dark, was close to her head, making her lovely eyes and cheekbones even more prominent.

"It's ravishing, you should wear it like this more often."

"Oh, you," Leri poked Fane in his ample stomach. "You flatterer. Come on, let's go."

Walking by the back of the Ambassador's Residence, Fane said, "I forgot completely. An invitation to the July 4 party came for us a couple of days ago." Leri stopped dead in her tracks.

"You forgot? You forgot? Something like that and you forget? It's only three days away!" She was only half joking. Fane made himself smile. "Yes, I forgot. Is it important?"

"Important? Is it important? It's only 'the' event of the year, to be on that guest list. As Assistant Director, my husband, Assitant Director...but what about Dr. Dragomir?"

"He was invited, of course, but he sent his regrets as always. He doesn't enjoy that kind of thing."

"He probably can't stand for that long or walk the distance required," said Leri then she stopped herself. "I shouldn't be unkind. He probably can't help his weight?"

"What do you mean?" asked Fane curiously.

"I mean that there are some body types that are simply fat, whether they want to be or not. I was reading..." Leri went on about her new discovery for a bit before moving to the next important question, what to wear. This occupied them to the entrance of the part of the park by the lake, a favorite summer destination ever since they had moved into Ady Endre.

"How many years have we been coming here?" Leri asked, tucking her hand into Fane's elbow in spite of the heat.

"I can't remember, exactly, maybe twenty? And I need to talk to you about how much longer we might be staying there."

"Do you think we should move?" She stopped to admire some ducks on the water then looked at Fane. He looked into her eyes for a moment, then looked back at the ducks.

"Not exactly. Well, maybe. It's a long story. Let's walk."

So they continued around the lake, over the Japanese style bridge, by the Village Museum as Fane told Leri about Emil's 'accident', that he, Fane, had been given information about it which was valuable to the Americans, that the Americans were proposing they, he and Leri, leave the country but he didn't know how they would do it. He tried carefully to tell her enough but not so much she, or anyone else except himself, could be in danger from his knowledge. What a damnable situation, he thought to himself in passing, to have to edit my words to my wife. Finally, he came to the end.

"And so...I'm not sure what we should do. Things have been getting worse here. Not just the food and heat," he anticipated Leri's agreement, "but...there seems to be some rivalry I'm getting caught up in with the...Services...I don't know what it is but it worries me." And the burden of knowing about Emil. And the idea of leaving Romania. And how hard it would be for you, Fane thought but didn't say. At least he thought he hadn't said it until Leri spoke.

"Oh, it wouldn't be hard for me at all!" Leri's eyes were shining when Fane turned toward her. He took a step back in surprise. "Not hard?"

Leri took his question as seriously as he had meant it. "Fane, listen. You know I grew up in a different family than yours, you knew my parents. We were bourgeoisie, educated. We never had any hopes for this system but I haven't said much because...because it was useless to complain about things you can't change and I always hoped you might be right, that perhaps we were only going through a phase. Phases. Endless phases," Leri's voice trailed off. "And I know that some really good people—like you— benefitted from the system but...you know, I talked with Rodica about it, both before and after Emil was killed, because Emil was like you, hopeful until...until the last couple of years. And by the way, neither Rodica nor I thought it was an accident, ever. It was because he knew something about the nuclear system, wasn't it?" Fane stopped again, this time in dismay.

"How do you know? What do you know?"

"Only rumors, and Rodica's belief. Sometimes I thought her idea that he was murdered was only hysteria, but down underneath, I knew she was right so we talked. But getting back to leaving, I'll miss some people and our apartment but think of it! Think of the adventure, seeing new places. Do you realize we've never been out of Romania except to Bulgaria and Hungary?"

Fane didn't know whether to be dismayed or relieved. Leri continued. "And this regime...those dreadful creatures, 'The Great Leader' and his wife...the stupid decisions they have made, the misery they have caused. I'll never forgive them for preventing me from having children. You know that, don't you?" Leri looked at Fane fiercely. "If we'd been able to use contraception like normal people, I wouldn't have had those abortions and..." she choked momentarily, then calmed a bit. "I've always blamed them, especially Her, for those dreadful policies, trying to force women to have children, now they're even checking women at their workplaces to see if they're pregnant or not...I hate them. I hate what they've done here. When," Leri turned to face Fane, "when do we go?"

Taken aback by this torrent of feeling and thought that she'd never shared with him before...how much else didn't he know about this woman, his wife, he had lived with, loved, made love to, been with for over twenty years?...Fane could only say, "I don't know...and I didn't know...why haven't you told me how you felt...?"

"Because," Leri was her normal self, "because it wouldn't have done any good and might have made you unhappy. But now we have a chance to get out and..." Leri did a few dance steps in delight, "Look," Leri motioned to a couple walking toward them, shadows long in the last of the evening light, "isn't that your friend who got the asparagus that time..." Fane looked up and saw Antonescu and his wife coming toward them.

"Good evening," he said inclining his head in greeting. "Do you enjoy walking here as well?"

"Fane!" Antonescu turned his attention from his wife to the other man, looking pleased, Fane noted. "How nice to meet you here! Let me introduce my wife...and I believe this is your wife — we met once." Leri smiled and said something about asparagus, all four chuckled.

"You seem very happy tonight and your husband looks rather serious," Antonescu said to Leri.

"I'm literally dancing with delight," Leri answered, "because Fane promised to take me to Prague this August if we can get permission. I've never been and I hear it's so beautiful. And Fane is probably thinking about the money!" The foursome chuckled again. "I'm sure he'll be able to manage," said Antonescu reassuringly and glanced at Fane approvingly. "Look, we're celebrating our anniversary tonight, we have a reservation for four at the Pescarus but our friends...she's sick with the grippe, they couldn't come... why don't you join us?"

"We'd love to," replied Leri before Fane could refuse but in spite of his doubts and fears the evening turned out to be remarkably pleasant. Walking back Leri tucked her arm in Fane's. "Those are such nice people. If we weren't leaving, I think we could be good friends. Where does he work?" Fane changed the subject and his stomach began churning again.

Bucharest — July 4, 1985. There, I think everything is ready. The music we taped, old Big Band music, I think the Ambassador and his wife chose well, the Romanians should like that. Emil has the sound system set up. The Color Guard is ready for the Presentation of the Colors, we have the Star-Spangled Banner and a decent recording of the Romanian National Anthem ready, funny how hard it was to find one. It looks like the food will be decent and someone must have mentioned something because it also looks as if there will be plenty. Thank goodness we have a new Ambassador. I do love this enormous garden, it's so well kept and lovely, nice trees, a really pleasant place. I wonder if it will rain, but I don't think so. There are a few clouds but not too many. There...I see the Codel coming in, three Congressmen and their wives...I must...no, Scott is going to greet them.

And I'm ready, I guess. I think I have the Romanian words and phrases...it's so important what I need to tell Stefan, maybe while they have the Color Guard. I wonder what he's said to his wife. I suppose he has talked to her...they've seemed like such a close couple. She is lovely, I think she works as a teacher but I don't know exactly where. It was so nice at their house day before yesterday, they were so gracious but I wonder...Stefan has to be Securitate. I mean, when the Congressman's wife told the Ambassador that they'd really like to see how an ordinary Romanian lived, visit in a house, no one knew what to do. Why do they always call me in those situations...of course, they didn't actually call this time, I was there for coffee. They wanted a female officer to talk with the wives. So much for equal opportunity. But when push came to shove I was the only officer who was able to call up someone and ask if the Codel could visit. Then we waited for Stefan to get back to us...it only took ten minutes and in the afternoon we went to their house. It would have been easier in the morning, we could have just walked from the Residence but I suppose they needed some time to get ready. I would have. Needed some time to get ready, that is. So we went to their little apartment on that charming shabby street and the Codel was enchanted. Score one for Embassy Bucharest, they said they hadn't been able to do this in Moscow. I suppose it's harder in Moscow, the Romanians are Latins, after all.

And now it's almost time. I'm nervous about talking to Stefan. Should I do it when Valeria is there or wait until I have him alone? I wonder. Surely he must have told her.

Leri took Fane's arm to negotiate the cobblestones on their street. "If you didn't wear such thin, high heels," said Fane. Leri's look was enough to fell a goat, he thought, so he shut his mouth.

In any case, it didn't take long to arrive at the gate of the Ambassador's Residence. No matter how many times he had been there—well, two, Fane admitted to himself, three counting this time—it was impressive to go in... foreign territory. He felt Leri's hand tighten on his arm as she saw

340

the American flag and could read her mind. Now it was going to be her flag.

The line at the gate moved slowly but there were enough friends and acquaintances that conversation made the time pass quickly and it carried on into the walled garden of the Residence. Brightly decorated booths, all sporting the red, white and blue of the US flag, dotted the grounds. "Oh, look," said Leri, "I think those are for food. I've read about American food, 'burgers' and 'hot dogs'. I think hot dogs are some kind of sausage, that's an odd name."

"Trust the Americans to have odd names," they heard behind them, "for ordinary things like *carnati*." It was Dan from Slatioara who fell into exchanging news of mutual friends spiced with a bit of gossip—Dan was excellent at spicing things with a bit of gossip—while Fane chatted with his attractive wife. The line, forming and reforming as people spied other acquaintances, moved on to allow each person to shake hands with the US Ambassador, his wife, the Congressmen and their wives, and senior Embassy officers. The line halted as Fane and, especially, Leri reached the visiting Congressmen who greeted them as old friends. Maybe I'll have somebody to call on in the US, Fane thought. Finally they were moved on by an American functionary, sent on along with promises to talk later.

"You're quite a star!" Fane told Leri, pleased that she had made such a good impression. "I didn't know you would take to public life so easily." Leri laughed delightedly. Fane wished he felt as lighthearted. He searched covertly for Ellen and spotted her talking to Carol. The couple moved in that direction, arriving just as Ellen and Carol were bidding each other good-bye.

"Don't break up the conversation just because we're here," said Fane with a genialty he didn't feel. Carol laughed, kissed Leri, and said something about taking her to try a hot dog. "Unless you've already had one." "No," she replied, "I haven't had anything to eat—we've" she glanced meaningfully at Fane, "been too busy talking to half the world."

"Go on, then," smiled Ellen. "And you must also try a hamburger as well." The two turned to each other and the ceremony of the Color Guard started, halting conversation. The Marines in their tan uniforms, gold and blue and red accents, moved forward smartly and presented the Colors. Fane moved Ellen back a few steps, into a grassy area away from trees. Forunately, he thought, the sun is far enough down that it's shaded even here—otherwise it would look odd to stand in the sun. As the speeches began Ellen looked steadily at the speakers with great attention and said softly, "There is to be a ship visit in early August. If you wish you can leave on the ship."

"How would that be managed?"

"You'll be invited—half the world is being invited— to tour the ship. That's why it's coming. During the tour you'll just be taken off to see something at a certain point and disappear."

"Will you be there?" asked Fane. Ellen drew a deep breath. "Yes, I'll be there. Do you want to do it? I need to know...apparently it takes some time to make arrangements. But," she added hurriedly, "if you can't say right now I can wait a couple of days. You only have to say yes or no then."

Fane was so tense he could hardly make himself look relaxed and wave discreetly back at a friend who had just seen him. The friend began to make his way in their direction.

"Yes, we'll do it." he told Ellen. "Can we take anything with us?"

Ellen had asked about this. "No," she said sadly. "Just what you'd normally carry on an afternoon's outing. Does your wife know? Does she want to go? It must be an enormous, terrible decision to make." Fane suddenly wanted to sit down and talk and talk with this kind woman but the friend came within earshot before he could do more than say, "It's okay. We'll go."

Bucharest — July 1985. All right, Stefan will go, the Other Agency is making the arrangements with Defense, apparently there is a lot of red tape and I'm glad I'm not involved. I'm involved enough as it is. This country seems to bring responsibilities I hadn't dreamed of, I feel responsible for uprooting this man and his wife from their lives, their lovely little home, whatever friends and relatives they have, this beautiful, torn, sad country...I know they made the decision, I didn't force them. I know they will have a better life in the US... I hope they will have a better life. Could it be he's a double agent? What have I done?

'What have I done?' Fane asked himself. 'What have I done? What will I do?' He looked around at his library, now expanded from the front room into the hall and a bit of it, well, bedtime reading, into the bedroom, and sat down heavily in one of the chairs.

He and Leri had done an accounting, so to speak, of what they were leaving. It was mostly *who* they were leaving, actually and it was easier, it seemed, for Leri. "It's funny," she said, "but though I have a lot of 'friends' I don't have anybody really close to me except Rodica and that one teacher at work...family, yes, but my parents are gone, I'll miss Aunt Sanda terribly but we hardly see her these days. I like my work but there are other teachers, the students move on, and a teacher's job is a solitary one except for Party meetings. There's so much work, so many papers to correct that I don't have time to talk to people in the Faculty Room..."
Fane thought of the Institute, what it represented, his work, his renown in this small world of medieval Romanian history. Carol. Carol's father. Uncle Vanya and Aunt Anna all the last three growing old and he would never see them again...Father Augustin, Dragomir, Popescu, Antonescu... yes, Antonescu...Andrei...the list went on in a web of being that had not only caught Fane but made him what he was, given him importance...and then there was his library.

"What shall I do with my library?" he asked Leri. "Give it to Carol," she said. Even though Fane had already made the decision he felt a bolt of surprise at the idea.

"Give it to Carol? He doesn't read this kind of thing." Carol's reaction was, word for word, the same and Fane's reply was what Leri had told him. "I know, but still you value books and learning and most of all, you're my friend and will keep them for my sake." But Carol wasn't Leri and didn't know why Fane was asking the question at this point. "Look, you brought this up before...what in hell is going through your head that you're even asking me?" was his next sentence.

Leri had also thought of this answer. "Because Leri is insisting we make a will, in case something happens to one or both of us. If it's just me who goes, there's no problem, but what if there's a train wreck or something that takes both of us? We have no children, I have no brothers or sisters..." Fane paused, thinking of Mioara for the first time in years, wondering what ever might have happened to the girl who was in love with a village boy...what was his name?...and then taken by a Russian officer far...Carol must have had the same thought for he caught Fane's eye in sympathy and forged ahead. "All right, if it will make Leri feel better." And that subject was closed.

Eventually invitations to the ship visit came to Fane and Leri and Carol and, it seemed, half of Bucharest as well as most of Constanza. "Did you get an invitation to the Americans' battleship?" asked Carol, relaxing in Fane and Leri's front room after a Sunday dinner. Leri nodded enthusiastically. Carol wasn't as taken with the idea. "It's going to be a total zoo. Apparently they're bringing people on to this ship in tranches. I'm not inclined to go and I'd advise you to stay home as well."

"Can't do that," said Fane before Leri could speak.

"Why not...oh, never mind."

"It's simple, Dragomir doesn't want to go but he wants the Institute to be represented."

Carol gave Fane a skeptical look and went on. "I'm scheduled for what must be the last group of the day, what about you?" Leri went into the other room and came back with their invitation. Both of them had read it several times without noting this detail.

"So are we," she said, at least I think so, from four to five in the afternoon?"

"I wonder what there is to see that will take an hour. I can't imagine they'd show us anything of, um, importance," said Carol.

"It's probably because there will be long lines getting on and off."

"Oh, great. Half an hour getting on, half an hour getting off, welcome to the American ship visit. I'll drive down if you're going—you'll come with me?"

"We'd be delighted. Do you think we should stay overnight?"

"I'm not sure...it's on a Saturday...let me check and see if we can find hotel rooms. Perhaps we could go to Mangalia and look at some horses..." Fane groaned.

Constanza—August 1985. This is an interesting town. I read that Ovid was exiled here but seeing Greek and Roman fragments in the Museum makes it real. We don't connect, we Americans, we don't connect parts of the Old World the way they should be connected. Romania in Greek and Roman times...I'm nervous. I've been told what to do, and it seems simple, but what if it doesn't work? What will happen to them if they're caught by the Romanian authorities? What will happen if Stefan just...doesn't show up? I must stop worrying this torn cuticle or it'll get infected...

The tire of Carol's Trabant blew just as they left Hirsova. With great good luck, it was outside a tire repair shop, one of a row of small, dirty and probably illegal establishments along the national highway. The three walked up and down while the tire was being repaired.

"Don't worry," said Carol. "if we don't make the visit we can still have a good dinner and perhaps go for a swim." Fane smiled and thought he'd like to kill Carol. The tire repaired, the party set forth again across the wide beige plains and chalk escarpments of the Dobrogea, chatting about this and that as if, Fane thought, everything was completely normal. It was as it should be. It was as it had to be. Fane wanted to shout in frustration as minutes ticked by in the traffic jam going in to the port area of Contantza, but he didn't. He didn't shout in exultation as it became apparent they were in time for the visit. He chatted normally as if nothing at all was out of joint, as if his stomach weren't so tight it hurt, no longer even churning, just tight. All he had to do was survive the next two hours.

Part of it was spent in a line shuffling into the ship. Once up the long gangplank they were divided into groups by a ship's officer. Behind the officer was Ellen who caught Fane's eye. She moved forward, floating through Fane's bad dream..."Stefan, Valeria, Carol! What a pleasure to see you here." Ellen turned toward the ship's officer, "Charlie, these are special friends of mine, can we give them the VIP tour?" Fane saw Dan from Slatioara further back in the line with his wife looking at them, ready to leap forward and claim special status as well then heard Ellen again, "Here, come this way..." The three went through a door and joined a group of ten or fifteen Romanians with three Americans. There were explanations, they moved to another area, more explanations. Ellen caught Fane's eye again and looked toward a new person with the group, another American naval officer, some rank, Fane couldn't make out the Navy ranks. This man, who spoke passable Romanian to Fane's surprise, moved forward and began explaining things to them while Ellen engaged Carol in conversation. The group moved off. Fane, Leri and the officer followed, talking about the ship. The hallways were narrow, a gray metal, stifling and confusing as they wound their way through the great vessel. At a certain point the officer said, "I understand you need to use the, uh, facilities...please come with me. If we can't rejoin this group, we'll catch the next one...you needn't worry, there's one more." Ellen and Carol, at the rear of the others, talking, rounded a corner while Fane and Leri were led down another corridor, then a turn, then another, further into the depths of this maze, this hiding place, this...Fane's increasingly wild thoughts were interrupted when the strange American opened a door into a double berthed cabin. As they entered his voice changed from a guide's patter to real conversation.

"We have prepared this cabin for you. I do need to ask you one more time if you are sure you want to do this. We could return to the tour and no one would know."

Leri, not Fane, answered firmly. "We do. We've thought about it and made our decision."

The American smiled with genuine warmth. "Welcome to US territory if not yet to US soil. You'll find drinking water in the cupboard. I'm sorry there aren't better accommodations but this isn't a passenger ship. We sail in," he checked his watch, "an hour and a half but all passengers will debark in the next twenty minutes."

"What if we're missed?"

"Someone from the Embassy saw you go down the gangplank...you left early because Mrs. Vulcean didn't feel well and are probably at the hotel. Or perhaps you've found a doctor." The American officer smiled. "Don't worry. Oh... I have a message for you." He pulled an envelope out of his pocket. "I am going to leave you now. I am going to lock the door—I hope it won't make you nervous but we must be sure no one comes in."

"We understand," said Fane who managed to find his voice and take the envelope at the same time. The American smiled reassuringly, touched his cap and left. Fane looked at Leri and then at the close-in gray metal around them. "He didn't say if we could talk," he said softly.

"We'd better not", whispered Leri, "in case someone's outside." Fane nodded, looked at the blank envelope and tore it open. Inside was a single page with two sentences in familiar handwriting.

"I'm sorry I can't be with you at this moment but I'll meet you in Istanbul. Welcome to the free world." It was signed simply, "Mihai." Fane handed it silently to Leri, tears rolling down his face.

Epilogue

Ellen and Carol stood side by side in the shadow of a nameless metal building, watching the ship pull away and gather speed in the deepening evening dusk, leaving Romania behind, the last of the guests also leaving in the opposite direction, their backs to the sea, talking, fixed on the dinner or cocktail party or drive back to Bucharest ahead of them. Quietly, Carol took Ellen's hand and held it, both their hands hidden in the folds of her skirt. There he traced the ball of his thumb across her palm and caressed the mound at the base of her own thumb. She stood taut, meeting the heat of his desire with her own, willing it to go away. There were still secrets to keep, even from Carol, maybe especially from Carol, and soon Stefan and Valeria would be safe.

"Ellen, dear, darling, they're never going to allow me to see you again." Ellen tried not to flinch as they both continued to watch the ship with neutral faces. "I know. You don't need to tell me." Carol continued, the finality of his voice making the subject clear.

"I don't understand," she managed to say. Carol continued to rub the base of her thumb, slowly, regretfully, with enormous tenderness and great passion.

"There is a little plate that hung in Fane's house," Carol said, his voice only reaching Ellen's ear, so softly that even she could only feel rather than hear what he said. "A little plate he carried with him to Transylvania in the war, through the *liceu*, brought to Bucharest to the University, hung above his table in his home. When I went to pick him and Leri up, he didn't know I saw, but he looked at it, then he took it off the wall and put it in his pocket."

"You have no idea what we have gone through, during the war, afterwards, but Fane is like my brother. I won't betray him and I won't betray you. I haven't betrayed you. I have loved you as I have never loved a woman before. And this," Carol moved his head a fraction of an inch toward the ship, out in the water and becoming smaller, "this will take you from me."

"What will happen to Robespierre?" Ellen said, immediately appalled at her thoughtlessness. Carol glanced at the clear tears trembling at the corners of her eyes with the shadow of a smile.

"That's why I love you, always practical, always the American. Do you care?" His tone changed, became rough.

The tears began to spill onto Ellen's cheeks, drying almost immediately in the seabreeze. She moved closer to Carol in response. "Can I even answer that? I know you in one way, I've seen you almost every week for two years. We have talked and laughed. Once..." her voice trembled..."you kissed me,"

"I caress that thought every hour."

"Now you are being dramatic." Carol smiled without looking at her and squeezed Ellen's hand. "My Midwestern American," he said. "I can't have even the smallest flight of fancy in the way I love you."

"But I don't know you, don't know much about your family."

"You met my father."

"I guessed that, but...would it work? If we could be together?"

"Oh, yes, it would work, as you say. It will. Some day. Not now but some day things will change in Romania. Then

350

I'll see my brothers Fane and Mihai again. And I will find you."

Carol turned, lifted her hand to his lips, then walked away.

Notes

Romanian is a romance language and much but not all pronunciation is similar to Italian. It isn't necessary to pronounce everything properly, but there are a few names and words that merit a bit of explanation and hints as to how they might be said and what they mean. As they occur in the text, and using English orthography (e.g. our alphabet, not theirs) these are:

Stefan Vulcean (Shteh-FAHN Vul-chay-AN) is the name of the protagonist.

Fane (FAH-nay) -- the diminutive for Stefan, used by family and friends but not official contacts.

Carol (CAH-roll) -- a man's name, the Romanian equivalent of Charles

Mihai (Me-HIGH) -- the Romanian equivalent of Michael

Radauti (Rah-dah-OOTZ) -- a town in northern Romania. Before World War II the home of a large Jewish population, much of which was deported to camps and not exactly cared for lovingly. Large numbers perished, many who survived never returned to Romania and the territory where the camps were located was acquired by the USSR.

Soba (SO-bah) – large tile stove for heating a room. Often the tiles are beautifully decorated.

Tzuica – prune brandy, often homemade

Chernovitsky – A town in northern Bukovina now in the Ukraine. The pronunciation is less important than the fact that the Russians, at the time, used this name while the Romanians called it Cernauti. It was Czernowitz (with various spellings) under the Austrians. It is now

Cernivtsi. Romanians in Bukovina still dream it might be returned to Romania....

Timisoara – (Tim– ee-SHWA-rah) – City in SW Romania

Ploska (PLO-shkah) – a jug, often wooden, used to hold liquor

Palinca (Pah-LING-kah) – The Transylvanian version of tzuica, much stronger and usually double distilled. Drink with caution.

Marasesti (Mah-rah-SESHT) – Monument to a battle where Romanians beat the German army in WWI

Colinde (Co-LEAN-day) – carols

Anticariat (Ahnt-ee-car-ee-aht) – Used book store. Often sells postcards and prints as well as books.

Martisor (Martz-ee-SHORE) – small trinkets on red and white string, given to ladies, mostly but not always, by the men in their life, during the first week of March

Urzici (Ur-ZEECH) – Nettles. Cooked when young can be delicious. Not great when fully developed.

ODCD – The Government of Romania office that provided services to foreign embassies during the Communist years. More or less.

And now a word about geography. National boundaries in Eastern Europe are changed with the speed of summer lightning but people are not. There are several major changes to Romania's boundaries that are important to this story:

1920: Romania is officially awarded Transylvania, Bessarabia, Bukovina and other territory on the basis of national population.

June 10, 1940: Molotov draws a line across the map in pencil and not only retakes Bessarabia for the USSR but part of Bukovina (now part of Ukraine) as well.

August 30, 1940: A large chunk of northern Transylvania was returned to Hungary.

September 12, 1944: The territory in Transylvania is returned to Romania but not that taken by the Russians in Bukovina and Bessarabia.

Made in the USA
Las Vegas, NV
13 November 2023

80797078R00208